Jules Wake's earliest known declaration that she planned to be a writer came at the age of ten. Unfortunately the urge to actually get her backside into gear and write a book didn't revisit her for quite some time after that.

After a twenty-year career in the glamorous world of PR, working on luxury brands, she switched professions to give her more time and energy to write. By day she works in a junior school and by night writes romantic comedy and happy-ever-after stories, which are the sort of books she's always enjoyed reading.

You can follow Jules on Twitter @juleswake or visit her at www.juleswake.co.uk.

By the same author:

From Italy With Love
From Paris With Love This Christmas

JULES WAKE

Escape to the Riviera

This novel is entirely a work of fiction.
The names, characters and incidents portrayed in it are the work of the author's imagination. Any resemblance to actual persons, living or dead, events or localities is entirely coincidental.

AVON
A division of HarperCollins*Publishers*
1 London Bridge Street,
London SE1 9GF

www.harpercollins.co.uk

A Paperback Original 2016
1

A catalogue record for this book is available from the British Library

ISBN 978-0-00-818529-9

Typeset in Sabon by Palimpsest Book Production Ltd, Falkirk, Stirlingshire

Printed and bound in Great Britain by Clays Ltd, St Ives plc

For Super Agent Broo,
thank you for everything x

CHAPTER ONE

Surely, no judge in the land would send her down for giving in to temptation and throttling her niece? The phrase 'justifiable homicide' rattled around Carrie's brain with pleasing harmony. Yes, she'd almost certainly get away it. Teenagers were tricky little sods, although her sister might have something to say about it. Angela managed her daughter's strops with understated equanimity, but then she was very good at putting up with things. Carrie, on the other hand, found it difficult not to react. How come she could cope with a class full of other people's kids but was ready to strangle her own niece for being a first-class, there was no other word for it, madam? It would be wrong to come right out and call her that, strangulation was therefore entirely reasonable. Her fingers twitched. So, so tempting.

'Told you we wouldn't get in,' Jade pointed out for the third time, in her loud 'I'm disgruntled voice', attracting pernicious interest from the people in the queue behind them. No doubt a score of parents were heaving fervent sighs that she wasn't theirs.

Did Jade have any idea how close she was to having the very living breath choked out of her?

'You should have booked the tickets online, like I said to. It's ridiculous,' moaned Jade, contradicting any pleasure she might have gained in being right.

Carrie scowled at her niece. One, she flatly refused to pay a two-pound fee, per ticket, mind you, for the luxury of booking tickets in her own home and two, especially not for a film you could flipping well see for free on television. *Breakfast at Tiffany's* had been around for fifty years.

'Now, now, I'm sure there's something else we can see,' said Alan, stepping back to look up at the bank of screens advertising at least another eleven films being screened.

'Yes,' said the girl at the desk, with a touch of desperation, trying to hurry them along. 'One of the films starts in two minutes.' Whose side she was on? She'd soon be out of work if people paid the over-priced booking fees and didn't buy tickets at the desk.

If that happened and you had to do it all online, there'd never be any chance to be spontaneous and decide to see a film. Take pot luck. Not that Carrie had done anything that random in ages. With sudden dismay it occurred to her that spontaneity was in short supply these days. Did that happen to *everyone* with age? Was it growing up? Maturing? Or just her getting duller?

'Which one starts in two minutes?' asked Carrie, straightening up and flashing the girl a brilliant smile. 'Wait. Don't tell me.' She turned to the others. 'Let's go for it. It'll be a surprise.'

They all stared at her as if she'd gone mad. As well they might, where had that crazy thought come from?

'What! We can't do that,' said Angela. 'We don't even know what it is. We might hate it.'

'That's the most ridiculous thing. Why would you do that? That's so lame.' Jade shook her head. 'Anyway there'll only be tickets left for the crap films no one wants to see.'

'And also rather risky, darling,' added Alan.

'Or it could be fun!' Her voice lifted with enthusiasm, looking back at the united front of three deeply sceptical faces. 'We might see a film we'd never normally choose and enjoy it. Broaden our horizons. A voyage of discovery! You might love it and you'd never have known. And what about that sense of anticipation?'

'Like who does that?' Jade punctuated every word with a different facial expression.

If displeased gurning ever became an Olympic sport, she'd surely clean up. 'Sounds a pathetic, losery sort of thing to do.' She continued.

'Erm, if you could . . .' the girl at the desk nodded her head, indicating the restive queue. 'Or perhaps step aside while you're deciding.'

'No. Not happening. There's no way I'm queuing all over again.' Jade turned to the girl. 'What tickets are left for anything that's not totally shite?'

'Well there are two screens showing *An Unsuitable Man,* which is pretty popular.'

'Done.' Jade gave Alan an unapologetic smile. 'Sorry Al, it's a chick flick.'

'That's fine, I think I'll cope,' replied Alan, amusement glinting in his eyes.

Carrie shot him a grateful smile and got her purse out. 'Four tickets for that, then.'

'Does anyone know what it's about?' asked Angela.

'Not a clue, but it's got Mr Delicious Arse in it, so if all else fails we've got man candy. Sorry, again Al.'

All was right again in Jade's world.

'Isn't that a tad sexist?' teased Carrie, on safer ground now.

'Sue me.' Jade grinned. 'But I bet you agree. Sorry Al, again, but the man with the oh-so-yum butt is serious sex on legs.'

'Jade!' said Angela with a half-hearted exclamation of consternation, before adding, 'But we still don't know what it's about.'

'I'm guessing,' said Carrie, paying for the tickets and tucking away her purse, 'there's a clue in the title, which probably contravenes the trade descriptions act. Cute unsuitable man reforms to become cute suitable man.'

'And there speaks the scriptwriter,' said Alan, wrapping his arm around her as they walked towards screen seven.

'Then it sounds like a very good alternative,' said Angela. 'Although perhaps a bit unfair on the sole male in the party.'

'Well Al would prefer that to a shoot 'em, beat 'em and kill 'em, fast and furious thing, wouldn't you? You're used to all that *Pride and Prejudice*, *Far From the Madding Crowd* stuff.' Jade shuddered. 'I'm so glad, once this year is finished, I never ever *ever*, have to do English Literature again.'

'So too, I suspect, is your teacher,' said Al with a wink. 'And no, I'm quite happy to watch something undemanding. I'm sure there'll be some lady candy for me.' His hand resting on Carrie's shoulder squeezed her.

Thank goodness he was used to teenagers. Carrie lifted her hand and wrapped her fingers around his, squeezing him back. Being a teacher at the same school as where she taught drama part-time meant Jade's behaviour, thankfully, didn't faze him or put him off.

*

They shuffled into their seats and sat down in the semi-darkness. The ads had already started but the audience, blasé and indifferent to the stylish mini-films, paid no attention. Jade's phone glowed as she scrolled through pages on the internet, reminding Carrie to switch hers off. Next to her, Alan did the same.

'Richard Maddox,' announced Jade, showing her phone to her mother.

Carrie heard Angela's quick, sharp gasp.

Her stomach flipped. In the dark she saw the light from the phone reflected in Angela's wide-eyed expression.

Angela grabbed her arm on the rest between them.

'He's Mr Delicious Arse,' explained Jade, leaning over her mother to show Carrie a picture of Richard Maddox's naked backside.

All the air whooshed out of Carrie's lungs and someone had removed the bones in her legs. Thank goodness for Angela's grip on her arm, otherwise she might have slipped out of her seat like a slick of jelly, sliding right out under the seat in front of her all the way to the bottom.

'It's a YouTube vid. Him buck-naked on a beach in California. All you can see is his butt.'

An image of a tiny heart-shaped mole wormed like a determined maggot into Carrie's head, and no matter how hard she blinked, she couldn't dispel it.

'Not the meat and two veg, thank you. That would just be vile. Don't look, Al.' Jade waved the phone at him.

'Thanks, Jade, I won't.'

A sudden burst of music, ebbing from left to right of the cinema in a cacophonous wave, silenced the chatter and Jade snapped her phone off.

Angela's hand crept into hers with a limp grip. Carrie

clung on to it, her heart leaping about in her chest like a bucking bronco on acid. Her stupid brain insisted on replaying an image of a finger tracing that blinking mole, the tip of her index fingernail a perfect fit for each side of the heart, which nestled on the top left side of a right buttock. She squirmed slightly in her seat and stiffened when she realised what she was doing.

'You okay?' whispered Angela.

In the darkness Carrie shook her head, unable to speak. A sense of dread and anticipation rolled around in her stomach. She sat straighter. It seemed a miracle she could keep her body still when inside it felt like someone had switched on a blender.

It was bound to happen one day. A miracle that she'd managed this long. Richard Maddox starred in one blockbuster after another.

Sickness and curiosity warred. It had been a long time. She'd been good. Not stalking him. Not Googling. Managing to avert her gaze from the front of *Hello* magazine at the checkout in Marks and Spencer, training herself not to flinch when someone in the staff room talked about his latest movie or when his name was linked with yet another blonde bombshell of dubious intelligence. Okay, that was her being a bitch. They might be very intelligent, but couldn't they give everyone else a break and not be completely gorgeous as well?

Maybe she'd built it all up in her head and seeing him on screen wouldn't affect her at all. She hadn't seen him for years. Eight years, ten months, give or take a day or two. And she only knew that because it was July 1st and he'd left on the August bank holiday. No other reason.

Why the hell hadn't she done this before? Put her demon

to rest? Except he wasn't a demon. Or even a bad person. Just someone from her past. She should have done this ages ago.

She squeezed Angela's hand back to show she was fine. Absolutely fine.

Carrie approved of the sassy character of the female lead, a willowy blonde, who kept the hero on his toes. The well-written screenplay had lots going for it. Entertaining. Good snappy dialogue. Gorgeous location. New York without the traffic, the noise or the humidity. She liked the conflicts that kept him and the heroine apart, and the will-they-ever-get-together moment, where he cast a wistful backward look at her sitting alone on the Highline. Carrie was doing really, really well. Focusing on the film. The mechanics of it. Stoic and impassive. She was doing well, right up to the point when on the Staten Island Ferry, Richard Maddox's character removed the suitcase from the heroine's hand, turned her to him, cupped her face in his hands, pushing her long windswept curls out of the way, and leaned in. The camera homed in on the wistful, longing expression on his face, his lips centre-screen as he uttered the words, 'I love you,' before leaning in to bestow a kiss of heart-rending intensity.

He might as well have punched her right in the gut. She almost doubled over with the impact.

A flush of heat raced through her as memories loosened, tumbling down like an avalanche. The way he'd lazily snake one of her curls around his finger when they were lying in bed in the mornings. His eyes holding hers when he kissed her, the quick nibbles at the corner of her mouth, those spontaneous public pecks on the Tube as if he couldn't hold them back and the long, slow langorous preludes to love-making. A myriad kisses danced in her head.

The pain sliced hard and sharp, like a crack suddenly tearing its way through her heart. She tensed, her diaphragm clenching as she fought to hold in a shuddering sob, which threatened to launch itself into orbit.

Mindful of Alan on her right and Angela on her left, she swallowed hard. She clamped her lips in a mutinous line, wrapped her arms around her chest and shut her eyes, praying that these precautions would succeed in repelling the emotion fighting to leak out. Tears streamed down her cheek, gathering speed and a single hiccoughing sob escaped.

Al slipped an arm along the back of her chair. 'You big softie,' he whispered.

Blinking back the tears, feeling all kinds of fool, she ducked her head to scrabble around in her bag at her feet to find a tissue. It gave her time to take her attention away from the screen and to get a grip.

'Aw, Auntie Carrie's been crying,' teased Jade as they filed out of the cinema, blinking as they emerged into daylight. 'You big wuss, you.'

'She's an old romantic, aren't you love?' Alan shrugged into his jacket as they stepped out into the early-evening drizzle.

'It was a lovely film,' said Angela, her eyes anxious as they scanned Carrie's wan face. 'Made me cry too.'

Carrie winced at the blatant lie. She did love her sister.

'Mum, what are you like? Seriously? What was there to cry at? Honestly, you're a pair of saps. I'll give him hot, though. Up in the old Fahrenheit register. Hot, hot, hot,' she paused with a cheeky raise of her eyebrows, 'for an old guy.'

'Old?' chorused Angela and Carrie at the same time, exchanging secretive smiles.

'Yeah, he must be at least thirty. Old.' She grinned. 'Obvs, not for you geriatric crustys, of course.'

Carrie and Angela each linked an arm through Jade's.

'What do you think?' Carrie said to Angela. 'Bread and water for the next ten years?'

'Ladies, you can do better than that.' Alan frowned as if giving it serious thought. 'How about no phone upgrade for another year?'

'Nooo!' howled Jade, dramatically locking her hands in mock prayer, 'anything but that.'

'Or we could give her away?' suggested Angela

'Who'd have her?' Carrie shrugged as Jade poked her tongue out.

'There is that,' agreed Angela with a long-suffering sigh. 'Look's like we're stuck with the brat.'

'You know you love me. Both of you.' Jade tugged at their arms, pulling them closer to her.

Her mother placed a kiss on her cheek. 'We do.'

Carrie followed suit. 'Course we do.'

She pushed back at the sense of melancholy hovering over her, as if ready to snatch her away.

She had plenty of love in her life. What more could she ask for? She had a tight-knit family and a lovely man, who adored her.

CHAPTER TWO

'You coming in for a coffee?' asked Carrie, opening the car door.

Alan shook his head, as Angela and Jade stepped out of the passenger seats in the back. 'No, it's a school night and I've still got a stack of marking to do.'

So did she. Guilt pricked at the thought of 8G's navy-blue exercise books heaped in a pile in the kitchen. They ought to be done tonight.

She came round to the driver's seat and Alan climbed out of the car to face her. She was lucky to have him. Good looking in a forty-watt sort of way. Every feature created a harmonious symmetry that fell a touch short of dazzling. Nice brown eyes, with thick dark lashes that begged the question was he wearing make-up, good skin, hair mid-brown but slightly limp and a nice neat nose. He was the same height as her and quite possibly the kindest man she knew.

'Okay. Thanks for coming with us. Sorry about the film choice. I'm sure it wasn't your cup of tea.'

'What? And *Breakfast at Tiffany's* was?' He tilted his head to one side.

With a gentle laugh she tugged at his jacket. 'Yeah, but it's iconic and you said you'd never seen it. And everyone should see it at least once.'

He put his arms around her, pulling her into an embrace.

'Well, the other one wasn't so bad. Though who knew you were such a closet romantic? Tears, Miss Hayes? I always thought for a drama teacher you were incredibly emotionally stable.'

'Thanks, I think. That was supposed to be a compliment?'

He grinned at her. 'Of course it was. Not that you need them.'

He leaned in and brushed his lips over hers. For a minute she clung to him, her heart lifting in anticipation. She wanted him to kiss her. Properly. Chase the demons of fantasy away. This was real.

She deepened the kiss, needing that connection with him, but he pulled back.

'I need to go. Those books won't get marked by themselves. Sleep tight. See you at work in the morning. Only three more Mondays and we're home free.'

She bit back disappointment. Alan was being sensible. In a few weeks' time they'd have a whole summer off, although they'd yet to decide what to do. He'd got a cycling holiday in the Swiss Alps booked and, despite the invitation, it didn't appeal. She could've gone along but Angela and Jade still hadn't sorted out a holiday and it felt wrong to abandon them.

'Thank the Lord.' She hugged him. 'This summer term is always a killer. There's so much going on. Exams. The leavers getting too big for their boots. I can't wait until we break up.'

Jade had already gone up to bed when Carrie sank down at the kitchen table opposite her sister. She let out a weary sigh and reached for the cup of tea Angela had made for her.

'You okay?'

Carrie rubbed her hand over her face, trying to summon up the right words. She didn't want to worry Angela but no she wasn't okay. Nothing like okay.

'I'm fine. That last bit got to me. But I'm fine.'

She should be fine. After all, she'd worked in the business. Written her own scenes designed to engineer an audience's response. Should be impervious to a scene where the director had brought every cinematic trick in the book into play, expressly to create a total heart-stopping, heart-fluttering scene.

'Are you sure?' Angela's soft voice penetrated her thoughts, her gentle grey eyes glistening with sympathy.

'Am I fuck?' Carrie laid her head on the table and bashed it a couple of times. It hurt.

'Carrie!'

She lifted her head and said with a weary sigh, 'I'm not fine at all. I feel pants.'

Seeing Richard had knocked her sideways, out through a glass window seventy-five stories up, and she was still hurtling through the air.

Her response was ten times worse than she could have imagined. Out of sight, out of mind had worked pretty well for her to date. Whoever talked about opening cans of worms had known their onions. She wished she'd walked out of the cinema as soon as she'd heard the name Richard Maddox.

'Probably the shock of seeing him again, as it were.' Angela lifted her shoulders in a helpless shrug, her brave attempt at reassurance at odds with her bewildered expression.

She and Carrie were so different. Angela's mild disposition and gentle approach meant that she sailed rather serenely through life on a gentle swell, never plunging into the lows or cresting the highs, despite the constant pain and difficulties she suffered with her rheumatoid arthritis.

Her affair with a married man that resulted in Jade was the most out-of-character thing that Angela had ever done and even now Carrie had difficulty in believing that her sister had been swept away enough to commit adultery. 'Maybe it's because you never had proper closure. When I got pregnant with Jade, I knew that it would be over with Clive. With you and Richard, it never ended properly. Just drifted to a halt.

'I'm sure that's what it is. How long ago was it since you last saw him? Seven, eight years? You can't possibly be in love with him, not after all this time.'

Carrie swallowed a protest. What if she could? She'd never tested the theory before today. 'Yes, you're right. It's the shock of seeing him in all his twelve-foot celluloid handsome glory.' That's what had made her heart beat a thousand times faster and deepened the hollow feeling in her stomach all the way to Australia.

'No one's that good looking. Do you think he was wearing loads of make-up?' Angela said knowledgeably, as if she spent hours on a film set.

'Probably,' agreed Carrie, nodding as if her life depended on it.

'And I *bet* he had a body double.' Angela leaned back in her chair, waving her cup about in her usual feeble grip, sloshing tea over the sides. 'His body can't be that good.'

Carrie nodded again. If she wasn't careful someone would stuff her in the back window of a car.

Angela had a point, though. It certainly hadn't been when he was in his twenties but then he wasn't leading a superstar lifestyle then. You don't exactly fill out a scrawny frame when you're existing on baked beans and fish-finger sandwiches, living in an unheated, mould-ridden flat off Cold Harbour Lane in Brixton, shivering off any muscle tone to keep warm.

'Alternatively,' Angela was her in stride now. 'he could have a Rottweiler of a personal trainer who dogs his every step-making sure he lives on horrible Hollywood-healthy milkshake things, like wheatgrass and alfalfa sproutings or that keen squaw stuff.'

Carrie smiled as Angela pulled a bleurgh face.

'And he must wear contacts. No one's eyes are that blue.'

Richard's were. To hide the ping of protest her heart made, Carrie let out a mirthless laugh, cupping the mug of tea to take a sip.

'Sweet of Alan to come with us.' Angela's eyes were guileless and her smile kind.

'Subtle.'

Angela shrugged. 'He's lovely. You've been seeing each other for a while.'

Carrie didn't say anything.

'Do you think something might happen there one day?'

'One day. I guess.' Carrie had been giving it more thought recently. He made her happy. So happy. They were good together. She loved him. Not in the crazy, helter-skelter being-at-a-fairground way she'd loved Richard but in a stronger, more enduring fashion.

'What if one day is soon?'

Carrie was missing something. Angela's eyes were bird-bright, beady with expectation.

'What do you know?'

'Oh.' Worry crept across her face. 'Shoot, I've given the game away.'

'Well you hadn't but you have now.'

'If he did ask you, you know, to marry him, you'd say yes, wouldn't you?' The lines in her forehead deepened as she realised she'd dug herself into an even deeper hole.

'Angela. What do you know?'

'You mustn't tell him I told you.'

'Like I'm going to do that.'

'He asked to borrow one of your rings, to get the size right.' She sighed. 'And he showed me lots of pictures, to check he'd get something you'd like.' She brightened. 'But he didn't say when. Although, now I've spoilt the surprise. You're going to have to act surprised when he asks you.'

'You muppet. How could he not know you are the worst person at keeping secrets?'

'I kept one.'

Carrie sighed. 'You did.'

'If he asks, what are you going to do, about, you know? You'll have to do something.'

'Yeah, I will and I should have done it years ago, instead . . .' she paused. Instead of deliberately ducking the issue. 'I need to do something about Richard Maddox.' See, if she said his surname, it made it less personal, as if he wasn't *her* Richard. As if she wasn't entitled to call herself Carrie Maddox. 'It's time we got a divorce.'

CHAPTER THREE

Carrie dragged herself up the stairs to the staff room, consigning whoever had timetabled double drama for Year 7's last periods on a Friday to the very far reaches of hell. As usual the staff room looked as if a cyclone had torn through, followed by marauding Vikings, hotly pursued by random burglars. The cupboard was bare of a single clean coffee cup and the biscuit barrel offered nothing more than crumbs.

Glad it was the end of the day, Carrie retrieved her bag and phone from her locker and a yellow post-it note fell out. With a smile she scooped it up from the floor. Alan had a habit of slipping them through the crack in the door.

Dinner tomorrow night? Prezzo or Pizza Express. Both have offers on. Lots of love Ax

He was out at a quiz night this evening with his cycling buddies and she'd promised herself a curry, a glass of wine and an hour with her laptop. Since she'd won a playwriting competition a few months ago, she'd been tasked with making a few changes so that it could be considered for a West End run. She had until September to get it sorted. So far, good ideas had been elusive. Thank goodness for the long summer holidays.

She tucked the note in her bag and checked her phone to find a text message from her sister, assuming it would be the usual *can you pop to Tesco and pick up . . .* she scanned it quickly.

Exciting news. Grab a bottle of something French!!!!!

'Why French?' she asked walking through the front door and into the living room holding out the bottle of Macon Villages, currently being feted on the supermarket shelf as reduced from £9.99 to £5.99. A bargain, no less, although she was sceptical that this bottle had ever been sold at £9.99.

'We need to start getting in the mood,' said Angela, bouncing out of the chair beside the fireplace.

'The mood for what?' Carrie flopped gratefully into the small two-seater sofa piled high with mismatched cushions. Friday night was batten-down-the-hatches night. Once her shoes were kicked off, she wasn't going anywhere, although in her head she fondly imagined she still went out dancing. With a sigh she nestled into the comforting embrace of the cushions. This was her favourite room in the house. The only one not co-ordinated to within an inch of a paint chart.

'A holiday. I've found us a free cottage, villa, house thing in France.' Angela sat back down, clasping her gnarled hands, the joints ravaged by arthritis, on her lap.

Carrie's ears pricked up at the magical word. 'How free?'

'Proper, real free,' Angela giggled. 'Oh, Lord, I sound like

Jade. Marguerite, at Winthorpe Hall, offered me the use of her house in France for the whole summer.'

Angela worked at a rather swanky residence for distressed gentlefolk of advancing years. Basically it was an extremely posh old people's home with an army of carers, an à la carte menu for dinner each evening with wine and its very own private cinema with screenings every night.

Her duties, as far as Carrie could work out, involved making up a fourth at bridge, completing shopping runs to the Clinique counter at the local Boots for age-defying potions, managing library visits and accompanying the residents on cultural excursions to the Royal Opera House or the Victoria and Albert Museum. It was a tough job but someone had to do it. Although, to be fair, Angela's work opportunities were fairly limited.

'And does Marguerite have all her mental faculties? Actually own the house? Or did she sell it years ago and she's forgotten that minor fact?'

'Marguerite most definitely has every last marble intact.' Angela nodded her head to emphasise the point. 'She's so sharp she could slice slivers from a block of ice for her six o'clock G and T. With all her airs and graces, she's like one of those old Hollywood stars. You should see her slippers, I swear they're trimmed with marabou, or whatever that fluffy stuff is called. She has a different pair every day, to match her outfit.'

'She sounds quite a character.' Carrie could imagine her quite well tripping down the corridors of the very grand Winthorpe Hall. It was more like a luxury hotel than a home for the elderly.

'She is.'

'This place she has in France, I'm sorry, but why would

she have a place out there and not live there? Or not sell it?'

'She keeps it for her family. And she does go out there, when they visit, but she likes company. That's why she moved into Winthorpe. Anyway the whole family are going to America this summer. The house will be empty and she said we can have it. What do you reckon?'

Carrie reckoned that it sounded far too good to be true, but in the absence of anything better coming along in the next few weeks before the end of term it was definitely worth considering. Blimey, once upon a time, she'd have happily leapt on the back of a scooter with a tent and a sleeping bag on her back and gone. Being cautious had crept up on her. Maybe it was all those risk assessments they were so fond of at school. You couldn't take a trip anywhere without seven levels of form filling-in. OV8s, SF9s and a triplicate V13a.

'Whereabouts is it?'

'South of France. Provence sort of way,' Angela paused, wrinkling her nose in thought, 'Or around there. It's in a village.'

'And what sort of accommodation?'

'I think, from what she said, it's all on one level, a bungalow. She said it's got fabulous views.'

Estate-agent speak for 'it hasn't got much else going for it'.

'And the market in the village is wonderful and there are plenty of lovely places nearby to eat.'

'The kitchen is dire you have to eat out.' Carrie could see it now. No wonder Marguerite's family weren't keen on going.

'What do you think? Do you want to come with us?'

'In principle, yes' Carrie said slowly, not wanting to let practical considerations dim Angela's enthusiasm, 'it sounds wonderful. Can I let you know? Perhaps you need to find out more.'

Angela's face fell and her mouth crumpled into a mutinous line that was horribly reminiscent of Jade when she didn't get her way. Except, unlike Jade, Angela wouldn't voice her emotion, she'd button it up in disappointed, accepting silence. Angela didn't complain about much and she had plenty to complain about.

'Nearest airport. Train station. Things like that, so that you can work out the best way to get there and how much it will cost.'

'Marguerite says you can fly EasyJet,' Angela beamed. 'And then it's not far from there.' With Angela's smile restored, Carrie felt slightly less of a killjoy. Her sister and niece depended on her. They needed her and it was important to remind herself of that occasionally. Especially when thoughts of Richard intruded. Swanning off to Hollywood had never been a realistic option for her and she didn't begrudge staying for her family. They'd needed her far more than he did, as all the pictures of him with his leading ladies had soon proved.

'I can't wait to tell Jade,' said Angela. 'She worked hard for her exams. She deserves a proper break.

'Now, what time shall I order the curry. What do you fancy? Your usual.'

Carrie stretched, luxuriating in the fact she didn't have to leave the house again today. She might even go and put her pyjamas on.

'Chicken Biryani? Sag Aloo? Basmati rice?' Angela had already picked up the phone. God, they were predictable.

She sat up quickly, or as quickly as she could. It wasn't that easy to gain purchase on a mountain of cushions.

'No, let's have something different for a change. Where's the menu for the Tandoori Cottage?'

'But we always ring the Banani on the High Street.'

'I fancy a change.' Carrie cringed inside. A different curry house constituted a radical change? She really needed to get out more.

CHAPTER FOUR

'Blimey, you're up bright and early.' Carrie rubbed her eyes, as if trying to clear the mirage that was Jade in the kitchen before nine o'clock on a Saturday morning.

'I'm on a mission.' Jade flicked her head up from her laptop. 'Sort out flights to this place in France before Mum gets all uber-twitchy and comes up with a gazillion reasons why we can't go. She's finally got the deets of the village where this place is. And I've got an early shift at the café today. Babysitting tonight. And working at the hotel tomorrow. I'll be rolling in the Benjamins when I get paid. Primani here I come.'

'Not paying for your flight?' asked Carrie and immediately regretted it when she saw her niece's crestfallen face. She shouldn't tease her; she was a good kid who most of the time pulled her weight. Her positive work ethic couldn't be denied. If you asked her to do a job, *and* she wanted to do it, or acknowledged she had time to do it, you could rely on her. The trick was finding the right job and mentioning it at precisely the right moment.

'I should, shouldn't I?' She turned to Carrie with a worried frown.

'No, honey.' Carrie laid a hand on her shoulder. 'I was teasing you. I'm sure flights to France won't be that expensive and you can be completely flexible about dates. Means we can get the cheapest flights.' She winked at her niece. 'And still be able to afford a pair of new jeans.'

Jade pushed her hand off, laughing up at her. 'You're mean.'

'What's this about a new pair of jeans?' Angela wandered in carrying a mountain of washing. 'You've got enough clothes to sink a fleet of cruise ships.'

'Actually,' Jade tilted her nose in the air and said with a smug tone, 'I told Auntie Carrie that I'd pay for my flight to France instead of buying a new pair of jeans.'

'Really, darling, that's sweet of you but you don't have to.' Angela put an arm around her daughter. 'You're saving up for your own car. That's more important.'

If she wanted to drive, Jade would need her own car, as Angela's automatic, with its specially adapted steering wheel, wouldn't be suitable.

'What time do you need to be at work?' Carrie took a quick peek at the clock. 'I can drop you off at the café when I go to Alan's if you'd like.'

'That would be ace, thanks. I need to be there for ten-thirty. Crikey Moses, I'd better do this and get ready.'

Carrie bit her tongue. She knew better than to query how long it took to get ready. Jade's make-up, admittedly a work of art, took a minimum of an hour to achieve. Perhaps that was where Carrie had gone wrong in her younger days. She hadn't cared enough about that sort of thing. Looks, appearance. There was never enough time to think about them.

She was too busy living life. Teenagers these days had lots more opportunities and yet the boundaries of their lives were limited by their addiction to social media and what everyone else thought of them.

'Right Mum. Sleezyjet. Luton to Nice. Piece of . . . cake. If we fly out on a Thursday evening its thirty-two quid. Come back on a Saturday night. Only twenty-four pounds.'

'That sounds very cheap.' Angela frowned.

'Cos, no other bugger wants to fly then. Market forces. Supply and demand.'

'Wow that Economics GSCE level is really paying off,' said Carrie in mock admiration as she sauntered out of the kitchen. 'Leave at ten-twenty.'

'Sure.' Jade was already busy tapping away at her laptop, Angela craning over her shoulder as Carrie went upstairs to take her shower.

With a quick review of her wardrobe, Carrie yanked out a pair of jeans and her favourite pair of Converse High Tops, covered in gold sequins. She'd bought them on a whim and she adored them, despite the comments both Angela and Alan had made. She didn't care, they were utterly gorgeous. The fact that they were comfortable was a happy coincidence. If she and Alan were going into St Albans for the day to take a look around the Cathedral and the Roman Museum, comfort was the order of the day.

After her shower, Carrie gathered up her hair and with a ruthless tug secured it in a ponytail before wrapping it round several times into a messy bun that she skewered with a couple of decorative wooden chopsticks. She sometimes wondered if perhaps she should have it all cut off, it wasn't as if she ever wore it down and it nearly reached her waist. She spent half of her life tidying it back into its bun. It was a constant battle, like trying to tame a small animal into submission and failing.

Grabbing her jacket, she called for Jade. 'Are you ready?'

'Nearly,' came the expected response from Jade's bedroom next door.

'See you downstairs. I'm leaving in two minutes.'

'Okay! I said I'd be ready!'

With a roll of her eyes, Carrie pounded down the stairs and went to retrieve her handbag from the kitchen.

Angela pored over the laptop with an unhappy frown.

'What's the matter? Are the flights too expensive? Did Jade get it wrong?'

'No. They're fine. We can get flights for around sixty-five pounds return, which is fantastic, if we fly at funny times but that's okay. No, the problem is getting from the airport to the village. There's no public transport – or none that connects. And a taxi from the airport would be rather expensive. I'll have to ask Marguerite what she does.

'Are you back tonight?'

'No but I'll be back early tomorrow. Marking and planning.' She caught sight of the clock. Easy-going and laid-back in most things, Alan did have a bit of a thing about punctuality. Being late showed, he thought, a lack of respect for the other person.

'Jade! I'm going.'

'Alright, keep your hair on. I'm coming.' Jade shouted back.

Angela and Carrie exchanged eye rolls. 'Bye Angela, see you in the morning.

*

'I'd forgotten how lovely it is here,' said Alan as they strolled arm in arm around the nave of the ancient stone building. 'No chance of bumping into any kids from school, either.'

'Always a bonus,' agreed Carrie with a sigh, drinking in the calm, quiet atmosphere. It seemed difficult to believe the cathedral was a step away from the busy high street.

Above them, the sun shone through the rose-stained glass window glistening with brilliant colour.

'Now, do you fancy the guided tour? There's a highlights tour in a few minutes.'

Carrie checked the time on her phone. They'd already been wandering around for an hour. How much more was there to see?

'Why don't you do the highlights tour and I'll sit in one of the pews?' She'd be quite content to gaze up at the window. 'I can wait for you but I don't think I'm up for a tour. My brain's turned to mush.'

'Why didn't you say? Come on let's go to the refectory. Tea and cake.'

'No, Al. You stay. I don't mind.'

'No,' he took her arm in a gentle but insistent grip. This was forceful Alan. Not exactly a force to be reckoned with, he did everything with calm understatement. 'We can come back here any time. Besides cake solves everything.'

The Cathedral café, Abbots Kitchen, offered a very fine selection of cake.

'Excellent. Coffee and walnut. Perfect. What do you fancy? I'm starving.'

She burst out laughing as the woman behind the counter served him a huge slab.

'You're always starving. It's all the cycling.' She gave him a quick, teasing glance. 'You've been out this morning already, haven't you? What are you like?' He put her to shame, not that he ever bothered about her single-minded aversion to exercise.

He responded with an impish grin. 'I'm making sure I'll be in peak shape for the holiday.'

'Rather you than me.' Carrie shuddered. She couldn't think of anything worse than a week toiling up and down the mountain roads of the Alps.

'I've been thinking. You know we were talking about perhaps going to Cornwall or Wales later on in the holidays.'

'Yes, I think I'd prefer Cornwall, bit more chance of sunshine.' With the whole summer break in front of them, the holidays had seemed ages away and they hadn't booked anywhere yet and now she had Angela's offer to think about.

'Well . . .' Alan looked a little sheepish. 'I was thinking . . . that maybe we should wait and save our money . . . go somewhere in the half term in October . . .' A flush ran up his cheeks and the coffee cup in his hand shook, '. . . for maybe a honeymoon.' He put the cup down in its saucer with a clatter and started fumbling in his pocket, tugging as the lining came out, ejecting a red velvet box onto the floor. It tumbled under the table, coming to rest beside her foot.

Biting back a smile, she bent to retrieve it.

Alan sighed and grinned. 'I messed that one up, good and proper.'

Carrie laughed and handed it back to him. 'Possibly not your finest hour. Do you want to start again?'

'I'm not sure you're going to have me, after that fine example of my total ineptitude in the romance department.' He shook his head and pulled a self-deprecating face. 'I had it all worked out. Planned. I was going to go down on one knee on the lawn outside, but there were too many people. I got nervous. So I decided I'd do it later . . . and then it came out. All wrong.'

He twisted the box in his hands as he spoke and then, with a start, glanced down, as if suddenly remembering what it was. Placing it on the table, he took her hand, serious now.

'Carrie Hayes. Will you marry me?'

No fuss. No drama. Just Alan. Quiet, steadfast and true. She'd had drama and fuss and look how that had worked out. With Alan, she knew exactly where she was, while it might not be thrills and spills, his gentle love was like a warm hug. He would always be there for her.

'Alan Lambert. Yes, I will.'

They stared at each other, smiling for a minute.

'Oh, you need this.' He opened the box and started to take out the ring and then half way through changed his mind. 'Here, you'd better do it. I might drop it and then the damn thing will go flying across the room and get lost before you've ever seen it.'

Carrie took the open box and went to take the ring out.

'Don't worry if you don't like it. I can take it back. If it's not right. And say so, won't you. If you don't. Like it, that is.'

She leaned over the table and kissed him to shut him up. 'Shh. It's beautiful.' And it was. A single solitaire diamond in an elegant raised setting. She handed it to him. 'Go on.'

As he slipped it on to her finger with a shaking hand, a warm rush of love filled her heart. He was a good man. He'd look after her. Be a good partner. She'd never have to worry about him leaving her. 'We're engaged,' she said with a giggle, suddenly giddy and light-hearted. It seemed rather staid and sober to be sitting there when they should be bouncing around with excitement.

'We'll need to talk about some of the practicalities,' said Alan, taking her hand and tracing around the ring on her finger. 'Like where we're going to live. My flat's a bit small . . .'

'And bachelory,' added Carrie with a smile.

His face fell. 'It's not that bad. I was going to say, I know it's small but I think we should live there. Think how much money we could save, with you paying half the mortgage and the bills. I mean, we could carry on, but I think getting married makes a lot of financial sense. You know, pooling our resources. Later maybe, we could think about getting a bigger place. I'm loathe to throw my hat into the ring for the Head of Department job and have to suck up to Johnson.'

Alan was a brilliant teacher, but he had no ambition when it came to his career.

'Actually, I've got some money set aside.' Carrie wasn't sure that she wanted to start married life in Alan's flat. 'When my parents died they left their house to me and Angela. She bought the house with her half of the money and my rent money covers the mortgage, but I still have my half of the proceeds.'

Alan sat up. 'I'm marrying an heiress. Well that's even better. I had no idea.' His forehead wrinkled. 'Hmm, well that will put us in a better position financially.'

The moment was in danger of going flat with this boring talk of jobs, mortgages and money.

'Come on,' she grabbed his hand.

'But I haven't finished my . . .'

She dragged him out of the café, pulling him along by

his hand, bumping into chairs as they went. She wanted to run, jump up and down and get rid of some of the energy crackling through her before it burst out through her skin. Her arms prickled with it.

As soon as they emerged outside, Alan tugged back, slowing her to a halt.

'Carrie!' he said, smiling down into her face with a slightly reproachful shake of his head. 'You're crazy.' He lifted her hand and kissed it.

'Yes. Crazy. Alive. Happy.' She grinned up at his familiar face, her cheeks stretched a tad wider than comfortable, ignoring a little voice telling her rather peevishly that she wasn't as happy as last time.

Happiness last time had propelled her down Primrose Hill, running too fast and giggling so hard she could barely breathe, but it didn't matter because there wasn't room in her chest to take a breath with all the fireworks exploding and whooshing and crashing inside her. She'd thought she might explode from sheer joy, which only became giddier when they fell together, arms wrapped around each other, rolling down the hill. And when their pell-mell flight was halted by a hawthorn bush, with a bump that forced the air out of them, they stared at each other with the kind of hungry intensity that made you want to crawl inside the other person because you couldn't get close enough.

Carrie ducked her head to look at the ring on her finger, fighting the sick thud in her stomach. She didn't want to remember that. It was in the past. A different time. A different person. This was now. *This* was what she wanted.

CHAPTER FIVE

How the hell did you divorce someone when you had no idea how the hell to get hold of them in the first place?

Carrie pulled her laptop closer. Sitting in the kitchen felt a little precarious, Jade could get bored with her Netflix binge at any moment and appear behind her, but apart from the lounge, it was the only place you got a decent wi-fi signal.

According to the government website, you could have a DIY divorce for very little money, which sounded great until she started doing more digging. Initially she'd hoped she might get away without having to get a solicitor involved. It wasn't as if she and Richard had anything to fight about. No shared belongings. No children. Not even a marital home. A solicitor wouldn't be interested. Or maybe they would be if they thought major pound signs might be involved. She'd soon disabuse them of that thought.

Richard wasn't likely to contest it, surely not after all this time. He was established, a big-time superstar.

Years ago she'd suggested a divorce. Richard said he

didn't want to. Neither did she, but with gritted teeth, she'd pointed out it was the practical, obvious thing to do because they hadn't seen each other for eighteen months. The rush of relief, when he said he didn't want to call time either, had only been eclipsed by her heart breaking into tiny pieces when he explained that it might hurt his chances of landing the next role.

Stupid idiot, she'd held that last-chance-saloon prayer that they'd work things out, but even though he'd smashed up all her hopes, having not worked in the theatre for eight months, she knew how precious every opportunity was. Who was she to deny him his big break?

She twisted a curl in her hand as she stared at the laptop screen. A divorce certainly wouldn't hurt his career now. Getting a divorce was surprisingly straightforward providing you had an address.

She didn't have a clue where Richard lived. It wasn't exactly something you could look up on the internet. Google was amazing, but she didn't think it was quite that amazing. Deciding to give it a go, she typed in *Where does Richard Maddox live?* What she loved about the great god of search engines, was that it never admitted it didn't know anything. Wouldn't it be great if occasionally a message would pop up, *Google does not have a clue*?

Article after article about Richard Maddox popped up, but not one of them handily said he lived at 3025 Pacific Beach Highway West, Malibu or 95a Beverley Hills Avenue, Hollywood, Ca.

The third from top mentioned that he was about to start filming a new film, *Turn on the Stars*, a romantic comedy, scheduled to go into production in the summer and to be filmed on the Cote D'Azur in France. Carrie winced. Where else but the Cote D'Azur? Although quite where it was in France, she was a bit hazy. Geography had never been her strong point.

'Hey Carrie.' Carrie jumped as Jade sauntered into the kitchen, working hard to resist the urge to slam the laptop closed. 'You okay? Is there anything to eat? I reckon Mum's hidden the rest of the chocolate biscuits.' She crossed to the cupboard, peering into the empty biscuit box with an air of utter disbelief.

'No, I'm pretty sure *you* ate them all.'

'That's ridiculous, I've only had a couple.' Jade pulled a disconsolate face. 'You don't get many in a packet, do you?'

Possibly not when you munched two or three every time you passed the biscuit barrel. Carrie decided it was best not to voice that thought out loud.

'Your film finished?'

'No, got bored. It was lame. What you doing? Don't tell me you're still working?' Jade squinted at the screen.

'No, just surfing.'

'Did Mum tell you about the holiday?' Jade threw herself into the chair opposite.

'No. We haven't spoken about it.' On the one hand free accommodation sounded wonderful for a whole summer holiday, but if something sounded too good to be true, it probably was.

'Looks like it's a no-go.'

'Why's that?'

'We can't get there, not without a flaming helicopter. It's too complicated. No public transport, which means it must be some crappy, middle-of-nowhere place.'

'How does Marguerite, the woman that owns the place, get there?' asked Carrie, used to Jade's dramatics.

'Chauffeur-driven from the airport.' Jade wrinkled her nose. 'Alright for some, eh?'

'Ah. And there's no other way?' Carrie was a great believer in where there was a will there was a way.

'Feel free to try. I've been on the web for hours trying to work it out. Basically we're stuffed. No cheap holiday on the Côte D'Azure.' Jade's downturned mouth almost formed a perfect semi-circle. 'Mum's found a,' she did speech marks actions, "cottage"– polite speak for caravan without wheels, in the Forest of Dean.'

'Côte D'Azur?' Carrie straightened.

'No, Forest of Dean.' Jade glared at her in that full-frontal, pay-attention manner teenagers were so good at adopting.

'No before that. Marguerite's place. I thought it was somewhere on the French Riviera.'

'Yeah, that too. Same place, two names. Why? Just ridiculous. Although makes no difference cos I'm never going to find out what it's like.' Jade slid lower down in her chair. 'Would you bloody Adam and Eve it? First time in a gazillion, trillion years that there's a chance of me actually going abroad. i.e. needing my passport. And it's snatched away from me in the nick of bloody time.'

As Jade had been talking, Carrie had done another quick search.

'Apparently, Riviera is the Anglicised version of Côte D'Azur.'

'For all I care, it could be the Welsh, Scottish or Irish version. It's no good to me.'

'How many does this villa of the famous Marguerite sleep?' asked Carrie, narrowing her eyes, a prick of excitement stirring.

'Doesn't matter as the Hayes family will NOT be going.'

Jade slid down her chair, arms folded, glaring across the table. 'My life officially sucks. Charlotte is going to the Hamptons. Becky is going to Paris. Eliza is going to Canada. I, on the other, rubbish, hand am going to a pathetic caravan park, without Wi-Fi, in the middle of nowheresville.'

'Could be worse.'

'How so?' Jade slouched even further down, her chin now level with the table.

'It might rain every day.' Carrie smiled, getting up and walking behind Jade to flip on the kettle behind her.

'That's mean. Thanks a bunch for that cheery thought.' Jade, now loose-limbed and droopy, looked in danger of melting across the table.

'Always good to share.' Carrie pulled a couple of mugs out of the cupboard, holding one up to Jade in offer of a hot drink. 'But, if you could get to Marguerite's, how many bedrooms does it have?'

'Oh God, you're not going to bring Al are you? He'll spend the whole time encouraging me to read.' With a sudden start, Jade straightened, realising that perhaps there was renewed hope. 'Not that he isn't a great bloke and all that but not . . . to go on holiday with. Bit too much of a teacher.'

'And what does that make me?' asked Carrie with a lift of one eyebrow.

'Ah,' she said, with an air of being terribly knowledgeable about such things, 'being an aunt is much, much worse.'

Carrie stuck her tongue out at her niece, and looped an arm around her neck in a wrestler's headlock. 'Is that so?'

Jade promptly dissolved into giggles.

'Mum's still not sure of the details but she thinks it's six.'

'That'd be two bedrooms and a sofa bed in the lounge,'

guessed Carrie out loud. This could be her best chance at tracking Richard down. Sleeping in the lounge was a smallish price to pay.

Jade shrugged. 'I guess.'

'What if I drove? Hired a car at the airport. Nice, did you say? Cinders and her mother could go on holiday somewhere hot and sunny.'

'Seriously!' Jade jumped up and threw her arms around Carrie. 'Auntie Caz you rock. That would be awesome. Even with Al. Not that Al is not nice. He's lovely. But . . . well you know.' Occasionally Jade knew when to stop. This moment was clearly one of them. Al was a teacher. Fifteen years older than her. One day she would understand.

'Good job Al is cycling in the Alps, then.' Carrie's stern look communicated that she'd gone far enough.

'Is that in Russia?' asked Jade, looking away.

'Did they teach you anything at that school of yours?' Carrie shook her head, but Jade gave her a cheeky irrepressible grin.

'Yup, Poker, Spin-the-bottle and how to top up your lunch card with someone else's account.'

Turning her back on her niece, Carrie poured boiling water over her teabag and waited for it to brew, tuning out Jade's excited chatter. How hard could it be to find out where a film crew was working? Surely she could discover where Richard was staying and hand-deliver a letter. She wouldn't even have to see him. This was the best possible solution. This way she'd be sure he'd receive the letter. She could spend weeks waiting for letters to go back and forth to the States, even if she had his proper address.

'Come on then, Princess Jade. Show me where we need to get to and what the flight times and prices are.'

CHAPTER SIX

Coming down the metal steps as dusk fell, the balmy heat enveloped her in that familiar holiday-warm embrace, immediately making her smile. In the distance lights twinkled, winking through the heat haze pouring off the tarmac of the runway. Overhead a plane roared as it took off. Despite the petrol fumes in the air, she could also smell that indefinable mix of Cypress and the Mediterranean.

Jade, who'd moaned for much of the flight, now started hopping up and down and asking lots of questions. Angela answered them patiently. Carrie tuned out. She had other things on her mind. She clutched the travel wallet closer to her. The car-hire papers were all in there. Booked online. Her diving licence as instructed. They weren't delayed. The car-hire office expected them. They were used to people arriving at all hours.

She had her phone. It had maps on it. They'd work in France, wouldn't they? She'd already programmed the address of the villa into the app. Carrie didn't feel as sure about driving as she made out to her sister.

Her hand tightened on her carry-on luggage.

Angela turned anxious eyes on her. 'Do you think we'll be able to find the car-hire place okay? They won't have closed yet, will they? It's peak holiday season. They must be used to people flying in at this time. It will be alright won't it?'

'Of course it will. Once we're through, it will be dead easy.' Carrie smiled, hoping that her sister couldn't see the mild panic in her eyes. She'd never ever driven on the wrong side of the road. Why the hell had she thought she could?

'Do you think you'll be alright in a left-hand car? And with the French drivers. I've heard they're mad.'

Nerves danced in Carrie's stomach, taking up a full-blown jig instead of the slightly agitated rumba of a minute before. 'It'll be fine. I'll take it nice and steady.' And pray that there wasn't much traffic on the road at this time and that the sat-nav on her phone would be patient with her and that she'd be able to manage the gears with the wrong hand.

They crawled at snail's pace through passport control and then it took forever for the noisy juddering carousel, like an angry caterpillar, to disgorge their luggage with ill grace.

'I can't tell you how grateful I am that you offered to do this.' Angela squeezed her arm as they walked out through the 'nothing to declare' channel, pushing a heavily laden trolley. It had been impossible to persuade Jade that, in the heat, she wouldn't need that many clothes, even if they were going to be away for nearly a whole month.

Carrie had halted at the 'nothing to declare' sign, fancifully imagining that she might get stopped and turned back to go through the other channel. *You should have declared your marriage.* The jury was still out on whether she should have told Al. Not telling him was cowardly, but how did you go about telling your fiancé that you were already married? She couldn't face the questions. Why hadn't she mentioned it before? How long were you married? When did you last see him? Why didn't you tell me?

'I'm not sure that if I was driving out here, I would have been brave enough.' Angela's voice penetrated her thoughts. 'You've always been so adventurous compared to me.'

'No I haven't,' Carrie responded, slinging her bag over her shoulder. 'It was easier for me to leave home.' She hadn't had a chronic illness to contend with. 'And I had a reason to go. A place at drama school.'

'Yes but you could have turned the place down. Not gone to live in London. It was a big step. You were marginally older than Jade and yet you went and embraced it.'

'I was hungry then. To perform. To act. It wasn't necessarily being brave, more like young and stupid. Foolhardy, even. I had no conception of what I was getting into. I assumed if I wanted it enough, it would happen and that, against the massive odds, I might be good enough and get work.'

'Yawnsville. We're on holiday here, guys. There's proper French on the signs and everything and you two are having a history lesson.'

They emerged into the airport departure lounge. What was it that made you aware that you were in a different country? Was it the people? Their indefinable Frenchness, which made them look different.

The familiar logos of Hertz and Eurocar loomed and there was the company name and logo that matched her paperwork. Hurdle one successfully surmounted.

'Why don't you wait out here?' suggested Carrie, looking

at the tiny goldfish bowl of an office, dwarfed by its big-brother branded counterparts on either side.

'Bonjour,' said Carrie, retrieving the pages printed from the internet.

'Bonsoir,' said the middle-aged man on his feet behind a tall counter.

'Yes. Do you speak English?'

'Oui Madam.' His dark eyebrows drew together in a ferocious, rather off-putting, slash suggesting that Carrie had committed a faux pas already. What he didn't realise was that if she'd attempted to speak French they'd have been here all night.

Rather than upset him any further, she laid the paperwork on the counter with an encouraging smile, hoping that managing the transaction with minimal dialogue might make him feel better.

He took the folded sheets and held them close to his face, his nose almost touched the paper.

With a nod, he looked up at her and then back at the paper before busying himself typing at his computer. 'Permis du conduire,' he said without shifting his gaze from the screen. Her mind went blank for a second trying to deconstruct the sentence. He'd spoken so quickly the words ran into one another and could have been a sneeze for all she knew.

'Driving licence.' He repeated in perfect English.

Like a chastened school girl or the stupid tourist she obviously was, she dug into her bag and pushed it across the top of the counter, smiling like an idiot in the vague hope it would soften him up. She could do with a friendly face right now.

The fears, which hadn't been fears at all when she'd first

suggested they hire a car and she drive, had been given life by relentless questioning from both Angela and Jade.

Dammit. It was an adventure. A summer on the Riviera. An escape from everyday life for a whole thirty days. She should be grasping it with both hands and wringing every last bit of fun and happiness out of it.

'What sort of car have we got?' she asked. She'd always been good with people. Why should one measly, grumpy Frenchman be any different? 'The four-wheeled variety I'm assuming but what make?'

He narrowed his eyes and glanced up. 'A Renault Clio.'

'Fabulous. Something with a bit of va va voom. I don't suppose Thierry Henri comes as standard?'

Who knew that Thierry Henri was the French equivalent of Open Sesame?

'Unfortunately not, Madame.' The words were said with a wry smile.

She lifted her shoulders. 'Oh well.'

He studied the screen. 'You're staying in Gassin. It's not too far from St Tropez. You perhaps will see a famous face or two during your time. They're filming a Hollywood movie near where you are staying.'

Carrie's pulse quickened. 'Really? That would be interesting to see.'

Lifting his fingers to his lips, he shifted his gaze from left to right, which was rather hilarious as there were only the two of them in the office, before saying, 'The production company has hired rather a lot of vehicles.' He nodded. 'Next door, on either side. They did not have sufficient. We have supplied several cars.'

'Wow,' said Carrie. 'Do you know where they're based?'

'No, there was a lot of secrecy about that.'

'Yes, I guess there would be. They wouldn't tell many people.'

'However,' he continued, straightening and leaning forward, lowering his voice, 'the director took one of our cars. He asked about parking for some of the locations. The harbour in St Tropez, the market in Ramatuelle and at a restaurant in Grimaud.'

Carrie wondered how many people he'd imparted that self-important information to in recent weeks.

'God, were you building the car or what? You've been ages.' Jade scrambled up from her position on the floor, where she'd half-sprawled across the cases on the luggage trolley.

'These things always take forever. But we have wheels. A red Clio. Out in the car park, bay 57.'

'A Clio. I hope it's going to be big enough.' Angela prodded the pile of luggage.

'It will be fine,' said Carrie and then with a wink at Jade. 'We can always leave Jade behind and come back for her tomorrow. Or we could ditch one of her cases.'

'Yeah, right.' Jade nudged Carrie. 'Mum, chill. It'll be fine. And,' she poked her tongue out at her aunt, 'I'll sit on one of my cases if I have to. I'm not leaving a single thing behind. I need everything.'

'No one *needs* ten pairs of shorts,' said Carrie.

'Wanna bet?'

'They do have washing machines in France, Jade,' said her mother.'

'Yeah, yeah. Are we going to get out of here or what?' asked Jade, seizing the trolley.

'Or what,' answered Carrie, her spirits suddenly lifting. 'Let the vacances commence.'

'Please don't try to speak French when we're out.' Jade groaned. 'It sounds sooo embarrassing.'

'I'll do my best.' Carrie exchanged a look with her sister, who burst out laughing.

'I think the chances of anyone understanding her are extremely slim.' Angela smiled, linking an arm through Carrie's. 'Lead us to our chariot. I'm ready for a nice cup of tea.'

'Tea? We're in France. On holiday. I'm ready for a large glass of wine.'

'Yeah, Mum. And I'm allowed to drink here. There's none of that being eighteen and identity card crap here. Hallelujah.'

'Like it's ever stopped you before.' Carrie often received a texted plea for a bottle of wine for a party. She and Angela were of the view that banning something made it more enticing and as a result had a fairly laid-back approach to alcohol, which thankfully Jade had respected.

'Isn't this fab? It's eight o'clock at night and it's still lovely.' Jade peeled off her cotton top. 'I wish I'd got my shorts on now.'

'We'll be in the car in a minute. It's got air con.' Carrie spotted the numbered signs. 'Here we are.'

Jade let out a sigh. 'Seriously. Why are you going so slowly?'

Carrie examined the speedometer, they were doing a respectable speed but it did feel painfully slow.

'I'm doing seventy.'

'The French obviously don't give a toss about speed limits, then, because every other bugger keeps overtaking us.'

'Let Carrie do her own speed, Jade. She's driving on the wrong side of the road. She's concentrating.'

'I also don't know what the local speed limit is, to be perfectly honest.'

'Easy, peasy.' Jade tapped away at her phone. '110km unless it's raining. Isn't that funny? Our speed limits don't mention rain and I bet we get far more than here.'

Carrie started to laugh as she put her foot down on the accelerator, watching the speedometer creep up. 'I forgot the speedo was in kilometres. I've been sticking to 70 thinking it was miles.'

'You muppet.' Jade shook her head.

In the back Angela laughed. 'Although you probably needed to go slowly at first to get used to the car and driving—' Jade and Carrie exchanged a look before joining in unison 'on the wrong side of the road.'

With the help of the phone and Carrie's new-found understanding of the speedometer the journey passed more quickly, the roads getting progressively smaller as they left the motorway. In the dark it was difficult to see much of their surroundings. They could have been in Milton Keynes, but as the miles on the signposts counted down to St Tropez, Jade suddenly shouted, 'The sea! The sea!'

Down below them a concentration of lights crowded around the water, outlining the coast.

'We're nearly there.' Jade began to bounce in her seat. Carrie gripped the steering wheel.

'I can't believe it! St Tropez. It sounds incredibly exotic.' Angela's tremulous voice held buttoned-down excitement.

Too damn right. It was exciting. And the minute she peeled herself out of this car, Carrie would be celebrating with something cold.

They circuited the outskirts of St Tropez and began to climb the hill up to Gassin, following the directions of the disembodied voice on the phone.

'I hope it's going to be nice,' said Angela. She'd edged to

the front of her seat, holding onto both head rests on the passenger and driver seats. 'Marguerite said not to expect too much but she wouldn't send us anywhere horrible.'

'Angela, as long as it's dry and has beds, it will be fine,' said Carrie, resigning herself to the prospect of an uncomfortable bed and very basic surroundings for the next four weeks. It wouldn't matter. When it was hot, you didn't spend much time inside. They could go out every day. Take picnics. All they needed was somewhere to sleep.

'Yes. You're right.' Angela sighed. 'And if it's awful, we can go home early.'

'It won't be awful. It will be fine.' And hopefully the heat would be good for Angela's arthritis. They'd have to make sure she had the most comfortable bed.

'It had better have a shower,' said Jade. 'I can't be doing with it being this hot and no shower.'

'I'm sure it will,' said Angela. 'Marguerite has owned this place for a while. I remember her saying something about new tiling in the bathroom being done last year.'

The directions on the phone were becoming more frequent and they all shut up so they could hear them. The road climbed and twisted and turned more frequently.

'Destination on your left in two hundred feet,' announced the map lady.

Carrie slowed right down, thankful there was nothing behind them. The road was completely black with absolutely no sign of habitation nearby. To the left, falling away down the hill, were lights in the distance but nothing nearby.

A horrible sense of foreboding clamped around her. Surely Marguerite's place had basic facilities like electricity. Or maybe it was all switched off and they would need to turn on the fuse box.

She drove slowly, still unable to see any sign of a house. 'Destination on your left.' The voice on the app held a note of desperation. 'Turn left. Turn left.'

Carrie couldn't see anything and it was only after the car crept past, she spotted a square of light embedded into a brick wall.

'At the nearest point perform a u-turn.'

Jade tutted. 'We've gone past it. You've missed it.'

'Well, it wasn't exactly obvious.' Carrie kept driving, looking out for some handy place to stop, but the road was narrow with too many bends. After about a mile she spotted a driveway, pulled in and did a quick three-point turn, to return back up the road.

This time she pulled in and realised that the blur of light was a keypad on the edge of two large gates.

'Ah,' said Angela, in sudden realisation. 'Marguerite said there was a pass code. I thought she meant for the house. Thirty Oh Six.'

'Are you sure this is right?' Carrie eyed the wooden gates, no wonder they'd passed them earlier, they were so dark they melded into the night, their solid size and dimensions designed to repel the hordes and keep out unwanted visitors. She had visions of angry Dobermans chasing them off someone's property.

'I think so.'

'Oh, for God's sake. Put the code in, if it works we know we're in the right place. If not, we're stuffed.'

For once Jade's prosaic approach agreed with Carrie's.

Leaning out of the window she tapped in the code with nervous apprehension. The drive had taken it out of her and now she wanted to be there.

To her slight amazement and utter relief, like magic, lights came on and the heavy wooden gates opened with slow, ponderous eventuality until the gap between them was wide enough to take the car.

Carrie inched forward, not quite knowing what to expect beyond, taking a leap of faith rather like stepping through the wardrobe into Narnia, except she had no idea what was on the other side. Luckily the smooth tarmac continued and the road curved downward in a wide sweep before coiling back upwards. Solar lights lit the road like sentries posted at regular intervals along the way.

'Whoa,' Jade leaned forward, her nose almost on the dashboard.

'That's Marguerite's little place?'

'Erm . . . I think so. She was quite vague. Talked about the view a lot.'

'You mean you heard the word 'free',' said Jade laughing. 'Mum, that is so typical.'

'Now let's not get carried away. That might be the main house and we're in an annexe or something. I know she said it was all on one floor.'

'All on one floor is somewhat different from a bungalow, Mum!'

Carrie stopped the car and all three of them stared at the house ahead of them, sprawled across the top of the hill in a halo of light, looking rather like something out of a Bond film.

Angela sighed with happiness, or perhaps relief, that they weren't staying in a dilapidated cottage falling down around their ears. Even Jade, never short of words, stared, drinking in the sight in wide-eyed silence.

Carrie drove carefully up the hill in second gear, not wanting to miss a moment of the delicious sense of anticipation. The little car wound through the landscaped grounds, lit here and there with uplighters, showing off ornamental grasses interspersed with gravel paths and evenly planted bay trees in huge pots, like sentries watching over the land.

It seemed rather untidy to park the poor relation of a car in front of this glamorous house. There was probably a garage for the sexy convertibles or huge four-wheeled things that ought to be here. As Carrie got out of the car, stretching her legs with catlike satisfaction, the scent of herbs filled the warm night. Sod the car, they were here and had possibly fallen into the lap of luxury. Whether they were in the gardener's cottage or the maid's flat, judging by the size and stature of this house, they were going to be alright.

Two enormous terracotta pots flanked the front double doors, twin concierges welcoming them, which might have been slightly intimidating if it weren't for the whimsical touch of tiny fairy lights threaded through the miniature olive trees in each one. Carrie smiled, it softened the rather grand and very contemporary landscaping along the rest of the front of the house, where artfully grouped smaller pots held a variety of precision-trimmed shrubs, scenting the air with a cocktail of fragrances including rosemary, thyme and bay.

Her face broke into a broad smile as she nudged her sister.

'I think this might do nicely. What do you reckon?'

'I had no idea it was going to be like this.' Angela twisted her hands together, as if she couldn't quite believe it either.

They stood together examining the house. 'I love the roof. Terracotta tiles. So Mediterranean. So romantic. I have a good feeling about this.'

'It looks wonderful.' Carrie squeezed her sister's arm.

'For Pete's sake are we going inside or not? Listen to you. It's a house. It's flipping gorgeous.'

Angela rummaged in her bag, pulling out the precious envelope, crumpled from the dozens of times she checked it was still there during the journey. Opening it, she pulled out the keys.

She held the key gripped between twisted thumb and finger, eyeing the lock with the intense concentration of a surgeon about to make the first incision. Jade and Carrie hung back with practised patience, determinedly not looking at each other. It was a familiar routine, where neither acknowledged the slow, painful attempts that any fine motor skills demanded or made any attempt to speed up the process. Although Angela's rheumatoid arthritis limited her in many ways, she never complained and had never once said, 'why me and not you' to Carrie.

The door opened, light streaming out and Angela stood poised on the threshold, a triumphant smile on her face.

'Looks like we're in the right place.'

They crowded in through the door, their feet echoing on the polished marble floor, blinking in the light thrown by a huge dandelion clock of a lighting fitting, with what looked like hundreds of brilliant bulbs. For a second they stared around the high-ceilinged hallway, larger than the whole of their semi-detached home.

On a console table of painted wood, in a cracked glass vase, spilled a blousy, extravagant bouquet of flowers, a white card tucked into the foliage.

Angela plucked the card and read out aloud.

Dear Angela and family, you are most welcome to La Maison de Clemont. Please do make yourselves at home. The fridge is fully stocked to get you started but please do let Marisa, our much-loved maid, know of your preferences and she will shop accordingly. She'll pop in to say hello. I hope you have a happy and joyous holiday here and I look forward to hearing all about it on your return.

Enjoy
With much love
Marguerite

CHAPTER SEVEN

'How lovely, said a rather shell-shocked Angela.

'This is going to be ace.' Jade threw her arms around her mother.

Carrie stepped forward, opening a set of double doors to reveal a spacious lounge. No, lounge sounded too mundane, this was a salon, a sitting room . . . just gorgeous. Looking up she traced the bleached-blonde wood beams criss-crossing a high-pitched sloping ceiling, smiling at the wonderful sense of light and space.

'Come and look at this,' she called, taking the three broad, shallow steps down into the room, unable to resist the temptation to sink into one of the two taupe-linen-covered sofas, each of which could have comfortably seated five people. Contrasting arm chairs in cream were dotted around the modern wooden coffee table opposite the sofas. Understated and classical, Carrie could imagine the key words, in capitals, on the interior designer's brief had been 'style', 'taste' and 'elegance'.

'Get a load of that TV,' said Jade with a squeal of delight, crossing to the flat-screen television framed within the wall above a fireplace with a log burner in it the size of a small bath tub. 'Whoa! That is fab-u-lous.' Almost reverently she reached up to touch the sixty-five-inch, or, whatever it was, screen. 'Much better than our piddly little thing.'

Personally Carrie thought the thirty-inch screen at home was more than adequate, although she had to concede the size of this room meant you did need a monster screen this big.

Angela came and bounced on the sofa next to Carrie, letting out a happy sigh. 'Oh my days. I never imagined it would be like this.'

'You pulled a blinder, sis,' said Carrie, hugging her.

'You certainly did, Mum,' agreed Jade, coming to join them on the sofa.

With a sudden squeal, Carrie threw herself backwards, taking Angela and Jade with her, kicking her feet up in the air.

'Woohoo!' she shouted as the other two burst into giggles and copied her, all three bicycling their legs like mad.

Euphoria fizzed in Carrie's stomach like an errant Catherine wheel, spinning so hard it had taken flight. 'It's like that scene in *Pretty Woman* where Vivienne throws herself on the huge bed.'

'OMG. What do you think the bedrooms here will be like?' Jade sprang up. 'And the bathroom?'

'I suspect bathrooms as in multiple. Which will be great. You can spend as long as you like in there.'

Jade stuck her tongue out her aunt.

'And what's out here, do you reckon?'

Soft flowing linen drapes skirted the room on two sides. Jade tugged at them to reveal a complete wall of French doors. It was too dark to see beyond the patio area and the dark shapes of furniture. Lights dotted on the hillside were testament to a potentially fabulous view in the morning.

'I'm starving,' announced Jade.

'Why don't I find the kitchen, while you two go and bring in the cases and then you can explore the bedroom situation?' asked Angela, falling into her usual mothering role.

'Okey doke.' For once Jade was happy to follow orders without arguing the toss. 'I reckon there'll be a bedroom each.'

'I hope so,' said Carrie, laughing. She'd been worried she'd have to sleep in the lounge on a sofa. These sofas were bigger than her double bed at home.

Angela stood uncertainly. 'Which way do you think the kitchen is?'

They burst out laughing, looking around them, all of them amused by the thought of being in a house so big that it wasn't obvious where the rooms were.

In unspoken agreement they retraced their steps.

'Blimey, this is fancy,' said Jade as they walked along a glass corridor linking the first building to another on a slightly different level. 'I think Marguerite's idea of everything being on one floor is slightly different to mine,' said Angela as they tripped up a set of three steps. 'Oh!' She gasped. 'Isn't this lovely? Look at the range stove. I would love one of those at home. It's got seven rings on it.'

The range, which didn't do much for Carrie, sat under a wooden cream-painted canopy, no doubt hiding the extractor fan. The styling of the kitchen was very much French provincial with its distressed wooden cupboards and plate filled racks. It was the sort of room that everyone gravitated to, perfect for cooking and entertaining at the same time, with its central island, a sink on one side and rustic wooden bar stools on the other.

What she loved about the room was the roof, similar to the lounge, open to wooden beams, which met in a high ridge running the length of the room, finishing above a contemporary-styled bay window. Under the window on all three sides was a built-in seat with brightly coloured cushions in patterned fabric.

Carrie's eyes were drawn to the full-height wine fridge, filled with bottles. 'Do you think she meant it when she said "help yourselves"? I think we should celebrate.'

Angela had already pulled open the doors of the American-style fridge.

'It's got an ice-maker. That's cool.'

'And enough food to feed five thousand,' said Angela faintly, looking around at Carrie, with a slight frown. 'I wasn't expecting this. I'm rather overwhelmed.'

'Bin that Protestant work ethic, Catholic guilt attitude right now. Marguerite's note was quite explicit and from what you've told me about her, she meant every word. We are going to enjoy every last minute of this wonderful house.

'Now you get cracking and rustle us up something fabulous and choose a bottle of wine. While me and the brat here will unload the car.'

'And bag the best bedrooms,' added Jade.

'I think, given your mother has come up with this gem, she should get the best room,' said Carrie, poking her niece in the back.

'Oy.'

'To be perfectly honest,' Angela shook her head in wonderment, 'I think the worst bedroom here will still be better than any of ours.

'I need to check out the wi-fi code.' Jade shook her phone. 'Crap signal up here. Please say this place has internet.'

'There you go.' Angela pointed to a note tagged to the fridge door with a magnet, rather bizarrely in the shape of the Statue of Liberty, among all the other local tourist magnets.

'Holey Moley, thank God for that.'

CHAPTER EIGHT

Sumptuous didn't begin to describe the bedrooms. They were all decorated in the same subdued colours which Carrie imagined would be very cool during the hot summer days, with pure-white cotton, plumped-up bedding.

Jade darted from room to room, now wired for comms, snap-chatting her friends asking their opinion as to which she should choose. While she was doing that, Carrie fell in love with the bedroom at the furthest corner of the building.

Like the rest of the house, it featured the same stripped-wooden beams, cool neutral colours and light airy feel, but what swung her decision were sets of French windows on two walls which met at the corner of the room. Opening one set, she stepped out onto a balcony and it felt as if she were stepping right out into the night air as the hill fell away beneath her. Someone had cleverly built this house to maximise the contours of the hill.

She unpacked quickly, laying claim to the room, although she couldn't believe that either Angela or Jade would be that fussed about this one. It was easily the smallest but it felt right, down to the little dressing table, which would double perfectly as a desk, although she suspected the view might be rather distracting.

Lavender perfumed the air when she opened up the painted-wood wardrobe, filled with fancy, silk-padded hangers and lace sachets of herbs. It seemed almost sacrilege to bother it with her meagre collection of clothes. She didn't do quantity but where quality was concerned, she had an aptitude for mixing expensive with dirt cheap and making it look good. Most of the things she'd brought with her, T-shirts, strappy vest tops and flippy skirts didn't need hanging up and certainly not on hangers as posh as these.

The tiled floors were cool to her hot feet when she slipped off her beloved converses and yanked down her jeans, which now clung to her legs. Folding them up, she consigned them to the back of the wardrobe. They could stay there until it came to going home. Just think – she could wear dresses and skirts every day without once having to worry about being cold or taking a coat or an umbrella everywhere with her. If it did rain here, it would be the sort of rain that you didn't mind getting wet in.

Slipping her feet into her well-worn flip-flops, she cast a quick, longing glance at the en-suite bathroom and its walk-in shower that she didn't have to share with anyone. Absolute bliss.

The beep of her phone with yet another text welcoming her to France providing details of how much it cost to send a text or make a call, reminded her that she ought to let Alan know they'd arrived safely and alleviate his fears that their free accommodation wasn't a shanty house after all.

A quick flurry of texts between them confirmed he'd had

a great day's cycling and that he was pleased that the house wasn't falling down around her ears.

All that was needed now, to finish the day off in perfect style, was a long, cool glass of wine. But first she wanted to look up where the village of Ramatuelle was and when market day was.

Angela had wasted no time. With the instincts of a born nester, she'd unearthed a table cloth, pretty napkins and china to lay the table in the bay window. To Carrie's delight a condensation-coated bottle of white wine wedged into a terracotta cooler took up prime position in the middle of the table flanked by a pair of large wine glasses.

With picture-perfect design, a basket of rustic bread waited alongside a wooden board of cheeses, some of which already scented the air with their pungency, a platter of sliced meats and two round dishes of pâté.

'Can I do anything?' asked Carrie, with a raised eyebrow, knowing that Angela was in her absolute element.

'Nothing. Apart from getting that bottle open and pouring us both a glass. Oh and you can put these olives on the table.'

'When are the others arriving?' asked Carrie. 'Did you put everything in the fridge out?'

Angela laughed gaily and threw open the fridge doors. 'You've got to be kidding. There's enough food here to withstand a siege. It's heaven.'

Every shelf was packed with unfamiliar branded bottles, unusual-shaped jars and beguiling paper-bag-wrapped parcels.

'There's gallons of stuff in here. Merguez sausages, compôtes, duck confit, Cassis and myrtle jam, a million different cheeses and meats.' Angela threw open a cupboard, almost skipping with joy. 'Here, look. There are stacks of tins, every kind of bean you can imagine, haricot, flageolet and green beans, cassoulet, Tartiflette and even tinned Dauphinoise potato!'

Carrie opened the bottle and poured two glasses, sticking her nose deep in the first glass before sampling it. The clean fresh straw-coloured wine tasted every bit as good as its heavenly smell.

'I'm going to have so much fun in this kitchen.'

'It's supposed to be a holiday,' said Carrie, offering up a glass with a dramatic shudder, grateful as always that her sister loved cooking.

'It is but I don't have the time to think about cooking properly at home, which means we have the same old. With all this inspiration, I can go to town.'

Carrie smiled, her heart lighter just listening to her sister.

'Are you sure? I know you love it but don't overdo it.' Her eyes rested on the knobbly joint at the base of her sister's index and middle fingers.

Angela flexed her fingers, the fine lines around her mouth tightening. 'I'm fine.'

Carrie smiled at her sister's stubbornness, but then she'd had to be to fight against the regular pain that her condition brought with it. 'I know you're fine. But I don't want you to end up in here all the time. Jade and I need to help out otherwise it isn't fair. Now come sit down.'

'I bet the view out of this window is fabulous in daylight,' said Angela, perching on the window seat and twisting around to peer through the glass. 'Can't see much now. No wonder Marguerite kept going on about the views.'

'My room's the same. I can hardly wait for the morning.'

'Glad you came?'

'Of course I am.'

'I'm very relieved this place is okay—'

Carrie let out a laugh. 'You are the master of understatement. This place is a-ma-zing with capital everything.'

'Thank goodness. I wasn't sure you wanted to come with us. Not so soon after you and Al got engaged.' She leaned over and laid her hand on Carrie's. 'Thank you.'

'For what?'

'For driving. We couldn't have come without you.'

'You don't need to thank me, you daft bugger.' Carrie shook her head as her sister's eyes shone suspiciously brightly. 'Honestly, what are you like? I'm getting a holiday. I've got my play to work on. And . . . I might be able to track down my errant husband.'

'What. . . Richard?'

'How many husbands do you think I've got? Although I need to get rid of him pretty quickly.' Carrie let out a peal of laughter. 'Oh, Lord, that sounds like I'm planning to bump him off.'

Angela snorted into her wine glass. 'It does a bit. Murder aside, why the hurry?'

'Al wants to get married in October.'

'Yikes! Can you get a divorce that quickly?' Angela shot a quick look towards the door. 'Although if you can't, he'll wait.'

Carrie studied the way the light refracted and danced from the solitaire diamond of her ring.

'You haven't told him.' Angela suddenly accused. She put her wine down with a firm chink, liquid slopping everywhere. 'I don't believe you. Why didn't you tell him?'

Carrie winced, still looking at her ring. 'Because it sounds weird. Hey Al, guess what? I'm married to an international A-list superstar actor. Have been for the last ten years.'

'See what you mean. He's bound to wonder why you never mentioned it before.'

'It's not that, it's confessing the whole impetuous-marriage thing. How do I explain that?'

'You were young and in love?'

'I know but he thinks I'm sensible and responsible.'

'You are . . . now.'

Carrie loved her sister, even though they couldn't be more different. Trust Angela to pass over her wild, impetuous youth with one brief word.

'He's so decent, I don't want him to think badly of me and I don't know how to explain that I'm not that person any more.'

'I think you're worrying unnecessarily. That's my department, remember? He asked you to marry him. He loves you. Alan's a lovely guy. Of course he's going to forgive you a youthful indiscretion. I think you ought to tell him.'

Carrie sighed. 'I think I'll wait until I've at least got the divorce under way. It sounds pathetic not being able to divorce your own husband because you have no idea of how to get hold of him. I've checked – you can't do anything without an address.'

'How are you going to get that?'

'He's here.'

With an almost involuntary movement, Angela checked the corners of the room.

'Not here, here, you noodle. In France.' Carrie took a swig of wine. 'Filming on the Riviera.'

'Really?'

'Yes, for the next two months.'

'The Riviera's quite big you know, it stretches all the way up to Monaco, about a hundred miles.' Angela had been reading guidebooks from the library for the last two weeks with the intensity of a student cramming for finals.

'I know but, stroke of luck, the man in the car-hire place told me some of the places they'll be filming. And one is down the road from here.'

'What are you going to do? Camp out there, until they show up? How will you know where to find the film people? And will he even be there? How will you find him?'

'He'll be in the biggest trailer,' said Carrie flippantly.

'But what if you don't find him?'

'Then I've lost nothing. It's not as if I've got a better place to start. Besides the car-hire man said they were filming in a market near here, Ramatuelle. All I have to do is go and hang out on market day.'

And when is market day?

Carrie grinned. 'Thursday and Ramatuelle is the next village.'

'What this Thursday, as in two days' time, Thursday?'

'Well, I don't know if they'll be filming this week, but I figure it can't hurt to keep visiting each week until they do turn up. Besides, I thought the tourist office would know if there's a film crew on the loose, especially with a star as big as Richard.'

'Smart thinking. Very smart.'

CHAPTER NINE

Dust motes danced in the brilliant beams of sunshine that streamed in around the edges of the drapes. Carrie couldn't help the smile that stretched across her face. With delicious anticipation she lay in bed for a few minutes, wondering what lay beyond the curtains, before padding across the floor and flinging them open, her eyes blinking into the high sun.

Squinting until they grew accustomed to the intensity of the light, she drank in the view. What a clever, clever design. Her corner balcony hung over the incline, where the hill fell away, leaving the sensation of being on a platform suspended above the valley. Ahead of her, in the still morning air, she could see the curve of green hills, interspersed with glimpses of hidden properties among the wooded slopes and beyond that the sea, azure-blue sparkling with white-crested waves.

Sitting down on the terracotta-tiled floor, nicely warm already, she slipped a leg each between the bars, letting them dangle, swinging each leg in opposition, with the sheer pleasure of being able to do nothing but please herself and pretend that she was almost in mid-air. It had almost been so long, she'd forgotten the simple and unique pleasure of the sun kissing her limbs. She leaned back on her arms, tilting her face upwards, like a flower.

'Carrie! Carrie! Over here?' Jade's excited voice came from the terrace. 'There's a pool down here and everything.'

She waved lazily, wondering quite what 'everything' entailed.

'You've got to come down and see it. Mum's made breakfast and there's an outdoor table. Come on.'

With a sigh Carrie hauled herself to her feet. Plenty of time of peace and solitude in the next few weeks.

'Good morning.' Angela, of course, had laid the table. Before Carrie even sat down, her sister picked up a cafetière brimming coffee, the grounds at the top almost frothing over the lip of the glass.

'Coffee,' groaned Carrie, 'that smells amazing.'

She sniffed and clutched the cup to her. 'Bliss. Did you sleep well?'

'Ish. I woke up early. Strange bed.'

'Carrie, Carrie come and see the pool.' Relinquishing her coffee and charmed by her niece's sudden childlike enthusiasm, she joined her at the poolside. For once Jade didn't have a scrap of make-up and was still in her pyjama shorts and vest top. She looked her age for once, without that world-weary smartarse cynicism she often adopted.

'Isn't it awesome?'

Carrie laid an arm across her shoulder and took in the view, the pool in the foreground, with its red-and-white stripy, padded sun loungers and the low, lean lines of the house in the background. 'Absolutely. Awesome.'

Replete with croissant and coffee, Carrie sat on the edge

of the pool, her legs stretched out in the sun watching Jade dipping her toes in the water and shrieking with the cold and begging her to come in.

After breakfast, they settled in the sun loungers, sticky with sun cream, smelling slightly of coconut. Jade plugged herself into her phone, lying prone on one of the sun loungers, in outsize Jackie Onassis sunglasses, holding the screen up to read out periodic text messages of sheer envy from her friends. Delighted with the stash of cookery books she'd commandeered, Angela sat in the shade with a note pad, scribbling things down and occasionally tearing off a strip of paper and tucking it into the pages and asking random questions, such as 'Have you ever had duck à l'orange?' and 'What do you think of bouillabaisse?'

'Did you know Kim Kardashian has three hundred and eighteen pairs of shoes?' announced Jade, reading from the screen on her phone. 'That's mad.'

Carrie tried to concentrate on next year's drama text, wondering how on earth she was going to interest her Year 10s of the political depths of the play and the tragic characters of Mother Courage and her children, when they were more concerned with the antics of a mad American family, rich idiots in one of London's wealthiest suburbs and has-beens in a pretend jungle.

'Eeuw! That bloke from Towie got a new tattoo on his you-know-where.'

The day set a pattern of lazing on the patio by the pool, occasionally retreating into the kitchen to get more soft drinks.

Over dinner, cooked by Angela, as happy in the kitchen as out by the pool, they talked about their plans for the rest of the week.

'The lovely thing about being here all this time, is there's no rush to do anything,' said Angela. 'I don't feel the least bit guilty for not going off and exploring.'

'We've got to go to some of the famous places, though,' said Jade. 'I want to tell my friends I've been to St Tropez. Do you think we could blag our way onto one of those big yachts?'

'I doubt it very much,' said Angela, putting a bowl of salad on the table, alongside a platter of garlic-cooked prawns gleaming pink in their shells.

'Mmm, those smell heavenly.' Carrie's stomach let out a yowl of support, making Jade and Angela giggle.

'Sorry.' She rubbed at her middle.

'Sounds like Chewbacca on heat,' said Jade. 'What's the plan for tomorrow?'

Angela and Carrie exchanged a quick glance.

'Let's play it by ear and see how we feel,' suggested Angela. 'We've got this lovely pool and it's so peaceful. I'd quite like to chill for a few days. Perhaps we can go out somewhere the day after tomorrow. Maybe explore Gassin. It's supposed to be beautiful.'

After dinner Jade plugged herself into her phone

'You going tomorrow?' asked Angela, sotto voce, even though Jade couldn't possibly hear.

'Yes, I thought I'd leave early. I'm more worried about finding somewhere to park than finding my way. I've got my phone.'

'That's all you're worried about?' asked Angela, her eyebrows almost taking off. 'What if the film crew isn't there?'

Carrie swallowed, that was about the only thing she wasn't worried about. If the film crew didn't turn up, then her worries stopped right there. She wouldn't have to worry about looking like a crazy fan, trying to blag her way through minders, security people or some clipboard official in charge of cordons. She wouldn't have to worry about what would happen if she did get through. She wouldn't have to worry about someone passing her message on to him. And if, after all that, she got that far, she wouldn't have to worry about what to say to Richard on the phone if he called her.

CHAPTER TEN

She gave the butterflies in her stomach a stern talking to as she crept along the hall. They had absolutely nothing to get in a tizz about. Now all she had to do was pray that she could leave the house before Jade woke up and she had to answer any awkward questions.

Of course, no one paid the least bit attention to her prayers.

'Carrie, wait! Where you going?'

She'd taken two scant steps out of the front door. Her heart sank like lead weight plummeting to the absolute depths of the ocean. Seriously? Was someone having a laugh?

'I thought I'd pop out for an early-morning drive, perhaps bring us some fresh croissants back.' Carrie kept walking, the car keys in her hand. 'Quick explore.'

'Great idea. I'm starving. Get me to la boulangerie. That's French for bread shop isn't it? Ooh they'll have chocolate croissants. Pain au chocolat. I'll come with you.' Jade stooped down and slipped on her flip-flops and padded down the steps.

'You don't want to do that. Stay here. I might be a while.'

This was as bad as that time when she was eighteen and almost at the front of the queue in Boots with a pack of condoms and her mother bearing down despite arranging to meet outside Woolworths.

'That's okay, I don't mind.'

'Yes, but I might stop somewhere. A market.' Carrie had reached the car door, narrowly averting disaster by remembering at the last minute not to get in on the passenger side. 'Visit a couple of churches,' she said, with the flourish of a poker player producing a Royal flush. There, the C-word. If that didn't put her off, nothing would.'

'No worries. I've got my phone, my sunnies.' She waggled her sunglasses up and down from where they'd been perched on top of her head as she drew level with Carrie on the other side of the car. With a sudden grin, she added, 'And I can scrounge some cash from you if I need anything.'

'What about your Mum? You can't leave her on her own all day.'

'It won't be all day, will it?' replied Jade, with infuriatingly correct logic. 'Besides she's happy as anything in that kitchen. She's not going to miss me. Probably like having the place to herself.'

Jade swung open the passenger door and plonked herself in the seat, reminding Carrie of an over-eager family dog in anticipation of a day out.

This was going to be a disaster. If she did stumble across the film crew by some incredibly happy and coincidental accident, how the hell would she get rid of Jade? These days a Mars Bar and illicit Coca Cola wouldn't cut it as a bribe. They weren't quite as alluring as they'd once been. Jade's taste had broadened as well as going up dramatically in price, although these days you needed to take out a loan for a simple chocolate fix.

'I think we should wait for your mum to get up and see if she wants to come too. At least tell her we're going out.'

'That's dull. Where's your sense of adventure? Carte blanche. Seize the menu. We should go now. Mum won't mind.'

Carrie paused. Her sense of adventure had long since got up, packed its rucksack and two-man tent and hiked out of Dodge. Seizing a menu was much more her style. Sadly.

'It's carpe diem—'

'Duh! I know that. Anyway it's too late because there's Mum.'

'Morning! You two running away already.'

'Hi, I'm heading off to see if I could find a bakery and bring back some fresh croissants but Jade stopped me. Would you like to come too? We can wait if you want to get ready.'

Angela immediately understood.

'That sounds lovely. Jade, have you switched off your hair straighteners?'

'Yeah.'

'Are you sure?'

Jade shrugged.

'I thought not. Go back and check them now.'

'Mummm!' She slouched back into the house.

Carrie shook her head. 'Your daughter's a blinking limpet. I thought I'd never shake her off.'

'If I come with you, you can ditch both us and you can check out the market.'

'Or I could do a runner now?'

'And what . . . your life would be worth living for the next few days?' Angela laughed. 'Give me five minutes and

I'll be ready. You can treat us to those croissants for breakfast.'

Carrie took it slowly. It was a gorgeous morning and the views around each bend were distracting, with their frequent glimpses of sea, when she needed to focus on the task of changing gears with the wrong hand.

'It's mega-blue. Do you think its bluer than other places?' asked Jade from the back seat. 'Is that why they call it Côte D'Azur? Azure's a posh word for blue.'

'I've no idea, but it's lovely.' Carrie was concentrating on the road, to be honest.

The drive didn't take very long at all and suddenly they were on the outskirts of the village.

'Sing out if you see a car park,' said Carrie, manoeuvring carefully as the streets closed in, the high kerbs and unfamiliar position on the road making her slightly nervous. And there was traffic, lots of it, some of which demonstrated an unnerving style of driving. A horn blared from the Mercedes behind them when she slammed on her brakes to avoid a small white van veering out of a side street, cutting right in front of them. It wasn't even her fault. She glared in the mirror, not that the owner of the great white beast behind them could see. Angela's hands twisted on her lap and she shrank back from the door, her shoulder touching Carrie's.

'I did read in one of the guide books that you take your life in your hands driving on the Riviera.'

'You did, did you? Thanks for the heads' up.'

Angela coloured. 'I didn't . . .'

'I'm teasing.' Carrie reassured her, knowing that her sister would worry that her comment had been misconstrued. It had the potential to worry Angela for days. 'The drive from the airport turned out absolutely fine. You get idiots like that at home.'

Angela relaxed and Carrie heaved an internal sigh.

'Let me entertain you, leeet meeee . . .' Jade burst into song, thrusting her arm through the gap between the front seats to indicate a blue parking sign pointing to the left. 'Let meeee spot the car park for you.'

'Oh dear god,' muttered Carrie. 'Thanks, Jade, for your timely directions.' She swerved into the turning, to a fresh cacophony of horns. She might as well join the mad local drivers.

'You said sing out . . . I did.'

'I don't think yelling in her ear is terribly helpful, Jade. You might have distracted her.'

'Might have, I almost hit that cyclist.'

Jade shrugged. 'You'd have driven straight past it, if I hadn't.'

Why saying in a normal voice, 'there's a car park over there,' wouldn't have worked perfectly well, Carrie didn't know.

'Isn't this lovely?' Angela kept stopping to examine the flowers overflowing and trailing down from window boxes perched on the stone stills of sun-baked houses and peering up at the vines growing from pots that crowded into the narrow streets. The lush greenery tracing its way across the walls with fingers of ivy and tendrils of wisteria was thrown into vibrant contrast by the warmth of old brick and peach washed stone.

They wandered up the hill, their shoes slipping slightly on the smooth old stones, along the streets that held an air of otherworldliness with their secretive recessed doors opening onto geranium pot-filled steps and tiny windows, with painted shutters like wings on either side. Carrie imagined that if you picked up a pot you might find a trefoil curved copper key to unlock one of the wooden painted doors and transport you to another world.

'How much further'? Jade stopped and rubbed at her toes. 'I'm getting a blister. The signal here's rubbish. Can't even send a text and there's no 3G.'

Carrie closed her eyes and counted to ten. It would be pointless trying to point out to Jade that she hadn't been invited in the first place.

'Maybe there'll be an internet café, where we can stop later,' said Angela. 'Come on, let's see if we can find a baker.'

As if the fairies in the elaborate tracery of plants had been listening, the artery of streets joined a larger one and suddenly they were in a street of cafés and touristy shops.

'Time for a coffee and a sit-down,' declared Angela, with a telling look Carrie's way. 'And we might be able to find some plasters for your toe, Jade.'

'And while you're doing that I'll see if I can find the tourist office and get a couple of maps of the area.'

'Great idea,' said Angela, almost bundling her away.

Abandoning them, with Angela musing over what coffee to order, Carrie hurried off before Jade could decide she might be missing out on something and decide to limp after her.

Following the directions, the owner of the coffee shop had given her, after a few false turns, she turned down what should have been a dead end and suddenly pitched into the noise and bustle of the market.

Striped canvas roofs covered stalls piled high with food

so bright and colourful, her mouth watered. Angela would be in seventh heaven. The nearest stall exploded with a cornucopia of fruit and vegetables, displayed with artistic precision. Ruby-red fat strawberries squatted next to scarlet redcurrants and white-blushed blueberries, while grapes, red and green, jostled together in between rows of shiny plums.

Across the way a stall stacked high with salamis like Jenga caught her eye. What if you removed one and the stack stayed upright, perhaps you could have it for free? The thought made her smile. And if you sent the pile tumbling to the floor, you had to buy the whole lot.

Next to them were baskets filled with a variety of cured meats from linen-wrapped Bayonne hams through to the local thinner sticks of meat, Bistouquette Provençale and then short fat salamis available in different flavours, Sanglier, Piment, Canard, Chèvre, Fumé or aux cepes priced at four for ten euros.

It would have been nice to have her own basket and she could fill it with all the amazing goodies, like the other French women scurrying along, weighed down with bags, haggling with stall holders and exchanging ribald banter.

The crowd, busy with purpose, jostled and pushed, propelling her along as part of the tide of shoppers. She didn't mind. For the first time it felt like she was in France proper, stepping into another world with the smells, the sights and the sound of French spoken at a machine-gun-rattle pace, the guttural consonants flowing into each other – a stream of incomprehensible words.

When she reached the end of the row and turned into the next one, the throng of people slowed its pace, like liquid wax cooling, and the path through the market steadily became more congested. Whispers and nudges, nods of 'come see this', rippled through like a Mexican Wave. It was difficult to see what was going on but as she craned her head, she spotted the unmistakable fluffy torpedo of a boom mic.

With a gulp, she swallowed hard and smoothed down her skirt. This wasn't supposed to happen. Happy, no, convenient, coincidences happened in films and books, not in real life. When she'd set out this morning, in her heart of hearts, she hadn't expected to find the film crew. It had been one of those deliberately fooling-yourself moments that you're doing something positive when you know it's no such thing because it's never going to happen. Now it had and she was totally unprepared.

For a while she stood, happy to hide in the crowd, far too scared to worm her way forward because she hadn't the foggiest what she would do if she got to the front and spotted Richard. With the inevitability of the ebb of the tide, as people became bored, they relinquished their place and Carrie found herself sucked to the front of the crowd, two rows back. Artificial light cast from several arc lamps lit up the shaded market stalls on the right-hand side and beyond them, a row of vans and trucks lined the road.

The butterflies, she told herself earlier not to get in a tizz, suddenly took flight in a frenzied rush, bouncing around her stomach, leaving her breathless and wide-eyed. She'd never imagined she'd stumble across the filming, although she'd made a massive assumption about it being the right film and that Richard might even be here. The dammed butterflies didn't give two hoots about that. They were making a do-or-die attempt to escape right through her stomach wall.

There was no sign of any filming taking place, although quite a lot of people buzzed about, zipping backwards and forwards, looking terribly busy and important. A girl with a clipboard and headphones was nodding urgently with two men, both of whom looked as if they'd been sleeping rough in the streets for the last couple of nights. Over in the corner, a cameraman was laughing with a small group of people who had to be extras and the soundman was dismantling the long pole of the boom.

Carrie squeezed behind two women of indeterminate age, who were excitedly whispering to each other in English. Both were dressed as if they'd recently stepped off a golf course, in smart chino shorts, matching T-shirts and peaked sun visors. One was slightly taller than the other and Carrie heard her addressed as Hilary.

'That was definitely him.'

'Are you sure?'

'Well, no, but it might be him,' said Hilary.

'Excuse me?' The two women swung round. 'Do you know what they're filming? Or who's in it?'

'Shh, you have to be quiet,' said Hilary nudging her and nodding towards one of the two scruffy men. 'The director keeps getting shirty because we're making too much noise. He keeps threatening to move us on.'

'Hmph,' said the other woman with a disdainful sniff, 'I don't know why. It's a public place. What does he expect? And, quite frankly, he looks as if he should have been moved on. A good wash and scrub wouldn't do him any harm.'

'Apparently,' said Hilary, in a confiding whisper, 'it's an American film. Hollywood. Blockbuster. Big names.' Her eyes widened with each phrase making Carrie wonder whether she might dislocate something.

'Is it anyone famous?' Carrie asked, her words almost sticking in her throat.

'Famous? Oooh yes! It's that fella from,' Hilary turned to her friend, 'what's that film he was in? You know thingy.'

'Oh, that one. Yes. The one where he drove that—'

'—silver car.' Hilary nodded. 'And it had a dog in it.'

Carrie bit back a smile at their conversation, as incomprehensible to her as it was clear to them. They reminded her of a married couple, together for so long they didn't need to converse in whole sentences.

'Yes. Now what's his name?' mused Hilary.

Carrie waited, shifting from one foot to the other, trying to hide the fact she wanted to grab Hilary and give her a damn good shake.

Hilary scrunched up her face. 'He was also in . . .'

Carrie bit her lip. God give her strength. 'Do you mean Richard Maddox?' she asked, sounding normal and sane and not wanting to rip the woman limb from limb.

'That's the one.' Hilary's friend hissed in a carrying whisper. 'You clever girl. Ooh are you alright? You look rather pale.'

'Have you seen him?' Carrie stood on tiptoe but there was little going on. The two tramp look-a-likes had gone, leaving the girl with the clipboard moving from group to group, gesticulating madly.

'Not now. He was here earlier. I bet he's gone back to his Winnebago.'

'Do you think you'd get a Winnebago up these streets, Kathleen? I'm not sure.'

'Maybe he's dropped off in his chauffeur-driven Bentley each morning.'

With nothing very much happening now, the crowd began to thin and Carrie had a much better view. A jolly market tradesman in an apron, who clearly wasn't a trader, sipped coffee and chatted to a couple of other decidedly French-styled people with string baskets and shopping trolleys. Definitely extras, Carrie guessed. The crew worked around them with that busy precision of people who know exactly what they're doing. Some peeled the gaffer tape securing the cables to the floor, others were dismantling the lights and others consulted schedules while packing things into large padded boxes.

To a man they ignored the crowd around them, they might as well have been behind a sheet of bullet-proof plate glass, a deliberate policy to discourage the general public from getting too close, as if they were an alien species apart from everyone else.

Carrie hesitated, imagining the crew might dismiss her as yet another fan or a lunatic stalker but she couldn't let this chance slip by. For a minute, a smile played around her lips. What if she marched up and told them she was Mrs Maddox, Richard's wife? It would be worth it to see their reaction, before she was carried off to the funny farm.

Thing was, she had once been in this world. Okay, she'd had a few walk-on parts in a couple of films, none of which had been spotted by a director and propelled her to instant stardom or even a bigger part, despite her vain hope that one of them would say who is the girl with the curly hair?

It had been such a long time ago; she'd virtually buried that part of her life. Being on set had been such a thrill, despite sometimes being tedious. There could be a lot of hanging around to get one small scene in the can but she'd loved being part of something, working alongside the whole crew all beavering away to achieve that goal. It had always been fascinating watching all the separate parts; the sound guys making sure they'd got what they needed, the camera men anxiously checking the light and conferring and most of all watching the director in action and comparing how she might approach a scene instead.

Added to all that, there was something quite indulgent about being on set, apart from the horrifically early hours. You didn't have to do anything but focus on what you needed to do, your scene. Not like in her job now, when as a teacher you were pulled in a thousand different directions on a daily basis. On set you might spend hours between takes but you had nothing else to do apart from learn lines or rehearse and there was always someone to talk to, someone else having to hang around. No wonder food was always plentiful. The catering guys worked non-stop and there was always a never-ending supply of bacon butties. Did they have salami baguettes here instead?

With a mental rap of the knuckles, she told herself to stop stalling. Here was her best chance to track Richard down and she'd done nothing for the last five minutes but hop about from leg to the other like a demented stork. If she didn't get a wiggle on, they'd have packed up and left.

She forced herself to wander over, picking the youngest-looking member of the crew, on the basis that she hadn't been doing this long enough to be blasé about her job and therefore would respond to the friendly chat of a passer-by.

'Hi, looks like you've been hard at it since the early hours.'

'God, yes,' the girl, in her early twenties, brushed her hair out of her face, straightening up from the coil of wires she'd recently gathered. 'We started at five, but it's a wrap now.'

'Got much more to do today?' Carrie summoned up a sympathetic tone.

'A couple of takes with the extras to get some general shots. But most of the crew are going on to the next location to do a recce.' Carrie bit back a smile, the girl didn't look as if she'd had that much experience, but she was certainly up to date with the jargon.

'The talent did it in a couple of takes. Which is always nice. They're done for the day.'

Inwardly Carrie cursed Jade. If she'd left when she'd planned, she might have got here in time.

In time to do what, mocked a voice inside her head? March right up to Richard and then what?

'Who is the talent?' For her own peace of mind, she had to check. She didn't quite trust Hilary and Kathleen. 'Anyone I would have heard of?'

The girl laughed, producing a bag of cable ties from her back pocket. 'You're kidding. Unless you've been living in a cave for your whole life.' She lowered her voice, 'Richard Maddox and Savannah Murray.'

'Wow. What is it? A big feature film?' Carrie was starting to enjoy herself, getting into character of friendly star-struck person who happened to be walking by.

'*Turn on the Stars*. It's a romantic comedy. Great script. We were lucky to get them both on board, it's taken a while for their schedules to coincide.'

'Are you out here for long? You sound English? Where are you filming next?'

'I'm from Essex. This unit is from England as most of the filming is here. I think there are a few scenes set in the States and they use a unit there. We're here for the next six weeks.' She grinned cheerfully. 'Not a hardship. Summer back home looks crap.'

She stooped down and started disconnecting some of the

cables from each other and tying them up with the plastic ties. 'I've got no complaints and for the next week we're down on the harbour at Port les Pins. Less busy than St Tropez, thank goodness. It's a pig to park the vans down there and the traffic is horrendous this time of year. The local authorities are helpful, though, it's good for tourism. The tourists love it when they see . . .' The girl faltered.

Carrie laughed. 'Yes we do. But many years ago I was an actress. I know the drill.'

'Oh, sorry I didn't mean to . . . you know.'

'It's fine. The film world looks glamorous to the outside world. They don't see the long hours and the hard work the crew put in.'

'God no, I mean I love it but its non-stop. We're back on set again tomorrow morning at five. The early mornings are killers.'

'I remember having to travel miles between sets, as well.'

'This isn't too bad, our base is in St Tropez.'

'Nice,' teased Carrie. 'Posh hotel?'

'Yeah, right! We're in the Ibis. The director and the big names are staying in Le Chateau de la Messardière. Now that is posh.'

'And of course, that's where Richard Maddox and Savannah Murray are staying?' Carrie twinkled, a sudden fizz of excitement at how easy this was turning out to be. Her first attempt and she'd discovered where Richard was staying. This Mata Hari lark was proving to be rather enjoyable.

'Of course, not that I've been there.'

'You done with these, Lorraine?' A thick-set man with a sharp buzz cut came up, barely even glancing at Carrie.

'Yup, they can go in the van.'

'Can you go and give the sound guys a hand?'

'Sure.' She flashed Carrie a quick grin. 'Gotta go, nice chatting with you. Might see you down at the harbour. We're filming on one of the floating gin palaces down there. Be interesting getting the power generators on board.'

'Lorraine,' the man gave an impatient nod of his head.

'Bye.' She turned to her colleague and handed him one of the coils.

With a casual wave hiding her excitement, Carrie turned and walked away, trying not to skip. *Result.* She wouldn't even have to see Richard, she could simply go to the hotel and leave him a letter there.

While she'd been talking her phone had buzzed several times. There were three impatient texts from Jade.

Where are you?
Have you got lost?'
Your coffee's going cold.

Jade and Angela were sitting outside the café, Jade scrolling through her phone and Angela leaning back in her chair, her eyes closed, soaking up the sun.

'Where've you been?' Jade scowled up at her before looking back at her phone. 'We've been here ages.'

Angela sprang to attention, her eyes asking a million questions as she mouthed, 'Did you see him?'

With an imperceptible shake of her head, answered, grateful that Jade was more interested in her phone.

'Sorry I got distracted by how amazing the market was. Even made me want to cook.'

Angela raised an eyebrow.

'Almost,' she ducked her head. 'Okay, chop things up and have them with bread.'

'I'm too lazy to move at the moment and we've got plenty of food in the fridge, I'd better not go and take a look. I know I'll be tempted.' Angela shunted her seat up, so that Carrie could squeeze in.

'They have a market on Sunday as well. We can come back then. Urgh.' The coffee was stone-cold.

'I'm too hot,' said Jade.

'You do look very pink, did you put any sunscreen on?' asked Angela.

'No.'

'And I didn't bring any with me.'

They decided that as the temperature had hit the 90s already, they'd head back to the villa for a swim to cool off and then have lunch.

Halfway back to the car, as they emerged from the shady streets, Jade suddenly realised she'd left her brand-new sunglasses behind. Seeing that Angela was wilting in the heat, Carrie offered to go back and get them, giving the car keys to the others so that they could at least put the air conditioning on.

The sun was at its highest now and most people had sensibly stopped in some of the pavement cafés, leaving the streets mostly deserted.

She'd got used to having the street to herself when a man in dark sunglasses came abruptly around a corner and she almost cannoned into him. For a minute they did that very English side-stepping dance.

'Sorry,' said Carrie, lifting her sunglasses as she spoke, immediately realising she should have said 'pardon' and regretting taking them off as she squinted into the sun at him.

'Carrie?' He took off his sunglasses.

The butterflies were back with a vengeance, rising with a great fluttering kerfuffle and then en masse sank back with a great thunk. It was *him*.

She swallowed, completely struck dumb. It was as if her jaws had gone into spasm and absolutely refused to move.

'Carrie? My God, it is you.'

She stared and stared and stared. The face, once as familiar as her own, looked exactly the same. Those so bright, they couldn't be real, blue eyes, that she'd seen filled with first-thing sleepiness in them, alight with laughter at a stupid joke and sharp with thought at a serious question. Now they registered surprise. Her heart almost stopped as she drank in the sight of him. Still utterly gorgeous, with that perfectly chiselled jawline, which she used to tease he'd borrowed from Action Man.

The years vanished and, as if it were yesterday, she remembered walking hand in hand across Westminster Bridge in the dense drizzle of autumn. Yesterday, when they'd sat at the top of Primrose Hill, surrounded by the green shoots and early daffodils of Spring, unable to stop kissing each other. Yesterday, when he'd received the call. Yesterday, that painful stiff-upper-lip parting at Heathrow.

He stepped forward, reaching out a hand, as if to touch her, and then paused.

'What . . . are you doing here?' he asked, looking equally discomfited and confused.

'I . . .'

'You look . . . well.' His mouth curved into the sudden easy grin she knew, his eyes dancing with mischief. 'I like the dress.' And then he frowned, the dark brows drawing together in a sudden slash, as if trying to work something out that wasn't right. 'But not the hair.'

With a sudden movement he pulled out the chopstick anchoring her hair. With the slight touch of his forearm against her face, her world turned upside down as her curls cascaded free, dropping down her back.

He stood there, holding the chopstick, looking like a young wizard who'd performed his first spell and now wasn't sure what to do. Carrie let out a breathless, musical laugh. It was typical of Richard: act first, think later.

With a triumphant smile, he gave an approving nod, 'That's better. Much better. Now you look like you.'

Carrie wanted to come back with something witty and snappy, half of her desperate to put him in his place for his sheer cheek and the other half wanting to impress him with her sang froid. Instead she smiled stupidly back at him, her heartbeat bursting into breakneck speed and a flush racing through her.

'How are you? You look well.'

'You said that already.'

'I did, didn't I? It's amazing to see you. You look . . .'

'You said that already.'

'It's not every day you run into y . . .' Panic flashed in his eyes as if he realised he was about to step into dangerous territory. The W word would make it personal.

'Your wife,' said Carrie tartly, a punch of pain ricocheting around her chest. A wife he'd conveniently forgotten all too quickly once he'd got to Hollywood. By his second feature film, the phone calls and texts started to dry up, the conversations became more stilted and the pictures of him and his leading lady started to get regular billing in the gossip columns. As far as she was concerned, it had been a case of out of sight and very much out of mind.

His face crumpled with something that might have been regret or at least she liked to think so. How the hell did she know? she hadn't seen him for eight years. Now she studied him more closely, she saw the signs of self-possession. The clothes sharper and more chic, the blue of his shirt no doubt picked out specially to enhance his eyes and the trousers, linen and tailored, fitting him like a glove. Despite his urbane elegance, she couldn't help remembering a time when he'd lived in baggy jeans and laughed at men who used personal-grooming products. The man in front of her looked as if he used them by the articulated lorry-load.

He wasn't the man she'd fallen in love with, the same as she wasn't the person he'd fallen in love with.

She glared hard, to make him back off, and snatched the chopstick back, bundling her hair up and spiking it through viciously.

'I didn't mean . . .' He took a step towards her.

'Look, it's him. I told you I'd seen him.' From around the corner a coachload of young teenagers came and like locusts descended on them, homing in on Richard, their number forming around him, pushing her away until she was the outsider looking in, which was exactly as it should be.

Over the tops of their heads he caught her eye, as she began to back away.

'Wait Carrie. W. . .' his voice was swallowed up by the excited chatter of the girls waving bits of paper and trying to take selfies with him.

The sudden physical barrier was a welcome reminder of the divide between them. They were different people. That was a lifetime ago. There was absolutely no need to speak to him or have any contact with him. Thanks to the friendly film-crew girl, she didn't need to. She knew where to find him.

'Auntie Carrie. Auntie Carrie!'

As she turned she saw Jade half-running and half-walking up the hill towards her. With a fleeting backward glance at Richard, who was still watching her, she strode forwards to meet her niece.

'I found them,' crowed Jade. 'My sunglasses. They were in my bag all the time.'

Desperate to get away and praying that Jade hadn't caught sight of the commotion behind her, Carrie began to hurry towards her.

'OMG. Carrie. Look, it's someone famous,' Jade stepped around her to look up the hill at where the girls were surrounding Richard, who had been spun round with his back to them. 'I've got to get a selfie.'

'Jade, no.' She tried to grab her niece. 'Leave the poor man alone, he's already besieged.'

'Do you know who it is?'

'No idea,' Carrie snapped.

'I'm going to find out,' Jade grinned with youthful determination. 'One more selfie won't hurt him, whoever he is.'

'Jade!'

'What?'

'I'm leaving right now.'

'Don't be boring. I'll never, ever get the chance to see a sleb this close again. Come on, you can get a picture too. Your students will be dead impressed.'

'I'll go without you.' She tried to put a hand on Jade's, but she was off like a greased whippet, phone out.

'Jade!

'I'll catch you up.'

Carrie decided this was a lost battle and it would be better if she left – and quickly, before Richard turned around and linked the two of them together. Would he remember Jade from all those years ago?

She hurried down the street, fighting the temptation to take one last look back. A few streets later, a piercing stitch stabbing into her side forced her to stop. Her whole body hurt but it had nothing to do with the stitch. Her face crumpled and she bent double trying to ease the pain.

'I say, are you alright?'

Jade loomed over her. 'You look terrible.'

For Jade to notice, she must have looked horrendous.

Now that she stopped, dizziness overcame her and she swayed on the spot, praying that the light-headed sensation would recede. With her knees trembling and nausea dancing in the pit of her belly, she wondered if she might pass out. It had to be shock. Her body reacting after the see-sawing of emotions she'd put it through this morning. The up of fearful anticipation and down of abject relief.

'Auntie Carrie,' Jade's voice held a note of panic. 'Are you okay? Can I . . . Shall I . . .'

Uncertainty flashed in her expression.

'I'm fine. Just a bit faint. Probably too much heat.' She wasn't going to confess to Jade, it was more likely a post-shock, adrenaline hangover. The aggressive punch of chemicals which had rolled through her system, setting all her senses on alert, had now evaporated like a magic genie rescinding its powers, leaving her with an overwhelming sense of being unutterably tired. She clung to a nearby wrought-iron hand rail.

'Are you sure?' asked Jade doubtfully.

'Let me catch my breath a minute. I've overdone it, that's all. Too much sun. Not enough fluids.' Carrie sounded like an aged great aunt well into her dotage rather than an auntie scant years older than her niece. There were plenty of occasions when Carrie had been taken for Jade's older sister. As for fluids, she could do with a shot of something to put some fire back.

'Do you want me to get Mum?'

'No, I'm fine, honestly. I . . . let's get back to the car.' The sooner they got away the better.

'If you're sure.' Doubt filled Jade's face.

Despite the sick sensation churning around her stomach, which was stupid, it wasn't as if she'd got up close and personal to real danger, she picked up her pace and almost marched down the hill back to the car park. Every now and then she threw anxious looks back over her shoulder.

Jade threw open the back passenger door and hurled herself in, pushing her phone out to her mother. 'Guess who we saw? Look I got a selfie with him. Richard Maddox. Isn't he gorgeous? He's even more gorgeous in the flesh, isn't he, Caz?'

'You saw Richard?' Angela's eyes went wide, studying Carrie with concern.

'Oh God, yes,' said Carrie, limp in her seat, now that she'd reached the air-conditioned haven of the car. She put her head in her hands and leaned over her knees. 'I walked right into him.' Reliving the moment as she told her sister was every bit as bad as the moment it happened.

She straightened up and took a peek at herself in the mirror before turning to Angela. 'What a nightmare.'

Jade leaned through the gap between the passenger and driver seats, like a fox scenting a chicken, her nose almost quivering.

'I don't believe it.' Carrie rubbed at her forehead as if that might dissipate the band of tension which had tightened around her forehead. 'Blood, bloody, bad luck.'

'Why? I don't understand.' Jade flicked through her screen. 'I got two pictures with him and they're both great. I'm going to WhatsApp them now to Becky, Charlotte and Eliza.

Carrie groaned, still unable to believe what had happened.

Jade caught her eye in the mirror. 'Hang on.' Her eyes narrowed and she examined Carrie. 'Have I missed something?'

Angela looked from Carrie to Jade and back again.

'Mum? What's going on?'

With a sigh, Carrie said, 'Let's wait until we get home.' She gripped the steering wheel with purpose. 'I need to concentrate on driving and finding our way back.'

'Why can't you tell me now?' whined Jade.

'Because,' snapped Carrie.

CHAPTER ELEVEN

'I can't believe you never told me,' said Jade for the ninety-fifth time, slurping a tall glass of coke noisily. You're married to Richard Maddox. *The* Richard Maddox. That's awesome.'

Carrie contemplated the view from the bay window overlooking at the valley, absentmindedly sipping the large glass of wine that Angela had poured her as soon as they arrived home.

'That's unreal. You're married to Richard Maddox.'

'Jade,' her mother interrupted in a warning tone, which made no impact on her overexcited daughter.

'Yes, but Richard Maddox.' She paced around the kitchen. 'That is sick. And you never said.'

Carrie tightened her jaw.

'I can't wait to tell the others.'

'No.' Carrie swung around and shot a fierce glare at her. 'You can't tell anybody.'

'Okay, okay.' Jade held up her hands. 'No one's died.' She sank into the chair opposite and drained her glass before looking at Carrie in an unashamed examination, as if trying to work out how the hell her aunt had ever snagged an international sex symbol. 'Can I just ask . . .'

'No,' chorused Angela and Carrie together.

'. . . why don't you want anyone to know? If it were me, I'd tell everyone.' She leaned back in her chair, a dreamy expression on her face.

'What happened?' asked Angela.

'The film unit was there but he'd finished filming. However I did get chatting to one of the crew and I found out where he's staying.'

'Are you going to go and see him?' Jade leaned forward. 'Can I come?'

'No, I'm not going to see him,' said Carrie tightly. 'I needed to contact him.'

'Why don't you want to see him? He's your husband.' Jade emphasised the final word. 'It's not like we've got many in the family.' She shot a sly look her mother's way. It still niggled her that her mother had never married her father, who by all accounts had been desperate to marry Angela. It still surprised Carrie that she'd turned him down.

Angela didn't rise, instead she took a steady sip of her wine. 'Jade, we got married when we were both young and stupid.'

'How come you're still married and why haven't you ever said anything? I mean, if I were you I'd be living it up in Hollywood. He must have, like, a million homes.'

'He went to Hollywood. I stayed here. We drifted apart. At the time I wasn't planning on marrying anyone else. I left it and left it and after a while I, sort of, forgot.'

'You forgot you were married to a superstar? Man, that's nuts.'

'I didn't forget, I put it out of my mind.'

A horror-struck expression hit Jade's face. 'OMG! Alan. Does he know?'

'Of course he doesn't know,' said Carrie, hurriedly.

'When are you going to tell him?'

Angela raised an eyebrow. Carrie realised that Jade was asking all the questions that Angela wanted answered.

'I'm not going to. I'll tell him I was married before and that it didn't work out. That's all he needs to know,' she narrowed a fierce stare at Jade, 'and you are not to tell him or even breathe a word to anyone.'

'What no one? Not even my friends? That's ridiculous. They won't . . .' Jade winced. 'Yeah they would.' She pouted. 'That's mean.'

'Tough. I don't want anyone knowing. Everyone would talk, there'd be all sorts of comments. Can you imagine it at school? Alan would hate it and it's unnecessary. He never needs to know who I was married to.'

'What are you going to do? You've got to see Richard.'

'I don't want to see him and I don't need to.'

'But what if he still loves you?'

Carrie nearly spat her wine out. 'That's crackers. Jade, we haven't seen each other for years.'

'Yes, but you must have done once. You got married and if you haven't seen him much since, how do you know?'

'How do I know what?'

'That he doesn't still love you.'

Carrie's stupid heart did a little flip and a touch of grief whispered through her mind. He had done once when they believed in 'forever'.

'He might be bored with all those Hollywood bimbettes

and fancy a change. You're not bad looking and you're really kind and funny, sometimes.'

'Only sometimes?' Carrie hid a smile, even though she didn't feel like smiling at the moment. 'Thanks, Jade. That's very sweet of you.'

'Do you still love him?'

'No.' The finality in her tone should have made it clear. Today had stirred a lot of memories, but that's all they were, distant and long-buried memories that ought to stay six feet under, not be exhumed and re-examined.

'Shame.' Jade's shoulders slumped. 'He's awfully good looking. I wouldn't have minded him for an uncle.' She flounced out of the kitchen.

Carrie rolled her eyes and turned to Angela. 'I'm going to write him a letter and take it over to the hotel where they're staying.'

'What are you going to say?'

'Keep things formal, to the point. I need his contact details, an official address so that I can start divorce proceedings. Luckily we've been apart for this long, so it should be pretty straightforward. I'm not sure how long it will take. That's the only problem. The stuff I've researched online suggests it could take up to between sixteen and twenty weeks, in which case I'm screwed and I will have to tell Alan.' Hope gleamed in Carrie's eyes, 'But, if I can persuade Richard to speed things up, he might be prepared to pay for fancy lawyers who can push things through more quickly. You're always reading in the papers about celeb quickie divorces. That would be the best solution.'

'Personally, I think telling Alan the truth would be easier, but whatever you think.'

Carrie gave her a hug and they held onto each other for

a minute. Angela squeezed her back. 'I'm sure once Richard gets the letter, he'll be as anxious as I am to expedite things as quickly as possible.'

'Expedite! You sound all lawyerly already. Have you already written the letter?'

Carrie hadn't physically put pen to paper, or even fingers to keyboard, but she'd written an imaginary few lines several times in her head and each time the words sounded horribly bald, as if she were writing to a complete stranger. So much for being a writer, no matter how she phrased it, *I want a divorce* sounded final and cold. A miserable ignominious end to an incandescent love that had once burnt with such bright, brilliant, heartfelt passion.

'No, but I'm going to.' She sounded as defensive as Jade caught out for leaving her homework late on a Sunday evening.

Carrie took another sip of ice-cold coke and dreamily watched the passers-by. Today, after two whole days' lounging by the pool, they'd ventured to the beach beyond Ramatuelle, which had been recommended according to Marguerite's guest book of tips. She'd enjoyed the drive down to the coast as they skirted pine-clad cliffs with the sea shimmering in the background.

Jade, looking at her phone, gave a sudden guinea-pig-like squeak, her eyes widening and her cheeks puffing out.

Carrie waited for her to announce the latest Google fact or show them her Instagram feed or regale them with some celebrity gossip.

Nothing. 'You alright?'

'Fine,' said Jade, clearly bursting with some intelligence. 'I need to go to the loo.' She jumped up and almost ran to the toilets at the back of the room.

Angela shook her head. 'I think Eliza's got a new boyfriend. It'll be some juicy bit of gossip.'

'Doesn't Eliza have a new boyfriend every week?' asked Carrie.

'I've lost track. To be honest, I don't pay that much attention. Just nod. I've learned that if I do show much interest I'm doing the wrong thing and if I don't show any, I'm still in the wrong. It's best to keep things vague, not offer an opinion.' Angela shrugged. 'So far the strategy's working.' Angela let out a long-suffering sigh. 'I think I'm doing it right. It's a shame they don't come with manuals.'

'Hey, you're doing a great job. She's a pain in the arse but she's supposed to be. Perfectly normal and she has her good points.'

'Remind me of one. Three days we've been here and her room is trashed already. I was mortified when the maid turned up yesterday. I would have made her tidy up.'

Carrie giggled. 'That's the whole point of having a maid. To do that for you.'

'Well, she'd better not get used to it. Marisa had folded all her clothes, put them away in drawers and unpacked the rest of her things.'

'I suspect it was because she didn't have anything else to do and felt guilty being paid.'

Marisa, the maid, appeared the day before to change the sheets on the beds, provide fresh towels and to clean up as well as to check on the provision situation in the fridge. A diminutive whirl of energy, she'd roared up the drive in a very battered Peugeot, bounded into the house with a pile of white, pillowy towels nearly as tall as she was and carrying several bulging carrier bags. Introducing herself in perfect but very heavily accented English, she proceeded to whip through every room at an astonishing pace, gathering towels and sheets, to Angela's horror.

'We only slept in the beds two nights and she changed them. We're very spoilt,' said Angela.

'I love being spoiled,' said Jade, returning to the table. 'Can I ask you a question, Auntie Carrie?'

Carrie scrunched her face up. 'Like what?'

'So you and Richard Maddox. Are you really Carrie Maddox, then?'

Carrie closed her eyes, she didn't want to talk about this. 'Officially yes.'

'What, you got properly married, in a church and everything?'

'Register office.'

'When?'

'June 28th,' said Carrie, with a long-suffering sigh, hoping it might stall this line of questioning.

Thankfully the waiter arrived, bearing three plates.

'Phone away, please.' Angela nodded at Jade, who ducked down as if to put it in her bag under the table but Carrie caught her sliding it under her thigh on the chair. Like every other teen, totally attached to her phone. Rather sobering to see how dependent they all were on them.

'Jade, put the phone away.'

With a sulky pout that she'd been caught, Jade slid it back under her leg. Carrie raised an eyebrow but Jade stared back with a defiant glint in her eye.

Jade wasn't her daughter. She let it go. She was Angela's problem and sometimes it was best to pick your battles. Going head to head over a phone was the equivalent of a declaration of all-out war. Not worth the aggravation.

Carrie and Angela chatted together over dinner, while

Jade stared off into space in between checking her lap was still there.

'Jade,' Angela, tapped her plate with her knife, 'if you get that phone out once more, I will take it away.'

'You can't, it's my phone.' Jade clutched it protectively to her chest and Carrie was hard pressed not to laugh.

'I can and I will if I have to. I've told you umpteem times. No phones at the dinner table.'

'This is lunch.'

'You know exactly what I mean. Now put it away before I get cross. Honestly, what is so important that you have to keep checking it.'

'Nothing.' This time Jade put her phone in her bag but as she ducked her head, Carrie caught a sly smile on her face. Carrie was very glad she wasn't her daughter. She was definitely up to no good. No doubt plotting something with her girlfriends as there was little she could do out here. She didn't know anyone.

CHAPTER TWELVE

The smash of glass on tiled floor startled Carrie as she lay by the pool the following morning and she jumped up to go and help. Angela's grip was precarious at the best of times and at home there were various rubber grips and tools designed to help remove the lids from jars and tins.

Gathering up tiny chunks of broken glass was often beyond her twisted fingers, although it didn't stop her trying. Carrie admired her fortitude but found it equally frustrating because inevitably Angela would cut herself.

Picking up her pace, she hurried into the kitchen to help the clean-up operation.

'How could you?' Every scrap of colour had leeched out of Angela's face as she stood there, facing her daughter, hackles raised like a dog about to leap in to the fray. Carrie stopped dead, not wanting to intrude but as she arrived both Angela and Jade turned towards twin expressions of guilt and horror on their faces.

At Angela's feet lay a smashed jar of olives that she'd made no attempt to tidy up.

'I was trying to help. You're always going on that people should talk face to face about things. Not rely on texting and stuff,' said Jade defiantly.

'This is totally different. And you know it. Plus, you certainly didn't have to take it this far and invite him here,' said Angela, her face taut with fury, slipping a sidelong glance at Carrie.

Jade didn't answer, looking stony-faced at the floor.

It sounded like one of those arguments about Jade's dad. Periodically Jade would start up, about wanting to meet her father. Although Carrie would rather have left them to it, she needed to tidy up the mess. She ducked her head and grabbed a roll of kitchen towel.

'Oh for God's sake, Carrie, leave it,' snapped Angela. 'I don't need you tiptoeing around me.' She glared at her daughter and Carrie. 'Jade can do it after she's told you what she's done.' Angela folded her arms, uncharacteristically militant.

Jade peeped up at Carrie from under her brows, head ducked down, as defensive as a turtle about to tuck back into its shell.

'It's fine, I'll leave you guys to it.' Carrie held up her hands in surrender and backed out.

'Jade!' Angela snapped. Carrie didn't think she'd ever seen her sister quite this cross. What on earth had Jade done?

Jade, every bit the naughty child, couldn't meet Carrie's gaze. She swallowed hard and tears began to well up in her eyes. 'I thought . . . it would be nice . . . that if you saw him . . . you.'

'I saw him?' Why would she want to see Jade's father? She'd met Clive many years ago. He was considerably older than her.

'She's only invited Richard Maddox here for dinner. Tonight.' Exasperation rolled off Angela in waves, as she bent to start picking up the debris from the floor. 'What were you thinking?'

'You did *what?*' There was a rushing in her ears.

'I invited him. For dinner.' Jade lifted her chin and met her aunt's eyes.

Carrie repeated the words as if that might make sense of them. 'You've invited Richard Maddox. Here. For dinner.'

'Yes,' said Jade warily but without any discernible sense of shame.

'And what? He said yes?' Sarcasm permeated every syllable of Carrie's words. She could strangle her niece. What a bloody stupid thing to do, although Richard Maddox probably received thousands of far more salacious invitations on a daily basis. It was highly doubtful he'd even noticed Jade's amongst his fan mail.

'Actually he did. Said he'd be delighted. He's coming at seven-thirty.'

'What!' screeched Angela frantically, looking around the kitchen. 'You didn't tell me that. Seven-thirty, tonight? Here for dinner?'

'Yes.' Jade spoke with a touch of pride. 'I sent him the address.'

In a daze, Carrie sank into the nearest kitchen chair, trying to get her head straight. This couldn't be happening.

'You invited Richard for dinner and he's agreed?' Carrie lay her head on the table, wanting to pound it with her fists. 'That's . . . ridiculous.'

Jade smirked.

'What the hell did you say to him that made him agree?'

And how come she managed it so bloody easily? Talk

about galling. Carrie had done weeks of research on the internet trying to track down his sodding agent or management company.

Jade tilted her head with a touch of cockiness. 'I tweeted him. Twitter. Said I had information about the significance of 28th June and for him to DM me.'

Bloody hell, the little toad had tucked that fact away quicker than a hamster hunting down the last sunflower seed in captivity. A vision of her and Richard laughing and kissing on the steps of Kensington and Chelsea Register office after they'd come out of the ceremony ran through her head. With a pang, she wondered where he'd been on their last few anniversaries.

'You asked him to direct message you? And he did?'

'Yeah, straight away. I was gobsmacked, to be honest.' Jade gave a modest shrug, as if to be congratulated on her cleverness. 'I wasn't sure he would.'

'Bloody brilliant!' snarled Carrie.

'Well, I thought it was.' Jade folded her arms.

Carrie shook her head. 'What did you say?' She almost didn't want to know. Could this get any worse?

'I told him who I was, that we'd seen him in Ramatuelle and that you were my aunt and that he should come and have dinner. He said it sounded a great idea.'

Carrie glared at her niece, relaxing a touch. 'He agreed to come have dinner with someone who could be anyone. I don't think so.' She could breathe easy again. 'Someone's having you on.' Of course it was a wind-up. Richard's Twitter account was doubtless managed by some PR person or some digital agency. They were used to this sort of thing.

'I'm not stupid.' Jade turned her nose up and rolled her eyes. 'I asked him for proof that he knew you.'

Carrie sighed, a horrible sense of foreboding weighing over her. 'And what did he say to that?' She crossed her fingers behind her back.

'You've got long curly hair that's always in your face,' Jade pulled a face, as if less than impressed, 'and your eyes are sometimes hazel and sometimes green, depending on your mood, but when you're cross there's a little vertical frown line that appears right in between your eyebrows.'

Carrie froze, her stomach turning inside out.

Shit. It really was Richard.

God, he used to tease her. She remembered him stroking the little line with his index finger, coaxing her back into humour. He called it her cross patch. Which had been bloody annoying as half the time it was him doing something silly or crazy that had put it there in the first place. It was impossible to stay cross with him for long, though. There was never time. There was always so much going on, cramming every minute with living, that there wasn't time to waste being cross. They'd lived life at a breakneck pace, desperate to sample all the good things as quickly as possible.

Queuing for cheap seats, seeking out hole-in-the-wall dives, hosting experimental theatre, rehearsing themselves, auditioning, performing, cycling, pell-mell and crazy, through London in a constant, fun-filled battle against the clock.

The memories spawned another and another until she thought her head would explode with all the poignant images cramming their way in.

'So, you did what, invited him here?' Carrie blinked, gnawing at her lip, 'What exactly did he say?'

'That he'd be delighted to accept the invitation and he was very much looking forward to meeting me and seeing you again.'

'That's it. Nothing else.'

'Yup.'

'Seven-thirty.'

Richard was coming here. Tonight.

Carrie rolled her eyes at Angela, who gave a weak shrug.

'What were you thinking?'

'I thought it would be romantic. Meeting again. You're still married so you must still like him. And he hasn't divorced you, so he must still like you.'

Carrie exhaled noisily, wondering at the simplicity of Jade's thinking. That's what had got her and Richard into this mess in the first place. 'And it never crossed your mind that there might be other reasons for us never getting round to divorcing, like the publicity that it would cause. That it might damage his career. That we were perfectly happy not having anything to do with each other.'

Jade shook her head. Although why Carrie even bothered, she didn't know. Jade had never yet admitted to being wrong.

'I'm happy to cook something,' volunteered Angela, as if that would help break the stalemate.

God give her strength. 'He's not coming. Jade's going to have to cancel him.'

'Why?' asked Jade petulantly.

'Because I don't want to see him.'

'Why not?'

Angela held her gaze.

'Because . . .' and suddenly she couldn't think of one good reason.

She stalked out of the kitchen and up to her bedroom.

Leaning on the balustrade, looking out to the sea, she half-laughed to herself, trying to imagine Richard's reaction to a text from Jade. Why had he agreed to come? What would he have thought? The whole evening had disaster written all over it in screaming capitals. It would be better to cancel him. Tell him not to come. Except, would that look like she cared one way or the other?

It would be weird seeing him again after all this time. She'd changed so much; he was certainly bound to have done.

Dragging the wicker chair to the front of the balcony, her knees touching the railings, she sat down, her thoughts pushed and pulled by insistent memories that refused to be shut out.

Her thoughts were interrupted by a tentative knock.

'Yes.'

Jade peered around the door. 'Can I come in?'

Her eyes were suspiciously bright, although her mouth held a touch of defiance tinged with doubt. Carrie knew the look well. It was that crisis of confidence when Jade's absolute certainty that she'd done the right thing suddenly came crashing down.

'You okay?' asked Jade, loitering in the doorway.

'I'll live,' said Carrie, her jaw tightening. Her fury had died away, replaced with dull acceptance and a burgeoning curiosity.

'I'm sorry. I thought it was dead romantic and I couldn't understand why you wouldn't want to see him again. I mean, he's one of the most gorgeous men on the planet and he's your husband.'

Oh to be a teenager again.

'I realise now, it's probably awkward. Rather like, that *my mate fancies you but she's too scared to say anything*.'

Carrie sighed. That hadn't even occurred to her. She'd

need to make it clear to Richard that this had all been Jade's hair-brained idea. In some ways Jade was still so young.

'Well you can apologise to him yourself. That's your penance. I want you to explain that what you did was without my permission or my knowledge.'

Jade swallowed. 'I will,' she said in a small voice. 'I am really sorry. Do you think he'll be super-mad too, when he realises that you didn't invite him?'

'I suspect he already knows that, which makes me cross with him. He's taken advantage of the situation. He shouldn't have responded to you and made arrangements, knowing that you were a minor.'

Which confused the hell out of her. Why on earth had Richard agreed to come? He had the whole of the Riviera jet set to play with, why would he want to come and slum it with them?

Jade's bottom lip quivered. 'I am really sorry.'

'You've sort of done me a favour,' at the brightening of Jade's expression, she added, 'but don't get carried away. I'm still furious with you. You should know better. Interfering like this. I'm resigned to seeing Richard tonight and maybe it is a good idea to face him and get it over and done with, but I'd rather have done it my way than been forced into it.'

'Sorry.'

'Hmph,' grunted Carrie, crossing her legs and leaning back into the chair. 'If you ever pull a stunt like this again, I'll post that picture of you on Facebook when you were five with the pudding-bowl haircut.'

Jade gave a ghost of a smile. 'I promise I won't. I am really, really sorry. I didn't mean to upset you.'

'Come here,' Carrie shifted in her seat, allowing Jade to

squeeze in next to her. Carrie put her arm around her shoulders and pulled her niece in to her.

'What's he like?' Jade asked quietly.

'Richard?' Carrie stilled. 'You don't remember, but when you were little he was around quite a lot. He came to your seventh birthday party. He's likely to have changed since I knew him, but then,' she smiled, 'he was brilliant fun. Full of energy, get up and go. Life was one big adventure and we weren't missing out on any of it.' They'd been so impulsive and ready to embrace all life had to offer. 'I remember, on the spur of the moment a friend of ours inviting us to see a play he was doing at the Fringe in Edinburgh. We got on the next train, even though the city's notorious for being 'no room at the inn' that week,' Carrie laughed. 'And the director invited us to stay at his parents' place, which turned out to be a proper Scottish castle with turrets and everything.' They'd stayed for a week, with Richard charming the Laird and his wife. 'I even tried fly-fishing.' Carrie shook her head. 'We were always doing things like that. We lived in a tiny flat in Brixton. A real dump, not that it bothered us. It was handy for the Tube and there was always a party to go to, or friends kipping over.

'Is he as good looking as all the pictures?'

Carrie wanted to say no. That he bore a passing resemblance to the Hunchback of Notre Dame when he woke in the mornings, was as hairy as a gorilla and had webbed feet as well as belched and farted like a trooper. It would have been good to tell her impressionable niece that film stars weren't God-given handsome in real life, that their looks were attributable to hours in make-up and their svelte figures achieved with the help of personal trainers, nutritionists and photo-shopping.

Unfortunately, when it came to Richard, she'd be lying. The good-looks fairy had dropped her entire quota of magic dust smack bang on his head when he was born, along with a bucket load of charm and a total disinterest in mirrors.

'Fraid so.'

'But is he nice? Eliza met John Ryan once and he was dead arrogant and up himself.'

In a way, Carrie hoped so. It would be a shame if stardom had spoilt him. 'He used to be. I wouldn't have married him otherwise.'

'I guess. How did you meet him? And how long were you together?'

'It was in the first term at drama school. Talk about naïve. Most people had had a few years out but I went straight from sixth form. I was seriously wet behind the ears. The tutor in improvisation class put us together to do a piece together. For some reason Richard decided the scene should have a passionate kiss in it. And, of course, I was trying to be terribly cool and blasé and pretend that I could handle it.' Carrie laughed. 'The mean sod told me after the first rehearsal that I was a dreadful kisser and that I needed to practise.'

Jade's eyes almost bugged out. 'Oh no, what did you do? I'd have cried.'

Carrie grinned at her. 'No way. I told him it was his lousy technique and he was the one that needed to practise.'

Jade giggled. 'That's cool. What did he say?'

'He laughed, he'd been joking. It was his way of asking me out. He suggested we go out, get a few drinks and get some practice in. And that's how it all started. We moved in together and then after about eighteen months, we got up one day and decided to get married.'

'What? Just like that.'

Carrie's stomach clenched. No, not just like that. Not like that at all. It hurt too much to remember the intensity of those days. The utter do-or-die emotion that she felt for him.

'We got married and then a month later, a week after we'd graduated, Richard was invited to do a screen test in LA. Flown out first class.'

'Wow and did he get the part?'

'No, he didn't. It took a while for him to pick up again when he came back. He really wanted to prove to his dad that he could make it as an actor.

'He came back with his tail between his legs.' Carrie sighed at the memory. 'God he was miserable for those few weeks. I'd landed a very small part in *Blood Brothers* and—'

'Back up a minute. You were in *Blood Brothers*? What? In London? How come I never knew that?'

'It was only a small part.'

'Yeah, but even so. That's cool.'

Carrie smiled. At the time it had been more than cool, it had been amazing. Working in a proper theatre six nights of the week, doing what she loved. Richard came to watch three times in the first week.

'Then what?'

'Richard got another call. He'd been back barely two weeks. This time we made a big joke about it. He said he'd bring me the first-class goodies back from the plane and he'd see me in a week's time.

'Only he got the part. God, we nearly wet ourselves with excitement.' They'd squealed like toddlers in a ball pool when he told her. 'He came back, with the champagne from first class.' And they'd made a grown-up plan. He would go back out, make the film and then she'd either join him or he would come home.

'What happened?'

'He made the film and then, while filming, he got an agent, who helped him audition for a part in a play in New York. He got that and during the run another director saw him and offered him another part, being filmed on location all over the place. I was still in the theatre. It turned out to be impossible to keep in touch. Phones weren't like they are now.'

And Angela's arthritis took a turn for the worse. But she wouldn't tell Jade that. Leaving Angela with a young child hadn't been possible. And she thought Richard would come back one day. But he never did.

A full-scale production had commenced in the kitchen and Angela was in her element when Carrie, having absorbed the worst of the shock, had come back down to the kitchen. Now a frisson of excitement danced low in her belly as well as outright curiosity. Richard wasn't the man/boy she'd known all those years ago. He was new and reinvented but there was no reason why it couldn't be fun getting to know him again. However contrarily she didn't want Angela or Jade to think that she'd accepted the situation yet. Although she'd forgiven Jade, her niece needed to realise the consequences of what she'd done and Carrie was relying on Angela to reinforce that message.

Marisa, who'd stopped by to check on the towel situation again, had been drafted in as sous chef and chief confidante. The two of them sat at the breakfast bar, perched on the stools, poring over recipe books spread out across the counter.

'If we did the pork loin, we could do a goats' cheese and walnut salad for a starter.'

'Or what about ze petite quiches as hors d'oeuvres?'

They batted ideas back and forth like good-natured tennis players keeping a volley going for the sheer pleasure of it.

Angela spotted her. 'Richard's not allergic to anything, is he?'

'Not when I knew him, but for all I know he might have gone all Hollywood and eat some weird diet. He probably exists on a macrobiotic diet of grains and raw fish with a portion of bean curd on a good day, washed down with wheatgrass. Don't they all have almond milk instead of dairy these days?'

'I'm sure he'll have a very sophisticated palate as well,' said Angela staunchly. Carrie had a vision of her picking up her recipe books and clutching them to her as if they were her babies and challenging Richard to eat her food.

'I bet he eats in posh restaurants all the time,' she said. 'And if he doesn't he might be grateful for some home cooking.'

'When I knew him, he was grateful for a tin of beans,' said Carrie acidly. Personally she didn't think they should make any special effort or any fuss, but that would have denied Angela this special moment.

'Where's Jade? She should be chained to the sink and be your galley slave for the next fifteen years.'

Angela wrinkled her nose. 'She's trying to decide what to wear.'

'Sackcloth and ashes, if I have anything to do with it,' muttered Carrie darkly.

'I'm sorry.'

'For what?'

'For what Jade's done.'

'It's not your fault. Besides, she's already apologised.'

Angela's mouth dropped open. 'And you've forgiven her?'

Cassie threw herself moodily against the kitchen cabinets. 'I didn't have much choice. Besides she didn't do it to be malicious.'

'No she did it because she wanted to meet Richard Maddox and boast about it to all her friends.'

'There is that,' said Carrie. 'But it's done now. I have to get through it. If he even turns up.'

'He'd better.' Angela cast a look at the food on the side.

'Why does he want to come? That's what I don't get. He could have got in touch with me at any time.'

'Maybe he wants a divorce too. Realises the time is right. He might have met someone else.'

Carrie felt slightly sick.

Angela added, 'That would be handy. He'd be prepared to speed things up. You won't have to tell Alan about not being divorced or,' she paused, 'about being married.'

She ducked to one of the cupboards, pulling out a selection of brightly coloured cloths. 'Ah, here we go, just the thing. This will look lovely and there are matching napkins. I think we'll eat outside. We can hang lots of candles up around the verandah, make it look pretty.'

The Richard she knew had had to make do with candlelit suppers because they couldn't always round up enough fifty-pence pieces for the meter down the hall.

CHAPTER THIRTEEN

Angela had done herself proud, the table twinkled jewel-bright with a pink gingham tablecloth, solid royal-blue napkins and coloured wine and water glasses. Tea-light holders were suspended from every nook and cranny on the terrace overlooking the pool, waiting to be lit.

Little pottery bowls, dark with shiny tapenade, and plates piled high with slivers of unleavened bread awaited the guests. Cutlery lining each place mat attested to the courses that Angela had planned with her right-hand woman, Marisa. The menu had been arranged and prepared with military precision, leaving nothing to chance. Alternatives had been discussed and were on standby should Richard, in the intervening years, have become a vegetarian or, woe betide him, a vegan. Carrie found it difficult to believe that such a devotee of the bacon butty and Burger King's Whoppers might have undergone such an about-face, but Angela felt that anything was possible in the wilds of the Hollywood hills and Californian liberal (whacko, according to Jade) influences.

Carrie steadfastly refused to get in a tizz about Richard's arrival and spend hours getting ready. At six-thirty she was still in the pool. Her forty-sixth lap hadn't proved any more calming than the first, tenth or forty-fifth. Ploughing up and down, with only her thoughts in her head for company, had given rise to numerous imaginary conversations, all of which were accompanied by a hideous tinkly laugh that her imagination had introduced to every scenario. She wasn't going to get out of the pool until she'd reached fifty laps.

When she did get to fifty, she threw an extra one in out of sheer pig-headedness. Richard's visit was going to be a perfectly normal event. An old friend, she hadn't seen for years. Who happened to be gorgeousness incarnate, once the love of her life and now an international superstar.

Who was she kidding?

When she finally got into the shower, she opted for Marguerite's best Jo Malone soap to get rid of the smell of chlorine. Rather than spoil the rather divine smell of lime, basil and mandarin orange, she decided to go the whole hog and use the matching shampoo and conditioner and the body lotion afterwards.

Dressing was easy. She pulled out a navy blue cotton halter-neck sundress with large white daisies dancing across the bottom two-thirds of the full skirt.

The distinctive, almost, fifties style, had come from vintage or pre-loved clothes, as was the trendy term these days, shop, called *Vogue* in Berkhamsted. It was one of those mesmerising dresses that hints at all the things you might be, that you still could be and taunts you for being a coward. Displayed to advantage on the back wall by itself, it reminded of her of one of those clever portraits where the eyes are watching you from whatever angle you stand, only this was in reverse and from wherever she stood in the shop, she could still see it. In her drama-school days, she would have snatched it off the hanger and dived into the nearest changing room. She must have been hormonal or something that day because she kept circling around the shop and coming back to it. Even as she told herself she'd never wear it, that it was totally impractical and had it even seen an English summer, she was handing her card over to the shop assistant, who didn't bat an eye at her buying such an obviously unsuitable dress.

With a sigh, she let the fabric whisper over her head, settling like a second skin. When she stared in the mirror to add a barely-there touch of make-up, it was almost as if she'd gone back in time. With her hair down, she reminded herself of the Carrie Richard used to know. She tidied her room. Folded her underwear in the drawer. Rearranged her toiletries on the dressing table. Straightened the bed.

It was nearly seven-thirty. Would he be fashionably late? Or was that arrogantly late? For a minute she thought of Alan and his scrupulous punctuality. Richard would be late.

With absolutely nothing more she could do in her room, apart from open up her laptop again and check her emails, which she'd done two minutes before, she gave herself a last perfunctory look in the mirror, not examining her appearance too closely, and left the room.

Angela fussed in the kitchen, putting the last-minute touches to everything. She'd dressed for dinner in a pretty print dress that suited her colouring perfectly and her flushed face.

'Do you think he'll definitely come?' asked Angela.

'He'd bloody better after all this effort.' Carrie opened the fridge. 'I need a drink; does it matter what wine I open?'

'Yes, it does. The Sancerre is for the main course. You can open the Côtes de Provence.'

Carrie wrestled with the unfamiliar corkscrew, she was used to screw caps. It seemed rather undignified to have to fight her way into a bottle or maybe her hands were shaking.

'Just a small one for me,' said Angela, peering into the oven.

Carrie poured herself a large glass and handed her sister a second glass.

'Can I do anything to help?'

'I've asked Jade to light all the candles when he arrives. I hope he's going to be on time,' Angela checked her watch. 'I think everything's ready. You could stop pacing. It's making me nervous.'

'I'm not pacing.' Carrie stopped dead in the middle of the room and sipped at her glass.

'You're tapping your foot.'

Carrie huffed. 'I'll go and see how Jade's doing.'

As she walked through the lobby area, under the diamond-bright chandelier, the buzzer for the front gate sounded. She jumped and also, for no apparent reason, yelped. The buzzer sat beside the front door, innocuous and innocent. What if she pressed the intercom and told whoever it was, in the vague hope that they weren't Richard and someone stopping for directions, that the family wasn't home to visitors?

Jade came barrelling past. 'He's here. That'll be him. Let him in. Let him in. Quick.'

'Calm down.' She might as well have spoken to the wind, Jade skipped past her, depressing the button. 'Hello.'

'Hi, it's Richard Maddox. Here for dinner.'

'Come right in.'

Carrie raised an eyebrow as Jade blushed. 'What's with the American accent, all of a sudden?'

Jade giggled. 'No idea, it seemed sort of appropriate.'

Through the glass sidelights they could see the headlights of a car wending its way up the road.

'You can open the door, introduce yourself,' suggested Carrie, before adding, with a stern look, 'And make sure you confess and tell him that I knew nothing about this. I'll be outside on the terrace.'

She rushed outside so fast she tripped but managed to stop herself falling headlong into the table. Instead she splashed wine down her dress, leaving a Zorro-like streak across the skirt. Drawing on every breathing technique known to man or drama student, she staved off incipient hyperventilation but couldn't do a damn thing about the skippety-skip of her erratic heart, which had decided to play silly buggers.

She heard the deep baritone of his voice, a low buzz pitched against Jade's higher tones, which even from here she could tell were scaling Everest peaks of excitement.

'We've met before, but I don't suppose you remember.'

'Gosh, sorry. I was quite little,' said Jade.

'No, you were far more interested in the Peppa Pig that Carrie bought you.'

'Wow, I still have that.'

'Good because we walked the length of bloody Oxford Street to find the damn thing.'

Jade giggled as she and Richard came into view.

Every nerve ending stood to attention and then he was there, gliding towards her, his hand outstretched, a big stupid grin on his face and not an ounce of awkwardness.

'Carrie.' Behind him, Jade hovered, the last great romantic, in anticipation of some *coup de foudre* reunion.

'Richard.'

With consummate ease he planted a kiss on either cheek.

'Excuse the face. It's for continuity, although my co-star keeps complaining it's like being kissed by a pineapple.'

'You haven't improved your technique, then,' said Carrie, with a wicked glint in her eye.

Angela, appearing at the French doors, let out a gasp and Jade caught her eye, clearly trying to hide her laughter and also slightly shocked.

Richard let out a delighted laugh.

'You never let me get away with a single thing, did you?' he asked, stepping back and giving her a thorough once-over.

'Definitely not. Then or now. Don't think anything's changed because you're a big Hollywood hotshot.'

'I wouldn't dream of it.' Richard's eyes met hers and although he was smiling, serious intent lurked there.

For a moment she felt as if she were on a thin crust of ice that could give way at any second. On the surface everything was fine and dandy, underneath was another matter altogether.

Focusing on his face and meeting his gaze without flinching took every ounce of concentration, especially as all her senses were aware of the subtle spices of his after-shave and the electric hum of his closeness. Just that proximity was too close to the eye of a storm and everything whirling around them. It triggered sensations she'd forgotten and an immediate response from her body that appeared to think nothing had changed.

All their yesterdays were caught fast, like leaves in a

net. It was hard to believe that she hadn't seen him for so long. It was as if he'd walked out of the flat the day before and strolled back in a day later.

He smiled, his eyes crinkling, a few more lines than there used to be but, if anything, even more attractive. 'You've no idea how glad I was when Jade got in touch. You vanished so quickly the other day.'

'That was Jade's doing, not mine.'

'I think I realised that,' Richard teased.

'And you weren't above taking advantage,' challenged Carrie, narrowing her eyes at him, enjoying the exchange. It took her back to those days when they'd first met. Richard had been used to women fawning over him. She'd always kept him on his toes.

Richard grinned, his teeth white against the tan and dark bristles. 'Absolutely not.'

Angela came down and Carrie honestly thought she was going to curtsey.

'Angela. How lovely to see you. You haven't changed at all. I can't believe you've got a teenage daughter. Jade was about seven when I last saw her and Peppa Pig. Now look at her.'

Jade had retreated into star-struck silence, and despite the fact that it was so normal, it was surreal. Richard acted as if he were some long-absent relative who'd flown in from foreign climes. Carrie wanted to shake her head and rub this reality out, like she would the mist on the inside of the windscreen.

'Richard,' said Angela. 'It has been a long time. And haven't you done well? It's lovely of you to come,' she shot a glance at Carrie, 'when I'm sure you could have done all sorts of more interesting things this evening.'

Angela, oblivious to outraged glances, from both Carrie and Jade, carried on, 'Did you have to travel far?'

'Luckily I've got a driver, Philip. Actually,' he leaned forward and muttered in Angela's ear.

'Of course. I'll see to it. Now has Carrie offered you a drink yet? Come and sit down. We've got some aperitifs to start with. You're not allergic to anything are you?'

'Only porcupines,' said Richard, throwing a teasing grin towards Carrie.

'Please help yourself while I sort a few things out in the kitchen. Jade, I could do with a hand.

'Shades of Mrs Bennett,' commented Carrie with amusement as Angela dragged her daughter away.

'God, I remember that production. Hellish theatre. And who was that girl that played Elizabeth? Talk about miscasting.'

'I recall she was sleeping with the director. It helps,' said Carrie. 'Don't you see a lot of that?'

'Not much. Everyone's much more PC these days. California's a hotbed of litigation. That was a travesty, I recall. You should have got the part; your eyes were far livelier.'

'I don't think it was her eyes the director was looking at. She had other assets.'

Richard laughed, leaning back in his chair with negligent ease as if he popped in from next door every evening. 'She gave new meaning to the words "bodice ripper". There was serious danger of a major wardrobe malfunction every night. I worried about her bursting out of her frock, I could have been suffocated.'

Carrie hid a smile. 'Don't let the paparazzi hear you saying something like that, you'll be drummed out by the PC brigade. Are you allowed to say things like that?'

'I can say pretty much what I like here, can't I? I'm among friends.' He tilted his head in challenge.

It was as if the clock had been turned back and she had carte blanche to be the same as she was then.

'Friends? We haven't seen each other for years, don't you think that's a little bit on the presumptuous side? We're both bound to have changed. You especially. There's no reason why we might still be friends.' Ouch, so much for her attempt to be sassy and confident. She came across as sharp and strident.

'There are plenty of reasons we might be.' Richard stared at her. 'Although, I think I will fall out with you big time if you keep wearing your hair like that.'

With a swift movement, like a fencer taking advantage of her lowered guard, he swept the chopsticks anchoring her hair out and threw them across the terrace towards the swimming pool.

Like a Victorian maiden, she made a desperate grab to rescue the hair that came tumbling down.

'What did you do that for?' she said, gathering her hair in a ponytail, securing it in one hand.

'Because it looks much nicer down. Why would you wear it up?'

'It's practical, easier to look after.'

'And dull. I do like the frock, though. That's very you.'

'Funnily enough, I wasn't seeking your approval. I don't care what you think.'

'And neither should you. I paid you a compliment. Please don't tell me you've turned into one of those arch-feminists who don't think men should comment on their looks.'

'I haven't turned into anything,' said Carrie. 'I've matured and, hopefully, become much wiser.'

'Really? I suppose you were always the crazy one.'

'I was crazy?' That's not how she remembered things.

'Yes,' Richard frowned. 'Always ready with a creative idea. You got us into all the scrapes. Led me into mischief.'

'That's not true.'

He raised both eyebrows. 'Charity-shop rainbow challenge?'

She opened her mouth to deny it but had to smile at the memory of him wearing a rather sickly mustard yellow tank top over a teal and white-striped shirt with bright-red boot-leg jeans, a woman's fuchsia-pink jacket and a deep-purple scarf.

She put her hands over her mouth and started to giggle. 'Oh God. I do remember.'

'Now, if I'm not mistaken, Madam, I'm not the crazy one, that gem was all your idea. You came up with the budget. What was it? A tenner. We had to shop for an outfit and the person who had the most colours, not including patterns, won. But as an extra fillip, you dared me to meet everyone in the pub wearing the complete ensemble.'

'We caused such a stir, but the landlord gave us free drinks all night.'

'I'd completely forgotten about that.'

'And who's idea was it to buy Houdini?'

'Harry, you mean. It wasn't my fault he was an escapologist hamster.'

'It was your idea to give him a home. Everyone needs a pet, you said.'

She bit her lips, trying not to smile. She remembered saying it too.

'I nearly died when I woke up and he'd walked across my head, the first time he went missing.'

'You did scream like a girl that night.'

'So would you if you woke up with a mouthful of fluff and some creature pitter-pattering along and hauling its arse over your face.'

'That hardly makes me crazy.'

'Swimming in the sea in the dead of winter, taking me to a knitting club, ukulele lessons in a pub in Hoxton, kayaking up the Regent Canal.'

'They were cultural experiences.' And Carrie had forgotten about them. It was as if he triggered a trip wire releasing a whole load of memories, which had been tightly bound and tucked up out of the way.

'There was nothing cultural about the "escape from a zombie experience".'

Carrie snickered. 'That was a job opportunity. They were paying good money for people to play the zombies.'

'Carrie, the people that went there were nutters. There was a chance they'd slaughter the zombies.'

'Which is why we didn't do it in the end.'

'Not for the want of you trying to persuade me.'

'You enjoyed the make-up.'

'No, you enjoyed doing the make-up.' He rubbed his face, as if still trying to remove the grey face paint she'd enthusiastically smeared his face with one evening. 'And that fake blood tasted disgusting.'

She winced, remembering getting a mouthful when he'd decided to go the whole hog and lurch over to her, playing a zombie hell bent on kissing her. For a moment she was back in their scruffy flat, laughing helplessly as he staggered around, shoulders hunched with a fake limp, hamming it up for all he was worth.

'You looked hilarious.' She laughed.

'No, I looked scary and no wonder. The stuff you put on my teeth made me look as if I'd been feasting on dead bodies for months. That tasted foul too. I think you were trying to poison me.'

'I don't suppose you have that trouble with professional make-up artists these days.'

'No, they're much nicer to me. Show some respect.'

She sobered. They doubtless did. He was a big cheese these days.

'What are you doing now?' he asked softly. 'Are you still acting?'

The question was gently put, as if he knew damn well their careers had hurtled off in cosmically different directions, but at least had the sensitivity to ask.

'I gave it a good try. But . . . well, you know what it's like.' He didn't. Once he'd got to Hollywood, his career had gone stratospheric. Not for him the constant knock-backs, the fruitless auditions and the hopeless chasing for news. 'I'm a drama teacher now.' She shrugged. 'In a secondary school.'

'Do you enjoy it?'

A star winking high overhead caught her attention as she gave the question due consideration.

'I do, although I worry about the kids. The good ones. Will they make it? What can I do to give them the very best chance when I know a lot of it is down to luck?'

'I bet you're a good teacher. You always wanted to help everyone. And you were very good at giving critical feedback without being so brutal it hurt. I wouldn't have got through the first screen tests without you.'

'Rubbish. You had the talent.' She didn't want to take any credit.

'I also got the break. You were the one that made me do

that play, where J.C. Rogers saw me. If he hadn't invited me to the States, I wouldn't be where I am now. You drilled me when we practised my audition pieces.'

'Yeah, and didn't you complain.'

'Because you were bloody Attila the Hun. No, do it again. Feel the character. Did you ever think about going into directing?'

'I do plenty of that with school plays,' she smiled. 'And I've been doing some playwriting.'

'Good for you. What sort of stuff?'

'I'm working on one at the moment.' She couldn't help boasting. 'It's been taken on by a director, he's very keen.' Her mouth turned down in frustration. 'We're still trying to get a backer, but he thinks it's great.'

'But you did win an award for it,' chipped in Angela from behind her, as she appeared bearing a large pottery platter, the pungent scent of baked Camembert filling the night air. 'The gold medal for best new playwright.'

Richard raised an eyebrow, cocked his head and gave her a keen-eyed look. 'Not exactly small beer.'

Carrie lifted her shoulders 'It's nice to get that endorsement from people who know what they're talking about.'

'Have you written much?'

'A bit.' She didn't like to dwell on the pile of manuscripts that she never had time to do anything with, like submitting to agents, competitions or the open submissions run by broadcasters. Lots of opportunities but so little time.

Angela snorted. 'Her room is piled with manuscripts.'

'Still as talented as ever and far too modest,' commented Richard. 'That smells wonderful,' He gave Angela an enthusiastic smile. 'I miss home cooking.'

Angela put the plate in the centre of the table. 'Do help

yourself.' She watched him with hawk-eyed intensity as he dipped a slice of French bread to break the crust of the cheese, satisfaction dawning on her face as the creamy cheese oozed out. 'I'm sure you eat in fantastic restaurants all the time. This is nothing.'

Carrie wanted to roll her eyes, because Angela had been in the kitchen doing 'nothing' all day. She and Marisa, who'd left at six, had left no pot or pan unturned in their determination to put on a feast worthy of a Hollywood superstar.

'Another person who is too modest.' He took a bite and nodded, his eyes closing as his sighed. 'This is wonderful. Absolutely delicious.'

Jade followed suit. 'Not bad at all, Ma.'

For a few minutes silenced reigned as they all did justice to the velvety gooey Camembert, the tea lights flickering around them.

'And I can tell you eating in restaurants all the time palls. You only have to dribble your soup down your chin and some bugger captures it and shares it with the entire social media universe. And on location, I live on black coffee. I crave a good old shepherd's pie or a roast beef and Yorkshire pud.'

'Boring,' said Jade, helping herself to another slice of bread. 'This is yum. I hate shepherd's pie. Too much like school dinners.'

Angela and Carrie exchanged glances. That was the first they'd heard of it.

'If you eat in restaurants you never ever have to do the washing up.' She gave the numerous plates and glasses on the table a disgusted look. 'Although I guess you have servants to do all that.'

Richard laughed. 'Not exactly. I'm rarely home. Pretty much live out of a suitcase.'

'Where do you live? Hollywood Hills? New York?'

'Wherever I'm filming. Usually in a hotel.'

'Seriously?' Jade's voice held scathing disappointment. 'I thought you'd have mansions and penthouse suites all over the place. I mean you must be absolutely minted.'

'Jade!' her mother squealed, 'I'm sorry, Richard.'

She turned to her daughter. 'You know better to say things like that. It's very vulgar to say someone's minted.'

'Vulgar. Mum, no one says that sort of thing any more.'

Richard watched the two of them, amusement dancing in his eyes. 'It's fine, Angela, I've had far more intrusive questioning by a lot less charming people, who ought to know better.'

'So where do you live?' asked Jade, turning to Richard, with a hint of triumph as she placed both elbows on the table and leaned towards him.

'I rent a place outside LA, not a penthouse suite, I'm afraid, although it is a very nice condo. And I'm thinking about buying a place in London.'

'London!' Carrie's voice came out as a squeak.

'Yes, there's a lot of filming being done in the UK and I've been getting quite a lot of scripts for British TV dramas in the last year. One of which I got close to doing.'

Disquiet filled Carrie. Richard being thousands of miles away had made their separation logical and practical. Would things have been different if he'd had a base in London sooner? And now she was being ridiculous. A million different things could have happened in their lives. It wasn't as if they were likely to run into each other but for some unaccountable reason she didn't like the thought of him being in London.

'What about the West End? Would you do a play? Matthew Perry did a play.' Jade was an avid Friends fan and must have watched every last episode at least three times.

Richard paled. 'God, no. I haven't done any theatre for years and I don't intend to start now.'

'There's not the money in it, I guess,' said Carrie, without thinking, and then immediately blushed. 'Sorry I didn't mean to be . . .'

'Vulgar?' he teased with a show of good nature but Carrie got the impression she might have hit a raw nerve.

'No, it's a commercial reality. Sad but true, when you think how much hard work it is, having to perform and give a hundred percent every day, sometimes twice a day.' Theatre had always been her passion. She loved the fact that every performance could be different. Once a performance was captured on film that was it, there was no sense of engaging with an audience. It was a one-way transmission. Theatre allowed you to respond to the audience. 'I wasn't casting aspersions on your artistic integrity.'

'Come on, dish the dirt. Which stars have you worked with?' Jade's welcome interjection removed the taut line from Richard's jaw.

'Well I'm working with Savannah Murray at the moment. She's very lovely.'

'Well duh! You have to say that. Tell us what's she really like?'

Richard paused and then leant forward and whispered. 'Complete air head. Can't remember a line to save her life. But she's very sweet. Drives the crew mad because she's always losing her phone and half way through a scene she'll remember where it is and stop, to ask someone to go and retrieve it.'

'What about Kathryn Derringer? We saw *An Unsuitable Man . . .*' Jade paused and, with horrible certainty, Carrie could have predicted what came next.

'Auntie Carrie,' she turned to her, eyes shining with sudden discovery, 'You never said a word when we went to see it.' And then, as the last bit of the jigsaw locked into place, she added, 'That's why you were crying.'

There was a pause around the table, Carrie concentrated on the sound of the cicadas chirruping in the warm night air.

'Kathryn's a consummate professional,' said Richard, without looking at Carrie. 'More wine, Angela?'

'That would be lovely,' said Angela picking up her glass and, in her eagerness, almost smashing against the bottle as he lifted it in her direction.

Conversation moved onto more general topics, with Richard showing more than polite interest in Jade's A level choices and her views on school, boys and learning to drive. He had real charm, thought Carrie, as she listened to his gentle questioning and saw Jade blossoming and becoming more articulate and enthusiastic. She'd missed out on a male role model in her life. Alan treated her with the same casual attitude he would to any of his students. He was used to teenagers and didn't find them particularly fascinating. He made no bones when he came round to the house that he was there to see Carrie. Richard's interaction with the impressionable Jade was rather sweet. Not once did he show that her naïve questions were anything other than deserving of considered answers.

With the Camembert demolished, Carrie jumped up to help Angela, shaking her head slightly when her sister indicated that perhaps her daughter should be helping.

There was a strange man in the kitchen, tuned into the television, with a cup of coffee and an empty plate in front of him.

'This is Philip, Richard's driver.'

'Hello,'

'Good evening.'

'You're English.' And very well spoken with it, to her surprise.

'Well, I was the last time I checked.' He dusted down his well-pressed navy trousers.

'I thought you'd be a local. What, does Richard fly you wherever he goes?'

Phil laughed. 'Good Lord no, I've retired out here. Very early retirement, mind you, from the police force. And a friend of a friend asked if I fancied a job for the summer. Bit more interesting than watching reruns of *Only Fools and Horses* on cable every night.'

'Retired? You don't look old enough,' Angela said. 'Now, are you alright for coffee? I'm just going to serve the main course and I'll nip back with a portion for you.' She wrinkled her face in apology. 'I'm rather proud of this, I don't want to slice it up until I get to the table. Is that terribly silly?'

'Absolutely not m'dear. Let me give you a hand with those dishes.'

'No, you can't do that. You're a guest . . . sort of,' Angela added for Carrie's benefit, 'Richard asked if I'd give Phil something to eat. It seemed a shame for him to sit out in the car. I invited him in.'

'Which doesn't make me a guest at all.' Phil stood up, slipped off his jacket and rolled up his sleeves. 'He's a nice lad. Not like the girl, Sierra, or whatever she's called. Where's that washing-up liquid then?'

'There is a dishwasher,' said Angela.

'Even better. I'm a dab hand at stacking one of those fellows.'

CHAPTER FOURTEEN

It was almost easy to believe that this was a perfectly normal evening with drivers in the kitchen and a heart throb at the table, sitting outside in the balmy heat.

Carrie studied Richard as now he chatted easily to Angela, complimenting her on the delicious beef and asking how she'd cooked it and drawing out her interest in cooking. He was as smooth as a talk-show host.

Jade hung on every word, her hunger for celebrity gossip and inside news sated for the time being.

Carrie swallowed, trying to analyse the nugget of dissatisfaction. What had she expected? When he'd first arrived, a frisson crackled between them, lively with heat and fire as the memories of a different life had flooded her, but it had ebbed and faded. Like a chameleon Richard had fitted in and the conversation had stayed safe and bland. Nothing important was touched upon in the conversation and no one referred to any tricky topics.

Under the table she fiddled with her napkin, concertin-aing it into a series of folds, pressing firmly. Why the hell had he come? As if hearing her thoughts, he glanced up and his smile faltered as he saw the expression on her face, but with another question from Angela it slid back into place, which irritated Carrie even more.

Suddenly the situation seemed utterly absurd. This man from her past, sitting here holding court, pretending he was an ordinary person, while opening a door on another world that should remain shut to them, acting all the while as if he hadn't ripped her heart out. Pretending they were old friends rather than man and wife, married in haste because they couldn't live without each other, except it turned out he could. Very easily.

She frowned, needing to remind herself that this wasn't real. She, Jade and Angela were ordinary people, with ordinary lives that needed to be got on with. She and Alan had a future, a path as clear and steady as the one he was no doubt cycling along. After a hard day's cycling he would be taking it easy after a cold bath and a big meal of pasta, settling down with a good book. Making the most of his holiday before the term started again. She didn't want these reminders of what used to be.

'Do you think you could get me into the club in St Tropez?' Jade asked, 'My friend Eliza says George Clooney and Beyoncé hang out there. Do you know him? Although he's well old now.'

'What, George? Yeah, I've met him a couple of times. I was in talks with him about a possible project. He's doing a lot more directing these days. Nice guy.'

Carrie scowled at the casual name-dropping and wished Richard wouldn't pander to Jade.

'And have you been to Les Caves du Roy?' She turned

to her mother. 'That's the hippest night club in St Tropez, with resident DJ Jack-E. I bet it's banging. I'd love to go there.' Her wistful look was about as unsubtle as a bagful of sledgehammers.

'I think you might be underage,' said Richard, exchanging a discreet smile with Angela, 'And the crowd can be a little wild in there. I'm not sure it would be suitable.'

Jade pouted. 'I go to plenty of clubs at home.'

Carrie had a pretty good idea that the school socials, sans alcohol, she was used to, had about as much in common with a sophisticated French night spot as a donkey did with a thoroughbred racehorse.

'It'd be wicked if I could get in. Think what I'd tell my friends.'

Richard laughed. 'No dice, sweetheart. Your Mum would kill me.'

'Huh,' she turned to Angela, 'Things are different now. You don't understand.'

'I doubt you'd get in,' said Richard kindly. 'And the drinks are ferociously expensive in there.'

'I would if I went with you. Seriously, my life is dead. I never have any fun. Living with you two.'

Richard's stern expression, a gentle but clear rebuke, surprisingly halted Jade's complaints.

'Sorry, but it's frustrating being so near and not being able to see any celebrities.'

'That's told you,' Carrie chipped in.

'Oh God, I didn't mean you. Obvs you're a celebrity but . . .'

'I don't have quite the same cachet as George or P Diddy,' finished Richard.

'I don't know what cashay is, but you know what I mean.'

Richard gave Angela a quick glance. 'If . . . and only if, your Mum's in agreement. I'm thinking about throwing a party on one of the yachts in the harbour in St Tropez for the cast and crew, in a couple of weeks' time. If you behave, brat, I could send you an invitation.'

'You're shitting me. OMG. Will Savannah Murphy be there?' Jade jumped up and threw her arms around his neck, her body jerking with excitement. 'I'll be good for the rest of my life.'

'Please Mum. Please. Please say I can go.'

'The invitation would be for all three of you, of course.'

Smooth, thought Carrie acidly, very smooth.

Abruptly she pushed her chair back.

'I'll go and make some coffee.'

'No, I'll do it,' protested Angela half-rising from her seat.

'It's fine.' Carrie marched off, now cross with herself for being cross and letting it show.

Crashing about in the kitchen didn't make things any better, instead it brought home how childish she was being and not understanding why made it even worse.

She assumed Richard still took his coffee the same way and she certainly wasn't about to ask him. She paused over the sugar. They'd both taken their coffee black with two sugars then. She'd stopped sweetening hers ages ago. He probably had to. She'd give him that concession.

When she carried the tray out, Angela, sensitive to her sister's nuances, suggested that Richard and Carrie migrate to the veranda outside the lounge while she and Jade did some tidying up. A quelling glance killed Jade's protests and with well-meaning corralling, Carrie ended up on one of the rattan armchairs next to Richard.

The chairs on this separate veranda had been arranged

at right angles, allowing a view out over the hill but also to talk to a companion. The ideal spot to start a difficult conversation.

Lights grouped in clumps across the hillside below reminded her of constellations of stars, a ragged line down to the left, a cloud shape on the right and over there a single solitaire shining brilliantly.

'I didn't know if you took sugar any more,' she said as he took a sip of coffee.

'I'd forgotten I used to. Is that what you're cross about. Or is it because I said Jade could come to the party?'

'Who said I was cross?' She deliberately resisted the compelling urge to fold her arms across her chest, instead feigning an open-body posture as if she were totally relaxed. 'Although I don't think you should encourage Jade like that.'

'Why not? It will give her some major bragging rights and it's no problem.'

'Not to you.'

'And how is it to you, Miss Crosspatch?'

He had her there.

'I'm not cross.'

He leaned forward and rubbed at the spot between her eyebrows. 'Still a dead giveaway.'

She pushed his hand away. 'Don't be stupid. They're age lines.'

Richard laughed. 'Because you're ancient.'

'I'm definitely older and wiser,' she sighed. 'Which brings me rather neatly to . . .'

'To what?'

'Oh come on, Richard, don't be obtuse.'

'That's a great word isn't it? Obtuse. Layered with meaning.

It sounds less insulting than coming straight out and saying 'stupid', but if you think about it, it's even more insulting.'

'You're not flipping preparing a role here and analysing your character,' snapped Carrie, flashing her eyes at him, shocked at the sudden but very definite impulse to slap him. Extreme, perhaps, but her hands itched to do it. She could almost imagine the surprise on his face. It would jolt him out of this 'I'm comfortable and in command of the situation,' and a thousand times better than this awful sitting-on-the-precipice sensation. She didn't want to be the one to launch herself off. He should be the bloody awkward, out-of-place and uneasy one, not swanning in charming her relatives with promises of glamorous A-list parties and pretending that everything was normal.

As he turned his head away, taking advantage of the diversion of the view, she saw his jaw tighten.

Good. Her fist clenched on her thigh, waiting for him to resume the conversation. The silence stretched out. The bastard was going to make her do the work.

'Richard,' she started.

He turned to face her, one eyebrow lifting. Was it amusement or derision?

'Lovely as it has been to take this trip down memory lane, it's also time that we got around to getting divorced.'

'It probably is,' agreed Richard, who then turned away to continue his contemplation of the view and didn't say another word.

She wanted to shake him. 'Why did you come tonight?'

'Curiosity, I guess.'

It hurt more than it should. A lot more.

'Well, now your curiosity's been assuaged, perhaps we can discuss the mechanics of the process.'

'Did you ever wonder if things might have worked out if we'd done them differently?' Richard's words almost sounded absent, as if it were some philosophical question.

'No,' said Carrie, quashing the opposite thoughts that danced up and down in her head, saying yes, yes, yes. 'It never would have worked. We were far too young. Children still. We wanted different things out of life. You were much more ambitious than me.'

He swung around, his eyes fierce with some emotion she couldn't identify. 'Me more ambitious? That's not the way I remember it. You were always ambitious. We both were. I always thought that's why we understood each other so well.'

Carrie stared hard at the cloud-shaped collection of lights. 'I grew up. Discovered more important priorities.'

'You never gave us a chance you know.'

'I beg your pardon.' Slapping him had taken second place to pushing him off the balcony.

'You bailed, at the first opportunity.'

'I bailed,' her voice quivered, 'Excuse me. You were the one that went to Hollywood.'

'Yes.' He sounded angry now. How dare he? What right did he have to be angry? He was the one who left and never came back.

'With your support. You were the one who said I had to take the chance.'

'Oh and you weren't at all keen?'

'Of course I bloody well was. I'd seen one chance slip out of my fingers, I wasn't going to miss a second one. Remember what my mum said.'

Carrie did. It had been their mantra. Unbidden, the words came to her lips. 'Be like a terrier, shake every last opportunity to death.'

'Yes.' His expression sobered and for a moment they were both silent, as if remembering the horrible night when Josie Maddox's light went out for the last time. Richard's mum had always believed he'd succeed and, while she was alive, shielded him from his dad's scepticism that acting wasn't a real job.

'Once I was in Hollywood, there was no way I was going to let go. Mum always believed I'd do it. I couldn't let her down.' He turned urgent eyes her way. 'But you were in complete agreement that it was the right thing to do. You pushed as much as I did. You were the one who said I had to go. I thought you wanted it as much as I did.'

Shame-faced, Carrie ducked her head. That was love for you. Ambitious for herself, she'd understood how important it was for him. That last morning at the airport, when they'd clung to each other, she'd been the one who had to do the smart-talking. Talk him into letting go and walking through passport control. She'd been fierce with ambition for him.

'You never came out.' The bald statement laden with accusation made her stomach flip.

Carrie winced. 'I couldn't.' She took refuge in indignant rebuttal, ignoring the twin trammels of guilt and regret. 'You knew that. Being in the theatre for a six-month run. I couldn't say, I won't be in this weekend I'm popping over to the West Coast to see my . . .'

'Husband?'

Coldness settled in her stomach. A husband should have been important enough. For the first time the word carried the weight that she hadn't given it at the time.

'It's all by the by now, anyway. We should have got divorced ages ago.'

'Why didn't we?' asked Richard, his voice so quiet she had to strain to hear it.

'Because it didn't suit your career the last time we spoke about it.' A strained trans-Atlantic phone call, where much had been said but nothing at all.

'I remember it differently.' Richard's jaw tightened.

She didn't want to go there.

'I've met someone. He wants to marry me.' There was absolutely no point going into the whys and wherefores now.

Richard's smile wasn't kind. 'And do you want to marry him?'

How did he do that? Place some great import on the irrelevance of the way she'd phrased it. 'Yes.'

'So, it's rather lucky we ran into each other.'

'I didn't exactly know how to track you down.'

'You knew where my agent was.'

'He's not exactly my best friend.'

'He's not mine either. He's my agent. He looks after my career, not my love life.'

'You could have fooled me.'

'What's that supposed to mean?'

'When you were first in the States, he wasn't that great at passing on messages.'

'Film locations aren't always that handy for communication.'

Without realising it, Carrie had crossed her arms.

'What's he like? Your fiancé.'

'He's very nice. Lovely. Kind. A cyclist.' Why did she say that?

'What, like in the Tour de France?' Richard sounded impressed.

'Not professional, but that type of road-racing, yes.'

'Must be super-fit.'

Carrie's mouth twisted as she pictured Alan standing next to some elite athlete, half the size and stature.

'Yes, he is.'

'And do you cycle together? You went everywhere on that rattletrap thing with the wicker basket on the front when we were students.'

'God, I'd forgotten about that. I was heartbroken when we left and moved to London and we couldn't fit it in the van.'

'And you left that note in the basket.' He shook his head, as if still wondering at her foolishness.

'Please look after this trusty steed, her name is Flo . . .'

'. . . and watch the back brake, it has a tendency to work loose.'

They both fell silent.

'I ought to round up Phil. It's past his bedtime.'

'Yes but . . .'

Carrie didn't know what to say. Suddenly the task of getting a divorce seemed enormous and not quite as simple as posting a few papers.

She hadn't anticipated the huge sense of relief that came when Richard said, 'Look, why don't we meet for lunch tomorrow?'

CHAPTER FIFTEEN

Carrie turned over again, kicking at the deliciously weightless cotton sheets and cursing the light streaming in from the edges of the blinds. Another tangled dream. One of a series of dreams that had run into each other. Her pesky subconscious had a lot to answer for. The colours were fixed firmly in her head. Richard, in a bright-yellow jersey, cycling, legs pumping indefatigably, up a mountain leading the Tour de France while Alan trailed, a disconsolate expression on his face, at the back of the pack on the mountain stage. The rather obvious and unkind symbolism wasn't lost on her. Sighing and punching her pillow, she turned again, her back to the morning sunshine.

It was no good. She was awake, well and truly wide awake and unable to get last night's conversation out of her head. The words circled in her head like a nasty hangover. One, like all hangovers, she fully deserved. Honesty compelled her to admit her memory had conveniently used the years to paper over the facts, her improved version of events making it easier to hold him wholly responsible for them going their separate ways. The resulting bitter anger had insulated her sense of failure and helped her move on. It took a while to recover from a broken heart. How much longer would it have taken if she'd acknowledged that the break was as much her own fault as his?

But that was all in the past and it didn't mean, she decided, clenching her jaw, that it had to impact on the future.

She lay looking up at the ceiling and, with an exasperated huff, threw her legs over the side of the bed and sat up. Six o'clock! That wasn't getting-up time on holiday. She thought of all the times during term-time when she had to drag her sorry carcass out of bed at seven. Life wasn't fair.

Her laptop mocked her from the dressing table. She'd yet to open the document with the play. Coffee. And work. She might as well make the most of this unforgiving hour. For some cosmically funny joke in some realm of the universe, her brain was at its most fertile at this time of day but her body refused to co-operate. For once, she'd harness some of the ideas and attempt to wrestle them into submission by gluing her backside into the chair. But first coffee. And she needed to retrieve her hair slides in the daylight. She hoped they hadn't gone in the pool.

'You're up early.'

'Bejesus! You scared the daylights out of me. What are you doing up at this time?'

Angela smiled, a dreamy, secretive expression slipping across her face and sipped from a mug. 'I'm always up at this time. It's my favourite part of the day. I like the peace and quiet. The calm before the storm.'

Carrie wrinkled her nose. She and Jade had never quite managed to time their routines to suit each other. Inevitably there were fireworks in the mornings. 'And,' Angela added, 'it's my best chance of getting in the bathroom.'

'Well, at least here you've got your own bathroom. I'm not sure how we're going to manage when we go home, after a bathroom each and all this space.'

'Well, hopefully it's temporary. Have you and Alan decided what you're going to do? Are you going to move in with him?'

It hit Carrie, like a force-nine gale, that she hadn't even contemplated doing that until they were married. It wasn't that she was old fashioned, but it hadn't occurred to her.

'We're going to buy a bigger place. His flat is . . . a boy's place. And I've got the money from Mum and Dad. If we combine that, we could get a bigger place.'

'You could have bought a place ages ago. Used that money.'

Of course, Angela being Angela couldn't come right out and ask why she never had, which was a relief. After Richard had gone, the only thing that kept Carrie going was the handy realisation that she needed to keep an eye on Angela and Jade. As Jade got older and became more active and started school, it became harder for Angela to cope. Not that she ever said anything, but Carrie could see that things were challenging. It made perfect sense for Carrie to move in with them and even more so financially. It wasn't as if Angela could get a high-paid job. She'd trained as an accountant, which is where she'd met Clive, Jade's father, but continued ill health had forced her to take the offered redundancy.

'Did you sort everything out with Richard? Gosh he hasn't changed that much, has he? As lovely as he always was. And so good with Jade. I mean, he can't be used to teenagers, can he? But he handled her beautifully.'

'That's because she was on her best behaviour,' grumbled Carrie, thinking of how she normally behaved.

'True, but he did have a way with her. And as soon as he arrived, he asked me to look after Phil. What a nice man.'

'Who, Phil or Richard?' asked Carrie with a teasing grin which deepened when Angela turned a rosy pink.

'Phil. He helped with all the clearing away. What's happening?'

Angela nursed her coffee cup between both hands, with an expectant air.

Carrie rolled her eyes, 'We're going out to lunch today. He's coming at twelve-thirty.'

'That's good, isn't it?'

'I hope so.' Her mind strayed back to last night's conversation. It hadn't been as straightforward as she'd hoped. Richard didn't exactly bite her hand off to sign on the dotted line.

Making sure she kept herself busy throughout the morning, she decided to work outside, taking advantage of the pretty little summer house on the lawn below the pool. It was the first time she'd explored beyond the pool terrace and she quickly discovered the reason for the well-manicured gardens.

The summer house doubled as a tool shed, albeit a very grand one. The tools were all housed in wooden racks and neat cupboards. Beside it, in a little lean-to, a ride-on tractor was parked, no doubt used to cut the vast lawn, which was surprisingly level given that the rest of the garden sloped away down the hill.

Once she stopped being distracted by the view, which the

summer house had been positioned to enjoy, she lost herself in the story and managed to write a few scenes.

Angela made one welcome interruption mid-morning with a large glass of home-made lemonade. There was no stopping her newly discovered inner domestic goddess.

After a few hours, her back complained about her posture, bent double over the little mosaic table. As she stretched she caught sight of one of the gardeners heading her way. Dressed in baggy khaki walking shorts, trainers and a shabby T-shirt, with a canvas hat on his head, he shambled towards her. Curious, she scanned the rest of the lawn, expecting to see a few of his colleagues. The gardens were immaculate; she would have thought there'd be an army of gardeners to keep it looking like this, not this solitary fellow.

She nodded at him, unconvinced her schoolgirl French would make much impact. To her surprise, he walked right into the summer house, loitering in the doorway, silhouetted by the sunshine. It was one of those very British moments where she didn't know what the hell to say or do. With the full sun behind him, the floppy hat pulled low over his face and the mirrored sunglasses, it was difficult to see him properly.

She nodded at him again.

He nodded back and, for a minute, it felt as if she were in a French farce and she wondered who would break first.

'Bonjour,' she said.

He grinned, perfect all-American white teeth glowed at her.

'You!' She jumped up as Richard bent double with laughter.

'What the hell do you think you're playing at?' she yelled at him.

'I wondered how long it would take you to recognise me,' he wheezed, between delighted chuckles.

Oh Lord, how the hell did he do that — swap from Mellors, the gardener, to James Bond, with a mere tweak to his gait, straightening up and lifting his shoulders? Of course, he was an actor, a bloody good one. He could move seamlessly from role to role and she needed to remember that. Now he'd pulled his hat off and ditched the sunglasses, it was perfectly obvious. She had to admit, but wasn't going to, that he'd disguised himself rather well. She'd had no idea it was him until he'd flashed those glow-in-the-dark choppers at her.

With a pinch of her lips, she slammed her laptop shut, as his laughter eventually subsided. Honestly, it was worse than having to deal with the Year 10s at school.

'Are you ready for lunch?' he asked, pulling up a seat and sitting down opposite, drawing in a much-needed breath. 'Sorry,' he struggled to hide another threatened burst of laughter, 'but it was funny. You had that outraged, prim, "you're invading my space but I'm too English to say anything about it" look on your face.'

'I thought you were one of the gardeners,' she said, with a touch of disdain, but he grinned even more.

'Mission accomplished, then. Shall we go?' he asked, merriment still dancing on his face. 'Come on, Carrie. It was funny.'

'Only if you're about five,' she said, with an inward wince. What was wrong with her? When had she lost her sense of humour? She sounded horribly like a school teacher of a bygone age. Even her students wouldn't recognise her at the moment.

'Let me go and get my bag and say bye to Angela and

Jade,' she paused, adding with saccharine sweetness 'unless you fancied inviting them along too.'

'Not this time.'

As she stood up, he stepped in front of her, his eyes looking into hers. 'Shall we start again?'

Her eyes widened, as she wondered what he was . . . before she could complete the thought, his lips had touched hers with a fleeting but nonetheless electric-charged kiss, which sent a couple of thousand volts zinging through her.

'Hello,' he said, the husky timbre of his voice resonating like a tuning fork against her breast bone.

Oh shit, how did he do that? With as much dignity as she could muster, given that her legs were about to go on strike, she pulled away. 'I'll go . . . get my things.'

She hurried back to the house, conscious her face burned bright pink, a shade that owed nothing to the sun.

CHAPTER SIXTEEN

'Have you been here before?' asked Carrie, looking around. The restaurant simmered with quiet, low-level chatter. A few unoccupied tables dotted the sun-filled terrace, but most, including theirs, had reserved signs on the pristine, crisp white table cloths. The maître d' had seated them with an almost cavalier flourish, in a prime spot beneath a wide cream parasol, at a table on the edge of a broad patio with a commanding view of the Bay of St Tropez.

A week ago, she'd been drinking builder's tea in the staff room at work. It was a pinch-yourself moment and she was glad that she'd made an effort and put on a dress and strappy, heeled sandals.

Did the staff know who Richard was? Phil had dropped them off at the end of the street rather than bang outside the restaurant and Richard had kept on the ridiculous hat, along with the sunglasses, and maintained the shambling walk.

As disguises went, it was rather successful. In synthetic fabric shorts and sensible walking shoes he resembled a rambler who'd strayed off the path and lost the rest of his party, a million miles away from the suave movie star she'd bumped into in Ramatuelle a few days ago.

'Yes, I've been here a couple of times. Friends of mine have a villa down the road. They come here quite often. It's the best restaurant in Gassin and definitely commands the best view.'

Carrie took in the view, focusing on the intense blue, which darkened where the sea met the sky, a pure azure unmarred by a single cloud or white-capped wave. She gave a silent shudder of bliss, a smile touching her lips as she shifted her attention to the trees in verdant shades of green, massaging the contours of the landscape.

Sleek service accompanied the arrival of the menu as the waiter shook out her napkin and placed it in her lap.

'Aperitif?' asked Richard, consulting the menu and snapping it shut almost immediately.

She nodded, unsure whether he was asking or telling her.

'Would you like a Pastis? Or champagne?'

'Pastis? Isn't that liquorice?'

'Anise. Or aniseed to us.'

'I think I'll stick to champagne.' If her colleagues could see her now. Champagne for lunch, how decadent.

'Dom Pérignon?' Richard asked.

'T-that would be lovely.' She inclined her head graciously as if the champagne, she'd only heard of in James Bond films, was her go-to choice when it came to lunchtime aperitifs.

Richard rattled off their order in excellent-sounding French, upon which she commented.

He laughed. 'Down to a very good language coach, when I played a lieutenant in Napoleon's army in an unseen drama that never made it beyond the pilot. I can do a passable accent but the words are terrible. Ordering food and drinks is about the extent of my skill.'

Something she'd do well to remember. He could adopt another persona at will. He was an actor, that was what he did. The Richard she knew all those years ago no longer existed. Why was he suddenly showing an interest in her now, after all this time? It wasn't as if he hadn't known where to find her.

Perusing, or hiding behind, the menu, gave her somewhere else to focus on rather than looking across the table at the man who'd been, still was, her husband. She hadn't expected to enjoy herself. Not that that had anything to do with Richard. It wasn't every day you got to eat in a place like this. Her aim had been to get through this lunch, nailing down everything they needed to and then she could get on with the rest of her life and forget all about him.

The previous night she felt as if Richard, like some devious fairy or imp, had led her down a completely different path to the one she wanted to go, distracting her with spurious conversation. It was quite simple. They needed to formalise a divorce. And as quickly as possible.

Dealing with Richard was a bit like knitting with mist, she decided. It was up to her to pin him down and sort things out today, once and for all. She pulled a notebook out of her bag and put it on the table between their place settings.

Richard inclined his head but didn't say anything. The mirrored lenses were starting to bug her.

'I need an address for you.' She pulled out a pen and pushed the book over to him. 'Can you write it down, so that we can start.'

'Start what?'

'You're being obtuse again. To start divorce proceedings. It's all very straightforward. I need to fill in a divorce petition form but I can't do it without an address for you.'

'And then what?'

'You're sent a divorce petition. All you need to do is agree to it and return the form within eight days.'

'And that's it?'

'No, then I apply for a decree nisi to the court. They agree . . .'

Richard held up a hand. 'Hold your horses. How come the court decides all this? Don't I have a say in anything? I recall I was there when we got married.'

'Richard! When you get the divorce petition and return it, you are agreeing. And would you take those bloody sunglasses off.'

White teeth flashed as he peeled them off and lay them on the table with a flourish. 'That's more like the Carrie I remember.'

Luckily for him the waiter arrived, smoothly depositing a tall delicate glass of straw-coloured champagne in front of each of them.

Had he always been this damn irritating? She focused on her hands in her lap, knitting the fingers together. With a calming breath, she quickly separated them and leaned her forearms on the table.

'Salut,' he lifted his glass in toast. 'To new beginnings.' His face gave nothing away.

'Salut.' She took a sip and almost sighed. 'This is heavenly.' She took another taste, enjoying the sensation of sharp bubbles dancing over her tongue.

'So, this petition thing. I don't have to agree.'

Carrie swallowed her drink in a hurry, gasping slightly as it almost went down the wrong way.

'Of course . . . you have . . . to agree,' she wheezed.

'Yes, but what if I don't want to?' He looked reasonable. He sounded reasonable. 'Did you know fifty per cent of people regret getting divorced?'

He wasn't being reasonable.

'Are you being deliberately difficult about this?' The calming breaths weren't working.

'You've sprung this on me.'

'Sprung it on you!'

'Yes,' he put an elbow on the table and rested his chin in his hand, as thoughtful as a scholar, 'I'm trying to get my head round it. I've never been divorced before. I don't know any of this stuff.'

Carrie sighed and muttered under her breath.

'I heard that.'

'There are five grounds for divorce; we could go for any one of them. Adultery, desertion,' she paused, before adding with a hiss, 'unreasonable behaviour, or separation for two years or five years. I'd say we've got a full house there. Take your pick.'

'I'm not disagreeing that there might be grounds but I'm not sure we've given it enough of a chance. I thought we established last night we'd both made mistakes.'

'What?' Carrie stared at him. Was he mad?

'So, given we've been apart all this time and not got divorced, we should at least give it a try. After all, what's the hurry? We've been "not divorced" very successfully for the last eight years.'

'Only because you didn't want a divorce. You wanted a

separation, remember? You didn't want to formalise anything at the time.' She clenched her hands under the table but couldn't stop herself adding, 'You've had plenty of girlfriends over the years. Didn't any of them want to get married? Or was our marriage a handy excuse?'

Richard's eyes narrowed. 'Our marriage was never mentioned. And if you recall, you suggested a divorce. When I said I didn't want one, you then wanted the separation. You pushed for it, if you remember, and you assumed, at the time, I was seeing other people.'

Carrie tossed her head. 'You said, at the time, it suited your career.'

His face closed down but not before she saw an odd look flash in his eyes.

'And I don't have a girlfriend at the moment.' His face hardened. 'You shouldn't believe everything you read in the papers.'

'You're asking me to believe you've been a monk all this time?' She raised a sceptical eyebrow.

'No, I'm reminding you of how it played out. You called time first. Not me. I told you that I wasn't involved with any of those women. You wouldn't believe me but you wouldn't come out either. I couldn't win.'

'I . . . I . . .' Damn, he was right. It was a low, but honest, blow. She'd conveniently buried that truth.

'Richard. I'm engaged to another man.'

He raised an eyebrow.

'Alan wants to . . . *we* want to get married at half term. October.'

'Hmm. Sounds rather tight timewise.'

'Which is why we're having this conversation now.' Her voice rose. 'If you don't contest, there's a chance we might be able to speed things up, especially as there's no money, children or property involved. A good solicitor can help expedite the process. Keep things out of the papers.'

Richard leaned back in his chair, looking a little too relaxed as he sipped his champagne, the rest of him very still. Even with the silly clothes on, he exuded a touch of slight danger. A hint of storminess rolled in the deep-blue eyes and, with sudden prickle of awareness, Carrie wondered if she was taunting a tiger.

'Two weeks,' Richard sat forward again, putting his glass down with ungentle thud, sending champagne slopping over the side.

Carrie frowned.

'You give me two weeks.'

'What do you mean?'

'Two weeks to decide if it's a good idea to get divorced. I let you call the shots last time. It's my turn. Two weeks to make sure you won't regret it afterwards. If after that you still want a divorce, I'll pay a solicitor to get you the quickest divorce ever.'

'Don't be ridiculous,' Carrie snapped, ignoring the weird sensation of falling through the air.

'What have you got to lose? The Carrie I knew would never back down from a challenge. She'd have spat in her hand and shaken on it.'

'As I told you before, I'm older and wiser.'

'You keep saying. But surely this is a logical deal. Win, win for you. You get to prove me wrong and you get your quickie divorce.'

Any moment now, she was going to start hyperventilating. This was not happening. It should have been totally simple. The research she'd done described the process in three easy stages. File for divorce, apply for a decree nisi, apply for decree absolute. Job done.

She also recalled a section on *if your partner lacks the mental capacity.* Paying closer attention to that bit might have come in handy.

'Why are you doing this? And what do you get out of it . . . I'm not sleeping with you.'

With a lightning-quick reaction, he smiled. 'I didn't ask you to.'

She blushed, realising that her response made it sound as if she were considering his dumb-ass offer.

'Why two weeks? And why now?'

'Why not?' He shrugged and lifted his glass as if he didn't have a care in the world. In front of her eyes, he melted into the role of louche, devil-may-care actor. 'My schedule's quite light for the next couple of weeks. I'll be at a bit of a loose end. At least with you, I can be confident you won't set the paparazzi on us or sell your story to the press.'

What had she expected? That he still cared? Still thought of her? She was the dumb-ass but his flippant response still hurt a little bit.

'This is a game to you, isn't it?'

He shrugged again. 'If that's what you want to think. Like I said, I'm at a loose end.'

'We wouldn't want you to be bored, would we?'

Her icy sarcasm didn't even come close to hitting the mark. He responded with a cheerful smile and raised his glass in yet another toast.

With a discreet tug at the tablecloth, the waiter made his presence known. Carrie could have kissed him.

'Madame? Monsieur?'

'Do you want some more time?'

Carrie shook her head and buried her head in the menu.

'I'll have the scallops followed by the fillet de boeuf,' said Richard, handing his menu back to the waiter. 'Rare, please.'

Her vision a little blurred, she examined the choices with the intensity of finals' student opening an exam paper. Crevettes en cocotte, beignets de crabe, moules frites aux Pernod, canard à la bourguignonne. Her taste buds withered, unable to summon the energy to show any enthusiasm for the expensive, Michelin-star menu.

'I'll have the same,' she said hurriedly. Richard's choices sounded as good as any. 'Although not rare. Medium.' Rare in France meant blue didn't it? That sounded far too adventurous. 'Actually, well done.'

The waiter straightened, worry lacing his face, as if the prospect of facing the chef with that request held some terror, while amusement danced across Richard's.

Anger flared in the pit of her stomach. 'No, make it rare.' Carrie took a defiant gulp of her champagne, emptying the glass, the bubbles exploding in her mouth, along with the realisation that playing safe wasn't all it was cracked up to be.

'Two weeks.' Carrie seized the bottle of champagne from the ice bucket on the stand next to the table and topped up her glass and then his. 'You've got yourself a deal.' She picked up the glass and lifted it in toast to Richard, who followed suit, clinking it against hers. War had been declared and he'd won the first skirmish. From the grin on his face, he knew it too.

*

'Excuse me?'

The steak, oozing blood and smelling divine, arrived and along with it, a giggly woman clutching an enormous handbag, wobbling on high heels, which raised her height to all of five foot.

She peered at Richard, who before Carrie's eyes, slumped in his seat, his neck vanishing almost instantaneously.

'Are you Richard Maddox?'

Carrie examined her steak for all she was worth.

'D'you know, you're the third person who, asked me that?'

Her head shot up at the sound of his broad accent, it could have been Richard's father sitting opposite.

'I wish I had his money. Me and the missus would be cruising in the Med, wouldn't we, love?' He'd sunk even further into his seat, his whole shape changed. John Maddox might as well have been sitting in front of her. She had to credit him, Richard was a brilliant actor.

'That we would,' she answered suddenly filled with devilment, matching his Brummie accent, gravelly syllable for syllable. 'Although with you and your seasickness,' she laced the words with weary disappointment, 'you'd spend most of the time with your head down the loo. Terrible traveller he is.' She rolled her eyes. 'Sees a wave and he's gone.'

'Oh,' the woman shuffled a step backwards, her handbag raised above her chest, her earlier smile fading with uncertainty 'You look similar. Are you sure you aren't him?'

'I should know. Been married to the bugger for ten years. He's no Richard Maddox, I can tell you. Especially not first thing in the morning,' said Carrie with feeling. 'Ha! Can you imagine it? Like sleeping with a delinquent walrus. Snoring, farting. You have to be joking.'

With each phrase the woman took another step back. 'Sorry. My mistake.' She bolted as fast as her heels allowed back to a table, to an accompaniment of mouthed questions from her companions.

'Wasn't him!' she heard the woman declaim in a loud disgusted tone as the group crowded around her, their heads all craning towards her. A burst of laughter echoed around the restaurant along with a chorus of good-natured teasing and heckling.

Richard gave them all a cocky wave, in keeping with his sudden Northern persona.

'Delinquent walrus? Where did that come from?'

'I don't know.' Carrie lifted her napkin to hide her giggles. 'It popped into my head.'

'I think I'm going to have to ration your champagne intake from now on.'

'Just when I was getting a taste for it.' She took another sip. 'It's rather nice. I think I might enjoy the next two weeks after all.'

'While I am starting to have second thoughts,' teased Richard, his blue eyes twinkling down at her as amusement tilted the corners of his mouth, making her pulse behave very strangely.

Oh lord, she was going to have to watch her step.

'You sounded exactly like your dad. How is he?' She almost missed the tiny movement as his jaw tightened.

'Same as ever. Still thinks I need to get a proper job. The only way he's ever going to be proud of me is if I land the James Bond role.' Bitterness rubbed the edge of his words.

'I think you must be exaggerating. Surely by now, you've done enough to make him proud.'

'You think? "Still dressing up and poncing about at your age, it's not right." That's his view.'

At his bleak expression, she leaned over and put her hand on his and gave it a gentle squeeze. 'You know your mum would have been thrilled to bits with your success.' She saw him swallow, his eyes focusing on a point far beyond the edge of the terrace.

CHAPTER SEVENTEEN

'Did Richard say anything more about the party?'

Jade pounced on Carrie as soon as she walked through the door, making her feel like she was eighteen again and coming back after her date to face her dad.

'No.'

'Are you sure?' Jade folded her arms, her chin lifted in mulish protest.

'I'm quite sure.' Carrie walked towards the kitchen, her niece following. 'We had other things to talk about.'

'I can't believe you want to marry Alan when you're married to him.'

'I'm sure you can't,' said Carrie, asperity making her voice waspish.

Jade had the grace to look embarrassed. 'It's just that he's not exactly Mr Riveting.'

Carrie ignored that comment and crossed to the fridge, pulling out a jug of lemonade. Angela had been busy again.

'It's not fair, you get to go swanning off and I'm stuck here.'

Carrie laughed. She could think of worse places to be stuck.

'We haven't even been anywhere to see people,' Jade sighed. 'Eliza keeps asking me if we've seen anyone famous and you won't let me tell her that Richard Maddox came here. For dinner.' Her voice rang sharp with accusation, leaving Carrie in no doubt that she was responsible for Jade's terribly dull life and the injustice of not being able to impart the most important bit of gossip ever.

Carrie remembered being the same age, on holiday with her parents, and the utter disappointment when they'd eaten their picnic from tin-foil packets, sitting, bare legs sticking to the vinyl plastic leather-look seats, in the back of the car, instead of sprawling on a tartan wool rug, a wicker basket at the ready, on a sun-facing hillside overlooking the sea.

'I tell you what. Why don't we get all dressed up this evening and go into St Tropez, celebrity-spotting? We can have a drink in one of the bars on the front.' And hang the expense.

Jade's face brightened and like an exuberant puppy, she bounced on the spot. 'Yes! Can we? That would be ace. Yes! Let's.

'Hey, Mum, guess what? We're going out tonight.' Angela, used to Jade's lightning prophecies and announcements, nodded mildly. Carrie envied her equanimity as she said, 'Jolly good. You found the lemonade. What do you think?'

'It's delicious.' Carrie enjoyed the tart sweetness on her tongue. 'I could get used to this.'

'How did it go with Richard?'

Jade had skipped off back to pool armed with her phone. The promised excursion would keep her and her WhatsApp group occupied for the rest of the afternoon.

'Confusing,' said Carrie.

'Really?' Angela glanced over her shoulder as she perused the contents of the fridge. 'Shall we have dinner when we get back? What was confusing? I thought you'd researched everything. It sounded straightforward.'

'It would be if I was dealing with a sane, normal person.'

'What do you mean?'

'He's being difficult about it.'

'Why?'

'He wants us to spend time together.'

'What, after all this time?'

'Exactly.' Carrie hauled herself up onto the kitchen counter. 'I could strangle him, except he makes it all sound so bloody logical. He said not being divorced has worked perfectly well so far, so what's another two weeks.'

'Oh.' Angela's quizzical sigh matched her own confusion. 'What did you say to that?'

'What could I say? I need him to sign the petition. Plus, he said if I agreed to his two weeks, he'd pay for a solicitor to speed things up, which would help. And he can afford the best in the business. It would mean that Alan and I could get married in October as planned.'

'You agreed?'

'Yes. We're going out for the day tomorrow.'

'Anywhere nice?'

Carrie pulled a face. 'It's a surprise. I don't get it at all. I think he's being pig-headed for the sake of it.'

Angela lapsed into thought. 'Did you ask him why?'

'I tried.'

'It's quite romantic,' she mused, 'long-lost love.'

'There's nothing romantic about it. He's not used to being turned down or not getting his own way.'

'I guess he does have his pick of women.'

'Exactly.' Carrie slid down from the top. 'I'm going for a swim.'

Perhaps a good, energetic thrash up and down the pool would dispel this sense of disquiet. What did Richard hope to achieve?

He'd unleashed a wash of unsettling memories, their attendant searing emotions jostling for space in her head and punching into her heart. She needed to insulate herself and keep her emotional distance. He could have his two weeks, but it didn't mean he was going to enjoy them.

'OMG, have you seen the size of that yacht?' Jade craned her neck, no inhibitions about gawking at the boisterous group talking and chatting on the deck of the sleek, white cruiser.

You couldn't miss it, rising four decks high from the water, a glossy advert for unlimited wealth, dwarfing and outshining the faded umber facades of the three-storey buildings opposite. Radio antennae and radar-shaped gadgets were testament to the advanced technology on board, hidden from view by the tinted glass windows.

Even the crew in matching white polo T-shirts and navy-blue chinos, shorts showing off tanned lithe legs, were beautiful people with sun-streaked hair and gorgeous smiles.

Carrie had never seen anything quite like the harbour front with its row of billionaire's yachts moored side by side, each one bigger and better than the last.

In full view of the early-evening crowd of tourists, designer-clad parties on the decks of several craft illustrated blasé indifference to the spectacle they provided, almost playing to the open curiosity of the have-nots wandering along the quayside as they bayed with overloud laughter, the light glinting off their champagne glasses.

'It's like *Made in Chelsea*,' sighed Jade, snapping away with her phone. 'Do you think they're famous? Do you think Richard knows some of them? I bet he does. It must be brilliant to be on board one of those.'

'Unless you get seasick,' said Carrie with a giggle, suddenly remembering their lunchtime conversation.

'Like you're going to get seasick in the harbour,' scoffed Jade.

She had a point. Carrie wondered how many of these floating gin palaces ever put out to sea. This one, with its aerodynamic sharp, sleek lines, looked as if it could be readied for inter-galactic travel within seconds.

The names of the yachts fascinated her. *You Only Live Once. Loaded. Rich Pickings. Laura Cash. Nice n Easy. Maid in Diamonds.*

An impatient, lordly honk behind them was a terse reminder that they were wandering along the road and when they moved, a Rolls Royce Phantom, complete with silver lady on the bonnet, cruised past them and glided to a halt at the next berth. A middle-aged perma-tanned couple, diamonds glittering at her ears and a Rolex watch on his wrist, so enormous you couldn't miss it, strolled down the gangplank, on a red carpet, no less, and waited as the driver of the car leapt out, strode to the back passenger door and opened it. With regal insouciance they slid into the back seat, the driver closed the door on them and without acknowledging the audience of passers-by who had all stopped, mouthing 'who are they?' he slipped back into the car and it purred away, cutting a swathe through the thronging pathway.

'How the other half live,' observed Angela.

'Crazy isn't it?' replied Carrie. It was a shame, they seemed so aloof and separate from the rest of this vibrant world, where the night buzzed with excitement, anticipation and expectation.

'Where do you think they're going?' Jade studied the yacht they'd vacated.

'Some Michelin ten-star restaurant somewhere, I guess.' Carrie couldn't help thinking of lunch and the eye-watering bill that Richard had paid without a second glance. This was another world, overladen with wealth and conspicuous consumption but beguiling in its decadence, glitter and glamour. There was a part of her that would love to be on board one of the yachts, experiencing the high life.

Jade looked less than impressed. 'I'd be clubbing. Did you know the VIP Room is down there? Last year Rhianna and Chris Martin played there. You know the age here is sixteen, instead of eighteen like at home.'

'And you're not going clubbing here,' said Angela. 'Even if you had someone to go with.'

'The year after next year, when my exams are finished, me, Eliza, Charlotte and Becky are going to Ibiza. Wall-to-wall clubbing.'

'I can't imagine anything worse,' said Carrie.

'Well that's because you're old,' said Jade. 'You don't understand these things.'

'We were young once,' Angela cuffed her daughter lightly around the head. 'And your aunt was positively wild in her youth.'

'Were you?' Jade's exaggerated amazement stung.

'I wouldn't say wild but I had a good time.'

Angela's facial expression disagreed.

'Okay, I was a little wild.'

'Really.' Jade's interested was clearly piqued. 'What sort of things did you do?' Her tone suggested that it was absolutely impossible that her aged aunt, who was all of thirteen years older than her, could have done anything approximating wild.

'I once rode naked down a one-way street on a bicycle.'

'You never.' Jade stopped dead in the street, much to the annoyance of the German family behind her.

'I did.' Carrie grinned. 'For a good cause. It was to publicise a play we were doing in Edinburgh at the festival.'

'Was that the year you stayed in that castle with the Laird?' asked Angela.

'I never knew about that.' Jade frowned as if she were trying to work out a difficult maths question and kept having to check back over the figures because the answer didn't add up.

'No, it was the year after that. We needed to fill the theatre every night and we'd agreed it was a great publicity stunt. Thing was, when it came to it, no other bugger would do it. So,' she sighed, 'I did it.'

But only because Richard had dared her to do it.

'I never knew that.' Angela looked horrified. 'I'm surprised you weren't arrested.'

'So was I!' Carrie began to laugh as the memory of that day crystallised in her head. 'We were hoping I would be, as that would have made a better story, but the policeman was ever so nice about it, even though he didn't know where to look.'

'You nearly got arrested!'

'Yeah,' Carrie said with a sheepish smile, 'I avoided mentioning that one at home.'

'What was the play?' asked Jade.

'Lady Godiva.'

Angela burst out laughing. 'Please don't tell me the bicycle was done up as a horse.'

'Damn, I wish we'd thought of that.'

'Did it work?' Angela asked.

'It did, although there were a lot of disappointed Scottish men in the audience who were there to see the English bird with her kit off. They thought it was part of the performance.'

Angela smiled, 'I might have seen the funny side of it.'

'Not a chance I wanted to take, thank you.'

'Can we stop for a drink now?' asked Jade.

'Yes, where do you fancy going?'

'All of these places are packed,' said Angela, surveying the busy bars. 'We'll never get a table.'

'Mum, don't be boring.'

'We'll be better off on one of the side streets. Those places won't be as busy.'

'Yeah, because they're not exactly banging.' Jade marched over to the nearest bar to read the menu at the front entrance. A barrier of thyme-filled troughs separated the rows of low-slung chairs facing the water from the road, all occupied, mainly by young twenty-somethings, the girls wearing the skimpiest tops and tiniest shorts Carrie had ever seen, and the men rocking the camp, all-white linen look. In some cases, all they needed was a captain's hat and gold-fringed epaulettes to complete the look.

Angela hung back. Carrie read the prices over Jade's shoulder and winced. You could buy a crate of wine elsewhere for the price they were charging for a bottle.

'Look, they're leaving.' Like a Lab scenting food, Jade

shot off, wriggling through the tables and staking her claim on one of them before the last occupant had even risen to his feet. He gave Jade a lazy smile. 'Hey, babe. Take my seat.' He leaned over and whispered something in her ear. She turned bright scarlet as he sauntered off, tossing a jacket over his shoulder before blowing her a kiss.

'What did he say?' asked Angela, rushing over, shooting suspicious looks at him. Carrie didn't think he even noticed, he was too busy admiring himself in the wing mirror of a dark-blue Maserati parked outside.

Jade's blush fired up more heavily. 'Just that the seat was warm already.'

Carrie had a strong suspicion it was a lot lewder than that.

Angela picked up the menu and gasped. 'That's outrageous. Have you seen the price of these drinks?' she squeaked. 'We can't stay here.'

Jade's mouth turned down at each corner and her knee jumped up and down.

'Don't worry.' Carrie laid a hand on her sister's forearm as Angela struggled to get out of the seat, which was a bare inches from the floor. 'These drinks are on me.'

'But . . .'

'Chill, Mum. We're here now and like you said before we'll never get a seat anywhere else.' Jade nestled into the seat, like a cuckoo staking its claim. There was no way she was going anywhere.

'Ang, don't worry. We haven't had to spend any money on the accommodation or the food. Come on, kick back and enjoy. It's a great spot for people-watching.'

'But you paid for the car hire,' Angela muttered.

'OMG look at that.' Jade pointed to a bright-yellow

Lamborghini that even, while crawling along the street, still emitted a throaty roar. 'If I had a car that expensive, I'd at least get it in a decent colour.'

'If I had a car like that, I'd get the exhaust fixed,' said Angela flatly.

'If I had a car like that, I'd get the hell out of St Tropez,' said Carrie.

They all burst out laughing.

'That's so lame,' said Jade. 'This place is ace. I love it.'

'After I'd driven a hundred miles an hour along the highway first.' Carrie added with a huge smile. 'If you're going to drive something like that, you ought to go fast. You can afford the speeding tickets.'

Jade gave her a considering look. 'Liking your style, Auntie C.'

'I'd be terrified of scraping the paintwork or crashing it. Can you imagine the repair bill or the insurance premiums?'

'I don't think people who own cars like that are particularly worried about their no-claims bonus.'

'Drinks, ladies?'

'I'll have a sparkling water,' said Angela, closing her menu with a firm snap, a prissy punctuation to her safe choice.

'Jade?' Carrie prompted her niece, who suddenly shut the menu and put it on the table as if to shun temptation. 'I'll have the same.'

'Oh for God's sake, you two. Order something worthwhile. It's not like we do this on a regular basis. Push the boat out. I'll have a Kir Royale.' Carrie handed her menu back to the waiter. 'She,' she pointed to Angela, 'will have a gin and tonic, lots of ice, no slice and the young lady will have a . . .'

Jade's face lit up with an excited beam. 'Vodka and lime with soda.'

The waiter didn't even blink at this unorthodox choice. 'Merci mademoiselles.'

'Thanks Caz. This is so cool.' She took her phone out and took a few more pictures, before despatching them via WhatsApp to her friends.

As she took a sip of the Kir Royale, the fizz reminding her of lunchtime, she felt a sudden buzz. They were in one of the most glamorous, chic locations in the world. She was going to enjoy it.

CHAPTER EIGHTEEN

'Where are you going today?' asked Jade with the mournful look of a spaniel who knows it's about to be excluded from an outing. She reached across the table to snag a second chocolate croissant. 'Mm, these are yum. I love it when the chocolate is all soft in the middle.'

'From the sounds of Richard's text, I think it's a trip to the beach. He told me to bring swimwear,' as well as the added instruction, *Wear trousers and flat shoes.*

Bloody man. How the hell was that supposed to help her decided what to wear? Trousers encompassed a whole new dilemma. Jeans, Capri pants or white linen?

Dithering in front of the wardrobe, which was not like her, she'd pulled out a pair of pale-grey Capri pants, wondering what Richard would turn up in. Then she put them back and hauled out a pair of crisp white-linen trousers. What part was he going to play today? Movie star or itinerant gardener? With an annoyed tsk, she pulled out a red T-shirt and a patterned scarf. She'd look chic even if he didn't. And why did she even care?

'The beach.' Jade sighed and Carrie stopped worrying about her clothes. 'I'd love to go to the beach. I bet it's one of those private posh beach places.'

'Posh? What? There are different grades of sand quality. Sea purity?'

'Nooo.' Jade stabbed at a loose croissant crumb, obviously exasperated beyond belief by her numpty of an aunt, before picking it up with her finger and waving the finger at Carrie. 'There are these super-exclusive beach places, where it's private and there's a pool and chairs and a DJ, proper music and a bar. They're so cool. You have to pay to get in. Nikki Beach is amaaaazing. I saw it on YouTube. Like one massive party. Maybe he's taking you there. You should see the cars in the carpark.'

'They showed that on YouTube?' Angela shook her head across the breakfast table, as beautifully laid as if they were in a hotel. It had become her habit to lay out the breakfast table with a pretty tablecloth and matching tableware and serve warmed croissants with a large fresh pot of coffee, despite the swanky machine in the kitchen. It was rather nice having this leisurely breakfast together, instead of the usual chaotic dodgem-car approach at home.

'Yes. It's wall-to-wall Mercedes, Ferraris. All convertibles. Unbelievable.'

Carrie's idea of beach heaven did not include a bar, music or a pool. She wanted to feel hot sand under her feet, lie on a towel and wriggle until her bottom hollowed out a dip to lie comfortably and inch into the cold sea wave by wave. However, the idea of the wind tugging and whipping at her hair in an open-topped sports car, like you saw in the films, had definite appeal. If she pinched Jade's larger than large sunglasses, she'd really look the part.

Should she pack a book for the beach? Weighing a paperback in her hand, deciding she'd regret it if she didn't, it was tossed into the straw bag along with her towel, sun cream, hairbrush, sarong, flip-flops (she'd opted to wear her Converse, in case they had to walk anywhere) and a bottle of water. Oh, and phone in a little zip-lock bag to stop the sand and any water getting on it. Plastic bag. That would be good for her wet costume later. Maybe a dry T-shirt? Was that everything? Not knowing what Richard planned made it difficult to know what to pack for the day. Should she take shampoo and conditioner? On the Continent most places had shower facilities and her hair was a bugger to detangle. She studied the curls in the mirror. If Richard did his usual trick and pulled it out of her up-do, she'd be stuffed on the beach.

After a few days in the sun her face had a golden glow that had banished her British sallow tinge. Giving in to a sudden whim, she added a quick slick of mascara, waterproof of course, and a touch of lipstick, in case they did end up at one of those beach-resort places, where no doubt all the girls would be utterly stunning and in bikinis a fraction the size of her good old Marks and Spencer one.

She heard the buzzer announcing his arrival at the gates at the top of the hill and gathered up her bulging bag, hoping they wouldn't have to walk too far.

Jade loitered in the hall with a nonchalant, who-me air about her. Angela was no better, making a vague attempt at tidying up the flowers on the console table. A welcoming party for a diplomatic mission would have been outnumbered.

'You're ready.' Jade was clearly disappointed by that. 'Are you sure you've got everything?'

Angela chuckled. 'By the size of that bag, I'd say she's got an entire set of cutlery, a full dinner service and the washing-up liquid, as well as the sink.'

Carrie ignored them both and rifled through the top of the bag, checking her sunglasses had been included.

'I've never seen you do your hair like that before,' said Jade, studying Carrie's long plait with the intensity of Richard Attenborough discovering a new species. 'It looks nice but too *Sound of Music*. You ought to try one of those fishtail ones,' she grabbed the plait. 'I could do it for you. They show you on YouTube.'

Carrie removed it gently from her niece's hand. 'Not today. It's purely practical. For the beach.'

And hopefully, Richard-proof.

With a move devoid of any subtlety Jade opened the door, not wanting to put Richard to the trouble of having to press the doorbell himself and Carrie heard a buzzing whine like a lawnmower or was it a chainsaw? She knew that sound, what was it?'

Richard pulled up into view.

'You have to be kidding,' she muttered, as he pulled off a royal-blue helmet, proudly clutching it to his stomach with both hands, like a knight's helmet. He beamed up at them, as if he were astride some majestic stallion instead of a small white scooter.

'Morning ladies.' He swung his leg over, looped the helmet over the handlebars and loped towards where they'd gathered on the top step.

'Wow, that's so cool,' said Jade, before adding, 'How old do you have to be to hire a scooter, do you think?'

'Ninety-five and half,' said Angela, without missing a beat, before turning to Carrie and muttering, 'Rather you than me.'

'Seriously.' Carrie stared at the scooter. 'Oh shit.' Then she took a peek at him. Oh shit, indeed.

Memories collided, taking her back ten years.

Today he looked like the old Richard. Hair dishevelled, pointing in all directions, a thin cotton navy T-shirt, well-worn jeans, open at one knee from wear and tear rather than by design, and an ancient pair of black Converse, with the beginnings of hole in one toe. Old Richard had the same endearing grin but not the breadth of shoulders or toned physique under his T-shirt.

Carrie sucked in a breath. Please let the journey to the beach be very, very short. Her system was already querying how it was going to cope, for an extended period, sitting thigh to thigh and hanging on to that torso. Extended period? Who was she kidding? Just the thought of getting onto the scooter behind him had sent her pulse soaring into call-a-doctor beats per minute.

This wasn't supposed to happen. Her body, the big fat traitor, was letting her down big time. She did not fancy Richard. Absolutely, utterly did not. That boat had sailed. She was getting married, for God's sake, to another man. She loved Alan. Her libido was being led astray, or maybe it was the victim of a form of muscle memory. That was it. An old habit. And habits could be broken. Strains of a Rolling Stones song drifted into her head. Old habits die hard.

She pushed her shoulders back with renewed decision. Today was about proving to him that his two-week idea was very stupid, they were worlds apart, they had nothing in common any more and she didn't have any feelings for him whatsoever.

'Ready for a day at the beach?' asked Richard casually.

He grimaced at her oversize bag but to his credit didn't say a word. With relief, she realised she could put it between the two of them and at least create some kind of barrier.

'Did you want a coffee or anything before you head off?'

Carrie narrowed a glare at her sister's back, even though she knew that Angela couldn't help herself. Not offering food or drink to a guest might just have killed her or ruined her day.

'Do you know what? That would be great. I'd forgotten what thirsty work it is on a scooter.'

Really? Folding her arms and tapping her foot would have been childish so she refrained, but it took some doing.

'I might have swallowed a couple of flies on the way here.'

'Yeuch,' said Jade, eyeing the scooter with less enthusiasm.

Of course, coffee turned into home-made lemonade and croissants, which had to be heated, but Richard, in no hurry, happily chatted to Jade and Angela as he lounged in the shade under the veranda.

Watching Angela blossom in response to his compliments about her cooking and talking with great animation as she described making some pastry, waving her hands without any sign of self-consciousness, Carrie made herself relax into her chair. There was no hurry.

'Where are you going today?' asked Jade.

'A beach not too far from here,' answered Richard, stretching lazily, his T-shirt riding up. Carrie's eyes slid away. He'd made himself far too comfortable.

'Good, because I haven't been on a scooter in . . .' Her voice trailed off, she knew exactly how long it had been.

'Since that time we went to Brighton.' Richard's face lit up.

'Brighton, I used to love going to Brighton,' said Angela, a dreamy smile on her face. 'Shopping in the Lanes.'

'Carrie had a bee in her bonnet about visiting the Royal Pavilion.'

'No I did not. We were doing the *Madness of King George* at college, it was research. I wanted to get a feel for the Prince Regent. It was important.'

'Not at seven o'clock in the morning.' He turned to Jade, adopting a put-upon air. 'She bounded out of bed and announced we had to go to Brighton.'

'It wasn't quite like that.' Richard exaggerated.

'No, true.' He waited a beat. 'More like eight o'clock. We were on the road by nine. On a scooter to Brighton.'

Jade sat up. 'How old were you when you got the scooter?'

'It wasn't mine.' Richard gave a pointed look at Carrie.

Jade turned to her aunt, her eyebrows like twin caterpillars, rearing up in sceptical disbelief.

'We'd borrowed it . . . for the weekend.

Her repressive tone made Richard snort but to be fair he didn't elaborate.

'My friend Ralph was selling the scooter and said I could test-drive it for the weekend.'

'He'd have let you test-drive it for a year.'

'Are you trying to say I led him on?' She turned, narrowing her eyes at Richard, seizing on it as a reason to be cross with him, even if it was spurious.

'He did have quite a crush on you, although to be fair, you were very good,' agreed Richard a little too easily, before adding. 'You only had eyes for me, everyone knew that.'

'Ever heard of modesty?' asked Carrie.

'God, do you remember that trip? What a laugh.' His shoulders shook with gentle mirth.

'A laugh?' Carrie widened her eyes. 'You've got to be joking. We got absolutely drenched.' With a shudder, she remembered the soaked-through misery of wet underwear clinging to her skin. 'And my hair. Oh God, we thought we were going to have to cut the knots out, it was in such a state afterwards.'

Richard raised one eyebrow, his eyes dancing with secrets and amusement.

'So we stayed overnight. In a B and B. Do you remember the woman that ran it?'

It was no good, Carrie couldn't keep up being cross with him. 'Mrs Barclay.'

'You remember her name?'

'Because of the bank, I guess, but she was very kind.'

'She ran that hot bath and gave you a bottle of conditioner.' His eyes met hers and a flash raced through her. Richard's hands gentle on her scalp, massaging the conditioner with thorough attention as he sat behind her, she sitting between his legs, her bottom nestling up against him. Her nipples suddenly tingled and she made the mistake of looking at his hands, tanned with long, neat fingers, laying on the white-sprigged tablecloth. An image of his hands, slick with conditioner, moving down from the ends of her hair, sliding their way inch by inch down her front. Abruptly she closed her legs tight, as if it might quash the sudden sensation flowering there.

'Shall we go?'

He took the outsize beach bag from her, for which she was grateful, giving the contents a cursory glance. Alan might have, no he would have, questioned whether she needed each and every item. Richard tucked it behind his legs at the front of the scooter. Only as she threw her leg over the scooter to sit behind, his bottom nestling up against her crotch, did she regret her haste, the memories still too fresh in her head.

As they zipped up the drive, the air buffeting her face, making her duck behind Richard's back, other recollections trickled back. It was her who had insisted they make the spur-of-the-moment trip to Brighton, despite the weather forecast. She'd underestimated the penetrating power of driving rain. They'd arrived so wet and cold that the thought of driving back was too horrible to contemplate, instead making the impromptu decision to stay overnight. Doubtless one of her brainwaves too. It had definitely been her idea to go and buy a complete set of new clothes from the charity shop for the evening while theirs dried over Mrs Barclay's radiators, although she'd drawn the line at charity-shop knickers and bought new.

They went out to dinner, fish and chips on the pier, because of course by then it had stopped raining, she in a taffeta black dress with a puffed-out skirt, which didn't quite go with her biker boots, and Richard in a very spiffy pin-stripe suit, although the broad lines looked as if they been chalked by a rather drunk tailor.

They must have made quite a picture, sitting on a wooden bench in all their finery surrounded by seagulls begging for chips.

The dress, a real find for only a couple of quid, which she'd kept and worn lots of times after that, was still up in the loft somewhere, along with a whole load of other clothes that she hadn't been able to bring herself to throw away but she couldn't see herself wearing again. They didn't fit with who she was these days.

Lost in daydreams, she realised she'd relaxed into Richard without even realising it, abandoning her upright impersonal hold on his waist. Somehow her arms had slipped around his front, her legs had inched closer to his backside and she'd nestled into his broad back, laying her cheek against the soft cotton of his T-shirt with the scent of him right under her nose. Half of her wanted to jerk back, what the hell was she playing at, while the other half wanted to enjoy the smell and the sensation of holding onto a warm body. The fabric of his top felt soft, good quality and well worn, giving off a slight scent, one she remembered well. It was the smell of his neck in the mornings when she nuzzled in and, with a pang that struck her like a blow, the smell on the sheets on the nights he wasn't there, when he'd first gone to Hollywood.

She inhaled deeply, aware of a low-level dull ache in her heart, always lurking under the surface, an ever-present shadow dogging her sub-conscious, but nothing in comparison to the wrenching pain searing a hole in her heart in those first few months he'd been gone. She needed to get a grip, that was the past. Older and wiser now, she could protect herself against that level of intense emotion.

Determined to ignore the memories that insisted on surfacing like cheeky, persistent dolphins, she stared at the scenery as they passed. They dipped in and out of the sun and shadows as they passed huge tracts of trees, the dark-green boughs creating shady pools on the sides of the roads. Pine and cypress on the air made her nose tingle.

The whine of the scooter grew as they climbed a hill and

as they crested the top, almost at a snail's pace by this time, the view out over the sea took her by surprise.

'Want to stop?' yelled Richard over his shoulder.

She nodded and they pulled into a viewing area, already full of cars and people lining the walls, snapping away with their cameras. The spot maximised the view of the Gulf of St Tropez and the Mediterranean beyond. A cruise liner ploughed its way across the horizon, slow and stately, like a swan surrounded by unruly ducklings, the yachts, sails billowing, zipping this way and that, catching the breeze.

Richard came to stand behind her and leaned in, his breath lightly tickling her neck as he extended one arm and, resting it on her shoulder, pointed to an area of the coast. It seemed natural to lean back into him and follow the smooth line of his arm, indicating a spot where the sea met the land curving away from them.

'That's where we're going.'

She cast him a doubt-filled look. The sun had risen high in the sky already. The beach was going to be incredibly busy and only get busier.

'Haven't we left it too late? We won't get a sunshade or sunbed.'

'Don't worry about that. But it is getting close to lunch-time.'

'You've just had breakfast.'

'What can I say? I'm a growing boy.'

They got back on the scooter and sailed down the hill, the roads becoming smaller and smaller until they turned off down little more than a dirt track, which they bumped along for a minute or two before it petered out into a small car park. In the wall ahead of them was a tall, narrow gate.

They hopped off the scooter and Richard slung Carrie's bag over his shoulder, selecting a key from the ring of the scooter keys.

'Here we go.' With a quick twist he opened the gate and stepped back to let Carrie through.

On the other side of the gate, a decked landing area with a set of steps, led downwards and by the stairs sat a large blue ice box. A boardwalk stretched away to the right, to which Carrie gave a second curious glance.

'Ah, great.' Richard picked up and gave her a cheeky wink. 'Lunch.'

He led the way across the platform. The set of wooden stairs ran in two flights down to the beach, a small curve of pristine sand about the size of a football pitch. Two hammocks had been pitched under a huge parasol on one side and comfortable recliners on the other with large sun shelter almost like a Bedouin tent.

Apart from that the beach was completely deserted. Carrie stopped dead at the top of the stairs.

'Is this for us?' For you, she should have said.

'Yup.'

The sea lapping at the edge of the sand sparkled in the sunshine, clear and bright. Around the edge of the bay outcrops of rocks stood guard, protecting the privacy of the beach. Their very own private, perfect slice of earth. Her heart skipped with a quick kick of excitement. To have the beach and the sea to themselves was quite the most decadent thing she could think of.

'Belongs to a friend of mine.' Richard picked up the ice box and, with her bag over one shoulder, headed down the steps, looking back at her and beyond her shoulder to the hill behind. 'The path at the top of the stairs leads to the house,' he nodded, 'you can see the roof. It's unoccupied at the moment, apart from a couple of skeleton staff who are here all year round.' He put his head down and concentrated on the steps, his clear actor's voice carrying back to her. 'Keith and his family, grown-up kids from his first marriage and little kids from wife number two, are in Mexico this summer, but Keith said I could use the beach whenever I wanted. Well, he said I could use the house too, but I didn't fancy that. Not on my own. It's too big for one person to rattle around in. Christine, the housekeeper, gets bored. Means she's happy to knock up a picnic anytime for me.'

She stared at his back. Housekeeper. Skeleton staff. Having a picnic 'knocked up' for you. Her height of luxury was buying a Marks and Spencer' prawn sandwich on a Friday instead of taking a home-made one into school.

'Do you come here a lot, then?'

'Occasionally. I like to swim without someone trying to get my autograph or a selfie,' he stopped at the top of the next flight and turned to her, 'or worse, nick my swimming shorts.'

'Did that honestly happen?' Surely he'd made that up.

'A couple of girls have tried.' He offered her a self-deprecating smile. 'I managed to fight them off.'

'I can't imagine what they were thinking.' Or why they would want to. 'Do they seriously think your meat and two veg is better than any other man's?'

'Thanks for that. You're good for my ego. Keep me in my place.'

'My pleasure.' Now she was half way down, you could see the house more clearly. 'It's a terrible waste. There must be loads of places that are empty. Marguerite's family didn't want to stay in the villa, for which I'm very grateful, but there must lots more that stand empty all year.'

'Which is why I've never bought a place.'

'But you're buying in London?'

'I intend spending more time there.'

Carrie didn't want to ask any more questions.

She took her time on the steps, letting Richard march ahead, hardly able to believe that they had the whole beach to themselves. With a quick smile, she wondered whether it would impress Jade or not.

At the bottom, she took her time, enjoying the workout, walking in the shifting sand exercised her muscles. There was nothing quite like it, she thought, although she was rather grateful that she didn't have to carry anything. It was nearly midday and the sun had reached its peak in the sky. She picked up her pace towards the fancy shelter that Richard had already reached. *Homes and Interiors* had come to the beach. Under the white awning were two wooden full-length sun loungers, with thick padded cushions in white and sunshine-yellow bolsters.

'I wish I'd put a skirt on, my legs are cooking,' said Carrie, ducking into the shade.

'Sorry, but I wanted you to be safe on the scooter. I see lots of kids in shorts come off and badly mess up their skin.'

'Forgiven.' Just when she was all hot and bothered, he pulled it out of the bag.

He flipped open the lid of the ice box and pulled out two cans of lemon Pellegrino.

She put the condensation-dripping can on her cheek. 'Bliss.'

Everything was. The sand so clean, she wondered if someone came down and raked it on a daily basis. That was too fanciful, perhaps, but it was clear that nature alone was responsible for that incredible depth of blue of the sea. She could see exactly why this coastline was referred to as the Côte d'Azur and this tiny secluded bay might have been created for a scene in a film. The hilltop behind them had a few pine trees casting their shadows on the beach and the craggy rocks on the outer edges created added interest.

Waves rippled into the shore, playful and merry, winking and sparkling in the sunlight.

Carrie kicked the shoes from her hot feet, promising them a cool refreshing paddle, and began to unpack her bag. Why had she brought this much stuff with her? Richard hadn't brought anything and now she could see why.

On each of the sunbeds was a neatly folded velour towel, navy-and-white striped on one, pink-and-white striped on the other and on top of each a white hand towel folded cleverly to form a basket that held two bottles of Lancaster sun cream, a high and low sunscreen factor, a Lotus flower facial mist spray and two fragrances of L'Occitaine shampoo and conditioner.

All were still sealed. It seemed a shame to open them but she couldn't resist trying the refreshing facial mist.

She had no idea if Lotus flowers had any special properties but removing the seal and reading the bottle helped delay the moment when she was going to have to strip off to reveal her bikini under her clothes.

'Wow, that is gorgeous.' She closed her eyes, enjoying the cold hit on her skin, although its effect was fleeting. 'I bet most of the guests don't even look at these things, do they?'

'You are kidding.' Richard reached down to the hem of his T-shirt and started to pull it up. Carrie wanted to look away but as he'd buried his head in the navy cotton, she stole a good long look at the lightly tanned skin, the line of hair running down his stomach, and smooth abdomen with discreet muscles that hinted at definition rather than shouted, *check us out.*

His muffled voice carried on, 'The richer people are, the more they have, the more they're given and they all love a freebie.'

Carrie busied herself with arranging her towel. 'And here was I thinking I was a cheapskate for wondering if I could take a couple of items back for Angela and Jade.'

Richard threw the T-shirt on the sunbed and started unbuttoning his jeans. Carrie quickly looked away.

'You can take the lot, if we can get them on the scooter. You look like you packed for a week.'

'A briefing issue. Your instructions weren't exactly detailed. Not all of us are used to Ralph Lauren towels and designer toiletries being laid on wherever we go.'

He shrugged. 'You coming in the sea?' He pulled down his jeans to reveal black jersey undershorts and somehow managed to pull the jeans over his feet with graceful ease instead of falling about all over the place like most people would.

'Yes,' she said, shimmying out of her linen trousers and pulling her T-shirt awkwardly over her head, struggling to manage the plait, which managed to get itself wound up in the fabric.

When she emerged the black jersey shorts lay puddled on the sand.

CHAPTER NINETEEN

She swallowed, staring at them with the horrified fascination of someone faced with a spider, praying at any moment it might scuttle away of its own accord.

The shorts stayed put.

'Are you coming in or not?'

With a quick blink, she raised her eyes to focus on his face. Nowhere else. Look at his eyes. Just keep looking at his eyes. Don't let your eyeline drop. Look at his nose or his mouth, anywhere but down.

A mistake because he grinned, bold as a pirate, confident and that slight tip of his eyebrow raised in definite challenge.

'Someone already stolen your swimming shorts?'

Lifting her chin, she held his gaze, defiant at first. Did he think she was going to follow suit because she didn't want to look gauche? Or was he trying to imply she was too chicken to strip off?

'Whatever happened to gung-ho Carrie? The girl who took the world on, every day?'

'I told you I'm older—'

'Balls. She's still in there, I'm sure. What happened to you? I don't buy the older and wiser crap.'

She heard the disdain in his voice as his jawline hardened, making her stomach churn. 'What happened,' she snapped her hands to her hips, 'is that when you went off to never-never land, I stayed in the real world. Got a real job. Had responsibilities.'

'A real job?' His mouth dipped. 'Yeah because twelve-hour days back to back for months on end isn't a real job. Learning lines. Sitting in a sound studio for days on end. No, that's not real work.'

A shimmer of guilt bothered Carrie until he scowled at her.

'I worked damned hard to get where I am. Those first eighteen months were killers. Making sure directors knew I was Mr Reliable. Being amenable. Doing the publicity. Playing the game. All those shots of me with other women, that was work. Every spare moment I had, I called you. You knew it was going to be tough, but we both agreed I had to go for it.'

Under his narrow-eyed study, the knots twisted tighter but she was unable to look away as the wordless exchange became a battle of wills.

'Fine, you worked hard. I get that. But now, life must be pretty easy.'

'It's easier in some ways, yes, but not in others. It's hard to get to know people. Are they sincere? Do they want something? There's always someone with a camera. I'm public property. Finding any privacy is pretty hard.'

Carrie raised an eyebrow. 'So you trust me?'

He sighed, his eyes focused on her face with sudden intensity. 'The Carrie I remember wouldn't sell me out. And

I'm pretty sure she's still in there, even if she is older and *wiser*. I bloody hope I can trust you. It's not much fun on a beach on your own.'

Finding it impossible to read him, she started to drop her eyes but the mocking challenge faded, replaced with a gentler, searching assessment, as if he was trying to look right into her soul.

Sharp awareness scythed through her as something in her consciousness shifted. Was that disappointment on his face?

'You can trust me.' Even as she said the words, she knew she'd ducked the real issue.

When had she stopped taking on the world? Jumping into life with both feet? Taking chances? Regret pinched, so acutely it almost hurt, forcing its way through long-held barriers.

Once upon a time she wouldn't have thought twice about what anyone else thought, she'd have stripped off because she wanted to.

When was the last time she'd acted on instinct, followed her gut or been herself? With a rush of self-awareness, it came to her. Like evolution, she'd adapted tiny bit by tiny bit, infinitesimal adjustments that over the years nibbled away at the edges, eating into the essential elements of who she really was. A person she'd almost forgotten had ever existed.

Sure in her decision, with steady hands, she unclasped her bikini top and took it off, rolling down her bottoms and laying both on the bed with unhurried casualness. The Carrie Richard had married would have peeled her top off and tossed it aside with much gayer abandon, but maturity brought with it some limits.

'Last one in is . . .' she said, and with a cheeky smile

took off down the beach to the sea, her heart skipping with the joy of being alive, the touch of the sun on her skin and triumph at the shocked surprise on Richard's face.

Ploughing into the sea, she splashed through the shallows, flinching and wriggling as the cold water spat up at her. Even though she didn't look around, she knew Richard was right behind her. Funny, she was okay about him seeing her bottom, for some reason, even though he'd seen it all before, but a touch of self-consciousness about flashing him a full frontal made her charge forward, wading her way laboriously through the water as it grew deeper, dragging at her legs and slowing her pace. Knowing that there was only one way to brave the cold, she threw herself in, gasping as the sea water embraced her body in an icy hold. A splash beside her told her that Richard had followed suit. With a kick of her legs, she swam quickly into the sun, aware of the water coursing over her naked body and Richard alongside her.

With dark hair plastered to his head, and drops of water twinkling on his long eyelashes, the bloody man even looked good dripping wet, like some exotic merman. Had he got better looking over the years? Or was it that familiarity had stopped her seeing it?

For some reason, swimming nude felt very different, even though a costume provided a very brief layer, or perhaps it focused her thoughts more. Her nipples hardened in the water and she felt the icy touch of the sea between her legs as she swam breast stroke.

Deciding this was far enough out, she stopped, treading water as Richard swam ahead, doing a clean, swift front crawl, powerful shoulders and arms planing the water. With a sigh she flipped on her back to look towards the beach, treading water. Despite telling herself not to, she'd taken in long lithe legs, flat stomach and lean hips. Richard exuded good looks with every damn breath. Unfortunately, her libido had decided to duck the lesson on common sense and the cold water did nothing to cool her wayward thoughts.

Richard had turned and headed her way, shaking the water from his head.

'That's more like the Carrie I remember.'

When she was enjoying herself this much, it seemed dishonest not to grin back. 'This is heavenly. I'd forgotten how wonderful it is to swim in the sea and not to have to be anywhere or do anything. I think this is the first time I've felt properly on holiday. You know, switched off from real life. No responsibilities whatsoever.' She held up her hands. 'I'm not having a dig.'

Saying it felt a touch disloyal. She loved her sister and niece but with her being the driver, it was incumbent on her to be entertainment officer, making sure they were both happy and did the things they wanted to do. After all, it was their holiday too.

'I didn't think you were,' said Richard, 'but if it makes any difference, I've got Sunday-night blues hanging over me. I've got to work later or play at being at work.'

'What are you doing?'

'We're filming night scenes at the moment, hence being able to play hooky today.'

Carrie winced. 'I'm sorry about what I said earlier.'

'I can promise you, when it gets to midnight this evening and I've thrown myself out of a window for the ninth time, it will feel like proper work.'

He rolled over and floated on his back next to her.

She glued her eyes to his face.

'Do you do your own stunts, then? I thought movie stars were too important and valuable to let near anything dangerous.'

'I don't think I like being referred to as a movie star,' mused Richard, his brow wrinkling. 'It sounds a bit ubiquitous, as if we're all the same. I'm not doing the whole stunt, only the front end, where you see me go out of the window. I have a stunt double who does the thirty-foot drop on the other side but I still have to hurl myself through the frame enough times to please the director, Frank.'

'You should be grateful you're not the stunt double. I bet he doesn't earn a fraction of what you do.'

'True, but I think my dad would still prefer it if I were a stuntman.'

'Are you sure about that?'

'Yup. He's pig-headed, proud of his grandchildren and still waiting for me to get a proper job.'

'You said that the other day but it can't be true.'

'Want to bet?'

'I don't believe you.'

'He had the same job in the factory, from sixteen until retirement. He's got a decent pension. A family. Something to look back on. It doesn't help that I'm not . . . settled and given him grandchildren of his own. As he sees it, I'm self-employed with no job security. He can't comprehend what my life is like in comparison to his, whereas what Michael and Robert do, he can relate to.'

'How are they?' Carrie had met them a couple of times when she and Richard were younger and she'd be hard-pressed to spot them in a line up. She had a vague recollection of sandy hair, indeterminate brown eyes, average height and insubstantial personalities, but then anyone would be eclipsed standing next to Richard. It hadn't been his looks but his sheer energy.

'Dull but very nice. Both married to nice, dull girls and have . . . I admit the kids are cracking, although,' he added with a naughty smile, 'that's because they're still of an age where other people's feelings are immaterial and if they want something they scream until they get it. Much more interesting.'

'Sounds like a lot of actors I know.'

'You malign me. Although I do know a few who fit the bill.'

'Like who?' she asked, her feet drifting downwards to touch the sandy bottom.

'That would be telling.'

Rising out of the water, as they neared the shoreline, sudden consciousness of her nudity gave Carrie a frisson of awareness, a sense that she was alive, her breathing easier as she circled her neck, letting all the tension float away. She hadn't a care in the world, or certainly not on this beach. Richard had seen her body plenty of times before and in the intervening years, she'd been lucky, she could eat what she liked and it didn't show. She'd rounded out a tad but her stomach had stayed put, nothing had stretched and her boobs were small enough that they stood upright on their own. Not that any of that mattered; this was for her, not him.

She lost her footing in the shallows, faltering slightly as the sand shifted underfoot. Richard's hand came to grip her elbow and then, as she regained her balance, he took her hand, interlinking his fingers with hers.

Muscle memory again? Or no reason to fight against it. If she pulled her hand away she was making it into a big deal. She wanted to show him it wasn't.

'Do you fancy something to eat? I can guarantee Christine will have laid on something special. Let's see what she's lined up.'

Hand in hand they walked up the beach, towards the sunbeds. There was nothing quite like the heat of the sun streaming over skin chilled by the sea. Carrie tipped her face up to the sky and stood for a minute, conscious of being bathed in sunlight. Pure heaven.

Richard tugged at her hand and she caught an appreciative gleam in his eyes. 'Come on, sun worshipper. I'm starving.'

She banished the insidious doubt that asked what Alan would think of this. Loose-limbed and relaxed, she sighed. She was on holiday, on a once-in-a-lifetime private beach, silky sand oozing through her toes and over her feet and her arm swinging in tandem with Richard's, where they were linked at the hand. Her body tingled with awareness, as if her nerve endings had suddenly been fine-tuned to respond to the stimuli of the wind, the water and the air.

Real life seemed a very long way away. She'd hadn't felt quite this relaxed and at ease with herself in ages.

'God, Christine's a bloody marvel.' Carrie took another bite of the chilled butterflied prawn. 'This is a picnic to the power ten.' The cool box brimmed with bite-sized treats to tempt the most jaded of appetites but she was equally happy with the tiny triangles of cheese and salami sandwiches as the lobster claws and accompanying tart hollandaise sauce. She took a forkful of crisp cos lettuce drizzled with delicately flavoured Cesare dressing.

Opposite her, wrapped in a towel around his waist, Richard popped a whole mini quiche in his mouth, crumbs tumbling down and catching in the slight hairs on his chest. She resisted the urge to lean forwards and brush them off, instead picking up a cut-crystal glass of chilled Chablis, concentrating all her attention on the delicious cool liquid.

'Try one of these,' he said, offering her a miniature tart, spilling over with a rich, creamy wild mushroom filling. 'She has the lightest touch with pastry.' His fingers brushed her lips as he leaned forward to pop it into her mouth.

'Mmm,' she groaned, focusing on the flavour, trying to steer her thoughts away from the sudden static spark of his touch that tripped her pulse. 'That's divine.'

He grinned, wicked eyes glinting, as if he knew exactly what she was thinking.

She grabbed her glass and took a gulp, gazing away at the perfect view.

'This is a gorgeous spot. So peaceful.' And not what she'd expected. 'Jade thought we were going to Nikki beach or somewhere.' And so had she. What was he playing at? Was this another part he was playing? Amusing himself. Creating a romantic scene, like in one of his films. Closing her eyes, she swung her legs onto the sun lounger and lay back.

'I thought you might like it. You always loved the sea and the sand. And I'm being a little selfish, it's one of my favourite places. I'm on show all the time, it's good to be able to get away from everyone.'

Replete after lunch and two glasses of wine, she dozed, too lazy to pick up her book and read. When she woke, to the sound of the sea lapping at the shore and the keening cry of a solitary seagull circling the bay, Richard had stretched out on the sunbed next to her, a mere arm's length away. Surreptitiously from beneath her sunglasses, she couldn't help but take a closer look at him lying motionless on his front, his head propped on one forearm. Was he asleep? Her eyes roved over his body, with its tanned skin, his bottom lighter than the rest of him.

She propped herself on one elbow, almost giggling, to take a closer look at well-conditioned buttocks. What was it Jade had called him, Mr Delicious Arse? He hadn't moved for at least fifteen minutes and she reckoned it was safe. The heart-shaped birthmark was still there. It had always fascinated her. Would he notice if she touched it, like she used to do? Skim her hand over his buttocks, lingering there before gliding up his back to massage his shoulders the way she'd done before an audition?

Did he sunbathe nude often? There was so much she didn't know about him any more. His daily routine, what he drank. Where he went on holiday normally. Who he spent his time with? Was there a girlfriend? Impossible to believe there hadn't been anyone in his life recently. In the early days, when he'd first gone to America, it had been hard to avoid the pictures of him posed with glamorous leading ladies, the headlines speculating about their relationships. Despite knowing how the industry worked, seeing those pictures hurt, like a giant hand squeezing her heart with ruthless fingers.

With every shot of his arm slung around some starlet's shoulders, his face bearing a hundred-watt smile, a little bit more of her shrivelled inside. A hundred times she thought of hopping on a plane, but there was always something stopping her. Jade was ill. Angela was ill. The understudy chasing her part. And the worry that she couldn't survive parting with him again.

The award season, the Golden Globes, the BAFTAs, the

Oscars, should have inured her to any further pain, when there'd been after-party pictures galore. Everyone pictured Richard with a different drop-dead gorgeous actress, peering seductively up at the lens from beneath sooty lashes.

For some reason the picture of him and his leading lady, Natalie Howe, who'd picked up best supporting actress, had been different, or maybe it hurt more, because this time it marked the turning point. It featured Richard, his bow tie undone and hanging down his white shirt with his arm linked through Natalie's as he stared down into her eyes – a snapshot of intimacy that mirrored the picture on her bedside table, taken the day after their marriage. The precious picture was the closest thing to a wedding photo she had.

'You okay?' With a start she found Richard had turned his head and his eyes were now open and filled with concern.

She wiped away a tear.

'Sand in my eye. I'm going for a swim.' With a fluid movement she left the shelter and broke into a run, letting the tears fall freely.

She was an idiot, she told herself, as she dived into the sea, welcoming the shock of the icy-cold water, which drove all thought from her as she concentrated on swimming hard.

When she'd acclimatised enough, she faced the shoreline, watching Richard's solitary figure in the awning. A man alone. Was that what this was all about?

Providing him with company? Surely, a man like him couldn't be lonely, although he'd intimated as much earlier. He'd never be short of invitations, but could he trust those people? Today was one of the first times he could relax and let his guard down without having to worry about her motives.

Suddenly she understood exactly why he wanted these two weeks, it gave him a break from what was his real life, took him back to a time before fame and, no doubt, gave him a sense of freedom. However, she needed to make sure she protected herself. Far too many memories were being dredged up that were best left alone. She'd built a life with purpose, which she could guarantee was happier and more fulfilled than his. She had Angela, Jade and Alan in her life. A good job. Good people.

The sun had moved around, someone had pitched the shelter perfectly and now that the midday sun had dipped slightly, the sun lounger was out of the shade. That was clever. She flopped down to dry.

'How was your swim?' asked Richard using the script in his hand to shield his eyes from the direct sun.

'Lovely. Thank you for bringing me here. It has been a real treat. A whole beach to ourselves.'

Richard lifted his shoulders and retreated back behind the script. 'Pleasure.'

'Learning your lines?'

'No, it's a draft, done by the current scriptwriter on the film. She's a friend and wanted me to read it to see if I'd be interested. She's on at me to do theatre. I might consider it if they develop it into a screenplay. I said I'd read it, as a favour, but I won't do a play.

'Why not?'

He pushed his sunglasses up. 'I'm not a stage actor.'

'Why not?'

'Because.'

'Because what? You're an actor.'

'I'm a film actor. The two don't translate.'

'Bollocks.'

'Language, Mrs Maddox.'

She ignored the inflammatory use of their name. 'That's utter bollocks. You trained as an actor. I've seen you on stage. You can act. You know you can. You're being disingenuous.'

'What I do in front of a camera is completely different, and you know it. I can't do stage work any more.'

'Of course you can. You've chosen not to.'

'No, I can't. It would destroy my reputation. I can't risk it.'

'What do you mean you can't risk it?'

'A flop on the stage might ruin my future films. I have to stick with projects I know will deliver.'

'Isn't that rather dull?' It sounded horribly risk averse. 'I mean, haven't you got enough money in the bank?' Bringing crude dollars up seemed crass but surely he'd reached the point where money wasn't important.'

'It's not about money. It's about reputation. I'm a bankable star. The minute I'm in something that tanks, it makes getting the next job that much harder.'

'Rubbish.'

He tossed the script aside. 'I'm going for a swim.'

She watched him stomp rather sexily, she had to admit, down to the water, before picking up the script. It wasn't bad. Not bad at all. Although she'd have ramped up the conflict between the two characters a lot more and made the bad brother less evil and more complex. At the moment he was too black, as opposed to the good brother who was too whiter than white. Both characters needed more light and shade to them.

She frowned. She could bet her last penny that Richard had been offered the good brother. Clean-cut and horribly obvious. Playing the bad brother would be a much more challenging and interesting role.

When Richard reappeared dripping, she swung her legs over the bed, jabbing him with the script as he leaned forward to grab his towel.

'You should do this. It needs work but you should go for it . . . and play Derek.'

'Derek? They've offered me Frank.'

'Yeah and . . .'

'Frank's . . .'

'Dull. You could have a lot more fun with Derek. There's so much you could do to develop the character. At the moment, he's too one-dimensional but it's easily fixed. They need to sort out his motivation. At the moment he's successful because he's greedy. It would make the story much more tragic and tug at the heartstrings of the audience if you change it, making Derek become a victim of his own success but he needs that success to support Frank and his family, which is ultimately the cause of his downfall.'

'Bloody hell. You're good at this. I kept reading this, thinking something's not right, but you've got it.'

He pulled out a pen and pushed the script towards her. 'Write it down. I'll go back to Miranda. That's brilliant and exactly right.'

He raised a hand and she high-fived him. 'I might even do it.'

'I think you should.'

'I mean the film.'

'Whatever, but you should play a villain for a change, take a walk on the wild side.'

'What? Like you?' his eyes mocked.

She couldn't look away. Was it her imagination or wishful thinking that his eyes held a touch of longing?

She forced herself to take a deep breath and look away.

During the rest of the afternoon, Richard kept reading out chunks of dialogue and asking for her opinion.

They'd debate the pros and cons of the character's responses, with Carrie scribbling notes in the margins as they talked. Every now and then, he'd throw in a comment and tell her to write it down. Or she'd stop him half way through a line and ask him what he thought it said about the character and whether he believed it fitted.

'You're good at this. What's the play you're hoping to get put on in London?'

'It's a twist on the Cinderella story. Instead of being the downtrodden step-sister. She's a high-powered control freak who takes care of her much weaker step-sisters and step-mother, who are good but gentle people.'

'I like it. Good idea. Tell me more.'

'Ella does everything for them because she doesn't trust anyone to do anything as well as she does it. She's a corporate shark who doesn't believe in happy-ever-after.'

'Tell me, how does she meet Prince Charming?'

'Mr Charming. She runs the family business, a shoe factory, and he's the family solicitor who is sorting out the family estate and business interests after their father has died. Ella is all about streamlining the business and making shoes for the mainstream market. The sisters want to make fairy-tale bespoke shoes.'

'Sounds a great twist. I can see that would have genuine audience appeal.'

'That's exactly what Andrew Fisher said. He's trying to find a backer at the moment.'

'Hmm, I don't know that much about theatre. Is that hard to do?'

'It's not easy.'

When they climbed the steps towards the gate, sun-soaked and tired with the weariness that came from lying about and swimming all day, Carrie realised she also felt energised in a way that she hadn't for years. Her head buzzed with ideas and suddenly she itched to get back to her own script. She'd been fiddle-faddle farting about with it for weeks and in one diamond-sharp moment, it had come to her, the motivation of one of her character's was all wrong. Change that and everything would drop into place.

Happily, she took the wooden steps two at a time, following Richard, who grumbled at the top that she hadn't pulled the gate shut properly behind her. Had she? She was pretty sure she had but who cared? If she could write a few lines in scene one tonight, she could see the difference it would make to the play.

'Earth to Carrie.' He handed her helmet over. 'Do you want to stop somewhere for a drink?'

'No, I ought to get back. I've abandoned Angela and Jade for long enough.' They'd been at home all day on their own.

Maybe she was being ungracious; he had given her a lovely day.

'Why don't you come in for dinner?' They'd appreciate the company and no doubt Angela would love another opportunity to show off her cooking skills.

'I'd love to, but can we take a rain check?'

Carrie burst out laughing.

'What's the matter?' Richard looked around as if he expected an audience to jump out and yell 'surprise'.

'No one says 'rain check' in real life.'

'Don't they?'

Guilt pricked her at the confused, boyish look on his face.

'They might do in film scripts,' and then she realised that she was being unkind, 'and in America'.

'What I meant was I'd like that, a lot, but I've got to be on set for eight tonight. Some of us have to work.'

'Yes, you have, throwing yourself out of windows. I'll pack the Arnica next time I see you.'

Carrie realised, as the words spilled out of her mouth, how much she was looking forward to seeing him again.

'I'm working tomorrow, although my schedule's flexible, but I'll text you.' His mouth quirked upwards in a lopsided grin. 'You can always kiss my bruises better . . . like you used to.'

With that he switched on the engine and revved up the scooter, leaving her blushing brighter than a tomato with sunstroke.

CHAPTER TWENTY

She had to stop this. She pushed the phone firmly away across the dressing table-come-desk. Another glorious day and not a cloud in sight. She was *not* going to check her phone again until at least ten o'clock. No, make it eleven o'clock. No, twelve o'clock. With a nod of resolve, she tilted the screen of her laptop towards her and then paused. Damn it. She pulled open the drawer and slid the phone into it and slammed it shut. There, temptation banished.

Quickly, Carrie reread the last scene she'd written and smiled. Over the last couple of days, for the first time since they'd arrived in the villa, she'd written and written and written. It was more that she couldn't not write.

For the last few mornings, she'd woken with the words almost bursting out, like wind-filled sails billowing, ready to take a boat skimming at full speed across the waves. Ideas for the play that she'd been working on for months suddenly coalesced and she knew exactly how to finish it. The characters of another idea she'd been toying with had also decided to make an unscheduled arrival in her head, along with huge chunks of perfect dialogue.

Just as well, because she'd heard diddly squat from Richard. Complete radio silence. Which was absolutely fine by her.

She yanked open the drawer and glared at her phone before grabbing it and stomping downstairs. She poured herself a coffee, put the phone on top of the breadbin and stomped back to her room, closing the door behind her.

Angela and Jade were out by the pool. Both of them had got used to her holing herself up in her room and left her to it. A natural holiday rhythm had asserted itself. Whenever Carrie came to a natural stop, she re-emerged for a swim in the pool, playing ball or racing lengths with Jade and taking time to taste Angela's latest creations from the kitchen. She had no problem going back to work, knuckling down and finding her way back into the story.

At quarter to twelve, she closed the lid of her laptop with a decisive snap and jumped up, stretching aching shoulders, and wandered through the house out onto the terrace. Jade sprawled on a lilo, in the pool, drifting along with her eyes closed. Maybe it was the delirium of finishing the play she'd wrestled with for so long or high spirits, but some imp of devilment took hold. Stripping off the kaftan she wore over her bikini, she ran the full length of the terrace and, with a terrifying war cry, launched herself into the pool, dive-bombing the waterbed and breaking the surface of the water with an almighty splash.

The wash upturned the lilo, spilling Jade straight over the side. She emerged, spluttering and furious, and immediately began splashing Carrie with angry screeching.

'You, you.'

Carrie splashed her back, grinning like a loon.

Then Jade ducked under the water and yanked her legs from under her. Carrie emerged, spluttering and laughing, much to Jade's delight, and the two of them splashed each other even more wholeheartedly, until Carrie grabbed Jade and kissed her on the forehead.

'You're bonkers, Auntie Caz.'

'I know but I finished my script.'

'What, the one you've been working on forever?'

'Yep.' Carrie thrashed about in the water in a victory shimmy that had more in common with a wallowing hippo, but she didn't care.

'Thank God for that. Mum! She's finished it,' Jade yelled. 'Does that mean you'll stop being a grumpy cow now?'

'I wasn't grumpy,' protested Carrie. She waved to her sister.

'Do you girls want some lunch?' called Angela.

Carrie gave her the thumbs-up.

'You haven't been much fun. Mum said not to bother you. I've been dead bored. Can we go out again?'

'Yes. Sorry. Where would you like to go?'

Jade screwed up her face. 'Anywhere, I don't mind. Do you know if Richard's going to have that party?'

'I've no idea. I've not heard from him.' She hoped she sounded blasé and nonchalant.

Her phone had stayed resolutely silent for the last three days. Not a text, an email or a call. How many ways were there to not get in touch?

'Seriously?' Jade climbed out of the water and flopped forward onto a sunbed, spreading out like a starfish to dry off. 'Bet he doesn't invite us in the end. I knew it was too good to be true.'

As they lay, the water slowly evaporating from their skins, Carrie resolved that she would get Richard to come to dinner next time after the next date. Her niece was a good kid. She deserved to have some fun in life.

Although, in the meantime there was still time to torture the pesky child. With the water pistol she'd pinched from the stash of toys in the storage shed by the pool a few days ago, she lifted her head, took aim and fired a jet of water straight down Jade's back, stuffing it straight out of sight as Jade squealed and turned her head.

'What was that?'

'What was what?' said Carrie, not lifting her head from where it was propped on her arms.

'Water.' She shot her aunt a suspicious glare and dropped back down again.

Carrie waited for a few minutes and then fired again, ducking her head back down as she began to giggle at Jade's second scream of outrage.

'That was you.'

'Not me.' Carrie pretended innocence, but Jade wasn't having it any of it this time and came straight over and started tugging at the towel on the sunbed and the blue plastic water pistol popped out.

'Aha!' Jade grabbed it with a triumphant giggle and began squirting her aunt in the face. 'Got you.'

Carrie jumped up laughing, lunging at her niece to try and retrieve the gun, getting a face full of water for her efforts.

'Give the gun to your aunt,' she spoke in a low voice, holding out her hand in the best cop-show posturing. 'You know you want to.'

'No way José.' Jade jumped and ran, Carrie chasing after

her around the pool. She closed in on her niece, who stopped to squirt her again.

'Pants. Out of ammo,' said Jade when a pathetic dribble trickled out. She ran to the poolside to refill the gun but Carrie had had a much better idea. She darted into the storage shed. 'Come to mama,' she muttered, scooping her prize from the shelf. There was a tap and a drain in there, which the hosepipe for the gardeners could be hooked up to. Perfect.

Jade was still trying to fill the puny water pistol when Carrie took up her pose on the edge of the pool.

'Make my day, punk,' she shouted across the water. Jade's head shot up. 'Meet Big Bertha,' crowed Carrie as she opened fire with an orange plastic Super Soaker gun, sending a satisfying torrent of water in a perfect arc and drenching Jade, who squealed again before bursting into fits of giggles, clutching her knees.

Jade wasted no time retrieving a second gun, which she named The Terminator and the two of them chased each other around the poolside, screeching with laughter and good-natured insults until they spotted Angela watching them, hands on hips, with a decidedly superior expression.

'Shall we get her?' asked Carrie, winking at Jade.

Jade grinned and the two of them advanced on Angela, guns pointed, with a steady pace.

She held up her hands. 'You wouldn't shoot a defenceless woman, would you?'

Carrie and Jade looked at each other, weighing it up.

'And don't forget, I'm the woman who's making you lunch.'

The two of them stopped dead.

'Oooh, what do you think?' asked Carrie, pretending to frown and give the proposition great thought.

'Hmm, lunch?' Jade cocked her head.

They caught each other's eyes and, with a simultaneous nod, they opened fire and drenched poor Angela.

'I'm going to be huge when we go home,' said Carrie picking up a slice of French bread and smearing it with tapenade.

'Get away with you,' laughed Angela, who had forgiven the pair of them but had sworn vengeance, which was rather alarming as she would normally be far stealthier and sneakier about it.

'You never put weight on and with all the swimming, you're looking very trim. Alan won't recognise you if he comes out here. Oh, by the way, your phone's in the kitchen, it's been beeping.'

Alan. With a horrible jolt, Carrie realised she hadn't given him a thought for the last couple of days. She'd been so involved in her play. *You thought about Richard plenty of times,* whispered an insidious voice in her head. But, she argued back, because he would have an opinion on her writing, he knew about that sort of thing. Alan's an English teacher, the annoying whisper pointed out.

She helped herself to another slice of French bread. It was a real shame she couldn't rip her own head off and throw it across the room, or terrace, in this case. It sucked not being in charge of your own thoughts.

Rather proud of herself, she didn't pick up her phone until one twenty-five. It was a text message from Alan. Communication from him had been sporadic due to patchy reception in the mountains. He wasn't sure how much longer they'd be in the Alps but had realised that the Côte d'Azur wasn't that far away in the grand scheme of things. And as there was plenty of room at the inn and it sounded rather palatial, with a pool as well, he thought, if they managed the last few climbs in good time, he might call in and stay a few days. It was weather-dependent; he'd keep her posted.

Refusing to give her response any complicated, soul-searching thought, she fired off a quick reply, telling him he was always welcome and settled back with her book to read in the sunshine for an hour.

The book didn't hold her attention and she couldn't blame the continual interruptions from Jade.

'It's too hot to read.'

'Why don't you listen to a book on your phone?'

'Boring, and you have to concentrate.'

Carrie sat up. 'Why don't you look up that YouTube video and do me a fishbone plait?'

Hopefully that would entertain her for an hour or two. She'd had enough of watching the disconsolate teenager droop about.

'Fishtail, you numpty!'

'Whatever.'

'Brill.' Jade jumped up and disappeared back into the house, while Carrie resigned herself to having her hair tugged and pulled. At least it would keep Jade occupied.

CHAPTER TWENTY-ONE

Bloody man. Thoughtless. Selfish. Self-absorbed. Carrie hurled her phone to the end of the bed. What if she had plans for today? It would serve him right if she made him wait until she was ready. She'd give him eleven bloody o'clock. And she'd have all her guards in place today. The secluded beach stunt had thrown her and, somehow, he'd wormed his way into her thoughts far too often.

This was a two-week gig while he was at a loose end, she mustn't be lulled into taking him seriously. It had taken him four whole days to get in touch again.

His brief text, sent at eight o'clock, read, Pick you up at eleven. Lunch & other adventures. Richard's idea of an adventure could mean anything.

Playing safe, she co-opted Jade's new-found hairdressing skills and loaded her bag up with a cardigan, a shawl, a bottle of water, a book, spare make-up and perfume. Was there anything else she might need? He hadn't specified trousers today, hopefully that meant he'd forsaken two wheels in favour of Phil's services. She risked putting on a floaty skirt and halter-neck top with low-heeled sandals.

At eleven o'clock exactly Richard pulled up, confounding her completely by turning up in a magnificent scarlet monster with a throaty roar that rumbled through her sternum.

'OMG,' she muttered to herself. The little Ferrari was absolutely gorgeous. As soon as she saw it, she skipped down the steps to stroke the glossy paintwork.

'Nice car,' she commented with a laugh. 'A scooter one day, Ferrari the next.'

Through the back window she could see the engine, which took up two-thirds of the car.

'Just keeping you on your toes.' He opened the door and, like the perfect gentleman, waited for her to get in before closing it and walking round to the driver's door.

Which film had he'd borrowed that smooth move from? With a light-hearted giggle, she slid into the low-slung seat and strapped herself in. The small, enclosed space had more in common with the cockpit of a plane rather than a car, apart from the little black stallion on the yellow badge on the steering wheel. She put on her sunglasses, stroking the soft leather seats. She could get used to this.

Jade appeared on the doorstep.

'Hi, I've got something for you.' He leaned over Carrie and opened the glove box, pulling out three large white envelopes.

Jade barrelled over to the passenger door.

'Cool car.' Her excited smiled faded as she took in the fact it was a two-seater.

'One for you,' he handed one to Carrie, 'One for you and one for your mum.'

Like a kid at Christmas, Jade tore into her envelope and

screamed in delight as she pulled out the stiff card invitation. She went running back into house, calling to Angela.

'Mum, mum, you'll never guess what!'

'Nice save, mate,' teased Carrie. 'I thought she was going to demand you take her for a spin later. Quick, let's make our getaway unless you want to be deafened by teenage squealing for the next half hour. I take it that was an invitation?'

'Yep, I'm throwing a party for the cast and crew to coincide with Savannah's birthday. And what's with the plait again?'

She folded her arms. 'It's practical and it stops you yanking it free all the time.'

'The practical plait. I don't like it. Too tidy. You should wear it down more.'

'It gets too tangled up. After a whole day out, it's impossible to get a comb through it again.'

'Then I'd have to condition it for you and comb all the tangles out.'

Her heart hitched as she studied his face. With a quick grin, he dispelled the charged moment by waggling his eyebrows with a suggestive leer, which made her burst out laughing.

Light-hearted and silly Richard she could cope with.

He fired up the ignition, revved the car with a mighty roar and then swung it around the drive in one manoeuvre and gunned the engine up the track to the gates, the instant speed almost plastering Carrie to her seat.

'Show off,' she yelled, as they catapulted to a stop at the sensor, where the gates opened, in contrast, with ponderous slowness. 'Is it yours?'

'No, I hired it. I did have one in Los Angeles but it was a faff having to garage it and I never got to drive her because

I was away most of the time and when I was home, the traffic was awful.'

She dreaded to think how much it cost to hire this little motor but it wasn't her problem. All she had to do was sit back and enjoy the ride, which she had every intention of doing.

'How the hell do you go about hiring a Ferrari?' she wondered out loud.

'I have a PA. Or rather a virtual PA. Arla. She's a marvel. Books Ferraris, organises parties, has invitations printed and delivered.'

'Virtual PA. Does she exist or is it a robot or computer programme? You do lead a very different life.'

'Arla's most definitely a real person. You wouldn't mess with her. She does everything online for me. Hence virtual. I've met her about three times. And I don't lead another life, I ask her to do the things that I'm usually too busy to do. She has amazing contacts. If I ask her to find me a Ferrari, she does her best. If she can't, she can't.' He grinned, 'but most of the time she pulls it out of the bag. She is pretty amazing.'

'I can imagine,' said Carrie dryly, picturing some soignée iced blonde who wore size-zero clothes.

'Bet you can't,' he cast her a knowing look as if he could see right into her head. 'She's a single parent from Brooklyn, with three children, thirteen, fifteen and eighteen, and she's a good size twenty. I like her because she's not afraid to take the piss out of me. No respect. When I asked her to book me the Ferrari today, she immediately asked me who I was trying to impress. She keeps me grounded.'

'I like her already. Does she know you've got a wife tucked away?'

'Yup.'

He kept his eyes on the road. What on earth had the virtual PA said to that? From the way he'd described her, she could imagine Arla would have had plenty to say.

Pulling out of the driveway, Richard zipped through the gears and soon they were whizzing along the country roads, screaming into the bends, from which they emerged to be greeted by yet another fabulous view.

'Do you mind if I open a window?'

'We do have air con.'

'I know but it feels . . . boring. Dull. I want to feel the fresh air.'

Richard laughed, 'I did think about getting a convertible, but it's a bit posey and in this heat it's not that practical. Go ahead.'

'And a Ferrari isn't posey at all,' she teased, throwing her head back and laughing at his rather endearing logic.

Unable to contain her excitement, she opened a window and put her hands out to let the air whip through her fingers. As Richard took another bend at speed, the engine revving to a high-pitched whine, a burst of adrenaline crashed around her system, sending her heart rate pounding. The car held the road beautifully and despite the scenery rocketing by, Carrie felt perfectly safe. Richard drove well, with verve and panache, but not so hair-raisingly that she worried. She envied him his skill and rather wished she could take a turn in the driving seat.

As she was admiring his profile, he turned and smiled. Her heart skipped a beat. With his dark hair windblown and the designer aviators in place, he looked every inch the movie star today.

'Any clues as to where we're going?' she raised her voice,

the wind whipping her words from her. The wind swirled around in the car, the breeze toying with her heavy plait like a playful kite.

'Don't you trust me?'

'Hmm, jury's out on that one,' she yelled. The coastline in the distance glistened as white-topped waves coasted into shore. A private secluded beach took some beating but she was rather glad they weren't going there again. Hopefully wherever they went today would have plenty of people around.

Half an hour later, having enjoyed the journey thoroughly in the powerful little car, they pulled up into a car park outside a rather grand white building.

'A winery,' she exclaimed in delight.

'Thought we could do a wine tasting. I know you love your wine.'

She thought of the days when they'd turned out coat pockets and kitchen drawers to scrape together enough money to treat themselves to a bottle of Lambrini and thought they were doing well. Bottles of the good stuff, when they'd splashed out more than ten pounds for birthdays or special occasions, had been few and far between, but savoured with great appreciation.

A small glow burned in the pit of her stomach at his remembering.

The welcome contrast of cool air greeted them as they passed through a heavy glass door and walked into the refined, hushed atmosphere of the winery. It brought to mind a museum or an art gallery. Even though there were quite a few people inside, there was the same sense of reverent quiet, voices lowered in soft conversation. Carrie almost felt obliged to tip-toe to stop her sandals slapping against the glossy marble floor.

Someone had spent a lot of money making the place look perfect. The cavernous room had been designed to within an inch of its life. Glass, wood and stainless steel dominated. While admiring the sophistication, with the heavy wooden tables bisecting the space exactly down the middle, and the polished bar area framed by hundreds of wine bottles, Carrie thought it was too soulless and pulled her shawl from her bag, wrapping it around her shoulders. It felt constrained, a little too antiseptic and trying a touch too hard, especially after the heart-racing high of speeding along in the Ferrari, which had left her buzzing.

However, as the place was busy it must be doing something right. Lots of small groups of people sat at the tables, their noses in long-stemmed tulip-shaped glasses, obviously at various stages of tasting.

A petite and very dapper young Frenchman rushed forward to greet them.

'Bonjour. Welcome. Have you booked?' He spoke in heavily accented but perfect English.

'Yes. Name of Maddox.'

The young man nodded gravely but gave no hint that he recognised Richard or had made any association with the name.

'Ah, yes.' He selected two long, thin menus from a box on the wall and ushered them down the room to a section of the table at the end, where another couple were already seated. 'Madame, Monsieur.' He indicated two spare stools. 'Someone will be right with you to take your order. Please have a seat.'

The woman who'd been staring out of the window, turned and her mouth dropped open as she did a very unsubtle double-take, flushed and examined her hands.

Carrie noticed that Richard gave her a gentle smile before focusing his attention on her.

'What would you like to taste?'

The woman nudged her husband and whispered something in his ear, trying to look discreet. She failed but Richard pretended not to notice.

Carrie tapped him with her foot under the table in a gesture of solidarity and mouthed. 'You okay?'

He winked at her and edged closed, his thigh brushing hers. 'Fine. How about this one,' he pointed to the menu, 'it says it's a blend of Sauvignon and Viognier, with soft grassy aromas and a touch of melon and figs.'

The man opposite got up to leave, pulling his phone out of his pocket while his wife remained, sneaking glances at them.

Following Richard's unconcerned lead, Carrie read the menu and said with a teasing smile, 'I'm always up for an elegant, harmonious wine with low acidity.' Being recognised wherever he went was an occupational hazard but luckily this couple chose to respect his privacy.

Richard ordered the wine, which arrived in no time, presented with a great flourish by the dapper waiter, who slid the glasses in front of them with a polite, 'Salut.'

'Nice pale golden colour.' Richard stuck his nose in the glass and took a deep sniff. 'Smell that. Grass. Meadows.'

'Gosh you're quite an expert,' said Carrie, surprised by the sudden serious expression on his face.

He nodded with the haughty attitude of a sommelier from a Michelin-starred restaurant. She watched as he tipped the glass back and sipped the wine, swilling it around before swallowing. Her mouth parted with a half breath as her skin prickled at his obvious sensuous enjoyment. With his head tilted back, eyes closed, it reminded her of another moment, sending a little kick through her system with a flare of desire due south.

Sommelier became naughty school boy in a flash. 'It helps that the tasting notes are rather informative,' he said, a wicked twinkle dancing in his eyes.

She batted his arm. 'You! Do you know anything about wine?

'Only what I like.'

'You had me going for a minute.' Carrie shook her head, storing the moment away as another pertinent reminder of his chameleon-like ability.

He grinned, unrepentant. 'Good.'

Carrie tasted another couple of wines, Richard taking the odd sip, as he was driving. Their conversation flowed smoothly as they talked about the whereabouts of old drama-student friends, few of whom worked in the entertainment industry these days.

'Shall we have lunch here?' Richard checked at his watch.

'If you've got time,' said Carrie, raising an eyebrow.

'I've got all day for you,' he gave her a hammy smouldering grin, which made her burst out laughing.

'Then, that would be lovely.'

'I need a quick word with maître d'. Excuse me a moment.' As he got up, he levelled a quizzical stare at the couple opposite who'd managed to pretend that they'd forgotten who he was in the last half hour.

They had lunch at the winery, outside on a terrace under a vine-covered pergola, offering a shady retreat. Richard had swapped to mineral water but ordered her another glass of the white wine. She'd taken a few mouthfuls when he grabbed her wrist and pulled her to her feet, his narrowed gaze focused on something over her shoulder.

'Quick,' he tugged her towards the back of the winery, walking with a slow but determined pace.

'What?'

'We've got company.'

'Company? What sort of company?' She almost giggled at the clichéd lines, but Richard's pissed-off expression stopped her. Through the winery and the front windows, she spotted a man with a large camera peeling himself from the back of a scooter.

'Oh shit,' said Carrie.

'Don't worry. I thought that might happen when boyo opposite us got his phone out. I made a contingency plan.'

'You did?' Carrie raised her eyebrows.

'This happens a lot.'

'I guess.'

He hustled her towards a door at the back of the terrace, which despite being in French, clearly said *Staff Only.*

'This way,' he guided her to another door with another notice on it. This time Carrie couldn't read it but Richard obviously had a plan and directions.

As he ushered her in, she burst into giggles. 'You know how to show a girl a good time.' She moved a mop out of the way to take a second step inside the tiny space. 'The cleaning cupboard?'

With a shrug, he eased in after her and closed the door. 'It was the best he could come up with.'

'I hate to say this but that bright-red monster out the front is a dead give-away,' she whispered as it went dark.

'How do you think I got him to help? I offered him a drive. In a minute he'll be motoring off down to St Tropez.'

'Clever.'

'Brilliant.'

'Modest too. Now what do we do?'

'We wait for a little while.'

'In the dark?' asked Carrie, doubtfully.

'Sorry I left the candles and matches at home this time.'

'Well that wasn't very good planning, was it, Mr Boy Scout with the brilliant ideas?'

'I need to work on that part.'

'You do. I'm losing track of who the real you is.'

'What that's supposed to mean?'

'You slip in and out of parts easily. Gardener. Old Richard, movie-star Richard, Sommelier, Action Man.'

'They're all me. At the heart of it all I'm the same person. It's an external façade that I can pull on as the situation arises. Inside I'm the same.'

'Are you?' Her voice faltered. In the dark, his familiar voice tugged back the memories.

'Yes,' he answered, a husky note to his voice which sent quivers straight to her stomach.

She felt his breath ease out on a long sigh, whispering past her cheekbone. With a rustle, she heard him move and his hands encircled her, reaching for the plait down her back.

'This . . . this confuses me.' His hands wove into the bottom of her intricate braid and she felt a gentle tug as he released the band. With small, slow movements, his fingers worked their way through, loosening the hair with butterfly touches against her back.

'I always loved your hair.' He eased closer, a bare inch between them. 'Whenever I imagined you . . .' he burrowed his fingers deeper into the woven hair, the movement of his arms brushing her ribs beneath her breasts, 'I always had a mental of image of it wild and loose.' The weight of the braid lifted and the breath in her lungs shortened as his fingers worked upwards, vertebrae by vertebrae. 'Of it streaming behind you, crackling with energy, the curls bobbing when you laughed.'

His fingers reached her scalp, a zing tingling the skin.

'I missed you so much. I thought about jacking it in so many times. Once, I got as far as the airport.' His voice swirled around her in the dark. No matter how tightly she squeezed her eyelids, it wouldn't shut out the words she didn't want to hear. 'But then Dad would have been right and Mum would have been furious . . . and you? Would you have wanted me to give it all up?'

Damn, the question broadsided her. She pulled her hair out of his hands, trying to ignore the blanket of dull sickness descending.

'No, I wouldn't.' He caught a strand and wound a finger in and out of the ringlet. Grateful for the dark, she blinked hard, afraid to move in case the stabbing pain in her heart spread. 'You did the right thing,' she said, a slight break in her voice.

'And you?'

The sick sensation rose up, threatening to swamp her.

'There's no point dwelling on the past.' She shifted, turning sideways and grasped the door handle, opening it to let in a welcome chink of light. 'Do you think they'll have gone yet?'

'We ought to give it a few more minutes.'

'Can I have my hair band back? It's too hot to leave it down.'

He caught her eyes as he handed it back, but she ducked her head and fussed about pulling her hair into a high ponytail.

With a rueful smile, he shook his head and tugged a few ringlets around her face free.

'That's better.'

She rolled her eyes, grateful that normal service appeared to have resumed. Her stomach let out a yowl of hungry protest.

'Dear Lord,' Richard stepped back with a horrified expression. 'Chewbacca's still alive and well, then.'

'Oh, yes. Especially when my stomach's being neglected. Are you going to feed me or not?'

'Given that awful noise, I might be taking my life in my hands if I don't. I'd rather face the paps.'

CHAPTER TWENTY-TWO

Carrie reviewed her wardrobe. All very well being invited to a swanky party, but what the hell was she going to wear? Somehow, she didn't think the daisy dress would cut it and, yes, vanity dictated that she did not want to look like some dowd next to the glitterati that were sure to be there. She needed a steer.

> Any clues as to dress code at this fancy party of yours?

After she sent the text off to Richard, she re-read the last one from Alan.

> Feel like I'm king of the mountains. Conquered one hell of a slope yesterday. Thighs sore today but worth it.

He did love his cycling and while she wasn't about to don lycra and join him, she'd never stop him pursuing his heartfelt hobby, just as she'd never have stopped Richard going to Hollywood or let him come back. She'd done the right thing. If he'd come back and they'd stayed married, would they have even stayed together? Disappointment made you bitter. She might not love being a drama teacher but her life with Angela and Jade offered contentment, kept her busy and most of the time she could claim to be happy.

With a ping, her phone announced a new text.

Clothes are always good. ;-)

What sort of you clothes, you numpty.

Why don't we go shopping?

Now there was an offer. Shopping with Richard. Always an adventure. Her heart lifted.

He picked her up an hour later, the throaty roar of the Ferrari revving on the drive announcing his arrival. Today he was smooth-skinned.

'Had a shave?'

'We've been filming a couple of different scenes this week, so I get a reprieve. Ready for some retail therapy?' he waggled his eyebrows.

'Yes, but you have to be sensible.'

'Sensible. I don't know what you mean.'

'No showing me up in front of shop assistants or making me try on outrageous outfits.'

'Who me?' He held his hand up to his chest.

'Yes, you. You have history, mate.'

'That satin bustier. Fabulous, darling.'

'Only if you were a nineteenth-century courtesan,' she said with indignation, remembering the lime-green corset, frothing with cheap lace and uncomfortable boned seams that he'd dared her to try on in Soho one afternoon.

'Now, I recall, you looked better out of it.'

Ignoring him, she patted her handbag, looking for her sunglasses. 'Where are we going?'

'St Tropez, of course, my darling,' he said in an outrageously camp voice. 'The place to shop and be seen.'

Carrie settled back into the leather seat as Richard drove with his usual verve and swagger, nursing the car around the bends and revving into the straights. She arrived at the underground car park in St Tropez with a big smile on her face. There was nothing quite like living life in the fast lane, on occasion.

Still in an upbeat mood when Richard slipped her hand into his, she was too content to demur as they strolled along, wending their way through the busy colourful streets, full of well-dressed people walking along in flip-flops and open sandals, enjoying the sunshine. She smiled at the sight of men topless in shorts, some bearing barrel bellies best hidden and others swaggering with taut defined abs dusted with hair, who knew exactly what they were about, attracting second glances from women of all ages. The women, Carrie decided, casting envious looks, exuded style, some in tiny white dresses showing off deep-golden tans, girls in strappy tops and short shorts designed to expose the maximum amount of lithe, lean flesh and plenty of others wandering along in nipple-skimming bikini tops, quite uninhibited. It made Carrie feel overdressed and a touch dowdy. Every seat in the pavement cafés appeared to be full, with people checking out the menus at the kerbside entrances, making the air buzz with light-hearted chatter.

Richard seemed perfectly happy to weave their way through the crowds. It made a nice change to have company.

Alan wasn't a shopper; he didn't like crowds.

A spurt of guilt flared, which she tamped down.

They turned into Rue Gambetta, the familiar designer names headlining their way down the street. People clutched expensive shopping bags bearing the names and logos of Chanel, Longchamp, Dior and Cavalli. Carrie had forgotten how much fun it could be window shopping, wandering in and out of the expensive shops, gasping inside at the crazy prices while looking at the silk scarves in Hermes, the handbags in Louis Vuitton and the jewellery in the famous Gas Bijoux.

A couple of things in Ralph Lauren caught Carrie's eye but nothing she couldn't live without. She tried on a shirt which she wasn't sure about, even before she caught sight of Richard lurking outside the changing room, shaking his head and giving it the thumbs-down.

'Wrong colour and not very flattering at all. Made you look completely flat-chested.'

'Thanks!' It was hard to take offense at his matter-of-fact tone, especially when she agreed.

'You'd rather I was honest with you, wouldn't you?'

'I suppose so,' she laughed. 'But only this time because I knew it looked rubbish. It's always better to try things, then you know for sure.'

'The skirt would suit you,' suggested Richard, pointing to the rack behind her.

She wrinkled her nose and weighed it up again. She had checked it out a couple of times with longing but had decided to err on the side of common sense.

'It is lovely, but it's not something I could rock up to work in.'

'I don't know. I'm not much of a skirt-wearer myself.'

With a giggle, she punched his arm. He took her hand and tucked it in his and they ambled out of the shop.

As they twisted through the streets near the old town and harbour, Carrie spotted a dress in the window of a very upmarket boutique. Like her daisy dress, it was one of those dresses that calls to you. She stopped to admire it.

'That's gorgeous,' she breathed in admiration, studying the supple fuchsia silk fabric and the exquisite stylish cut of the dress with its unusual neckline. Utterly feminine and no doubt horribly expensive, but she couldn't take her eyes off it.

'Beautiful,' he commented.

'Yes,' she said, pushing out the voice of temptation, whispering sweet nothings in her head.

When she went to move on, he tugged her back. 'You should try it on.'

She shook her head.

'I dare you.' Richard nudged her.

'What? To try a dress on.'

'Yes. You know you want to. What's stopping you?'

Carrie laughed. 'That it's so blinking gorgeous. I'll try it on, fall in love with it and buy it.'

'I could buy it for you.'

She turned around and gave him a serious death stare, scowling down her nose with as much haughty disdain as she could muster.

'I can buy my own dresses, thank you.'

'You going to try it on?' There was a knowing smirk on his face. Either way she couldn't win.

She tossed her plait over her shoulder and marched into the shop.

'Bonjour Madam, Can I help you?'

How did French people do that? They always knew that you were English before you'd even opened your mouth.

'Bonjour. The dress in the window, do you have it in a . . .' Damn she had no idea how a ten or a twelve translated into continental sizes.

'A 38,' Richard piped up behind her.

The woman took one look at him and stiffened, her face giving away that she recognised him. 'Oui, monsieur.' She bustled over to a clothes rail and, with great panache, pulled the dress out, shaking and fussing over it as she brought it back to Carrie.

'The changing rooms are here,' and before Carrie could draw breath, the woman had guided her with the single mindedness of a sheep dog determined that not one of his flock should escape. 'And monsieur, you can sit here.'

She pulled back one of the curtains and hung up the clothes, shepherding Carrie in straight after it and yanking the curtain back into place.

'I want to see it,' called Richard playfully. She peeped out from behind the curtain and wagged a finger at him.

'Shame they don't sell lingerie. This is nice too.' He held up a turquoise sundress.

'Behave,' she said repressively, the man had exquisite taste.

His response was an unrepentant grin as he lounged on the mink suede sofa, making himself comfortable. Madame had even bought him a glass of iced water.

Carrie lifted the pink dress from its hanger, her fingers smoothing over the light-as-air silk. It whispered across her skin as she shimmied it up over her hips and then slid her arms through the sleeves. For a second she wrestled with the zip down the back, wriggling to get it done up to the very top before she dared look in the mirror. On a whim, with quick, nimble fingers, she undid her plait, the curls springing into life as she shook her hair free down the length of her back. Then she turned to face the mirror.

Damn. The dress took her breath away. Quite the most beautiful dress she'd ever seen. Smart, sophisticated and sensual. Wearing it made her feel wicked, all woman and capable of taking on the world.

She twirled, sending her hair flying as she came out of the fitting room, dancing in sheer delight.

Richard looked up and froze, the smile sliding from his face.

'What's wrong? Don't you like it?' Carrie asked. The sleeping tiger was back. Serious, intent and totally focused. Nerves shimmered in the pit of her stomach.

He rose slowly from the sofa and without taking his eyes from her face said, 'You look like my wife.'

For a second neither of them moved or said a word.

He followed the simple statement with a smile of such sweetness, it punched into her, stealing her breath.

Every slow step he took towards her signalled his intent, honing in, unerring and sure.

Time slowed and she watched, until his final step brought them toe to toe, her eyes fixed on his face. The intensity of the blue eyes made her shiver as they roved over her face with such searing impact. She wanted to reach up and smooth her fingers along the strong jawline, slide them across his skin and stroke along the defined cheekbones. It was a face known to millions, but her hands knew every contour of his face, the tiny scar in his eyebrow, the sexy bump under his lower lip and that, at this time of day, his face would be fine sandpaper, rough with tiny breakthrough stubble.

His eyes held hers as he slid his hands up either side of her head, sliding into her hair and then, as she watched, he leaned forward, and kissed her.

The world fell away, leaving nothing but the kiss. Soft lips moulded hers, teasing and testing with a slow, thorough exploration, leaving every nerve ending fizzing. Passive, she let his mouth rove over hers, enjoying the sheer pleasure of the touch of skin on skin. Absolute heaven and . . . the memories stirred. So familiar. The way the tip of his nose grazed hers as he deepened the kiss. Like dancers they moved together, making tiny automatic adjustments to fit with each other. She sighed into the kiss, wrapping her arms around him, her body going limp with grateful recognition, like a ship slipping back into berth after a long voyage away.

She kissed him back, savouring the gentle touch of his fingers feathering along her cheekbone. She'd missed this. Missed *him*. This intoxicating, beguiling sense of being cherished floored her as it had done from the start.

With a regretful sigh, Richard's lips slid away from her lips and traced along her cheeks, before pulling back and resting his chin against her forehead. She could see the pulse pumping in his neck and felt the slight shakiness in his arms as he lifted a hand to smooth her hair away from her face.

A discreet cough made them both turn. However, with rather stylish insouciance the woman had glided away, having made her point.

Carrie wasn't sure who burst out laughing first, her or Richard.

'You like the dress, then?' she teased.

'It's okay,' he shrugged, and then added, his eyes darkening, 'But you're gorgeous.'

Unsure how to respond, she glanced away. It had been a long time since she'd received such a heartfelt compliment. She walked to a better-lit mirror on the other side of the shop, her legs shakier than she'd realised. She'd strayed into the middle of a minefield and had no idea how to get out intact.

'It's a very beautiful dress, Madame.' The shop assistant smiled. 'It suits you.'

'Thank you.' Carrie let out a long sigh. A dress like this had no place in her life.

Richard grinned his approval as he waited in the curtained entrance of the fitting room as she turned to go back in 'Want a hand?'

She nodded and turned, watching him in the mirror as he gave the zip his full attention. She took a sharp intake of breath as his finger traced down the indent of her spine, as bit by bit, he edged the zip down.

'Thank you. I'll take this from here.'

'Sure?' Mischief glittered from the brilliant-blue eyes. Was it her imagination or did the colour deepen the more wicked he became?

'Quite sure.' With a last lingering look at the dress, she resigned herself to taking it off. It was possibly the most beautiful dress she'd ever tried on. She'd wear it once . . . and then it would be a permanent reminder of Richard, hanging forever more in her wardrobe.

With a sigh she put it back on the hanger.

The woman came to the curtain.

Temptation hovered.

With a heavy heart she handed the dress back. 'No thank you.'

Richard yanked the curtain back, uncaring that she

was half-dressed. Like a ninja thief, he bent down and scooped her own clothes, backing out with a triumphant shout.

'Give those back.' She tried to sound stern but it was impossible when faced with a lunatic grinning with unholy glee.

'Nope, not until you buy the dress.'

Hoping to snatch them back, she made the mistake of chasing him into the shop.

Teasing, he dangled her skirt in front of her, laughing as she grabbed at it with all the finesse of a bull chasing a matador.

Her aim might have been improved if she hadn't been laughing so hard. Even the frigid Frenchwoman had dropped her professional façade, a small smile of amusement playing around her mouth as she lifted her shoulders in a typically Gallic indifferent shrug.

'Richard!' she said, her voice low in warning, 'Give . . . me,' It was no good, she couldn't keep a straight face, 'those . . . back,' the giggles burst through, 'now,' robbing her words of any threat.

Like a naughty boy, beaming from ear to ear, with the success of his teasing, he shook his head, waving the skirt with even more delight as he backed away, closer and closer to the glass door of the shop.

Looking behind him at the door she said, 'Don't you dare!' As soon as she uttered the words, she realised she'd made a fatal mistake. When had he ever backed down from a challenge? It had been a game they'd played over and over in the playground of London.

Richard whirled and shot out of the door, taking her clothes with him.

'What the . . .' she exclaimed. She was going to kill him, once she'd stopped laughing.

'He's mad,' she said to the shop assistant.

The other woman's face softened. 'He's in love.'

'But do you know what? So am I. I will take that dress.'

'A very good choice.'

Carrie stopped, her legs a little shaky, unsure as to whether the shop assistant was referring to the dress or Richard.'

When Richard reappeared, smug but a touch wary, she greeted him, a picture of calm and serenity. She sat in a deliberately relaxed pose, wearing the dress.

He nodded and approached the desk, pulling a slim wallet from his shirt pocket.

'I'd like to pay for the dress.'

The woman smiled, exchanging a conspiratorial look with Carrie.

'It's all been taken care of.'

He glared at Carrie, although he couldn't quite carry it off. Still too full of mischief.

'I don't need you to buy my clothes for me.' If she lifted her chin any higher she'd have doubled as a giraffe. 'I've managed perfectly well all this time.'

'Ah, but think of all the Christmas and birthdays I've missed.'

'Too late. What have you done with my clothes?'

He grinned, his eyes lighting up with unholy glee. 'I dumped them in the harbour.'

She bit back the laugh bubbling up. Only he would think of that and get away with it. 'Any particular reason why?'

'So that you'd walk out of here with a new dress.'

'Mission accomplished, then.'

'But I still owe you for the ones in the harbour.'

'Yes you do, but I'll think of another way to make you pay. But I can't go out in this one. I want to save it for the party.'

'Can I buy you the turquoise sundress?'

'Yes you bloody can. And don't think that gets you off the hook. You'll still owe me.'

'Should I be worried?'

'Yes.' She rose in one fluid movement and crossed back to the fitting room to put on the strappy, turquoise sundress. 'You can take me for a drink to show off my other new frock. Somewhere nice, mind.'

'I know just the place.'

There were serious pros to being on a date (there, she'd said it) with a celebrity. Despite the queue outside the very popular bar, somehow the maître d' procured them a table on the balcony overlooking the crystal water in the harbour and the street below. It was the perfect vantage point from which to drink Bellinis under the shade of a parasol and people-watch from behind sunglasses.

Richard's aviators kept most of the curious stares at bay, although several people at nearby tables around sent sideways glances their way, but then everyone here was on the lookout for a celebrity. Heads craned with every new arrival, eyes strayed over companions' shoulders and people tried to mutter through half-closed lips. The celebrity-spotters provided entertainment in their own right. Carrie was too polite to call them 'poseurs' but most of them were. Luckily they were also too busy showing off and far too cool. No one made any attempt to approach Richard, content to mutter and nudge each other. It was a curious sensation being watched but not watched.

'What's your next project?' asked Carrie. 'Apart from the play—'

'— which I'm not going to do.'

'You should do it.'

'There are a couple of scripts I've been looking at. Part of me would like to take a break. I've been filming back to back for the last few years. The last film I did, a superhero one, part of the Marvel franchise, is in editing at the moment and due out next month. I'm flying back to LA for a round of publicity. This film is virtually in the can and the next one goes into pre-production in October and then we start filming in Los Angeles in November.'

'Busy boy. You deserve a break. Why don't you take one?' She propped her elbows on the table, her chin in her hands.

'You have to take every opportunity, remember.' He echoed their mantra from their student days.

'Yes but it's different now. You're well-established; you can pick and choose.'

Even from behind his sunglasses, she spotted his quick frown. 'There's always someone new out there chasing the parts.'

'Seriously?' Surely he didn't believe that. 'Do you ever take a step back and think about where you want to be in ten years' time?' It sounded as if he were on a treadmill, that he was too scared to step off. It couldn't be good for him. It was one thing to be driven by ambition but not fear.

'What are you scared of?'

Richard stiffened, the glass half way to his lips held in mid-air.

'I don't know what you mean?'

'Yes you do.' She softened her voice as she sensed his barriers going up and laid her hands on the table. 'This continual working. You've never had a break. Looking at how many films you've been in, you must have worked non-stop.'

He shifted in his seat and put his glass down. 'You're a fine one to talk. What are you scared of?'

'Me?' She reared back. They weren't talking about her.

'Yes. All those manuscripts lying around.' He pushed his sunglasses up onto his head and laid a hand on hers. 'Why haven't you done anything with them?'

The soothing touch of his hand stopped her when instinct had her prepared to change the subject, bolting away like a horse. 'I have . . . with a couple.' She winced at the blatant fib.

'You always had tons of ideas.' His low voice, infused with admiration, sent a flush to her cheeks. 'Such vision. Are you pleased with the play you were working on?'

She sat back with pride. 'Yes, although it's been a pig to sort out. The director wanted some substantial rewrites. Make Ella softer at the end.' She grimaced. 'I know he was right, but it's been hard work.'

'Faint heart and all that.' Richard teased. 'Have you got any more things in the pipeline?' He stroked his thumb idly over the top of her hand, sending a slight shiver up her arm. She wasn't sure if he was even aware of it, but she did know from the slight cock of his head to one side, the stance of his body leaning towards her and the slightly parted mouth, that she commanded his complete attention. The absolute focus, like being in a personal sunbeam, was almost as sexy and mind-fogging as the earlier kiss.

'Not really. I've got an idea in the back of my head about a teacher who befriends a young girl who's neglected at home. The girl runs away from home and there's a big hunt for her. She's discovered hiding in the teacher's house because she feels safe with the teacher, but of course, that's a huge no, no. So the teacher is arrested.'

'Interesting idea. Does it happen?'

'As teachers we have to make sure that we don't put ourselves at risk of doing anything that could be misconstrued, even by association. Our code of conduct has to be above reproach.'

'I can't see you as a teacher, you know. Aren't there lots of rules and regulations. I recall your favourite phrase, "rules were made to be bent".'

'I do my best.' She winced. Some of the endless policies they had to read at work drove her mad and Alan was always the voice of reason, explaining why they were so important. Most of the time, it was a question of stating the bleeding obvious.

'So what now for the one you've finished? When's that going to be put on?'

'It isn't. Not for ages, if then. The director, Andrew Fisher, hasn't had a chance to find a backer yet.'

'That doesn't sound like you. Waiting on someone else. I remember you marching along with a sandwich board outside the theatre in Worthing drumming up audiences, pestering the local papers and camping on the doorstep of the radio station until they agreed to do an interview – and you weren't even in that play.'

'Don't remind me!' Back then she'd been so eager and filled with a sense of righteousness and zeal. 'I was younger, then. Believed in it all.'

'And you don't believe in your work now?'

'I do but . . .' She wasn't going to say she was wiser but

she'd run out of energy, lost the passion, about the time that she realised Richard wasn't coming back.

'But?'

She pursed her lips.

'What happened to the girl who kept telling me I had to go out and make things happen. Keep knocking on doors and not give up. That's what kept me going that first year in Hollywood. I was so . . .' he paused, a bleak look crossing his face, 'lonely.'

'Lonely? You didn't look lonely.' She wished she hadn't said that, it sounded bitter and jealous. 'I mean, you seemed very happy.'

'I had to. Trying to impress agents, producers, directors, casting agents.' Richard grabbed her hand. 'I missed you every single day. I didn't give up on you. You know how the game's played. Those pictures were publicity.'

She steeled herself to say it, her head dropping to study his hand still caressing hers with that rhythmic stoke. 'Even the one of Natalie Howe.'

His voiced gentled and he pulled her hand towards him, forcing her to lift her head. 'We were working together. It suited the publicity machine to team us up. It developed later.'

His mouth drooped, sadness etched in his downturned curve. 'After *you* said that we should go our separate ways.'

'It was for the best.' Was she trying to convince herself or him?

'For whom?'

Had she imagined that slight break in his voice?

'For both of us.' Why did this still hurt so much? 'You wouldn't be where you are now, would you?' She'd done it for him.

'True, but at what cost?' He turned away and slipped his sunglasses down over his face.

He was the one who had been more successful, he was the one who had made it. Why did she feel so full of guilt?

CHAPTER TWENTY-THREE

'Another drink?' asked Richard.

Carrie cast a look at the skyline and the lowering sun. Early evening beckoned and she'd been out all day. 'Don't you have to drive?'

'I've already texted Phil and put him on standby.'

Carrie laughed. 'How lovely to have people on standby. I ought to get back. Angela and Jade.'

'They're big girls now. Besides, Phil tells me that Angela says I'm invited for dinner.'

'He does, does he?' Carrie rolled her eyes but she was having such a wonderful time, she didn't want to cut it short. Sitting on the balcony in her new dress, with a big fancy rope-handled shopping bag at her feet, with great company, champagne and in one of the best seats in St Tropez. What was not to like? Or enjoy.

'And you're not working tonight?'

'No, they don't need me. I've got an early start tomorrow and I've got to be on set all day. Tomorrow's going to be hectic but you should come over sometime and watch. You could bring Jade and Angela.'

'God, Jade would love that. She's very miffed that she's not allowed to say she's met you.'

'Why can't she?'

'I guess she can now. When you first came over . . .'

'All you need to say is that we're old friends from drama school.'

'True.'

'But if you did want to tell anyone I'm your husband, I'd be cool with it.' He leaned back, his arms folded, a smile playing at his lips as if he'd manoeuvred the queen on a chessboard into an unassailable position.

'I'm sure you would. But "old friends" will do.'

'Coward,' he grinned, motioning the waiter over. 'Can we have another two Bellinis, please?'

Carrie felt too replete and relaxed to respond to his teasing.

When Phil pulled up outside, with her third Bellini swirling deliciously inside her, Carrie had persuaded herself that 'old friends' described them well. She'd enjoyed spending the day with Richard. Perhaps he'd been right, spending this time together, re-establishing their friendship before they got divorced, was a good thing to do. They could part with good memories instead of bad ones.

'Oh my God, you've got a new dress. That's not fair.' Jade pounced as soon as they walked through the front door and then, all smiles, turned to Richard. 'Thank you for the invitation. Who's going to be there? I hear F.J. Franklin is in town.'

Behind Jade's back, Carrie mouthed, 'Who?'

'Is he?' asked Richard. 'I'll have to ask my people to see if he's free that night.'

'You have people?' Jade's eyes widened. 'That is sooo cool. And I'm so screwed. I don't have anything decent to wear.' She poked at Carrie's large boutique bag with its gold rope handles. 'What's in the bag?'

'I,' Carrie emphasised the 'I', 'bought a dress today. Two new dresses.' She did a quick twirl and opened up the bag for Jade to take a peek.

'For the party.'

'I'll wear it then, yes.'

'Damn! I need a new dress. Mum!' Jade yelled and raced off.

'People?' Carrie shot Richard her best class-teacher reproving glare.

'Sorry,' with a self-deprecating lift of his hands, he added, 'I didn't think Jade would be impressed with a virtual assistant called, Arla. "People" sounds a lot better. But who the hell is F.J. Franklin?'

'I think he's a rapper,' interjected Phil from behind them.

'Figures,' said Carrie. 'Jade likes that shouty type of music.'

'Knowing Arla, she'll have a hotline to someone who knows him.'

'Phil, thank you for coming to get us.'

'It was no trouble,' his eyes twinkled, 'particularly as I was here anyway and your sister had kindly invited me to dinner.' He paused. 'She's struggling today. I helped out.' Then he added, 'Not a problem is it, Mr Maddox, if I eat with you?'

'Enough of the Mr Maddox crap, Phil. You know damn well it's not a problem at all. Especially not if you've been doing the cooking.'

'Jolly good, I'll go and help Angie in the kitchen, then. We've been experimenting with a nice onion soup. Just got the toast and cheese to finish off.'

Angie? And an admission of weakness. Carrie blinked and stared after Phil disappearing back to the kitchen.

During dinner, Richard received an eyeful of the full family dynamics, with the added entertainment of Angela and suitor. Carrie watched, open-mouthed, as her sister and Phil flirted. Angela, light-hearted and giggly in a way she'd not seen before. In contrast Jade was at her most annoying, continually asking Richard who'd be at the party, what she should wear and whether she'd be allowed to drink or not.

Although her questions irritated the hell out of Carrie, Richard engaged in a full-scale discussion on suitable attire for the party and agreed to make sure that the bar staff stocked Jade's favourite tipple, *Wicked*.

In a swift sea change of conversation, Richard then talked to Angela about a restaurant he'd visited in Mexico, describing the flavours, the ingredients, bringing them to life for her. Throughout the evening, Carrie could tell he'd enjoyed himself, but found herself wondering whether when he went back to his normal life, this would be a tiny diversion in the road. She doubted that meeting up with her and her family would have quite the same impact as he'd had on their lives.

The next morning Carrie received a text from an unknown number.

Hi this is Arla. Richard has asked me to fix up a dress for your niece Jade for the party. I've arranged for someone to drop off a selection of dresses for Jade to try on this morning. Hope that's OK?

Carrie nearly dropped the phone. It was only nine-thirty. Arla worked fast. What time was it in America?

She found Jade in the pool.

'Did you know Richard has arranged for some dresses to be delivered here today for you to try on?'

'What?' Jade's muffled voice came from the swimming pool as she attempted to blow up one of the panels of the airbed without getting off the thing. It looked a decidedly dangerous manoeuvre, one that Carrie itched to help with and tip her annoying niece into the water.

'Sorry, I'm trying to blow this up, it's leaking water, which is going right down my pants and it's cold.'

'Richard's PA has arranged for some dresses.'

'Fuck me!

'Language, young lady!'

'Sorry but, that's amazing. You need to stick with him. He's a keeper.'

Carrie turned her back on Jade, bending to brush a stone from her foot.

'Don't give me that look.'

'I've got my back to you, how can you see my look?' She sounded as bad as Jade.

'I just know,' crowed Jade.

'He's not a keeper,' Carrie stood on the pool's edge, one hip thrust out, 'he's a multi-million-dollar movie star, who has women all over the world adoring him. We're old friends. Who got married when we were far too young and stupid.'

'He looks as if he still likes you . . . a lot. When you're not looking at him, he looks as if he could eat you whole in one delicious gulp. I don't know why you don't give him a chance.'

Carrie tried to hang on to her patience and remind herself that teenagers spoke before they thought.

'It'd be so cool to be able to tell everyone he's my uncle.'

'Well, he isn't,' snapped Carrie.

'Technically he is, at the moment.'

'Technically, not for much longer.'

'I think you're mad. Mum thinks he's lovely too.'

Carrie considered it a good day when she only fancied herself strangling Jade once in an hour. Today just turned into a very bad day.

'Why is it that everyone has forgotten that I'm engaged to Alan?' Carrie stomped off.

Jade's squeals later that afternoon were all Carrie needed to tell her that a delivery had arrived. She stirred from her chair on her balcony. She ought to go and show some enthusiasm, but she'd rather enjoyed a few hours of peace on her own. She'd spent a few hours day-dreaming away, during which the germ of an idea for a new play popped into her head, making her remember that she ought to ring Andrew. Richard's words about her not trying hard enough to get her play put on stung.

She worked full time, and these days had other commitments. Richard didn't understand. It wasn't as if he lived real life.

Her phone beeped. Had Richard got the day off, after all? She wriggled in her seat, stretching her arm out lazily to pick up her phone, already trying to anticipate his latest instructions. Where would they be going next? Yesterday would take some beating, although the beach had been wonderful and he had promised her a drive in the Ferrari. Had he meant it?

With a delicious sense of anticipation, she opened up her texts.

> Another fantastic day's cycling. Perhaps we could honeymoon in the Alps. The scenery is spectacular and it would be out of season for skiing, there'll be plenty of cheap accommodation.

Carrie frowned. Not her idea of a holiday and certainly not a honeymoon. Poor Alan, she'd really not given him much thought. What was she playing at? She shouldn't have let Richard kiss her again yesterday.

Or we could go somewhere hot and exotic and laze on a beach!!! She texted back guiltily.

That's what one did on honeymoons, wasn't it? Or you went to Blackpool for the night and ate chicken and chips on the beach at midnight after three consecutive rides on the big dipper.

> Where do you fancy? I'm open to suggestions. And I can see the pros of seeing you on a beach in a bikini.

Blimey, he was obviously missing her. She should count her blessings. What a lovely man, especially when she knew he would far rather be cycling up some one-in-four incline than lazing on a beach. Definitely a keeper and she'd do well to remember that.

*

Carrie emerged from her room to investigate the source of the excitement and came face to face with a full-scale fashion show taking place in the lounge.

'What do you think?' Jade did a catwalk strut down the length of the room.

'Very nice.' And totally unsuitable, but Carrie caught Angela's silent signal and knew better than to say what she really thought.

'Nice! It's the bomb.'

'How many dresses came?' asked Carrie, looking at the explosion of fabric and colour, tissue paper and expensive carrier bags piled on the sofas.

'Ten! And shoes.' Jade clapped her hands. 'Two pairs.'

'Let's see them all, then.' Carrie sank onto what felt like the only clear space in the room, on the corner of the coffee table.

'Anyone want a drink?' asked Angela, with a surreptitious wink at Carrie.

'Yes, please.' From the amused twist to her sister's lips, she was going to need one.

'I'll make it a large one.' Angela sailed out of the room with the speed of a motor launch at full throttle.

A full hour and fifteen minutes later, Carrie felt ready to tear every last hair out of every last follicle on her head. Jade hadn't been able to narrow down her choice by a single dress.

Arla was obviously used to far more sophisticated teens. Only a couple of the dresses had more than a nodding acquaintance with subtlety, which of course made them twice as appealing to Jade. The styles ranged from figure-hugging bandage dresses, strappy bias-cut dresses that dipped and fell in all the right places, or if you were Jade's mother, the wrong places and micro minis so short, one false move and an open invitation would be made to all and sundry.

'Wasn't that kind of Richard?' said Angela, an hour later.

Carrie rolled her eyes. 'Very but I'm exhausted. Although all he had to do was send a message to his PA. She's the one that did all the hard work,' Carrie smirked. 'And you.'

Angela sighed. 'I've had practice.'

'You're a master now.' Carrie had to hand it to her sister, her handling of Jade's dress choices had been a masterclass in damning with faint praise.

'The mistake is to say you don't like something or it's unsuitable. You're dead in the water, then.' Angela raised her glass and they chinked them together.

'Telling her that the silver-and-black bandage dress made her bum look a tiny bit big was genius.'

'Mm,' Angela laughed, 'Never worked with you. You didn't care what anyone thought. I remember Mum trying that type of reverse psychology when you brought a ratty old fur coat back from the second-hand clothes shop in Berkhamsted.'

'Oh my God, yes.' Carrie imitated her mother's tones, 'Any self-respecting prostitute would love that coat.'

'Funny, you used to dress quite flamboyantly.'

'It doesn't go down that well in school.'

'Even so . . .' Angela looked her up and down. 'I used to envy you that vintage, boho style. It suited you.' She tugged at her own dress. 'If you're not careful, you're going to end up as boring as me.'

'You're not boring.'

'Hmm, you've both got new dresses for the party. Maybe, I should have dropped some hints to Richard.' Angela's teasing smile made Carrie laugh. 'Although I'm not sure I'd want him guessing what size I am.'

'You're tiny,' protested Carrie. 'You wouldn't want him choosing for you.' She knew her sister well. She preferred to melt into the background. With a taste towards well-cut tailored dresses that showed off her petite, trim figure and tiny waist, Angela preferred to look neat and smart. Carrie could almost guarantee her sister would wear her favourite navy blue and cream sleeveless shift dress.

'True. Some of those. . .' she shuddered. 'I ought to get them packed up and shipped off in case Jade changes her mind and decides to go for the kingfisher blue, slashed-to-the-crotch one.'

'What do you want to do tomorrow?' asked Carrie after dinner that evening, conscious that she ought to offer to take Angela and Jade out for the day. There'd been no word from Richard. It would do him good to see that she'd already made plans. Show him he couldn't expect her to drop everything for him.

Angela swallowed. 'Er . . . Phil offered to take us to Port Grimaud. You're very welcome to come too.'

'No,' Carrie ignored the sudden pang of illogical emotion. She didn't need to ask Carrie's permission but she couldn't quite shake off the sense of being usurped. 'I'll be fine. Have a day to myself.' She could write. Swim. Take the car out. Explore. Lots to do. She'd enjoy being on her own. It would make a nice change.

'Aren't you seeing lover boy?' asked Jade, looking up from her phone.

'No,' said Carrie, a touch more waspishly than she'd intended.

'Oooh!'

Carrie gritted her teeth at Jade's sing-song teasing.

'Why not?'

Because Richard hadn't texted. Carrie pushed her phone further out of reach. She'd turned into Jade, checking it every five minutes.

'You haven't had an argument have you?' Worry lined Jade's face.

'No.' It felt good to be childish back. 'It's okay Cinders, you will still get to the ball.'

'Phew.' Jade went back to her phone, tapping away. 'I was worried for a minute, but then being an important movie star, he's in big demand. I expect he has loads more important people to see than you. Do you think he's got a girlfriend? I bet he goes out on dates all the time, don't you think?'

'I've no idea,' said Carrie, her vocal chords taut as she bit out the words.

'Yeah, he's bound to have a couple of supermodels tucked away somewhere.' Jade flashed her a cheeky grin.

'And just this morning you were saying he liked me.'

'Yeah, I think he does.' Jade's expression sobered and she shrugged. 'But, be honest, you're a school teacher in Hertfordshire and he's a hot-shot actor who lives in LA. If he had to choose, he's going to stick with supermodels. Stands to reason.'

'Thanks, Jade.' Carrie swallowed her wine in one hurried gulp.

Two seconds later her phone beeped and she snatched it up, trying to tell herself it was only Alan.

Can you be ready in ten? Rx

She jumped up from the table, catching her cutlery and sending it clattering across her plate.

'I'm going out. Richard's picking me up.'

Before Angel and Jade could ask her a single question, she darted away to her room, her heart singing with sudden happiness.

She tugged at her plait, in two minds as to whether to set her hair free or not.

CHAPTER TWENTY-FOUR

Water lapped, gentle and insistent, at the side of the boat, the white sail brilliant in the moonlight.

Lights twinkled in the early-evening dusk, outlining the coast further east. The night air, redolent with the scent of pine, shimmered with magic, starshine and endless possibilities. Wind-twisted trees cast eerie shadows across the rocky outcrops surrounding the bay. They could have been on the very edge of Earthsea or a step away from Middle Earth.

Since Richard had picked her up in an understated top-of-the-range VW Golf, driving a few miles to a deserted jetty, they'd barely exchanged more than five sentences. Weariness seeped out of him, his eyes haunted with shadows and his face drawn. The few words he did manage seemed to be dragged from him with great effort.

When they got out of the car, he reached for her hand and held it in silent apology as they boarded a small dinghy with an outboard motor. The rip of the engine, like an angry mosquito, echoed loud in the empty bay as they bounced over the gentle waves to a yacht moored a few hundred feet away in the centre of the sheltered bay.

'Champagne?' he asked, as he ushered her to the stern with two cushioned benches.

'Would a cup of tea be too much trouble?' Champagne seemed clichéd and glib, when she sensed he needed something more. Comfort, understanding, peace.

'Shall I make it?' she asked. It was as if someone had sucked every last drop of energy from him.

His weary nod signalled relief as he sank down onto one of the benches.

Bringing two steaming cups back on deck, she laid one on the floor beside him and sat on the bench opposite. He'd closed his eyes, his face an impenetrable mask. She lay back and marvelled at the hugeness of the sky and the star-spattered universe beyond.

She heard him stir and lift his mug.

'Tea. Exactly what I needed. Thank you.'

'Are you okay?' asked Carrie.

'Just knackered. We've been filming since dawn this morning. Quite a harrowing scene. My character's mother has died.'

'Oh, sweetheart.' In one fluid movement, she rose and crossed to sit beside him, taking his tea from him before threading her arm through his.

Thigh to thigh, rib to rib, fingers intertwined, just an exact tableau of that interminable night in the hospital, waiting and waiting, as the seconds crawled by at their cruellest pace, for Josie Maddox to breathe her last and slip away to peace.

'It still gets me.' He shifted to rest his forehead against hers, his breathing slow and sure. 'I wish she could see me now. Know that I made it.'

Carrie tried to smile at him, but the hitch in her heart made it too difficult. Instead, she linked her fingers through his and leaned into his touch.

Face to face, their noses brushing, for a few minutes they were one, the human contact pulsing with the gentle energy of a lifeline. A sense of gratitude swelled in Carrie's breast, and a kernel of pride. No one else could do this for him. With a dizzying burst of awareness, she realised moments like this mattered, this echo of shared emotion, stamped on their individual and shared conscious for all time. She squeezed his fingers, savouring the sensation of his heavy hand in hers.

A slight breeze lifted the lines of the boat, which chink, chinked against the mast with musical notes and rippled against the fabric of the pennant at the top.

After a while, they moved, shifting to lean back against the side of the boat, still thigh to thigh, cups of tea clutched in their hands.

'Thanks, Carrie.' He lifted his mug and with a self-deprecating smile drained the rest of it. 'I needed that.' He pulled a face. 'So much for champagne and roses. I was going to bring you out here for lunch tomorrow.'

'I'm not a champagne and roses kind of gal. You should know that by now.'

'Yeah,' he said, with a sad smile. 'But you might have been, given the chance.' He stretched and his eyes drooped, before his mouth widened into a full-on, knackered, too-tired-to-hide-it, gaping yawn. 'Sorry, I shouldn't have texted but . . .'

'It's fine. I'm glad I'm here. You need to sleep, by the looks of things.'

'I . . . missed you. I wanted to see you.'

She wished she could unhear the words.

'Why don't you lie down and have a doze?'

His eyes held hers and as he lay down he tugged her with him. 'Lie with me.' His eyes danced very briefly, 'keep me company'.

Like this, all the roles he played vanished. Just Richard. She could almost pretend that the last eight years had never happened. Relaxing into him, she lay down, her body sighing in recognition as he slid a hand over her waist, pulled her onto his chest and her knee slipped between his legs, each familiar move the steps of a dance they'd perfected years ago.

She closed her eyes and fought against the pinpricks of tears and the hollowness in her chest that threatened to overwhelm, concentrating instead on the pat, pat of the water lapping at the wooden hull, the rhythmic, somnolent bob of the boat and the oh-so-solid warm body underneath hers.

Cool air ruffled the hair she'd left down, but his chest radiated warmth, rising and falling with deep, even breaths. The steady thud, thud of his heart, pumping with rhythmic reliability beneath her cheek. She listened to the strong, sure beat. Why couldn't life be this simple? One beat after another, straightforward and sure of the job in hand. Affairs of the heart, so complicated and yet the physical organ a steady workhorse.

She felt the moment he relaxed into sleep, his muscles loosening, his face slackening and eyelids fluttering. Tilting her head to one side, she studied his face, shadowed and contoured by the stark moonlight.

With a sensation of free-falling, she swallowed hard. How on earth had she gone and fallen in love with him all over again? The lump in her throat felt insurmountable, as if she'd never be able to swallow again.

Tears threatened. Fighting them, she closed her eyes and nestled into him. His arms tightened around her and she stilled, terrified she might have woken him, but he softened his hold and sighed, his breath whispering across her face.

Aching with disquiet, her thoughts churning and winding back over themselves, she lay there, a thousand clips of their life together rushing through her head. Sleep almost as out of reach as Richard, but somehow she began to drift, the clips and sound bites in her head became muzzy and confused. She tried to wrap the elusive tendrils of thoughts into coherence but they escaped, seeping away like wraiths in the mist.

Warm and heavy-limbed, she woke to Richard's lips trailing a soft kiss across her forehead. Fighting the beguiling urge to go with it and sink back into him, she pulled back. Fatal mistake, she stared up into his face, his eyes still dazed with sleep and something else she didn't want to define.

'Hello you.' The sleep-roughened voice turned her insides liquid. When his lips dropped to hers, they sparked a sensation of exquisite sweetness, stirring memories like butterflies rising in one great rush. She wrapped her arms around him and pressed the length of her body against his, the way she had done a thousand times before, the entrenched familiarity like a conductor picking up his baton, a violinist his bow and the fingers of the flautist sure of each and every note.

Everything familiar and dear, but with the added excitement of passion and thrill. With a horrible jolt, the comparison with Alan swamped her with guilt. She paused, trying to gather her wits and rein in the wayward feelings, racing away with heady enthusiasm. She remembered this, the dizzying heights of euphoria, the blood rush of joy and the golden warmth of love, but she also remembered the ice-cold chill of loneliness and the hole in her heart so big it almost consumed her when he left.

She'd built a new life, one that beckoned a few weeks from now. Her future didn't hold yachts, starlight and handsome movie stars.

Heavy-hearted, she swallowed at the weight of the memory of sheer misery and the shadow it cast over her life. She couldn't do it again. Even so, with a defiant shade of the old her, she gave into one more heart-sizzling kiss, losing herself in the moment, before pulling away, regret pounding through every fibre of her being.

'Richard, stop.'

'You don't mean that.'

'I do. We have to stop. This is wrong.'

'Doesn't seem wrong from where I'm . . .,' he paused and stroked her face, 'lying.'

It would be easy for her to be sucked into this moment, to be held ransom to past emotion, but these feelings were echoes. Ghosts of a previous life.

She had to walk away now because she'd barely survived last time.

Like a swimmer throwing herself into the Atlantic, knowing it would be bracing, she took a deep breath, pulled away and sat upright.

'Richard. This isn't real. It has to stop. We have to be sensible. I know what this is.' She gave him a serious, grown-up look. 'Lovely as it is, you are harking back to a time when you and me were together, when people didn't know you. When you could be normal. This is a break from your reality as much as it is from mine, but for both of us it's a novelty. In a couple of weeks, you'll be back in the States and I'll be back at school.' With a lift of her chin, she straightened, ignoring the tightening of her gut and said, 'I need that divorce. We can't let this be any more than it is. A diversion.'

'Pardon?' As if the shutters had come down on every emotion, his face went blank. 'A diversion?'

'Come on, Richard. You heard. In a couple of weeks, you'll have moved on. Nothing is permanent for you, is it? You don't even have a home or a base. It's all transient. Like acting. You adopt a new role every so often. Another life. That's what this is.'

'Is that what you think?'

Quick and sharp, his words sliced through the air, at odds with his slow, weary demeanor as he rose to his feet and gathered the tea mugs. 'I can't even begin to tell you how shit that makes me feel, or how disappointed I am in you. You, Carrie. You know me, or at least I thought you did. Of all the people, you are the last person I thought would dismiss me as,' he mimicked speech marks, "bored movie star, having fun with nearest convenient female." It's a convenient cliché. Surely you could have done better than that, if you've decided to chicken out.'

Without another word he crossed, heavy-footed, down to the galley kitchen below.

Left on deck alone, she examined the clear starlit sky. Each of those pinpricks of light had been there for millions of years, shining down, steady and enduring. Before this week, she'd been steady and sure. Her direction all mapped out. Richard crashing in to her life was too much like a crazy meteor shower, in danger of pushing her off course. Hell, yes, she was chickening out.

A crash downstairs, and the tinkle of broken china had her crossing to the hatch.

'You okay?' she called down.

'Fine.'

'Do you need a hand?' She started to edge down the steps.

'No.' The growled answer made her stop in her tracks.

'Okay.' She sighed and crossed to the side of the boat. The moon's reflection licked across the surface of the waves, their silver tops spreading in a long slick out to the horizon. She held the side with both hands, her fingers gripping hard.

'Right. Shall we go?' Richard locked the hatch doors and was already crossing to the ladder down to the dinghy.

'Wait!' Her voice broke. 'Don't . . .'

He waited for her to finish. She hoped he'd break the silence and fill in the words. The coward's way out. She'd done this. Why should he rescue the situation when she'd deliberately brought things to a head?

She shrugged. He turned and climbed down the ladder.

Even though he 'radiated heartily pissed off' with her vibes, he still took her hand as she came down the ladder and steadied her into the dinghy, waiting for her to sit and be safe before he fired up the outboard motor.

He sat at the back of the boat, watchful eyes roving the shore and beyond, anywhere but at Carrie.

As they neared the jetty he killed the engine, letting the boat drift round into the wooden deck, allowing him to grab one of the bollards to guide them in.

Once the boat was tied up, he did finally look at her.

'I've never loved anyone the way that I loved you.' He

scooped a small pebble up from the bottom of the boat and tossed it up before catching it.

The sentence weighed heavy between them.

'It seemed so. . .' He tossed the pebble up before snatching it out of the air, 'at the time, I thought we'd burst from it, that sheer wonderfulness of it all, so huge, so big, so special. I thought it was unique. That you and me were forever and that nothing could . . .' The words spilled from him, strong and confident. Recognition hit her hard. That overwhelming sensation of the two of them being invincible.

His hands tapped a fast beat on the tiller of the motor.

'I hadn't figured that you'd change so much.' He dropped his voice, his mouth crumpled in a scornful line. 'You're not the Carrie I knew. Crazy Carrie. She was fearless, brave and adventurous, wanting to taste everything, try everything, live every beat of life and move with the rhythm of every dance.'

Carrie tensed, the words sliced deep.

'I thought if we spent some time together. . . she'd come back.' With a mirthless laugh, he tossed the pebble high and long into the sea, 'I was wrong.'

CHAPTER TWENTY-FIVE

Carrie woke for at least the ninth time in the night, tired but full of scratchy energy and not sure what to do with herself. When she hurled herself in the pool as the sun rose, welcoming the shock of the cold in the cooler morning air, it still didn't clear her head.

Regret burned hard and bright, despite the lengths she racked up, churning through the water with an almost desperate determination. Richard didn't still love her. She didn't love him. Her shoulders ached. Her brain hurt. She needed that divorce. Alan would be there in the future. Richard would be long gone, on location in Mexico, Australia, outer space, for all she knew.

Fifty-seven lengths later, her arms screaming in protest, she hauled herself out of the pool, lying on the side, gasping for a few minutes.

'There are easier ways to kill yourself.'

Angela sat on a nearby lounger looking faintly amused.

Carrie rolled over, wincing as her lungs complained with a pinch of pain.

She crawled to the sun lounger and sprawled face down on it.

'Coffee?'

'God, yes please.'

Her sister was the official coffee fairy. Managing to turn over and haul herself up, she cupped both hands around the cup. It gave her something to do and avoid Angela's candid observation.

Her sister would have been brilliant in MI5 or something. She didn't say a word, just watched with that bloody knowing look on her face, the you-know-you-want-to-spill-your-guts-and-you'll-feel-so-much-better-for-doing-it look.

'No I won't,' muttered Carrie.

'No, you won't what?' Angela's quick frown at least confirmed she hadn't acquired mind-reading tricks as well as Grand Inquisitor talents.

'Never mind.' Carrie took a long slurp of coffee.

'What went wrong?'

How did her sister do that? 'Who said there's anything wrong?'

'Twenty lengths are a holiday health kick. Thirty, sexual frustration. Forty-plus, pissed off. Fifty, mightily pissed off.'

'The White Witch of Swimming prophecy strikes again. Who knew?' Carrie glared into her coffee.

'Human psychology. . . plus I know you. Did you have a row with Richard?'

'You don't row with Richard. He lashes you with sentences without even raising his voice, which gets quieter and quieter. You have to strain to hear him tell you how disappointed he is with you.'

'I'm sure he didn't do that.'

'He did, but to be fair, he had a point.'

'Good lord, are you ill?'

'What's that supposed to mean?'

'Nothing.'

'I do concede people are right . . . sometimes.'

Angela pursed her mouth.

'Okay, I don't very often.'

'What did he say to upset you?'

'He didn't. It was me,' Carrie ducked her head, not wanting to meet her sister's frank query. 'I said that he was . . . I suggested that . . . I said that he was being . . .'

Angela raised a stern eyebrow in silent contemplation, waiting with that mothers-know-best attitude combined with the you-will-spill-the-beans-with-or-without-the-thumb-screws look.

'I told him he was using me as a diversion,' Carrie blurted it out in one garbled sentence, like a child thinking if I can't see you, you can't see me, except it was, if you don't hear it properly, you won't ask again. 'Which,' she added, 'is true.'

She traced the whorls on the towel on the sunbed. 'He's in the Riviera with a million different women to choose from. Why pick me? I know him. A spontaneous idea that he hadn't thought through. Typical Richard.'

'Or he's met up with his wife. The woman he loved enough to marry and he wants to spend time with her to see if that spark is still there.'

'Oh, bollocks. Whose side are you on?'

Angela let out a delighted laugh. 'Is that what he said? I was guessing.' She clapped her hands in delight.

'I don't know what you've got to be so happy about. Why is it everyone keeps forgetting . . . I'M. ENGAGED. TO. ALAN.'

Angela sobered. 'Sorry.' She frowned. 'It's tricky. Richard falling in love with you is just so romantic—'

'He hasn't fallen in love with me. It's not romantic.' Carrie waved her hand in front of Angela's face. 'This is not a film. It's real life. Rich, successful movie stars do not meet up with old flames, whether they are still married or not, and fall in love with them all over again.'

'Why not?' asked Angela, her head snapped up and she pinned Carrie with a piercing glare.

'Because.' Carrie clenched her fist under her thigh. Angela was supposed to be with her on this.

'I think you're doing him a massive disservice.'

'What? Richard?' Carrie's voice rose.

'Yes. He's been nothing but lovely to you.' Angela's knee jigged up and down. A sure sign she was about to say something she wasn't comfortable with saying. 'I'm sorry, but you should be ashamed of yourself.'

Ouch. That was strong, especially from her sister.

'He put a lot of thought into every one of those dates he took you on, organising things to make you happy. That doesn't sound like a diversion to me. And he's been very kind to me and Jade.'

'He's sucking up.'

'Really?' Sarcasm didn't become Angela, it made her way too scary. Relentless. 'Why?' She ticked off her bent fingers. 'Why would he want to impress me and Jade? Why would he want to impress you, if he was amusing himself? If you ask me . . .'

Which Carrie hadn't, but she didn't have much choice in the matter any more.

'And don't give me that look. He's done nothing but try to please you. A private beach. Wine-tasting. Being driven in a Ferrari. Champagne on the terrace on the waterfront in the harbour.'

Carrie stuck out her tongue at her sister's bloody annoying logic. Really, really annoying – doubly so because the old bag nailed it on every sodding count.

'When you put it all together. . .'

Carrie glared but Angela kept talking,

'He sounds wonderful and 'some might say' smitten. A very decent man, rather than your average movie star but then I wouldn't know, him being the only movie star I know and my brother-in-law to boot.'

'Do you know, I absolutely hate it when you're a little bit smug and satisfied.'

'What? When I'm right?' Angela beamed and jumped up to perch on Carrie's sunbed. 'I am, aren't I?'

'Yes, you bloody are and I've been a complete and utter shit and I'm going to have to apologise.'

'Hmm, yes, you have been rude to him.'

Carrie bit her lip. Angela was the fairest and most honest person she knew. If Angela thought she'd been rude, there was no doubt about it, she needed to make a proper apology.

'I will apologise to him, for misjudging his motives, but it doesn't change anything.'

'Doesn't it?'

'No, it might sound romantic but Richard and I are heading in opposite directions in life. It's never going to happen. Imagine hooking up with him again. I might as well throw myself out of a plane.'

'When you put it like that, it does sound rather terrifying.'

'But we can be friends and we can part on good terms. Besides,' she winked at Angela, 'Jade would bloody kill me if I jeopardised going to the party, even though I worry she's going to be very disappointed. It's going to be full of people who won't give us the time of day, they'll be very up themselves and horribly shallow.'

'Don't worry. Seeing the reality of celebrity life might provide a very valuable lesson.'

Damn. Even after cooling off with another swim, she still couldn't sit still. Richard had every right to be pissed off about last night. The more she thought about it, the more she wanted to spring into action and speak to him. Texting seemed inadequate. An apology, she'd always believed, should be delivered face to face and not shirked by ducking behind a telephone call or an email.

He was filming today in Port Grimaud. She remembered him mentioning it. It would be helpful if she knew when and where. And how did you apologise in grand enough style to ensure that the man who had everything would sit up and take notice?

Sending a ransom note made out of cut-up newspaper headlines, telling him that if he valued the other half of his only pair of shoes, which would meet a gruesome end if he didn't meet her in exactly five minutes in the park outside their flat, had worked once before.

She smiled at the memory of him hopping along the path through the shrubbery in the park to meet her on their favourite kissing bench. But that had been a stupid row about washing up, which hadn't mattered that much.

It was one thing kidnapping a shoe, not as easy to spirit away a whole movie star.

CHAPTER TWENTY-SIX

She couldn't have done it without Phil. Luckily his schedule included picking up Richard that afternoon and a little blackmail, namely getting Angela to promise to withhold all future food rations, ensured his cooperation.

Carrie had the engine idling at the foot of the steps, a pillowcase and an ice-cream scoop at the ready. She hadn't been able to get hold of any handcuffs, no thanks to Phil, who'd flatly refused to set foot in the local sex shop. He had his reputation to think of.

Precise planning for every eventuality had ensured that Richard, expecting to be picked up by Phil, had been diverted to a new pick-up point.

Her phone beeped.

The package is en route. ETA five minutes and counting.

She grinned as she read his postscript.

Should the mission go tits up, this is a black op, I will deny all knowledge and this message will destroy itself in ten seconds.

She didn't feel the least bit nervous, not in the slightest. No, her biggest concern centred on the dumb fact that she hadn't been able to get hold of a toy gun. Thanks to his extensive experience in action spy-thrillers, Richard might guess that he wasn't being held up by a real gun, but she hoped he wouldn't realise it was the opposite end of an ice-cream scoop.

She scanned the top of the harbour wall, pleased with her disguise. Hidden under a black baseball cap, Jade's sunglasses and wearing a black vest and black jeans, she looked suitably anonymous. Her heart quickened. He'd arrived, up on top of the harbour wall facing the road, where he expected Phil to glide up in a car.

Grabbing her props, Carrie crept up the steps, hoping there weren't too many people about. The last thing she needed was some have-a-go hero tackling her mid-way through her covert apology operation.

Offering up a very quick prayer that she hoped didn't give him a heart attack, she stuck the ice-cream scoop in the centre of his back and said in her lowest, sultriest French accent, 'Monsieur, if you value both shoes, whatever you do, don't turn around.'

Richard stiffened for a second, his head dipping as if to check his shoes, before letting out a startled bark of laughter.

'Madame, I'm at your mercy. I'm rather attached to these shoes, although of course I do own more than one pair these days.'

'Excellent. I will say zis once and only once.'

'Sorry, can you say that again? I didn't quite catch it.'

Carrie prodded him the back again, unable to stifle a giggle. 'At my mercy, remember.'

'Ah oui, Madame.'

'Don't turn around. Walk very slowly and move towards the top of the steps.'

His shoulders shook as he walked forward and Carrie smiled. She might be able to carry this off after all.

He stopped and she almost bumped into him.

'Of course, you do realise I'm a trained assassin. I have skills, you know. If I choose to, I could disarm you with one move, break your arm, dislocate your jaw and sever your femoral artery. You might bleed to death in less than sixty seconds.'

'I'll take my chances.' Carrie grinned and pushed him forward, towards the steps leading down to the stone jetty. At the bottom, free from the danger of falling down the stone stairs and breaking his neck, she pulled the pillowcase out of her back pocket. They made it look so damn easy in the movies. She could have done with an extra pair of hands. She stuffed the handle of the ice-cream scoop in her mouth, holding it between her teeth, and with both hands brought the pillowcase over Richard's head. He didn't make it easy for her and as she fumbled the damn scoop fell to the floor with bang and a clatter. 'I think you might have dropped your weapon.'

'I have back-up,' she lied, managing to bob down and pick up and ram it down the back of her jeans, where it dug into her bottom, proving that this secret squirrel business was no walk in the park.

'Would it help if we pretended my hands were tied?' asked Richard.

'You're not taking this seriously enough.' She nudged him in the back.

'Sorry.' He didn't sound the least bit contrite and she could imagine, under the makeshift mask, he was laughing.

'This way.' She stepped to the side of him and tucked a hand through his arm to guide him along.

When they reached the water's edge, she stalled for a minute before bundling him into the waiting speedboat.

'Please don't hurt me.' Richard's high-pitched falsetto made her laugh. She nudged him in the ribs.

'Quiet.'

'I'll go quietly,' he squeaked. 'You're not going to have your wicked way with me are you?'

'If you don't shut up, I'll toss you overboard and leave the body where no one will ever find it.'

'Promises, promises.' His voice deepened and she could picture the suggestive expression on his face. 'I can be tossed on board if you like.'

She screwed her face up, desperately trying not to laugh out loud.

'Quiet, prisoner.'

'Aye aye, captain. I say, you're not a pirate are you?'

'Sit still and be quiet, otherwise my associates will have to start removing shoes.'

'You have associates? Now I'm scared.'

'Yes, big bad, scary associates of a hairy-pirate persuasion.'

With a shake of her head, she turned her back on him, confident that he was quite safe perched in the middle of the seat in the stern of the boat. She couldn't remember the last time she'd been this silly and carefree.

But, she needed to concentrate on driving this thing. The rental guy had impressed upon her a few cardinal rules and although she'd driven her dad's boat in her teens, it had been a small dinghy with an outboard motor. This Formula 1 machine didn't compare to her Ford Fiesta experience. She turned her back on him.

With a determined push of the throttle, she rammed the boat into gear and roared away from the jetty side, leaving a wash of water spilling over the stone walkways. The vibration of the engine thrummed through her hands on the steering wheel. Within seconds they were clear of the harbour and she pushed the throttle back to full speed, aiming across the bay away from the yachting lane and let the boat bounce and lift, speeding away from the shore, skimming along the waves.

Fine spray danced like a halo around the boat, landing on sun-warmed limbs as her hair streamed along behind her. The combination of the cool mist on hot skin made her body tingle with exhilaration. She threw back her head, enjoying the speed, standing tall and proud at the helm, like a Valkyrie heading into battle.

The sun, refracting from the waves, dazzled and twinkled turning the water in the air iridescent, like a shimmering rainbow.

A hand slipped around her waist and she jumped.

'Oops, Mrs Maddox.' A voice growled at her ear, his lips almost whispering across her skin, sending a shiver through her. 'I think the prisoner escaped.'

He wrapped both arms around her, standing pressed against her, his chin resting on her shoulder, his stubbled cheek rasping against her sensitive neck, kicking her heart-beat up a notch.

She swallowed, almost floored by the hot flood of desire shooting through her.

'T-the prisoner needs to behave,' she spluttered, unable

to think of anything but the slow build of heat radiating from inside. She wanted to clamp her thighs together and cross her arms across her inappropriately raised nipples. 'I need to concentrate on driving this thing.' She looked back at him.

'I'll stand here and enjoy the ride, then.' The blue eyes danced, full of innuendo.

With a challenge like that, she couldn't resist ramping up the speed and turning the wheel in a sharp turn, tearing up the water. She'd spent enough time out on a windsurf board as a teenager to know the parameters on the water and steered a path away from other craft.

Richard's hands slid upwards, stroking her arms on the steering wheel. 'What if the prisoner gets hungry?' His hands skimmed across her skin in silken promise. 'Have you any plans to feed him?' His sultry voice shimmered with danger, turning her insides into mush and she hung onto the steering wheel as her knees threatened to give way.

Steeling herself, she gripped the wheel harder. Who was in charge here?

She tossed a look over her shoulder at him, suggestive and flirtatious. 'The prisoner will have to wait and see.'

Flipping her hair back, she turned, on the lookout for a couple of landmarks that Phil had showed her earlier.

Richard caught a hank of hair, coiling his finger through a curl, his hand catching her neck. Trying to ignore him she tilted her head, unable to avoid the gentle caress as his finger drilled gently into the sensitive hairline at the back of her neck. He gave up on the hair, stroking the back of her neck, exploring the smooth surface with insistent, roving fingers. With unerring precision they slid around to the column of her throat before sliding up to her cheek and the blade of his hand slipping over her lips and back along her cheekbone in a beguiling rhythm.

Bewitched, she kissed his hand and her hips swayed, mimicking the movement.

With a sudden, desperate gasp, she heaved air into her lungs and straightened.

'Stop.' Her breath hissed out. 'I need to concentrate.' The drugging kisses had dazed her and she needed to focus. With relief she spotted the church Phil had told her to look out for, perched high on the hillside, and as she guided the boat towards the shore, it lined up with the crooked tree on the top of the cliff. Phil had told her that these were the landmarks for a sheltered inlet and, sure enough, there it was. She slowed the engine right down and they drifted into the rocky creek.

She killed the engine, immediately aware of the chainsaw buzz of thousands of cicadas hiding in the pale-lemon, dry-grass meadows above the cliff sides.

Lowering the anchor, with a clean splash, she tried to ease forward but Richard had other ideas. If she turned around she'd be pressed right up against him. She closed her eyes, hoping that he might do the decent thing and step back. Give her some space. Let her get her emotions under control.

Of course he had no intention of doing so.

Her body burned at his touch, his groin tucked in behind her bottom. She wiped her hands down the side of her dress and stared hard at the bell tower of the little white church on the hill. He wasn't going to move and she needed to do this.

'I owe you an apology.'

'You do.' He didn't move or loosen his hold.

Not being able to see his expression made her nervous.

She had no idea what his reaction would be and couldn't see his face. She took a deep breath.

'You're not going to make this easy for me, are you?' she asked, closing her eyes with an inward sigh when he didn't answer.

'I'm sorry,' she whispered.

'For what?' His prompt, along with another sweep of his hands down her arms, made her even more aware of him.

Nope, he was going to make her lay it on the line and, if she were honest, if she were him, she would have done exactly the same.

'Richard, I've enjoyed spending this time with you and it was wrong of me to insinuate that your motives were less honourable than they were.'

'And?' He turned her to face him, his eyes hard and uncompromising. The tiger had been there all along.

He moved back and sat down, leaving her standing above him, alone, spotlit on stage, with a private audience. Despite his relaxed pose, one arm lying the length of the back of the seat and his legs crossed, one foot tapped up and down.

She twisted her hand in the folds of her dress.

'I was being a coward.'

He straightened, the foot dropping to the floor. 'Why?'

'Because . . . the memories are too much. It's all too much. It would be easy to slip backwards. I can't afford to fall in love with you.' She stared out over the bay, her eyes blurred, before adding in a quiet voice. 'Not again.'

'That's more like the Carrie I remember.' His smile softened with sadness but he didn't flinch or look away. She brought her gaze back to his face as he said, 'Brutally honest to a fault.'

'I have to be. This doesn't change anything.' She had to be tough with him. Make sure he understood.

'Okay.' His face was impassive.

She narrowed her eyes. 'I'm serious, Richard. In another few weeks, you'll have moved on, gone on to your next project. But,' she took a breath, so deep her lungs almost gave up on her, 'we can still enjoy the last week. As friends. We were great friends. We still like each other, but it . . . can't be more than that.' She straightened, rather proud of herself. That had come out rather well. Every last damn lying word.

'Okay.' He nodded, his eyes hooded. 'That sounds sensible.'

She waited, hoping he'd say more. Her fingers clenched, hidden behind her legs. Richard's easy acquiescence made her want to push him over the side.

'That's it? Okay.'

'Yes.' His head moved this way and that, as if he were looking for something. 'Is that food?' He spotted the bag tucked under her seat.

She nodded and dropped her hands to her sides. That was it? She frowned. The end of the discussion?

Surely he'd say something else.

'Mmm, these smell good.' He rummaged through the contents of the bag and as if the last half hour had never happened, his face creased into smiles, like a carefree young boy. 'Do I smell bacon?'

Incredulous, she watched as he pulled open the picnic bag to reveal several foil-wrapped parcels.

'Oh wow, these smell amazing. Please tell me . . . bacon butties.'

Carrie rolled her eyes and wondered if she should push

him overboard now. Bloody man. And how flipping contrary was she?

'They're bacon butties Angela-style, or rather, Riviera-style.'

She leaned past him and picked up one of the still-warm foil-enveloped brioche buns filled with the local fine bacon, dabbed with Maille wholegrain mustard.

With a sigh, she shook her head. She'd set this up as an apology and to try and win him over, thinking she'd have to do some serious grovelling. As usual, Richard had managed to confound her by being gracious and his child-like happiness with a simple item of food. But it had always been like that. He'd never quite done what she'd expected and once she'd been the same. Life had been a constant adventure. They'd been well-suited.

Like a magician unveiling her final headline trick, she dug into a different bag.

'I brought you beer.' She handed him over a bottle of London Pride. She leaned back against the dashboard, the last of her tension seeping away as the lines around his eyes crinkled in quick delight.

'You're amazing.' He laughed. 'Proper beer and bacon butties on a speedboat in the middle of the sea.' He threw back his head and chuckled. 'Everyone else for miles around is on the caviar and champagne.'

'I know what you are . . .' he hadn't changed that much, 'like. You were always powerless to resist a bacon butty. If you'd refused to get on board, that would have been plan B. Wave it under your nose until you followed.'

'What, like a dog?' He gave another shout of laugher. 'It would have worked too. He stuck out a hand. 'Friends it is.'

Ignoring the jolt in her stomach, she took his hand and shook it. 'Friends.'

Grabbing a butty and joining him on the seat, the boat bobbed as they munched together in mutual silence. 'Tell me about these skills? Have you really been trained to be a Ninja assassin? Do they get the Secret Service in to tell you how to do it all properly? All that ten four, the eagle's in the wind and get me a secured comms unit.'

Richard took a swig of beer. 'I'm afraid that's classified information and if I tell you, I'll have to kill you.' In that actor's way, his body language shifted slightly and he seemed harder-edged and awfully like one of his characters Jason Hendricks from *A Conspiracy of Men*.

'Do know how to break someone's neck?'

'Yes.'

'And sever their femoral artery?'

'Yes.'

She twisted her hands together. 'That's . . .'

'Of course. I also know how to lie through my teeth during intense interrogation.' His mouth curved upward in sudden glee and the subtle changes to his frame vanished as he became Richard again.

'You!'

He shook with laughter.

'Did you really have a gun?' He frowned. 'I couldn't figure out what on earth it was in my back.'

She let out a gurgle of laughter.

'No. I've got,' she pulled it out from her jeans, 'an ice-cream scoop and I'm not afraid to use it.'

CHAPTER TWENTY-SEVEN

The pink dress shimmered in the low light in the bedroom, it's beautiful cut emphasising the tanned column of her throat and the flattering colour complementing her skin tone, which over the weeks had turned a gorgeous honey-golden brown. She'd left her hair loose, not to please Richard, but for herself, enhancing the curls with the application of a little dressing wax. The sun had lifted the colour and rich copper highlights snaked in and out of the ringlets raining down her back.

She took another long, nervous look in the mirror and then told herself off. She should be excited, mixing with the glitterati in a gorgeous dress, an amazing opportunity she might never get again. Hell, yes. With a final twirl and one last peek at her reflection, she smoothed the silky fabric down her hips and lifted her chin. No, she felt bloody brilliant in this dress.

As the host, Richard would be busy with all his VIP guests. She, Angela, Jade and their trusty fourth, Phil, would no doubt sit in a corner admiring the finery of the other guests.

Oh and didn't that sound woefully Cinderella and big chip-on-the-shoulder territory? Tonight's adventure offered a bird's-eye view into another world and a huge treat, especially for Jade, who had been beside herself all day, desperate to know if Carrie had any idea who might be there aside from Savannah Murray and the rest of the cast.

An overhead whirring distracted her with its insistent airborne whine, which she couldn't quite place. Slipping on her watch, she picked up her clutch bag. The lift they'd been promised was cutting it fine, although this was the sort of the party to which arriving fashionably late was a given.

The sound intensified, coming from above the house now. Carrie ran over to the window as she heard her niece calling, 'Carrie, Carrie,' through the house.

A brilliant spotlight shone down on the flat lawn beyond the swimming pool, getting bigger and bigger. The shrubs around the edge blew back, straining to keep their purchase on land, pushed to the very limit of their grip by the down-blast of the wind from the helicopter hovering above and slowly coming down, squatting into place.

Wouldn't you know it? She'd wondered about that lawn and now she knew why it needed to be flat. Carrie hurried downstairs to join her sister and Jade on the terrace. All three of them staring open-mouthed at the royal-blue helicopter, looking rather like an exotic dragonfly perched on their lawn, the blades still whirring in a blur of movement.

'Oh my days.' Angela turned wide-eyed to Carrie. 'This is for us?'

'Can you believe it?' Jade had her phone out and her hand shook as she tried to get pictures. 'Eliza is going to go wild when she sees this.'

He'd done it again. Carrie burst out laughing. 'I love it. A helicopter. Whatever will he do next?'

'Richard sent this? Its sick,' said Jade.

'No, it was George Clooney. Or, wait, it could have been Brad Pitt. I forget. You know, being acquainted with lots of the rich and famous.'

Jade nudged her. 'Ha! Ha! You're so funny. Not.' Her niece stopped and gave her an appraising look. 'But, hello mama,' she deepened her voice in rapper mode and added with a cheeky wink, 'You look hot.'

'High praise indeed, brat. You don't look too bad yourself.'

Jade twisted her face in a half-smile. 'I had to put my nail varnish on three times because I kept messing it up and my hair wouldn't go and I think my bum looks a bit saggy and —'

'Jade, shut up. You look gorgeous.'

Angela exchanged a knowing smile with Carrie. Nothing they said would make any difference because what on earth did they know about anything?

'Hmph.' Jade tossed her spaghetti-straight hair, the GHDs had been doing sterling overtime, making it clear that Carrie's opinion carried about as much weight as that of the family cat, if not less. 'Are we going or not?'

Angela hesitated, eyeing the helicopter with trepidation. 'I'm not sure. Aren't they terribly dangerous? You're always hearing about helicopter crashes.'

'Muuum!' howled Jade. 'We might never get to go in one again.'

A familiar figure jumped down from the cockpit and, ducking under the blades in a crab-like run, came towards them, clutching a brace of headphones.

'Come on, ladies, your carriage awaits,' said Phil, looking rather dapper in a blue blazer, shining with gold buttons, and well-pressed trousers.

Angela hung back but Phil whispered something in her ear and to Carrie's surprise, she let out a very dirty laugh.

He handed them each a set of earphones. 'It gets pretty noisy in there. If you plug this jack in, you'll be able to hear the pilot talking to us.'

Strapped in, with a stomach full of kangaroos and the earphones wedged onto her head, Carrie gripped her knees together as the rotor blades stirred the air faster and faster, and then the cockpit lifted, hovering above the ground for a few seconds. Gradually, the blades screaming above them, the helicopter turned a slow, swaying half circle before rising and lifting right up into the sky, leaving her jumpy stomach behind. Even with her ears muffled, the sound was incredibly loud.

'Good evening, ladies. I'm Roger. We're flying east for a couple of kilometres. The trip will take no more than ten minutes. Relax and enjoy the view.'

Sitting next to her, Jade held her hand tightly and Carrie nodded at her, trying her best to summon up an encouraging expression on her face, which wasn't easy, given that she wanted to tap Roger on the shoulder and ask him how the hell anyone was supposed to relax in a tin can with its own wind turbine on the roof.

The unnatural motion of the helicopter, as it climbed higher, was quite frankly terrifying. It felt a lot less stable than a plane but then her sole experience of flying had been in very large planes – it was hardly comparable.

This was crazy, how often was she ever going to get to do this? She leaned over to the edge of the glass bubble and forced herself to take a look down at the once-in-a-lifetime view and smiled, fascinated by the sight. Beneath them a patchwork world of roofs in rainbow shades of terracotta spread out, hidden villas nestled in dark-green vegetation, their swimming pools shining sapphire-bright while sand-coloured fields wrinkled with green lines traced the contours of the land.

Over on the horizon the sea beckoned, looking bluer than ever and as they flew closer, a jewellery store of colours beckoned, the rocky contours below the surface creating darker emerald-green shadows interspersed with paler aquamarine shallows.

She pressed her forehead to the glass, drinking in the view, almost laughing at her earlier fears. It was official, she loved travelling by helicopter.

As they slid into smooth leather seats of the chauffeur-driven limousine after transferring from the helicopter, Angela, whispered, 'I could get use to this.'

The car purred its way along the road, taking the back route down into St Tropez and out along the narrow harbour road, with the sea on either side. After the noisy roar of the helicopter, the whisper of the engine was in stark contrast and, for some reason, the party sat in silence, not one of them saying a word until the car slid to an almost unnoticeable halt.

The driver skirted the front of the car, opened the door and one by one they filed out, each of them doing an identical one-step, look up, stop dead, combination, bumping into one another like comedy cartoon characters.

'Oh my days.'

'Rock and roll.' Jade whipped out her phone.

'Bloody hell.' Carrie's eyes widened as she looked up and up and up.

'Rather impressive,' said Phil faintly.

White lights outlined the numerous decks of the dark-blue yacht which rose like a wedding cake from the water. The reflected beams danced on the waves rippling into shore. It created a rather magical effect, softening the lines of the huge boat and making it seem like a fairy-tale vessel ready to float off to another dimension.

The first-floor deck, the biggest and the brightest, had been designated hub of the action. From there gay chatter and laughter bounced across the water's surface and it was alive with colour and shape as people mingled and moved, the light catching on glittering necklaces, flashes of jewel-bright dresses and the glow of white shirts picked out by ultra violet.

A black-suited man with ebony skin and the sort of chiselled face that belonged in a very expensive perfume advert, barred their way. Carrie was rather fascinated by the earpiece he wore, the curly wire disappearing down the back of his jacket. Serious security.

'Name of your party?' Nothing was going to be allowed to crack that face. Shame, he was rather gorgeous.

A smile played around her lips, it would have been fun to try and tease a reaction from him.

'Carrie Hayes.'

He spoke into a black strip at his wrist. All very FBI.

'Excuse me, ma'am.' He stepped away, turning his back on them.

When he turned to face them again, cool and impassive, he said, without any particular inflection in his voice, 'I don't have anyone by that name on the guest list.'

'But we have tickets and everything,' wailed Jade. 'Richard invited us,' her voice rose.

Carrie held a hand up towards her niece.

'We were invited by Richard Mad. . . Try Carrie Maddox.'

He tried again. To Carrie's satisfaction, a tiny flicker of surprise flashed in his eyes, before the smooth professional mask slid back into place.

'Welcome Mrs . . .er Maddox, I believe there are also a further three in your party. Jade Hayes, Angela Hayes and Phil Hillair-Brady.'

'That's correct.' Carrie inclined her head regally, a sudden thrill rushing through her.

'I do beg your pardon ma'am for the earlier—'

She waved his words away. 'Don't worry. It's not your fault.'

He ushered them to the gangplank, where a crew member dressed in a crisp white shirt and neat dark-navy shorts, waited.

'Evening and welcome to the Solander. Please come aboard. Drinks are available on the first deck, if you go right up these stairs with my colleague here. If there is anything you need during your visit on board, please don't hesitate to speak to one of the crew.'

Jade's eyes already as wide as they would go, darted about, trying to take it all in. 'I wonder who's here,' she muttered, bouncing on her toes. 'Do you think any celebrities will have arrived yet? Richard will introduce us to people, won't he? He will talk to us.'

'I don't know,' replied Carrie. 'You have to remember, he's the host. We can't monopolise him. Don't expect too much.' She looked at Jade's flushed face, pretty sure that she'd wasted her breath.

Hopefully, she wouldn't be bored or too disappointed or, more importantly, that none of the beautiful people here would snub the young girl. It was a safe bet to assume that there weren't going to be many, if any, people of her age. Carrie couldn't imagine that party small talk would interest Jade that much. At least she had her phone and no doubt taking lots of pictures for social media would keep her entertained. Ironic really. No doubt, she'd take more satisfaction out of being at the party and able to prove it, than actually enjoying it.

As Jade took another selfie, Carrie smiled at Angela. As usual, in the same way that she took everything in her stride, she was perfectly content to carry on a low-voiced conversation with Phil, almost oblivious to the excited buzz around her.

The group moved along the outer deck and up a small flight of stairs to the main deck. Jade gave an audible gasp and even Angela was moved to breathe a heartfelt, 'Oh my.'

The patina of the polished wooden boards gave off a warm, inviting glow and around the deck pale-suede couches and seating areas had been arranged. Every occasional table held a simple candlelit white orchid arrangement, which allowed the delicate flowers to shine for themselves, while longer-stemmed orchids decorated the bar area in the centre. At the far end of the deck, a swimming pool, glowing ultramarine with submerged lighting, gave the illusion of the water dropping away into the sea.

A prickle along her skin made her turn. She spotted Richard a few feet away, a statuesque blonde next to him, her arm wound through his, where they were talking to a group of three men. Almost immediately he unhooked himself from the blonde, his co-star, Savannah Murphy, and with a discreet apology excused himself, gliding over to greet them.

Her mouth dried as he crossed the deck in a few long strides. She stopped dead. Game over. Complete capitulation. Her whole body softened in feminine appreciation, her hormones surging in joyous surrender as a delicious fizz spiralled through her veins, spilling over and over as effervescent as champagne bubbles.

The sum of all his parts doubled equated to sheer gorgeousness. The cut of the dark-grey charcoal suit emphasised those broad, straight shoulders, not a crease or crinkle marred the wool fabric. She didn't know much about tailoring but she would guess that it had been made for him. The double-breasted jacket hung perfectly from his frame and unbidden, an image of his naked body, a very broad chest and fine hair tapering downwards, popped into her head, bringing with it a sudden flush to her cheeks. Hot and very bothered, she focused on his crisp, cool and very sophisticated white cotton shirt complementing his tan, an all-over tan that she'd witnessed, down to that familiar heart-shaped birthmark. Stop, she told herself, staring hard at the silk handkerchief tucked into the left pocket of the suit, but every part of her buzzed with sheer damn awareness of him.

'Good evening, ladies. Phil.' Despite encompassing the whole party with his greeting, Richard's eyes homed in on her and he didn't even spare a glance for the others. 'You look . . .' he lowered his voice so that only she could hear, 'like Carrie'.

As his husky, reverent tone shivered over her, she gripped her clutch bag, hoping he wouldn't notice the tiny movement of her swaying on her heels. Perhaps she could blame the movement of the boat.

'That's Savannah Murphy, isn't it? Gosh, she's tall. I thought movie stars were always short-arses.'

Richard shot Carrie a quick, regretful look, making her heart miss a quick beat. 'Language,' reproved Angela, who was trying not to stare at a woman to their left. 'Is that Helen Mirren?'

'Who?' asked Jade. 'That's John Baywater and Eddie thingummy and oh my God,' she paused and clutched her stomach, swallowing, 'its . . . its Fabio Stanza.'

Richard gave a brief frown.

'You know some proper famous people,' said Jade to Richard, nodding as if reluctantly approving. 'I'm impressed.'

'Thank you. One does one's best.'

'Do you like, know them, know them? I mean to talk to?' Jade asked Richard, without any pretence at being coy or discreet.

He laughed. 'A few. Who do you want to meet?'

'Fabio.' She clutched her hands together as she sighed his name.

'Jade, don't plague Richard,' said Angela.

'Yes, don't be an embarrassing brat,' said Carrie adding to her sister's plea.

'Don't worry, I'm sure we'll find a few people who will impress Jade, as I obviously don't count.'

Jade thumped him on the arm. 'Of course you don't count. You're family, that's different.' She shot Carrie a dirty look. 'Even if I'm not allowed to tell anybody.'

Richard leaned down and muttered something in her ear. They both turned and looked at Carrie, Jade with a calculating gleam. Carrie ignored them and turned to Angela.

'What would you like to drink? Our host is being rather slack.'

Richard grinned. 'Sorry, ladies. Can I get you something? Champagne? A cocktail?' He called over a passing waiter, dressed all in white.

'Come and meet Savannah. She's fun.' He tapped Jade on the nose. 'Will that do you, brat?'

She batted his hand away with a giggle. 'You're horrid to me, Uncle Richard.'

Savannah turned out to be charming and very friendly. Not at all film-starry, as Jade declared later.

'Hi,' she said, when they'd been introduced. 'Lovely party, isn't it. Richard's always so kind. Not like some of the co-stars I've worked with.'

'Really?' asked Jade. 'Isn't he old and boring?' She shot Richard a triumphant grin. 'Not like Jason Flemming.' She named Savannah's last co-star, a few years younger than Richard with something of a reputation. 'Is he that much of a bad boy?'

Savannah laughed. 'Jason's problem is that he's bonkers. Brilliant fun, totally unreliable and can't string more than three words together when he's off-camera. He's fine as long as you don't sign up to be his girlfriend.' She shared a couple of stories about his all-night party habits and his last poor girlfriend, who'd he forgotten to take home at the end of a party.

To Jade's delight Savannah happily name-dropped and gossiped as they gravitated to a small table. Despite Carrie's misgivings that the four of them would end up at a table tucked in a corner on their own all night, Richard turned out to be a consummate host and very good at introducing them to people they at least could talk to, even if they had nothing in common with them.

Before long Angela and Phil were chatting with a group of other people who had been extras in the film, many of whom were ex-pats and had taken part as a fun one-off.

Savannah seemed quite happy to talk to Jade and when her audience swelled with the addition of a couple of girls who were the daughters of the producer who'd flown out for the summer, she became even more loquacious, although it didn't stop her sending periodic glances Carrie's way.

'Shall we have a wander?' asked Richard. She'd expected him to do his bit and then disappear but he stayed with her, his hand straying to her back periodically or to stroke her forearm.

At first it had unnerved her, as he introduced her to person after person. No one questioned how they knew each other. He simply introduced her as Carrie, and then proceeded to chat away before excusing themselves and moving on.

Jade might be impressed and from where Carrie stood, she could see her still enthusiastically bombarding Savannah with questions, but she was getting a little tired of the meaningless chat. Some of the people took great delight in talking about people and events it was obvious she knew nothing about. It seemed rude, but they clearly took some sort of petty satisfaction from it. Others, so self-absorbed they didn't even realise they were doing it.

'You're very good at this,' she observed.

'At this?' He raised his hands in question.

'You know, social small talk. Chit-chat.'

'You don't make it sound like a compliment.'

She shrugged. 'They're not my sort of people.'

'Which is why I throw a big party, get it all out of the way in one go.' He ran a finger down the edge of her upper arm. 'Then I can spend time with the people I really want to be with.' He stopped in front of her and surveyed the room. 'It's part of the job. Networking. Schmoozing. Being seen. This way, I don't have to spend too much time with anyone. A quick chat here, a few words there.

'Come and meet Miranda, you'll like her. She was very interested in your ideas on her script.'

'Miranda?' A sense of foreboding trickled down Carrie's back.

'There she is.' He tucked his hand under her elbow and led her over.

'Richard,' Another tall blonde woman in among a small group turned and beamed at him, 'How are you? Lovely party, by the way. You managed to keep most of the riff-raff out, although I spotted Fabio oozing his way about earlier.'

Richard's mouth pinched. 'Much as I would have preferred not to, after consultation with our dear director,' he flashed a grin at the man next to the blonde, who Carrie recognised as one of the very scruffy men she'd seen on set in Ramatuelle, 'we agreed it would have caused on-set friction if I'd excluded him from the invitation list. My consolation is he'll find this party far too tame and will soon slope off somewhere more interesting.'

'Hopefully slither back into the sort of hole he came from,' said Miranda, her mouth turning down in disgust.

'Miranda, this is Carrie. She's the scriptwriter I was telling you about, the one who made the suggestion about Frank's character.'

Carrie braced herself, wondering what sort of reception she might receive. An amateur like her did not critique the work of someone like Miranda's work. This was Miranda Buckley, for God's sake. She'd won an Olivier last year for a play at the National.

'Hi, great to meet you. Richard, be a dear, go get us some drinks. I want to have a proper chat with Carrie.' With a push, Miranda sent him off like a bellboy to do his errands while she led Carrie to a leather couch on the far side of the deck, slightly away from the majority of people, who had accumulated in the centre. Was this how the sacrificial lamb felt when it was led off?

'Phew, its busy. I hate these shindigs, although Richard does it better than most. He gets that his guests might want to talk to each other. Usually the music is so effing loud at these things, I spend the whole evening nodding and smiling, I could be grinning away while they're tell me their dog's just died, for all I know. You have to be bloody careful. It's not that great and it's all about networking.' She let out a loud belly-deep laugh. 'It's pretty shit if you are trying to network and you piss off some major producer because you've laughed in the wrong place when he's just told you he forked out twelve mil in alimony. And I talk too much. Wish my bloody characters could speak this quickly when I'm trying to get the words down. The buggers all stay schtum. It's like pulling teeth, don't you find?'

Carrie laughed. 'Yes, or they don't say the right things.'

'I loved what you suggested. Although I hate you too,' she said, with a warm, open grin that almost took up her whole face, belying the words. 'It sucks when you've spent weeks rewriting the bastard and you can't put your finger on what's wrong and someone comes along and nails it. What you said about Frank's motivation. That was it exactly.'

'If it's any consolation, it was more of a help to me.' Carrie wanted to pinch herself. 'I was working on something and it highlighted what was wrong with mine.' Could she say that? Of course it would help, Miranda was the expert and here she was, some complete nobody.

'Isn't that a pig? I usually find when I get stuck it's because something like that is wrong. The structure, the character.'

Carrie couldn't believe she was sitting here talking to Miranda Buckley as if they were equals and that the other woman was so friendly.

When Richard reappeared with two long, tall glasses of Kir Royale, they'd established they both loved *Finding Nemo,* hated the film version of *Pride and Prejudice* with a passion and that *Memento* ranked in their top-ten films and that Miranda knew Andrew Fisher rather well. Carrie couldn't help letting her pride show when she explained about the Gold Medal award she'd won and that Andrew wanted to direct her play.

Richard hung about in front of them for a minute or two until Miranda said with a very wicked twinkle. 'Can we help you?'

'Am I being dismissed?' he asked.

'Yes, we don't need you. Go and talk to some other hapless guests.'

Richard raised an eyebrow and checked with Carrie in one quick glance.

'She'll be fine with me. I won't eat her, I promise, which is more than can be said for Savannah. The poor child might burst with curiosity, whereas I am taking my time, teasing out how Carrie has the misfortune to know you.'

'Be gentle with her.'

Miranda glanced from Richard to Carrie. 'She's a big girl, I'm sure if she can handle you, she'll be fine. Now run along.' She flapped her hands in dismissal and burst out laughing as he slunk away.

'He's a very nice man. And if I were that way inclined I might be tempted. How do you know him?'

Carrie hesitated.

'Don't worry, you don't have to tell me and if it's a secret I'd rather not know. Too many of the bloody things to keep, most of the time for the most spurious reasons. I have a hard job remembering what I am or aren't supposed to know.'

CHAPTER TWENTY-EIGHT

Food was served at nine and Carrie caught up with Angela and Jade at the buffet table.

'Having a good time?' she asked her niece, jigging about on the spot balancing a plate in one hand and a glass in the other.

'Awesome.' Her mouth moved but Jade seemed incapable of further speech.

'That good,' teased Carrie.

Jade nodded fervently. 'The girls on WhatsApp are going crazy.' She showed her phone, the screen featuring a scroll of more and more excitable emoji.

Clearly her street cred had hit stratospheric and likely to remain so until at least Christmas.

'You would not believe who I've been talking to. Savannah is dead cool. She, like, knows everyone. I met Eddie whatsit, the Oscar bloke, that woman from *Bridesmaids* and a guy who knows Kanye West. And Savannah's going to introduce me to Fabio, although I think I might faint, he's so gorg. And there's a disco on the deck upstairs. Starts at ten. Me and Dorrie and Carla are going to dance for the rest of the night.' She giggled. 'I might ask him to dance with me, what do you reckon?'

Carrie nodded, letting the words flow over her. She didn't think Jade would be half as impressed with Miranda, who'd been fascinating and interesting, with lots to say about a wealth of subjects. A far cry from her usual conversations, most of which focused on school, the students, assessments and exams.

After the buffet, Richard appeared at her shoulder again, where she was standing watching Jade on the dance floor.

'Disco or a walk on deck?'

'I love dancing but I think I might cramp Jade's style. She's having a ball. Thank you for inviting us all.'

Richard stiffened. 'Not sure I approve of her dance partner.'

'He's very pretty.'

'He's a pest.' Richard's words rang with irritation and Carrie wondered if there might be a little professional rivalry there and then recanted the thought. Richard radiated confidence, very much his own man and sure in his own skin. A very attractive trait. The difference between the young man she'd known and the man he'd become. A man she felt proud to know.

'There's a group of them. She's a sensible girl. She'll be fine.'

'What were you smiling about, just then?' he asked.

She blushed. 'Nothing, enjoying myself.'

'Having a good time?' He touched her forearm, inviting her to walk along with him.

'Surprisingly yes. Your friends, the real ones, are lovely.'

They weaved through the groups of people, sitting replete at tables, the detritus of empty plates being cleared by the unobtrusive but efficient staff.

'It's not always that easy to make friends in this business. You meet people, spend an intense period of time with them, then you spread out across the world. You tend to treasure those relationships where you click with people.'

'I liked Miranda, a lot.'

Richard ushered her through a doorway, passing one of the security people, and nodded towards a flight of stairs.

'You should hook up with her in London. She's going back there this weekend. Doing a writer-in-residence thing at one of the theatres.'

Carrie made a non-committal noise, knowing full well that the chances of her ever running across Miranda were marginal to non-existent.

At the top of the stairs, Richard took her hand. 'Up again.'

They emerged onto a much smaller private deck, with a semicircular couch tucked into the leeward shelter behind the bridge of the ship, where you could sit and watch the sea and the churning wake.

'Wow, this is rather nice. What an amazing view.'

'It is, isn't it? I love watching the sea. You can't ever think you're too important when you see the size of the ocean. Brings you back to earth.'

'There's nothing grounding about the size of this boat. Is it yours?'

Richard laughed. 'No, I chartered it for the party initially, for the one night. Arla found it. I was going to stay here for a week but,' he winced, 'it's too opulent for my tastes. It's mine until the morning.'

'What's opulent?' she teased.

'Lots of crystal chandeliers and satin-covered sofas. Gilt everywhere. Very rich oil sheikh. It's not very relaxing. Too formal. Some of the cabins are okay but the staterooms are more like a royal palace than Versailles.'

'Poor you.'

Richard reached out and swatted her bottom.

Despite the gesture being innocent, she was aware of the thin silk fabric. Did she imagine his hand lingered for a second?

'Where are your knickers?' asked Richard in pretend outrage. 'Not commando, surely?' He folded his arms as if waiting for an explanation.

She lifted her chin, about to say that she couldn't believe that all of his co-stars and the sophisticated women he dealt with on a daily basis didn't wear thongs, when she realised he was referring to the time when she'd left their flat to go to an audition without any underwear on. She gave him a superior glare, before giggling.

'You were the one that did that because you were too lazy to go the launderette. I did it once. And that was a VPL issue. I have plenty of clean underwear, thank you.' With an arch look she added, 'Are yours hand-pressed by an army of maids these days. Or do you throw them away and have a new pair every day?

Ignoring her question, his eyes slid to her bottom again.

'Not cheese wire?' He asked, referring to a long-ago conversation in the underwear department of River Island.

'Not at this price, Lord no.'

They smiled at each other, lapsing into silence as they studied the view. To the right, the darkness of the Med with the occasional winking light, and to their left the lights and noise of St Tropez, throbbing out into the night in the distance, could be heard above the bass of the disco below. The temperature had dropped to a pleasant cooler heat. The sea breeze picked up slightly, lifting Carrie's hair and blowing it across her face.

Richard brushed it away, his hand lingering on her face, his eyes darkening. Carrie's heart tripped, awaiting the inevitable kiss. Turning to face him, she pressed her back against the railings. There'd been a dull ache in her heart ever since the first day she'd seen him in Ramatuelle. And she was sick of it. Sick of the constant pull, the tug at her heart, the quiver between her legs, the awareness in her nipples.

She'd had enough. Friends be damned. Like a diver, she tensed in preparation and then let go, hurling herself over the edge. She wound her arms around his neck, sliding a hand into his thick, dark hair and pulled him down to her. Her lips roving over his. She didn't want to be kissed, she wanted to kiss him. She felt his lips curve in surprise but he slipped a hand around her waist and pulled her to him, his other hand skimming down her side, skirting the underside of her breast.

Arms and limbs entwined, their bodies one, they kissed, buffeted by the gentle wind. Searching and teasing, their soft sighs carried away by the airborne currents, until Richard tugged her over to the soft leather and they sank down, still kissing.

Lips, hands, whispering touches, soft skin, tongue to tongue, Carrie closed her eyes, her heart singing in recognition and pure pleasure.

Richard pulled back a little to trace her face with a gentle finger.

'We shouldn't be doing this,' whispered Carrie, 'But I don't care any more.'

'We should be doing this.' He stilled, cupping her face in his hand, the expression in his eyes boring straight into her chest. 'I was ready to throttle you the other night when you said we should be friends, but . . .' he gave a very masculine smile, firing up her nerve endings in a very delicate spot. 'I decided to play the long game.'

Her eyes met his and, with a feline smile, she reached up to trace his cheekbone, drinking in the familiar features, her heart singing with pleasure. 'I think your strategy might have paid off.' He turned his head to kiss her fingers. The soft touch sparked a reaction that tingled down her arm. She held up her palm and he laid his against it. Skin to skin. She wanted to press and press against him, their hands merging until neither of them knew where the other began or ended.

Her heart lurched and then, like an explosion in her chest as if everything burst out, there it was – the pure, unassailable truth. She loved him.

Stunned, she stared open-mouthed at him, trying to breathe normally, when agitated voices, like angry bees, floated up from the stairs, just out of view.

'Ma'am, wait.'

Angela appeared, looking like an indignant mother hen, closely followed by a very red-faced Phil and an agitated female security guard

'We can't find Jade. Anywhere.' Angela's voice rose as the security woman tried to speak too.

'I'm sorry sir, I tried to stop her.'

Angela shook her head. 'Phil has looked everywhere.'

'I have.' Behind Angela's back, Phil inclined his head, giving Richard a silent message. 'Everywhere I can.'

Richard stood up, helped Carrie to her feet and crossed to lay his hands on Angela's shoulders.

'I'm sure she's here somewhere. Don't worry. We'll find her.' He held up a hand to halt the guard.

'I'll get security to have a good look for her. When did you last see her?'

'She was on the dance floor.' Angela gave a rueful smile. 'She got her dance with Fabio and then she danced with the two girls. They were having a good time, the three of them. And then next time I noticed, she'd gone and they didn't know where she was.' Angela's mouth crumpled. 'You don't think she could have fallen overboard, do you. You hear about people falling off ships. She didn't seem drunk or anything.'

Richard's face darkened.

'Why don't you and Phil go downstairs to the main deck and wait there while I brief the security team to go through the boat.'

He waited until their steps receded and then turned with an abrupt movement to the security woman. 'Get James. Tell him to meet me *now*. Lower deck.' He spat the staccato words with precision.

She nodded and spoke her into wrist unit. 'Can you put me through to James? Richard needs to speak to him.'

Before she'd finished her sentence, Richard had taken Carrie's hand and pulled her with him, taking the stairs at a brisk, determined pace. His movements economic and focused.

'Should I be worried?' she asked.

'No, I doubt very much Jade has fallen overboard. As a precaution I'll get James to put a few divers overboard. I'd like to find out where Fabio is.'

'Fabio?'

'Yes,' he said, his lips firming into a forbidding slash.

'Him. I thought we were looking for Jade.'

'We are, but I have a hunch she's with him somewhere on board.' He paused at the head of the next flight of stairs, anger radiating from his rigid stance.

'On board.'

He nodded, his mouth twisting.

James met them at the foot of the stairs, his team waiting in the shadows behind him. Unlike the pretty security people dotted around the boat and at the gangway, his ready-to-spring stance suggested a much harder edge. The black uniforms of this small group of men, Carrie realised, weren't for show. Each of them had that quiet, watchful quality, their eyes alert, constantly on the move.

'Sir.'

'James, my niece has gone missing. Can you get a couple of men in the water, in case she's gone overboard?'

James shook his head. 'I've had men stationed on the lower deck all night. We'd have heard a splash, if anyone went over.'

'I thought as much. Can you get your team to check every state room, cabin and crew cabins? I think Fabio might have decided to take a little rest with my niece.' Taut anger shivered in the words. 'She's fifteen.'

'Right, sir. I'm on it.'

With a few brief words, the group scattered.

'Shit, I'm sorry Carrie. I should have kept a closer eye on them.'

'Richard, you're worrying me. Is Fabio bad news?'

'Not seriously bad news, but he's the love-them-and-leave them type, fine for women who know the score but not for impressionable teenagers. Jade definitely falls into the latter category.'

'Surely he's not going to be interested in a girl her age.'

'Who looks about eighteen tonight,' he observed.

'I almost said something to Angela earlier about how old she looked, but messing with Jade, hell-bent on making an impression tonight, would have been tantamount to taking a bath with a piranha and we'd already done an awful lot of fancy footwork to get near to an age-appropriate dress.'

'Hey, it's not your fault. We're in a public place. She's perfectly safe. They'll be necking in a corner somewhere. At the heart of it, she's a sensible girl.'

He shoved his hands in his pockets. 'I should have warned her that he's a sleaze-ball with women.'

Carrie snorted. 'That would have been the worst thing you could do, I promise you. Teenagers love nothing more than forbidden fruit.

They exchanged wry smiles.

'Not quite how I imagined things turning out this evening.' Richard said with a self-deprecating shrug. 'Or how I'd hoped.'

'Welcome to the family. Talking of which, I'd better go and check on Angela.'

Angela, determined not to make a fuss, sat with Phil on the edge of the deck, her eyes scanning the crowd, Phil sitting next to her, holding her hand.

'Any news?' asked Angela.

'No, but the security people are pretty confident that no one has gone overboard. They have people stationed outside to make sure that doesn't happen and to jump in if it does.

They haven't heard anything.' She paused. 'Richard is having the private areas of the boat searched.'

'What? I'll skin her alive if she's gone off exploring. That's very rude.'

Carrie tried to work out the best way of phrasing her next sentence. 'Richard thinks she might be with Fabio somewhere.'

'I'd have thought she'd be far too young and unsophisticated for him. Wouldn't he be more interested in someone like Savannah? It's not as if Jade can do anything for his career.'

Carrie would have been inclined to agree with her, if she hadn't heard Richard's opinion of Fabio.

'I'll go and have a quick chat with Savannah and the two Stacey girls. Maybe they know something.'

'That's a good idea,' said Angela jumping up, smoothing down her skirt and checking her handbag ready for action. 'Shall I come with you?'

'No you wait here, I've told James to come here with any news.'

'Honestly. I have no idea where Jade is, but she must have gone with him because I haven't seen him for ages either. I wonder where they've gone. It's so naughty of Fabio. She did seem rather smitten. I did warn her he was a bit of a lad, didn't I girls?'

The two blonde daughters of the producer nodded, although Carrie noticed one of them discreetly poke the other in the leg when she thought no one was watching.

'I'm sure she'll be fine. Chill, she's spreading her wings.' With a confiding whisper, which made Carrie want to slap her, this was her niece they were talking about, Savannah added, 'Probably, hiding out in a corner somewhere snogging.' She flashed her perfect cheerleader teeth. 'We've all done it.'

'Yes, but not with a Tyrannosaurus Rex in sheep's clothing.' Richard glared at her. 'You know what Fabio's like.'

Savannah coloured and ducked her head.

'If you see him, let me know.'

As they left, Carrie muttered, 'I think the girls might know something.'

'What makes you say that?'

'They were too happy to let Savannah do all the talking, as if they were relieved not to have to say anything.'

'Doesn't mean they know anything.'

'Richard, I teach teenage girls. Any drama, they love to be in on the act. These two seemed determined to shy away from it. That's not normal teenage behaviour, I promise you. Besides, I saw the younger one nudge her sister.'

'What do you want to do?'

'Let's wait a second and wait for Savannah to leave them. There you go.'

She approached the girl, Dorrie. 'Have you any idea where Jade might have wanted to go?'

Dorrie spoke quickly, as if desperate to unburden herself. 'I've no idea if she might have . . . but earlier she talked about wanting to go the VIP Rooms and asked Savannah if she'd ever been. Then Fabio said he'd been and she was asking him about it. But that was, like, hours ago. Then we were all dancing. Fabio went off with some other people. We didn't see him again.'

'Actually,' the older girl spoke, 'I did see them. They left the boat together.' Her mouth was bitter. 'Fabio asked me to go to the VIP Rooms with him. I said I needed to check with Dad.' She swallowed, looking close to tears. 'He said he didn't want to take a daddy's girl.'

Carrie squeezed her arm. 'Do you know what? I think you had a lucky escape.'

The girl nodded with a tremulous attempt at a smile. 'I'm sorry, I should have said earlier, I was . . .' her throat worked furiously and then in that candid innocent way of young girls, blurted out, 'jealous. Really jealous. Do you think Jade will be alright?'

'I'm sure she will. Well, until she gets home and then she's going to be in serious trouble.' Carrie's fierce scowl elicited nervous giggles from the girls, which faded when she added, 'And then I'm going to kill her.'

As they rounded the corner to join Angela, James came up.

'One of the lads has come back from his break. Says he saw Fabio and a female leave the boat.'

CHAPTER TWENTY-NINE

'I'm coming. The two of you need to get over yourselves. She's my daughter, my responsibility. She's a minx and she knows better. And you might be blaming this young man, but she knew exactly what she was up to. She's been on about this blasted club for weeks.'

Richard put a hand up to halt her flow. 'Fabio's no innocent.'

With a sour smile, Angela shook her head. 'You don't know teenagers. She'll have spotted him a mile off. He suited her purposes. Now, where is this club? Oh, silly me.'

The neon lights directly opposite were an obvious clue.

'I don't think they'll let Angela in,' whispered Carrie as they climbed out of the car. Angela marched with a purposeful stride, which boded ill for Jade. 'They're supposed to be pretty fussy.' And she hated herself for saying it. Angela's classic shift dress might turn a few heads in downtown Berkhamsted but here in the neon-lit, glittering evening, her non-designer, last-season's dress didn't cut it.

'Don't worry about that. They will let me in,' he said

without a trace of arrogance but with practical awareness of his VIP status.

'I wasn't worried about you.'

Richard grabbed a strand of her hair and tugged. 'They'll definitely let you in. I'd better stick with you.'

Carrie shook her hair to let it ripple down her back. Amazing what a touch of attitude could do for you. Tonight she'd felt she belonged and had been accepted, and it had nothing to do with the expensive dress, she'd just been herself.

The lengthy queue outside the nightclub snaked around the grey-washed walls filled with languid but loud party-goers, confident that they'd be let in.

Angela, ahead of them, trying to wriggle through the crowd, hoping to work her way through to the front of the queue, met with a series of disdainful and, quite frankly, rude stares. Not that she cared. With shoulders squared, ready for battle, she ploughed on, the girls in their strappy stilettos unaware that they faced the grave danger of losing a toe.

Almost as if someone had pressed a light switch, Richard straightened up, his shoulders broadening. She'd seen him transform plenty of time in recent days but this was different. Star quality and a definite swagger about him. A flurry of whispers rustled through the queue. 'It's him.' 'Richard Maddox. You know the guy from . . .'

He stepped in front of Angela, like Sir Walter Raleigh throwing down his cape and the magic of celebrity, parted the crowd, allowing the three of them to walk straight up to the large, rather breath-taking, bouncer, who Carrie could have sworn had a sixteen pack of ridged abs. She suspected the club employed much less attractive bouncers to do the real dirty work, if such work was required. She could imagine that might encompass the odd catfight if someone turned up with the same pair of Jimmy Choos or with last week's cast-off boyfriend. This gorgeous specimen wouldn't survive five minutes in a club in Leeds, Manchester, Birmingham or Southampton.

With his usual easy charm, Richard chatted to the doorman, who cast a dubious look at Angela, but before he could say anything, she tapped him in the chest.

'I'm sure you wouldn't want it known that Richard Maddox's underage niece was in your club.'

'No, mademoiselle,' he said, the cool confidence crumbling under her earnest stare.

'Do you have sisters?'

'Yes, mademoiselle, two.'

'Exactly. So you understand how your mother would feel?'

'Yes, mademoiselle.' He stood up a little straighter, as if he'd stepped into the headmaster's office. 'Go right on in.'

Richard's face made Carrie smile as she stepped aside to let him go in front of her.

'Seems like you weren't required after all,' she said cheekily.

'Are you two coming in or not?' Angela, who'd vanished ahead of them through the door, popped back, bringing with her the sudden increase in volume of noise. 'We're going to have to split up to find her, it's heaving in there.'

As soon as Carrie stepped in, it was like dropping into the underworld. The hammering bass rolled over them, the constant pounding waves, reverberating hard enough to make the hairs on her arms lift and move, like sea anemones underwater.

The driving beat and neon lights disorientated her and

the constant movement of people, arms in the air, a many-headed medusa writhing in time, made the club seem alive and otherworldly. Carrie stopped, the beat pulsing in time with her heart, resisting the urge to let her hips move and join in.

Angela was off, wriggling through the dancers, uncaring of who she upset.

Richard beckoned to Carrie. 'I have a good idea where Fabio will be.'

'Why didn't you say so?'

'I'd rather extract Jade before her mother gets to her. She's going to be embarrassed enough that we've tracked her down here and I'd rather Angela didn't see the sort of activity that goes on.' He suddenly took a lot of interest in a passing waiter with a tray full of drinks.

'What?' asked Carrie her voice sharp.

'Coke, I would suspect.'

Carrie closed her eyes. Jade was a sensible girl most of the time but in this place, where everyone seemed so alive and happy, and hip and happening, normal rules to everyday life didn't appear to apply. The thrum of the bass called with an enticing siren beat, once again inviting her to dance.

Richard eased his way through the heaving bodies, a task made easier by his commanding presence and the fact that most people did a double take the minute he approached and automatically stepped out of his way. Carrie had to admit it was rather impressive as she trailed in his wake.

They climbed a set of neon-lit stairs leading to an upper-level balcony, where the music sounded marginally quieter. On this level a series of half-moon-shaped leather couches in dimly lit alcoves were occupied by a mass of writhing bodies. In other circumstances, Carrie might have been amused by the sight of the acres of flesh on display, the multitude of tanned slim legs and long lean arms, reminding her of some enormous exotic octopus.

She turned away from the sight of a couple half hidden in a booth moving in a very definite rhythm, understanding exactly why Richard didn't want Angela coming up here. The dilated eyes and wild expressions on some of the faces worried Carrie. Flushed and giddy, would these young girls even remember what they'd been up to the following morning? Nausea rose from her stomach as she saw a well-tanned older man in his sixties feeding a young woman champagne, tipping the bottle into her mouth, leaning forward to lick the liquid spilling down her front.

Richard grabbed her hand and pulled her along.

'I don't think I like it in here,' said Carrie.

'Exactly. Now you can see why I didn't want to bring Angela up here.'

They moved through the room and then Carrie spotted a flash of lilac through the bodies.

'There,' she prodded Richard hard and they fought their way through to the far side of the balcony.

Jade clutched a pillar with one hand, a silly grin on her face. Next to her, a distinctly unamused Fabio tried to coax her to one of the nearby benches.

'Come on, Jade. You wanted to come here.'

'I . . . want to . . . go . . .' She started to slide down the pillar and with a giggle, 'oops. That thing's moving. I . . . go home.'

'Stop being a tease. It's cost me a fortune—'

With one seamless move, Richard slid between the two of them and glared at Fabio.

'Man, what are you . . .' Recognition dawned in the slight

second before Richard's punch landed right on his mouth. Blood spurted and Fabio wiped at his split lip.

'What the fuck . . .?'

'The lady wants to go home, you sleaze-ball. Plus, the fact she's fifteen. Underage.'

'What?' He shot a horrified look at Jade, who smiled like a dopey bloodhound up at him.

'You're very handsome.'

Panic filled Fabio's eyes.

'Seriously, she's fifteen.'

'Seriously. Yes,' snarled Richard.

'Hey man,' Fabio rubbed his jaw. 'How the hell was I supposed to know that? What am I supposed to do, get ID?' He asked with a sneer.

Carrie had crossed to her side and put an arm around her to prop her up. Jade's head dropped, halted with a bounce and lifted, only to do the same again.

'Carrie?' she asked, at last managing to hold her head up, her words slurred. 'I've had so much fun but I wanna go home now. Can we go home?'

'Don't worry, we'll take you.' Carrie shot Fabio a filthy look. 'Whether she's underage or not, surely if your date gets this drunk, you'd look after her?'

He shrugged. 'It wasn't that much. A couple of glasses of fizz, bloody expensive too. You might as well take her, then.' With an arrogant tilt to his head, he surveyed the crowd on the dance floor below. 'Plenty more fish in the sea. Of age, who can handle their drink.'

Richard grabbed his shirt, hauling him upwards. 'You really are a piece of work.'

Fabio held Richard's gaze for a second before pulling his head back and twisting his neck to look away.

'Look, man, she came on to me. Wanted me to show her a good time. That's what I was doing until you guys showed up with your morality police gig.'

'You didn't think perhaps the responsible thing would be to take her home.'

'Oh for Christ's sake. She's a nobody. If she can't take the pace, she shouldn't have signed up to the gig in the first place.' He stuck his chest out, the implication clear. He was a somebody.

'Wrong, she's not a nobody,' hissed Richard, pulling Fabio's shirt tighter. 'She's a somebody. She's also my niece. But next time you pick up some poor girl, remember that they're someone, a daughter, a sister, a niece, with people who care, who might come looking for you.' Richard's voice trembled with menace. With a blur of movement, he lifted one knee. Fabio went down, clutching his balls, howling in pain.

'Let's get out of here.'

He scooped Jade up in his arms.

'Can walk.' She said, her eyes moving in opposite directions.

'I don't think so.'

'Lemme.'

'Jade, let me paint you a picture. There's a fistful of paparazzi out there. They wait every night for a shot they can sell. You've got two options, one a candid shot of you staggering out of a nightclub looking like every other drunk teenager, or a picture of you in the arms of a famous film star being taken out of a nightclub after feeling faint.'

Jade snapped her mouth shut with a begrudging glare.

*

Carrie wasn't sure whether it was Richard's chilling tone of voice when he mentioned the underage drinking or the clear indication that Jade was his niece, but the nightclub manager and his staff were remarkably efficient about providing a private area for them to wait until Richard's car arrived.

Reunited with her very grim mother, Jade remained subdued, keeping her eyes closed and sensibly avoiding any conversation.

The car arrived and Richard carried Jade out to it, a few lights popping and flashing as he handed her into the car. Angela got in next to her daughter.

'Do you want to go back with them?' asked Richard.

Angela's odd, fierce expression stalled her and Carrie hesitated.

'Y . . . I . . . er, no.'

Angela dipped her head in silent, regal approval and closed the door of the car.

Carrie watched as the car slid away, taking in a sharp in-drawn breath at Angela's very clear, back-off-leave-this-to-me, message.

'What do you want to do? Go back to the yacht?' He checked the time on his watch. 'The party won't wind up for another half hour.'

'No.' She stared at the red tail-lights of the car disappearing down the street, unsettled by the change in family dynamic. They'd always been a unit of three, but if felt like Angela had slammed the door on her and shut her out.

With a shiver, she turned to face Richard.

They exchanged a long message-laden look.

'Do you want to go back to my hotel?'

The simple, direct question deserved nothing but the truth, one that she couldn't deny any more.

She was done fighting. Done thinking about tomorrow or the day after that or the one after that.

Holding his gaze, she said, 'Yes.'

How she managed to appear outwardly calm, she didn't know, when inside a carnival erupted. Whistles, bells, dancing. Her whole body combusted into joyous celebration as if to say thank fuck for that, we thought you'd never see the light.

CHAPTER THIRTY

'Nightcap?' asked Richard as she gratefully slipped off her shoes, letting her poor feet sink into the rich cream carpet. 'Cointreau? Tia Maria?

'Cointreau would be nice, thank you,' she said, looking around at the suite. Of course he had a suite, with its own well-stocked bar and complementary fruit basket. Newspapers and books scattered the surface of the coffee table along with a half-finished crossword.

'July 5th? You're not doing very well,' she teased, picking up the crossword.

'I've been busy. Working. I don't get that much free time, you know.'

'How long have you been staying here?'

'Two months. Filming is due to finish here in the next week, if we get all the scenes done. Then I fly to LA.'

In September she'd be starting a new term. She quashed the thought; that was then, this was now. Until then she was going to live. She walked across to the full-length French window leading out onto a balcony. 'May I?'

'Go ahead. I'll bring your drink out.'

The balmy heat of the night air enveloped her as she stepped out to touch the cool stone of the balustrade of the roomy balcony. The hotel, an oasis of understated elegance after the brash, full-frontal attitude of the jet-set crowd at the harbour front, nestled into the side of the hill a little way out of the town surrounded by windswept cypresses on the cliff edge. The night reverberated with the grating buzz of the cicadas revving up in the short dry grasses in the landscaped grounds of the hotel.

Richard stepped out behind her, the ice chinking in the fine-cut crystal glass he offered her. She took a sip of the cold oily liquid, the alcohol hitting the back of her throat with a pleasant punch.

He stood next to her, his shoulder brushing her arm and together they leant against the balcony's balustrade overlooking the starlit view of the sea and the sky. The distant lights shimmered and danced, reflected in the ripples of water lapping the shoreline. 'Thank you for helping with Jade. Leaving your own party.'

'She's still family.'

With a shake of her head, Carrie said, 'That's not true. She's never been family. Not really. We weren't married long enough.'

'We're still married.'

'You know what I mean.'

'No, I don't. We got married. It might have been a register office, but we made vows. A commitment. To look after each other, to support each other and to love each other. I'm sure that extends to the people we love.' He turned her to face him. 'I still think of us as married. I . . . he paused. The sounds of the night around them intruded, as his words hung with loaded portent in the air. 'It nearly killed me when you asked for a divorce.'

She stiffened, watching the lights of a boat wink as it slid across the horizon. 'That's not how I remember it. You said the timing didn't suit you.'

Gently he turned her to face him, taking both her hands, his eyes searching her face. 'What the hell was I supposed to do?'

The quiet question rocked her with its sincerity, demanding honesty.

It took a moment to frame the words, drag them out from the crevices in which the truth had been hidden, but she couldn't completely lay herself bare.

'I-I couldn't do it any more.' She teased out the soft admission, flinching. 'I . . . missed you,' her voice faltered. 'So much. It hurt . . . so damn much.' A flare of anger tinged her words. 'I didn't want a divorce.' Her jaw clenched and she threw her head up, tossing her hair over her shoulder, 'But I had to do something.'

With defiant entreaty, she met his watchful eyes. 'A do or die last-chance attempt.' She let out a mirthless laugh. 'Except you called my bluff and suggested a separation.'

'Shit,' he let out a long slow breath and leaned his forehead against hers. 'And I lashed out.' Shaking his head, his thumb ran over her wrist. 'I thought you didn't care any more. That you wanted a divorce.' His chin lifted, revealing the strong column of his throat, tempting her to lay a kiss on his skin. 'When I said it would damage my career, it was hurt pride talking.' He winced and lifted her hand to his mouth, brushing his lips across the soft skin on the inside of her wrist in silent apology.

'I left the next morning, to go on location. Three months

in the desert filming. When I came back you wouldn't answer my calls.'

A twist of pain circled her heart. Three months. She remembered them well. 'I didn't know you were away. I thought . . . it was what you wanted.'

"Never, not then.' His voice dropped. 'And not now. I . . .

She closed her eyes, trying to shut out the emotion threatening to rise up and swamp her.

'. . . still love you, Carrie.'

Knowing that almost hurt more. It didn't help.

She reached up and traced his lips with her fingers, wanting to shush him, wind the clock back, wishing the words could be unsaid.

A spark flared between them and he dipped his mouth to hers. Together they sank into the kiss, a lazy exploration of each other's mouths, slow and languorous, heat flickering around the edges which began to build. His hand slid down her neck, touching bare skin, skirting the side of her breast, skimming around her waist, cupping her bottom and pulling her closer to him. The kiss deepened, urgency rising.

Carrie savoured each gentle foray, basking in the recognition of his touch. They'd kissed a thousand times before and the memories came flooding back, crashing wave after wave after wave. Goodbye kisses. Hello kisses. Sexy kisses. Horny kisses. Desperate, passionate, can't-get-enough-of-you kisses. Languorous all-the-time-in-the-world kisses.

In one hot flashing burst, which burned from the inside out, desire rushed, it's molten heat threatening to consume her. Pushed by driving need, to take and taste, she pulled his head down and kissed him hard, her body demanding to know his again. Without finesse she pushed down his jacket, pulling his shirt from his trousers and slid her hands up his warm back, pulling him into her.

He responded to her fire, nuzzling the underside of her chin with a groan, setting the sensitive skin of her throat alight with sensation. When his hand strayed to the top of her zip, toying with the nape of her neck, in teasing circles, her insides turned liquid. She hauled him closer, impatient and greedy.

The slow dance of seduction done, she wanted to dive right in and race towards to the finishing line. Whoever said good things come to those who wait, had been talking about a different sort of good thing. And she didn't want good, she wanted wild and wicked. She wanted him now.

Working her hands over his belt, she un-notched it, sliding her hands over his crotch, caressing him through the wool trousers and smiling with siren satisfaction at his sudden gasp.

He pulled back, a question in his eyes.

'I was trying,' he took in a ragged breath, 'to be gentlemanly about this.'

'Bugger that.' She opened his shirt buttons and smoothed her hands across his chest, toying with the flat nipples.

He pulled down her zip with a pleasing slash of movement that had her squirming against him, welcoming the thrust of his hands inside the dress, which dipped to cup her bottom. She sighed, letting the pent-up pressure hiss from her lungs, welcoming the touch of his cool hands massaging her bottom with firm, proprietary strokes, hauling up against his erection.

Yes,' she breathed, the single word a siren call of invitation. Almost limp with relief, she gave a whimper of pleasure when his mouth descended, taking her lips, kissing her as if he might never get enough of her.

Passion ignited. They moved urgently now, kissing and fighting with each other's clothes. Richard pressed her back through the French doors towards the bedroom on the other side of the suite. Still lip to lip they stumbled, she walking backwards, trying to wriggle out of her dress while pulling his shirt off.

Her calves hit the back of the bed and she tumbled back, taking Richard with her, both of them moving in sinuous rhythm, trying to get closer to each other.

Frantic and breathless, both of them hell-bent on driving to the end, their love making took on a fast and furious pace, desperate rather than tender, as if they'd wasted too much time and needed to know each other again, now, this minute.

When Richard collapsed on top of her, with a drawn-out groan, she could barely think straight, conscious of her own keening cries. Pure sensation leaving her mind hazy and her body limp and boneless.

Afterwards, they stirred against each other and with her heart-rate still pumping hard, she shifted to lay back her arm across her eyes, trying to catch her breath. Next to her Richard panted, one arm tucked under her waist.

'Wow, I think you might have killed me.'

The moment turned light as if they'd burned through the weighted emotion that had erupted between them.

'Damn, does that mean that's it for tonight? You're not the man you used to be. I was hoping you might come back for round two.'

Being with Richard like this brought back feelings, the element of fun and inhibition, that had been tightly sealed away. A lock had been popped open and there she was, that abandoned twenty-year-old again. Confident, sure of her sexuality and not afraid to take every last bite of pleasure and passion. When had she lost that?

Richard propped his head on his elbow and twisted to lean down and look at her.

'Not the man I used to be. Is that a challenge, Mrs Maddox?'

She gave him a cat-like grin and stretched, pushing her breasts upwards towards him, fondling one with slow, supremely female, invitation. 'Too right it is.'

He skimmed a hand down her sternum, sliding past her waist to part her legs.

'Are you feeling neglected?'

'Not neglected,' she gave him an arch look. 'Just nicely revved. Ready for the main course.'

When had sex last been this suggestive, this joyous and about her having a good time?

'I think you needed a little intercourse digestive.'

He kissed his way from the vee of her chest with slow deliberation, his chin scratching her skin, teasing the tender skin. His tongue circled her belly button and she squirmed, instinctively starting to close her legs.

'Oh no, you don't.' He slid down between them, pushing them further apart with both hands before lifting her hips. Wicked promise danced in his eyes.

She took in a strangled breath and stared back, panting slightly now, her body burning for that intimate touch. He grinned and dipped his head, his tongue flicking with sure, firm strokes, over and over, making her clutch the bed sheets, whimpering in desperate need.

When he stopped she groaned a guttural, incoherent plea, her hips lifting and writhing with sheer want, until he surged up the length of her body and thankfully sank home.

This time, they made love with languorous indolence, a slow exploration of each other's bodies, kissing and nipping, stroking and teasing as they revisited old trails, unearthing secret paths, remembering that he was sensitive just there and that she liked to be touched right here. They explored each other, contour by contour, familiar and yet unfamiliar, satisfying and exciting, like coming home but to a home you'd forgotten how much you'd missed.

It made her want to cry when she realised how much she'd held back in recent years. How much of herself she'd subsumed. Had she done Alan a disservice by doing that or was it because of him? And what the hell was she doing thinking about him when she was in bed with Richard? She closed her eyes and shut him out.

When they sank into each other for a second time, their fevered cries swallowed by kisses, she held him close, skin to skin, as he stroked her hair. Heart to heart, the rapid beats in tandem, she closed her eyes and wished she could wrap up the moment, binding it in place for ever. Richard's eyes were already drifting shut but when she started to edge away, he tightened his hold on her.

'Please don't go. Stay,' he muttered, pulling back into his arms.

'I should go. I ought to get back.' The earlier events of the evening intruded with unwelcome persistence. Angela and Jade might need her.

He blinked at her, but understanding sharpened the planes of his face.

'They'll be asleep by now, won't they? I have to be on set at six. I can arrange a car to take you home at the same time.'

He kissed the top of her head and pulled her to his side. 'Sleep now.'

To her amazement, he dropped off almost immediately and she lay there smiling in the dark, listening to his deep, even breathing. Although tired, euphoria danced through her as if she'd conquered a mountain and reached a major landmark. For so many years, she'd blamed him for leaving her behind, allowing bitter regret to burrow its way in. Accepting that she'd been at fault didn't make the past any easier but it released a burden that had held her down, freeing her to make the absolute most of this brief interlude. Excitement fizzed through her. A summer holiday romance bursting with possibilities with someone who knew the real her and could let her be Carrie again.

CHAPTER THIRTY-ONE

She ought to turn over and ask Angela to put some more sun cream on her back, before she dozed off in the sun and deep-fried her skin. Lifting her head, she looked around and both Jade and Angela were in the pool, each of them splashing about by themselves, barely talking to each other. With a groan she dropped her head back down. A sloth monster had taken over her body, leaving her too lethargic and heavy-limbed to do anything, while her mind had taken over at a thousand miles an hour, determined to relive and savour every last damn minute of the night with Richard, leaving parts of her tingling with remembered sensation.

Angela padded up to the sunbed beside her, dripping water and leaving a trail of fast-drying footprints that winked out a step later.

'What time did you get back?'

Carrie shrugged. 'Not sure?' It could have been 7.05, 7.06 or 7.07.

She'd slunk in sometime after seven and might have attempted to pretend otherwise to Angela, except she'd crossed paths with Phil as she arrived and he left. With sheepish smiles, they'd nodded and, without a word, scurried off in opposite directions.

No doubt Phil would spill the beans at some point but she had ammunition of her own.

'So, is Jade okay?'

'She's fine.' Angela perched on the edge of the sun lounger. 'Although I think she's got one heck of a hangover. Or at least I hope she does.' Angela winced and touched her own temples as she reached for one of her flesh-coloured splints, fastening the velcro straps around her wrist. 'But she's learned a good lesson. Fabio refusing to bring her home when she'd had too much to drink was a real wake- up call. It's the first time, in her nice sheltered life, she's been in that sort of situation, where things are completely out of her control.'

'And I hope the last for a while. Despite the pretty face, Fabio's a pretty selfish excuse for a man.'

'She was very lucky.' Angela closed her eyes, shaking her head. 'Fifteen is far too young to go to a place like that. I saw some of the goings-on.' Her mouth firmed as she lifted her head. 'No harm done.' Angela let out a wry laugh. 'She might even understand now that I'm not always the killjoy she thinks I am.'

'She doesn't think that,' said Carrie, sitting up and leaning over to kiss her sister on the cheek. 'She loves you very much, like I do.'

'Thanks,' Angela held out a hand and Carrie took it, rubbing the swollen knuckles, aware that her sister's rare recourse to wearing her splints signified she was in some pain today.

'We had quite a few tears when we got in. She sobered up rather quickly and then slept in my bed last night.' Angela rubbed at the strapping on her wrist, the lines around her mouth deepening. 'She hasn't done that since she was a little girl.

'And then this morning she apologised and promised she'd never do anything else like that again. Apparently, from now on, she'll always listen to me and do as she's told the first time.'

'Yeah, right.' Carrie raised her eyebrows. 'And what did you say to that?'

Angela grinned, 'That she's still grounded for the rest of her life.'

'Fair enough,' said Carrie with a gentle laugh, glad to hear that mother and daughter were still okay.

'Although I'm not sure what I'll do if the picture of Richard carrying her out of the nightclub surfaces. There'll be a couple of mothers on Facebook commenting, I can bet. The usual it-must-be-hard-being-a-single-parent, saccharine-sweet digs.'

'You'll get over that. Besides, it will give them something to be jealous about, they haven't met Richard Maddox in person.'

'It's not that, more the fact that any picture is there forever. And then it's shared on Twitter, Instagram, Snapchat. Jade could be notorious by the time she goes back to school.'

Carrie frowned. Damn, her sister had a point. Gossip went viral in a matter of seconds on social media. Look how Jade found the picture on YouTube of Richard's bottom.

'I guess you're right. It's the times we live in. But we'll cross that bridge if and when we come to it. Let's hope the paparazzi will have bigger and better stories to sell.'

*

They'd settled down for lunch when the buzzer at the door announced the arrival of a visitor at the gate. Carrie shifted in her seat, an electric tingle of anticipation firing at the thought it might be Richard. Had he finished work early? Even as she half-rose from her chair, Jade had already jumped up. 'I'll go. I'll go.'

'I don't know who she thinks it's going to be,' said Angela, cutting another slice of bread. 'This turned out quite well, but it isn't quite French bread yet.'

'Tastes good enough to me.'

Angela was determined, with Marisa's help, to master making French baguettes before she left.

Carrie took another slice and loaded it up with the creamy goat's cheese local to the area.

'Hello my favourite ladies.'

She took a sharp, indrawn breath. A piece of bread lodged itself in her windpipe.

'A-A-A-lan,' she wheezed, the crust catching, razor-sharp as she tried to choose between breathing or choking.

Angela poured a glass of water, so hastily that it overfilled and splashed all over the table.

Spluttering and gasping, it took Carrie a good few seconds to stop coughing.

Alan dumped his cycle helmet on the table and crouched beside, her rubbing her back, looking extremely red-faced and with his sandy hair plastered to his head. 'It's okay. Breathe.'

Eventually she managed to bring the crumb up and swallowed down the glass of water.

Her face had turned bright pink and her chest felt rather tight.

'I wanted to surprise you but not quite like this,' he said with a perturbed frown. 'Are you okay?'

'F-fine. W-went down the wrong way.'

'Better now?'

'Yes, thanks. When did you get . . . I mean how did you get here?'

He beamed and pulled out a chair.

'Sorry, Alan, can I get you a drink or anything?' Angela jumped up.

'Anything long, cold and soft. Those hills are thirsty work.'

'You didn't cycle here?' asked Carrie in horror.

'I did.' He beamed. 'I got a train to Nice from Geneva. Put my bike on in Switzerland. Stayed in Nice last night. Left at seven this morning. Gorgeous trip. I thought I'd surprise you.'

'You've done that.' Carrie felt faint. 'How long did that take?

'Five hours' cycling but I took plenty of breaks. I wasn't sure how tough the going would be, which is why I didn't call. But it took less time than I thought. I decided to crack on until I got here. I must say, it's worth that cycle up hill. This a fabulous spot. You've certainly fallen on your feet here.'

He stood up and walked to the edge of the terrace, his hand shading his face as he took in the view. 'Very nice indeed.'

'It is. We've been very lucky.' How did it happen that she had nothing to say to him? Every word stuck in her throat.

'And look at you. Sun maiden. All tanned and golden.' He came forward, clasping her forearms, his eyes roving across her face, as if checking everything was still in place. 'Wow,' he took a surprised step back. 'You look amazing. So different. Is it your hair? I swear its grown, or maybe I'm not used to seeing it messy like this.' He gathered up a handful and pushed it over her shoulder. 'Must be a pain in this heat.'

'Thanks,' she cleared her throat and self-consciously touched her hair.

He leaned in to kiss her on the mouth and she closed her eyes, framing her lips to kiss him back with a sense of dread. Would he know? Could he tell that her kisses were different now? To her relief, he contented himself with a brief peck, although his eyes twinkled suggestively as he whispered. 'Time enough for that later.'

Her heart sank.

Angela bustled back, bringing him a long, tall glass of her home-made lemonade, which had become her holiday speciality.

'Come out on the patio, the view's wonderful.'

'It looks as if you've struck gold here. It's a fabulous villa. Plenty of space. And great cycling around here.'

'It is a beautiful villa,' agreed Angela, her eyes nervous and worried.

'Fuck me, Auntie Carrie, you should see . . .' Jade came running out of the house. Her mouth closed with a horrified snap when she saw Alan.

'Jade! Language.' Angela's eyes flashed fury. 'You're in enough trouble as it is, after your behaviour last night.'

Jade winced and tucked the phone she'd been waving behind her back, throwing Carrie one last mutinous, signal-laden look.

'What have you been doing? Getting drunk with the local teenage boys?' joked Alan, oblivious to the strained atmosphere almost vibrating between the three women. 'When in France . . . and all that. Were you very sick? Kiss a few boys?'

'Something like that,' said Angela, her face and neck taut with suppressed tension. 'In fact, Jade, why don't we go and have a little chat? Leave Carrie and Alan to spend some time together.'

Jade flounced off, Angela taking grim steps in her wake.

'Oh dear, have I walked in on a row? I suppose when we're married, I'll have to get involved. I'm not sure I want to be head of the family and the disciplinarian.'

Carrie could just imagine Jade's reaction to that. 'I doubt you'll have to. It's not as if they'd be living with you, at yours, ours, I mean.'

'We need to sort out our living arrangements sooner rather than later.' Alan laughed. 'You're getting very confused.'

He didn't know the half of it. Her brain had gone into complete melt-down and all she could think about was the way she smelled.

Could he smell sex on her? The bizarre thought wouldn't leave her alone. Could she go and discreetly shower again? She felt like an illicit smoker worrying about getting rid of the scent of nicotine and tar. Shame you couldn't scrub away a guilty conscience with soap and shampoo.

She shot a slightly resentful look towards Alan. If only he'd given her notice that he was on his way.

Then she pulled herself up short. Would it have made any difference?

'Do you mind if I go and freshen up? Unpack my things?'

'Of course not . . . I'll show you . . . the . . . my room.'

'I'll see you outside. There are towels and things in the en-suite.

She left him to it, almost running out of the room when he stripped off his black lycra cycling shorts.

Jade lurked down the corridor waiting for her, Angela in her shadow.

'Carrie,' she hissed. 'You've got to see this.' She held up her phone, wide-eyed with drama and mystery.

'What's wrong?' Carrie snapped. Jade's behaviour last night had left her on the stickiest wicket imaginable and her patience with her niece had all but evaporated.

'You're going viral.' Jade showed her the screen. 'I was trying to tell you earlier, except Captain Goody Two Shoes rocked up.'

'Don't be rude, Jade,' said Angela.

'Mum, her lame fiancé is the least of her problems. Look.'

Jade thrust out her phone. A picture of Carrie and Richard on the beach, completely naked, took up the whole of the screen.

The colour leeched out of Carrie's face. She could almost feel each blood cell being evacuated. Light-headed for a second, she grabbed the console table and tried to steady herself.

'Where . . . when . . .? Shit!' Carrie sank to the floor, her wobbly legs giving up the ghost, welcoming the cold slap of the white tiles on her bare legs.

'Where did you find this?'

'Where didn't I? It's on *Snackbitch Bites*, *Hub Bub*. You name it, every celebrity gossip website going.'

'Who can see it?'

'You're kidding. It's a question of who can't. Everyone's asking who you are.'

'Oh God.' She peered at the picture, dropping the phone into her lap. Absolutely nothing left to the imagination.

She sank her head into her hands and pulled up her knees. 'I don't believe it. I wonder how many people have seen this.'

Jade winced and sat down next to her aunt, putting her arm around Carrie's shoulders. 'This is from the *Mirror's* website.'

'Shit.'

Jade took the phone back. 'And on this one, and this one.'

'Well, at least it's not in the paper itself,' said Angela. 'At least, I hope not.'

'Great. That's not that much of a consolation,' Carrie snapped. Seriously? Angela couldn't honestly believe that less people surfed the internet than read a national newspaper.

She rubbed at her forehead as if it might ease the tension building there. This couldn't be happening.

'I wonder if Richard knows about this. I'd have thought he would have tex . . . oh shit I left my phone in . . .' She clamped her lips shut. Her phone currently lay on Richard's bedside table.

'*Hello*! He'll be well used to it,' Jade pointed out.

'He might be but I'm not. Oh God, what's Alan going to say?'

'He might not see it,' said Angela. She snatched the phone from Jade and switched the screen off with a reproving glare at both of them. 'In fact, it's highly unlikely.'

She took Carrie by the arm and led her towards the kitchen, her voice calm and level.

'Think about it. Alan isn't interested in those gossip and news sites and, no disrespect, but out of context, no one would know it's you. You look quite different. Jade's spotted it because the picture's of Richard and we know you were with him. If anyone else even noticed a resemblance they'd never imagine you know him.'

Carrie exhaled, the light-headed sensation receding. 'You're right.'

Her shoulders sagged and she gave her sister a hug. 'Of course you're right. And Richard's not going to tell anyone.'

She motioned Jade over. 'Is there a caption or anything? Does it say where it was taken?'

'Richard Maddox gets in the all-together with mystery brunette,' read out Jade. 'Richard, star of *Conspiracy of Men* and *An Unsuitable Man*, was spotted taking time out from his latest movie project, *Turn on the Stars* with a mystery beauty. The couple made the most of their secret beach hideaway and took to the sea in a cheeky skinny dip.'

'Phew. You're right, Angela. No one at home is going to have a clue it's me.' With a pathetic attempt at a smile, she added, 'Especially not if they're describing me as a "mystery beauty".'

Alan emerged looking clean and polished. 'That's a fantastic shower. Exactly what the doctor ordered. This place is fantastic. Do you mind if I have a look around?'

'No.' Carrie sat up. 'Did you want me to show you around?'

He laughed. 'No, I wouldn't want to disturb your sunbathing. It's too hot for me. I'll have a nose around, get myself acclimatised before I sit in that nice shady spot on the terrace with the paper.'

'Are you sure?' she asked. 'I should be a better hostess. Can I get you a drink or anything? There's heaps of food in the fridge. Soft and alcoholic drinks. We've been spoiled. Marisa the maid pops in nearly every day to check we've got everything we need and stocks up, even though there's plenty of food. Angela is in her element.' She frowned. 'I'll come with you.'

He dropped a kiss on her forehead.

'You stay put. I'm a big boy now. I'm not used to sitting still for too long.'

'I've been reading next term's texts,' said Carrie, crossing her fingers on one hand tucked behind her waist. One play counted, didn't it?

'Well that's very productive,' said Alan, tousling her hair.

Carrie held herself rigid. Why now, all of a sudden, did that familiar gesture feel patronising, as if he were patting her on the head like a dog? She had to get herself out of this rather resentful mindset. It wasn't his fault that his timing sucked or that she had no idea what to do.

She lay back on the sun lounger, trying to get comfortable. Her leg ached when she put it that way. Something dug in her back. Her arms felt too heavy laid by her side and then her shoulders itched on the chair. Sweat trickled down her cleavage and she swiped it away, her fingers fidgety and twitchy.

She turned again, sweaty limbs sticking to the towel. Now the sun's rays were too hot on her skin and her head throbbed as if it might explode at any second. Thoughts careered through her head, jostling for attention like voices in a crowd shouting to be heard, each one louder than the last.

She was furious with Alan for turning up and spoiling her lovely daydreams of last night with Richard and even more furious with herself for wanting to lie here, reliving every touch, kiss and peak of desire from last night.

Alan was a genuine, decent, kind man. She gnawed the knuckle on her index finger, biting down hard, welcoming the pain. She deserved it. Only a complete cow would be unfaithful to a man like him. She should feel guilty. Horribly, horribly guilty. Not keep going back to that warm glow inside her, worrying at it like a wobbly tooth. Alan was here. He loved her. Why, then, did her brain persist in replaying Richard's feather-light touch as he traced the outline of her collarbone, the weight of him when he collapsed on top of her or the sheer joy of falling asleep in his arms?

An insect buzzed close to her ear. Jade and Angela talked as they paddled in the pool and she could hear the paper rattle as Alan sat in the shade under the veranda by the kitchen. Should she go for a swim? Maybe a walk? Her legs, restless and agitated, moved again and she stretched her feet, wanting to kick at the bed.

Pages rustled, a shake and a slap of paper and then swift footsteps in sandals, flap, flap-flapping towards her. A shadow crossed her face and she blinked open her eyes to find Alan standing over her, a newspaper in his hand, which he kept slapping against the other hand.

Grim lines tautened his mouth, tiny fissures fanning out like cracks in stone.

'Carrie. Please tell me this isn't you!' The plea in his voice hit her hard as he held out the paper folded in half.

She took it and winced. In print, even with the little black strategic boxes positioned to create a semblance of modesty, the picture looked a whole lot worse – the way her head lifted towards Richard, a come-hither smile playing at her mouth. The image of them looking carefree and happy in each other's company, suggested much more beneath the surface. It was a picture-perfect snapshot of romance.

'Carrie?' In that single word she heard the entreaty in his voice, begging her to deny it.

She shot up into a sitting position, her agitated body grateful at last for some activity. With a sigh, she sought to frame the words. Alan frowned, the creases in his forehead working hard, as if struggling to find a logical explanation that would refute the damning picture.

'We need to talk.' She grabbed her wrap, needing to cover up.

'Talk?' Alan paled. Shock skittering in his eyes. 'Are you saying this picture is . . . real? That it is you?'

She led him around the end of the house to the little balcony with the rattan furniture, where she'd first talked to Richard. It had turned into her personal emotional battleground.

Perching on the very edge of one of the seats, she laid the paper down on the rattan table and clasped her hands. Alan sat opposite, spine straight, rubbing his knee with one hand.

'It's not what it seems.' No matter how she phrased the words, they'd sound like a cliché.

'What, that's not you? You're not naked on a beach. And that's not Richard Maddox.' His voice had a touch of acid now.

It was far more preferable to the wounded tone earlier. Convenient too. It loosened the noose of guilt if you were under fire.

'It is me. Yes.' She swallowed and rubbed her cheeks, trying to pick the right words.

'So talk me through it. How the hell did you meet him? And end up on a beach with him with no clothes on. Did you sleep with him?'

She closed her eyes, weighing up the truth.

'I didn't sleep with him, then. Believe it or not, those pictures are innocent.' Not that she could claim innocence, far from it but she didn't want him judging her on a lie. The truth was bad enough. 'People go on nudist beaches. It's not a crime to be naked. It doesn't automatically mean you have sex.'

'Was it a nudist beach?'

'I don't know. It might have been. It was private.'

'I'm not sure that's any better. What were you doing there with him?'

She closed her eyes and sucked on her lip.

'I knew Richard at drama school.' She took a breath. 'I should have told you before.'

'That you knew him? Why?'

She took in another deep breath. 'Because . . . I didn't just know him. We lived together. We were married.'

'Married!' Alan screeched the word. 'For how long?'

She traced the rattan pattern to the left of her knee. 'It's sort of complicated.'

Alan frowned, confusion filling his eyes. 'You were either married or not married. How can that be complicated?'

'We're . . . still married,' she said slowly, before adding in a rush of words. 'But in name only. We never got around to doing the paperwork bit. When I came out here, it was a way of tracking him down to ask him for divorce. I haven't seen him for eight years.'

'Eight years? Why are you still married? That doesn't make sense. And why didn't you tell me you were already married?'

'It sounds daft but I kind of put it out of my head. It didn't impact on anything. I put off doing anything about it. Until . . .'

'I proposed,' said Alan dully.

'Yes. I should have told you then but Richard was a dim-and-distant memory. It didn't have anything to do with us.'

'Nothing to do with us. You're married to a major star, a huge celebrity and you weren't going to tell me! Don't you think I deserved to know? I think that's rather patronising, don't you? Deciding what you would and wouldn't tell me. I guess it's too much of a come-down. A school teacher.' His lips curled with bitterness.

'I knew you'd be all funny about it.'

'Funny? What about you already having a husband? Well, there's a thing.'

'No, funny about him being who he is.'

'Hardly surprising. He's some 'A'-list wanker and I'm a nobody school teacher.'

'He's not a wanker. I admit he's very successful, but it's not a competition. You're two very different people.'

'Just as well. So this picture is the cosy 'let's get divorced chat' is it? Is that how celebrities handle these things these days. Obviously I wouldn't know.'

'I met up with him to discuss the divorce. He . . . he was being, well he wanted us to . . . he said he would speed things up, if I agreed to spend some time with him, so that we could part as friends. We went to the beach and he . . . dared me.' That sounded lame.

Alan rolled his eyes. 'Pardon?'

'Look. Nothing happened.' Honesty forced her to add. 'Not then.'

'You expect me to believe that?'

Sweat trickled down her back and she bunched her hands under her legs.

'No,' she said with aching sadness. He didn't deserve this. 'I don't and I don't expect you to forgive me either. I'm sorry. I should have told you that I was already married. I thought I could get the divorce sorted and you would never have to know.'

Panic stirred in Alan's face.

'It's not that I don't forgive you. It's . . . You do realise the seriousness of the situation. If people see this picture, you could lose your job. I could lose my job by association. The school's policies, Code of Conduct, Disqualification by Association.' His face crumpled. 'The last thing I want to do is lose you . . . but this could have dire consequences.'

He reached over the table and laid a hand on her knee. 'You know I love you. This has been a shock. I don't want to lose you.'

Sorrow filled Carrie's face. 'Alan, didn't you hear me? I didn't sleep with him that day on the beach but,' her leg jigged, she had to tell him, 'I . . . I . . . we have slept together.'

'I see.' Alan stared beyond her, his face a blank mask.

CHAPTER THIRTY-TWO

It would have been insulting to say she was sorry or to try and make excuses. She had none. They sat in silence for a few minutes, until Alan said. 'I think I'll go for a cycle ride.'

'Are you sure that's a good idea?'

'I think it's an excellent fucking idea,' snarled Alan with such venom that she sat back, 'especially when my fucking fiancée has been shagging someone else.'

She couldn't blame him. With a heavy heart she watched as he strode, radiating 'don't talk to me' vibes across the patio, skirting the pool and went back into the house. A few seconds later a crash reverberated through the building, sound bouncing off the water as he slammed the front door.

Angela brought her a cup of tea, popping it on the table and turning to leave before asking, 'You okay?'

Carrie half-laughed. 'I love you, Ang. Only you could bring a cup of tea and unobtrusively say, without a big drama, I'm here if you want me but I can bugger off if you don't.'

'I love you too. And if you want to be left alone, that's fine.'

'I've made such a muck of things.' She reached for the tea, needing the comfort of the hot cup despite the blazing sunshine. 'I've upset Alan. He's the nicest man I know and I've . . . made a mess.'

'Have you told him about Richard?'

Carrie screwed up her face.

'I told him we were married.' She faced Angela. 'I also told him that I slept with Richard.'

'You did. I mean you told Alan that. I . . . er . . . I didn't know you had. Not that it's anything to do with me.'

The brilliant thing about Angela was that even when she was dying to know, she refrained from asking.

'I went back to his hotel room last night.'

'I thought you were evasive about what time you got home.'

Carrie looked up at her. 'Partly because I crossed paths with Phil.'

'Oh.' Angela studied the floor with great interest. 'I guess I can't talk.'

'You're not engaged to anyone else.'

'True, but you are married to Richard.'

'I don't think on moral grounds, in this situation, that's going to cut it. I let Alan down. Badly. He didn't deserve that.'

'Does he know, that you . . . you know, slept with Richard?'

'Yes, I couldn't not tell him.'

'Is he very cross?'

'That would be far easier. If he were nasty and angry, I could be nasty back and we could have a huge shouty row and promise never to darken each other's doors.' She thought of the defeated hunch of his shoulders as he'd left.

'I've disappointed him and made him sad, which makes it a thousand times worse. I'm the villain and I can't escape from that, even though I never meant to hurt him.'

'What's going to happen?' asked Angela.

Carrie pushed her hands through her hair, tugged at the tangles, welcoming the pinching pain on her scalp. 'I get what I deserve.'

Angela rolled her eyes. 'What that's supposed to mean?'

'I've messed up things with Alan. Even if he wanted to, I can't marry him now.'

Angela's intense speculative stare made Carrie turn her head.

'Why not?'

'Because it's always going to be Richard for me.' Saying it out loud made her stomach flutter. 'I never stopped loving him. I tried so hard to pretend that I didn't. Some days I almost convinced myself, but it's like there's a constant dull pain always there hovering, on the edge of your consciousness.' She laughed, with a sour twist to her lips. 'Some days you think it's gone and then, bam, it's back, lurking again.'

Angela frowned and Carrie loved her for pretending she understood what the hell she meant.

'And what about him?'

Carrie wrapped her hair around her hand and wrist, letting it coil like a helter-skelter round and round. 'There's no future for us.'

'That's not answering the question.'

Carrie glared at her horribly perceptive sister. 'He says he loves me but . . . this is a holiday romance. We have our own lives now. And do you know what the worst thing is?'

Although the question didn't require an answer, Angela gave a dutiful shake of her head.

'It's my own fault. I let him go. And now it's too late.'

'Are you sure?' Angela asked, sympathy lining her face. 'Have you talked about it?'

'There's no point. He has his career. He'll be back in LA at the end of the month.'

'There are planes.'

'Yeah, and how long's that going to work for? Our lives are too different. I've got responsibilities. A job. I can't up and take off for a transatlantic weekend. And he's in big demand. He's at the peak of his career. You know what acting's like. You can't afford to turn any opportunity down. Besides being a married man wouldn't do. He needs to be the young, handsome bachelor. You can't spoil that illusion for fans.'

'I guess not,' Angela sighed. 'You're right. What a mess.'

'What's a mess?'

Carrie stiffened as Jade plonked herself down on the arm of the chair.

'Jade.' Her mother gave her a warning frown.

'If it's about the picture. I mean it's a bit bleurgh that you're naked.' She pulled a face. 'But, seriously, who's going to care? Chill Auntie Carrie. Everyone will be too busy wondering how you got to be on a private beach with Richard yum bum Maddox.'

'Thanks,' Carrie laughed. You had to hand it to her, she had a point. 'I have to hope no one at work realises it's me.'

'Yeah! Imagine. Your teacher naked. That is gross.'

'I didn't mean that. I could get the sack for improper conduct.'

'How? What's improper? He's your husband.'

'Yes, but they don't know that. If they realised it's me, I could lose my job and so could Alan.'

'Why? What's it got to do with him? He wasn't there, was he?'

'No, it wouldn't look good that he was associating with someone like me. Unfortunately, schools have heaps of policies about that sort of thing.'

'Sounds a load of crap to me. You can't tell me it's illegal or anything. You were in private with your husband. End of.' Jade bounced up. 'I'm off to get a drink. Want one?'

'No thanks,' said Carrie, tempting as it was to knock back a couple of stiff vodkas.

'Okey doke. But hey,' Jade bent and kissed her cheek, 'chill. It will be fine. He's your husband. That makes it okay. I promise.'

She jumped up, plugging in her earphones and dancing across the patio to a beat they couldn't hear.

'Bless her. She's a good kid, really.' Carrie smiled.

'Hmm, she's still on her best behaviour at the moment. It won't last long.'

When the buzzer sounded at the gate, Carrie, who'd been listening out for it with half an ear for the last two hours, jumped up. Alan had been gone for four hours.

'Livraison pour Madame Maddox,' intoned a voice. Carrie's heart sank back down with a resounding thud. Where was he? What if he'd had an accident?

A funny little Citroen van careered down the hill, pulling up outside the front door with a splash of gravel and an elderly man, who may have well cut his teeth on driving tanks in the First World War, sprang out of the car brandishing a huge bouquet of flowers.

'Madame Maddox?'

'Yes.'

'Voila!'

He bowed and presented her with the flowers and then, leaving her feeling slightly Alice-like on the steps, he jumped back in the van, revved the feeble engine, which sounded like an angry sewing machine, and hurtled back up the road.

Mauves, purples and pale pinks made up the arrangement, the scent of roses most noticeable. Nestled in the very centre of the display sat her phone along with a little white envelope.

'Sorry I can't be with you. Filming for next few days, but you might need this. Rx'

She left the flowers in the kitchen, clutching the phone to her as she slipped into the laundry room, not wanting to be disturbed. With the thrill of opening a love letter, she scrolled through the text messages he'd been sending her.

Morning. In case you forgot, I love you.

She touched the screen as if she could absorb the words through her fingertips.

Hey sleepyhead, spare a thought for some of us working hard. Missing you. Love Richard x.

With a smile and a lurch of her heart, she thought of him falling asleep, his hair tousled, his skin dark against the crisp white linen hotel bedsheets.

Had he been imagining her still in his bed?

There was a gap of a few hours before the next text.

'Thought we were never going to finish today. We're filming in Ramatuelle late morning. Would you like to meet there? Around 3pm? Café Berenice, Place du Marche.'

She clutched the phone to her chest. Damn. Had he waited for her? Had he wondered where she was? What had he thought?

There were a couple of missed calls in between the texts.

Hope everything is OK. Text me back to let me know you got home OK.

She winced. Damn, she wanted to speak to him. Hear his voice. How was it that she could miss him this much after one night?

I'd asked Phil to call in to check you got home safely. He says he saw you. Any reason you're ignoring my texts?

She clenched her fingers tight in a ball, cursing her stupidity in leaving the phone. 'Duh! Now I feel a muppet. Found your phone. Got a night shoot and all day tomorrow. Hectic schedule. Love Rx'

With a dreamy smile she clutched the phone to her chest, her head full of images of him and she pored over them like a miser counting pennies before tapping in a quick message.

Speak soon. Love Cx

As soon as she pressed send she realised she'd forgotten to say thank you for the flowers.

Thanks for the flowers too. Cx.

For a minute she ummed and ahhed as to whether to mention the picture.

No. Why spoil this lovely slushy puddle of warmth?

It would tide her over, like a secret balm, while she sorted out the fall-out with Alan.

Talking of whom, where was he? Had he cycled back to England?

CHAPTER THIRTY-THREE

'I really, really love you, you know,' slurred Alan, flopping forward, almost falling out of the car as Carrie tried to help him out of the little Clio. It was like to trying to make a puppet stand up when all the strings had been cut.

She hauled him upright, propping him up using her shoulder, and led him to the front door.

'Carrieeee,' he sang stopping and draping both arms around her and almost head-butting her as he attempted to nuzzle into her neck, leaving a wet trail across her ear. 'Donchoo love meeee? Tha's a song you know. Donchoo love me baby. Donchoo love me oooooh. Donchoo. Donchoo.'

'Shh. You'll wake the neighbours,' hissed Carrie, despite the fact that the nearest neighbours were the cicadas chirruping in the grounds, flinching as a waft of beery breath hit her full in the face.

'Sssorry,' said Alan, his head nodding and drooping. 'Shh. The neighbours.' He put his fingers to his lips. 'Shh.'

Disentangling himself from her, he began an exaggerated

tip toe towards the front door, waving one finger, whispering. 'Don't wake the neighbours.'

It took some manhandling, but she managed to get him up the steps to the front door.

'Hellooo Angela,' shouted Alan as her sister opened the door, holding it wide to allow Carrie to guide in the wildly flailing man.

'Alan,' she said in a faint voice, taking in his paralytic state with a horrified glance at Carrie.

'Found this bloody marvellous bar. The owner only bloody did the Tour. Wore the Maillot Ja-Ja . . . the yellow one. Fanshy a nightcap?'

With a stagger he tripped over the threshold, wheeled about for a minute looking like a bowled tenpin tottering on the edge of collapse, arms waving trying to balance, before he catapulted into the console table, knocking over the flowers, which Angela managed to catch, surprising herself, with the finesse of rugby player receiving the ball.

'I think you've had more than enough. Black coffee, perhaps?'

'Coffee, schmoffee. Let's party. I can party.' He narrowed his eyes at Carrie. 'I can party like any old film star. We can go dancing. Let's go dancing. You want to go dancing?'

'No, I don't, thank you.'

'You'd go dancing with *him*, though, wouldn't you? Dancing, schmancing with Mr Movie Star.'

'It's time for bed.'

'I need a wazz.' Alan started to unzip his trousers.

'In there.' Carrie shoved him towards the downstairs cloakroom and shut the door.

Angela sniggered and then clapped her hand over her

mouth. 'Sorry I shouldn't laugh but . . . I've never seen anyone in such a state.'

'Tell me about it. It took three burly Frenchman from the bar to get him into the car. He wanted to stay.'

'Has he been there all afternoon?'

'No, he was at another bar earlier and got to this one about eight.' Carrie had finally received a call on her mobile from the owner of a bar in Gassin at half-past midnight, asking her to come and collect Alan.

'Where's his bike?'

'Chained up outside the first bar.'

'Ouch. He's going to have a stinker of a hangover in the morning.'

'Serves him right,' said Carrie with feeling, and then winced at her own callousness. She'd caused this and it didn't serve him right. She hadn't served him well at all.

'Do you think he's alright in there? It's gone very quiet.'

'Although it's tempting to leave him in there, in case he throws up, we ought to get him into bed.'

'Do you want me to help you to put him to bed?'

'Yes please,' said Carrie, praying Angela's presence might dampen his ardour.

'Where do you want to put him?'

'He can go in my room and I'll sleep in one of the other rooms.'

'Hide, you mean.'

'Yes, that's the one,' said Carrie. 'I'll grab a few things and decamp.'

At last Alan emerged, his shirt tails untucked from his trousers, still pulling up his zip.

'Bedtime,' said Carrie, with the briskness of Matron.

'An exce-exce-cellent idea.'

Between them Carrie and Angela wrestled him along the corridor, uttering soothing responses to his increasingly incoherent comments.

'Here you go. Why don't you lie down?' Carrie pushed him to a sitting position on the bed.

'Come lie with me. My love. You know I love you.' He grabbed her hand. 'You still love me, don't you? I couldn't bear to lose you.' He squeezed her hand, pulling her to him. 'Don't go. Stay with me tonight.'

His eyes pooled with tears and his face crumpled. 'I couldn't bear it if you left me. You're amazing. We can get over this.'

She traced the lines of the tiled floor with her eyes, anything to avoid seeing the desperate appeal in his eyes.

'Alan, you need to get some sleep. Let's talk in the morning.'

Hurt eyes peered up at her. 'I want to talk now.'

'It's not a good idea. Let's wait until the morning.'

'Please.' His heartfelt plea made her feel seven kinds of bitch.

'Alan.' This was awful.

'Just lie down with me. Let me hold you.'

Her gut had knotted itself into a dense mass, like intricate macramé.

'Let's get your shoes off,' she said, shooting a look at Angela over her shoulder. 'Make you comfortable. Lie down.'

Without another word he flopped obediently onto the pillows and she lifted his legs onto the bed, taking her time to unlace his uncharacteristically scuffed tan brogues. She winced, touching the deep scratches in the polished leather – they looked as if they'd been through the mill today. By the time she'd eased them off, his eyes had closed but his face contorted with sudden frowns as if unpleasant thoughts kept jumping out at him.

'Spinning thing. Room,' muttered Alan and then groaned.

'I'll get a sick bowl,' said Angela, and disappeared with unsurprising alacrity.

Carrie stood at the end of the bed, watching him, not daring to breathe in case he opened his eyes again.

She crept backwards towards the door, grabbing her robe, praying he wouldn't open his eyes.

'Sorry, took me a while to find something suitable.' Angela returned carrying a large plastic bowl to find Carrie lurking outside the bedroom door. 'Is he asleep?'

'Close enough. He didn't open his eyes.'

'I'll pop this by the bed, shall I?'

'Would you mind?'

'That's what sisters are for.' Angela winked and slipped through the door and came back into the corridor within seconds.

'He's out for the count. Snoring gently. Nothing short of canon fire is going to wake him.'

'Phew.' Carrie rocked her head back, stretching the tense neck muscles. 'I'm a terrible person.'

Angela put her arm around her and hugged her. 'No, you're not. You're a good person. Don't forget it.'

'I don't want to hurt him, but I don't . . . love him . . . not the way I should.'

'And you can't help that. Better to realise now than later.'

'I'm not sure that Alan would agree with you,' said Carrie, conscious of a hollowness in her stomach.

*

It took her a while to orientate herself the next morning in the strange bedroom and a few seconds to peel her gritty eyes open. Surely she'd only been asleep for an hour. Something had woken her and she lay with her arm over her eyes. There it was again. Her phone. Despite being on silent mode, the damn thing had taken up the Samba. When she leaned out of bed to pick it up to find out who was texting, she realised it had danced out of reach with its constant vibrations.

'What the . . .'

It was half-past eight but the screen announced that she'd had umpteen WhatsApp messages, twenty texts and several missed calls.

Sitting upright she read the first text, the second and then a third.

'Oh shit.' Throwing back the covers, she jumped out of bed, thrusting her arms into her robe and ran through the house to the kitchen where she'd left her laptop last night.

'Bloody, bloody hell.' Pain pinched in the back of her shoulders as she leaned over the screen. How on earth had the papers got hold of this information? She was so screwed.

Yesterday's pictures had been enhanced with a new headline.

Mr and Mrs Maddox take a stroll on the beach.

But that wasn't the worst of it.

Richard Maddox's mystery bride has been unmasked as high school drama teacher, Miss Carrie Hayes. Capsholt High School, Head teacher, Mr Nigel Lyndon, 46, said that none of her colleagues had any idea that the glamorous Miss Hayes, 29, was married, let alone to an international movie star. 'We're all stunned. She never said a word to anyone here.' He refused to comment on Miss Hayes' future at the school following the publication of the revealing photos.'

Apparently the couple married in secret after a whirlwind romance on the Riviera, where Mr Maddox is filming at the moment. Mr Maddox's spokesperson declined to comment when or where the secret ceremony had taken place or how long the couple have been married.

A member of the cast, who didn't want to be named, said, 'It's all been terribly romantic. They were together at a party this week and he couldn't take his eyes off her.'

She stared at the screen, willing the words to vanish, wishing she could press the backspace button to delete them, word by word. Her throat closed as a sob of panic started to rise. The stark, uncompromising warnings of all those e-safety lectures at school came home to roost. Once a picture is out there on the internet, it's there for ever. You can't erase or remove it. Like some awful spell, the words had been cast and couldn't be pulled back. She couldn't even hope that no one might see them: an awful lot of people already had, judging by the state of her mobile.

Bloody thing. She shoved it out of reach. If she picked it up, she'd be tempted to look at the messages, like any of them were going to help. Gossip-mongering or official ones from the Head or his PA demanding an explanation and calling her into school. The Chair of Governors, Olive Martin, a mean old stick, who disliked the drama department on the principle that it wasn't academic enough, was no doubt revving up her broomstick and convening the coven to call for her to be sacked.

What was Alan going to say? What had Richard said? When had the newspaper spoken to his 'spokesperson' and why hadn't he warned her?

Wearily, she picked up the phone, handling it like a bomb about to explode in her hand and scrolled through the list of texts, missed calls and voicemails. Half of the numbers were unfamiliar but there was Richard's.

She listened to his voice message, urgent and low.

'I'm filming this morning; I can't get out of it. I'll be over as soon as I've finished. I've got Caroline, my press agent on it, trying to find out who leaked the story. We'll have to go to the media with our own story, to take the heat out of everything. Don't worry, she's a pro, she's done this plenty of times. Whatever you do, don't talk to the press or any friends, they'll quote you, you can bet. She's drafting a statement, which we'll issue later. I'll be there as soon as I can.'

Press agents. Statements. This wasn't her world. Talking to the media. She didn't want to talk to anyone, she wanted to bolt down a rabbit hole and stay there.

The gate buzzer sounded and Carrie flinched as she walked into the hall Angela had picked up the intercom telephone.

'Hello . . . who? *Oops Magazine?*'

'Don't let them in!' Carrie grabbed the phone from her and slammed it down.

'Okay.' Angela stepped back. 'What's going on?'

'The press found out who I am.'

'How?'

'I've no idea.'

The buzzer sounded again.

Carrie snatched it up. 'Can we talk to Carrie Maddox? Just an interview. A couple of photos. We pay well.'

She put it down without saying anything.

'Thank God for the gates.'

The buzzer didn't stop for the next ten minutes until, finally, Carrie took it off the hook. Unfortunately, that left the intercom channel open, allowing what sounded like thousands of tinny voices buzzing down the line. It added to the torture of being under siege, along with the dread of Alan waking up.

After a long shower, Carrie pinched a T-shirt from Angela, and took herself off to veranda at the side of the house. She turned up the volume full on her iPhone, plugged in her earphones and lay down on the rattan sofa, out of view from everyone.

There'd been no sign of Alan yet, for which she was fervently grateful, although she could only hide out here for so long, but she needed some time alone.

She managed to stay under the radar until eleven o'clock, when Alan tracked her down.

'Ah, this is where you're hiding. I've been looking everywhere for you.'

His usual ruddy complexion had a definite greyish tinge to it this morning.

'You and the world's press,' she sighed, removing her earphones and sitting up.

'How did they find out who you were?'

'I've no idea,' she lied. She'd been pondering that very question for the last two hours. Exactly five people in the whole wide world knew for sure it was her in that photo. One, being her, which narrowed the number down to four. She could scratch Phil from the list, as she doubted he even knew her surname, Richard again, equally unlikely, Angela even less so, which by the law of diminishing returns left

Jade, who had kept rather a low profile this morning, despite the fact that her own phone must be red hot with messages from friends, besides themselves at the celebrity-relation angle.

'Well, it's scuppered things. Have you heard from Nigel? I bet he's not best pleased. Wish you'd said something before. It makes me look an idiot. Proposing when you were already married.'

'I haven't checked. My phone's gone into meltdown.'

'But he's your boss.' He twisted his hands in and out of each other as he spoke, clearly unable to keep them still. 'You ought to check. Call him. He'll need to hear from you. God forbid, but you might have been suspended or something. You know how cautious the governors are.'

Carrie nodded. 'If they decided to suspend me, they'll have made that decision whether I speak to them or not. There's not a lot I can do about it from here.'

'Of course there is. You have to fight it. That's what the union's for. You need to get on to your union rep. I've been thinking and I reckon that you've got a good case. It was a private beach and you were with your husband. You and I know it's in name only, but no one else does. The papers think you've just got married, which means we'll have to postpone the wedding for a while. But that's just as well. Let things lie low. We don't want another media storm.'

He was a good man and she didn't want to hurt him, but she owed him honesty.

'Alan, I can't marry you.'

He took both her hands, his familiar face earnest. 'I know you think you can't, but this will all blow over. I still love you and I know we can get over this. Once the new term starts and things settle down, everyone will forget about this. The union will back you. It's not like you've broken any laws.'

'No, I'm sorry.' She pulled away from him as gently as she could. 'We can't go back to how we were. I'm so sorry, Al, but it's over.'

He grabbed at her hand, like a man scrabbling for a rope. 'Don't do this now. This is a knee-jerk reaction. You need to give us time. Out here, it's not real life. You'll see when we get home and go back to normal . . .'

Carrie shook her head. 'That's the thing, I don't want to go back to normal.'

'Well now you're being silly.' Alan sighed. 'No one wants to go back to normal. It would be lovely to be on holiday forever, but we all have jobs and responsibilities.' Carrie appreciated his tone about as much as twelve-year-old would have done and with heavy heart realised that trying to explain to him was pointless. He would never understand.

He stood up, about to step away, when he turned, his expression fierce. 'Seriously, Carrie, don't do it. We can get through this. You've had your head turned. Who wouldn't? It's gorgeous out here. This lovely house. Parties on yachts. Private beaches. It's not real. You're going to regret it when you get back to England and real life.' It was the most passionate and animated she'd ever seen him and she hated that it was for all the wrong reasons.

'I'm sorry.'

Alan narrowed his eyes, his mouth firming into a small, mean line before he said, 'It's him, isn't it.'

Before Carrie could deny it, he struck like a cobra, his voice full of venom, 'You do know that if he wanted you, he would have come looking for you before now.'

'It's not about Richard. There's no future there either. I realise now, that we, you and I, would be wrong.'

'You're sure.' He bit his lip, still hopeful as he pushed his hands into his pockets, standing his ground.

She nodded, unable to speak.

Eventually with the sort of look that would have made Eeyore proud, he turned and walked away.

She watched him, her breath catching with a tinge of sadness but also a sense of calm, knowing she was finally doing the right thing.

CHAPTER THIRTY-FOUR

With no fanfare or fuss, Alan gathered his things together and with grim politeness thanked Angela for having him. When Carrie went to kiss his cheek as he walked out to the waiting taxi, he turned his head away before saying stiffly, 'I hope you find what you're looking for.'

Watching the taxi trundling up the drive to the gates, she crossed her fingers. She hoped so too.

Angela linked her arm through Carrie's and they walked back to the kitchen, which felt like a command centre.

'Sit down,' said Angela. 'You look done in.'

'I think I've been scooped up by a tornado, done a few spins and chucked out.'

'Definitely over with Alan, then.'

'Yes. It wouldn't have worked. I should have realised that.'

'I was starting to wonder.'

'You were?' Carrie sat up straighter. 'Since when?'

'The day you came back from lunch with Richard. Your hair was down and the light had been switched back on. You used to look like that all the time. Bit like an eager and rather naughty lion cub on the lookout for the next thing to pounce on. I realised then.'

Carrie reached out and touched her sister's hand. 'Thank you.'

'For what?' Angela squeezed her hand.

Carrie laughed. 'For being you and for me not having to explain. I tried to tell Alan but he didn't get it.'

'What are you going to do?'

Carrie rounded up the crumbs on the table like a sheepdog, chasing down the errant ones at the edge of her place setting.

'Finish our holiday. Summon up the courage to look at all the messages on my phone and see if I still have a job when I get home.'

'I meant about Richard.'

'Nothing.' As Alan had helpfully pointed out, Richard had always known where she was. He hadn't bothered looking her up before. She knew where his priorities lay.

'Jade!' Her niece, who had popped her head around the doorway and then retreated when she'd seen Carrie, re-appeared, her posture ram-rod straight.

'Have you got something to tell me?' Carrie spoke in an I'm-very-disappointed-in-you schoolteacher tone, which usually worked. Jade stared at the floor, wrapping her ankle around her leg like a wayward stork.

'Erm . . . er. There's a man in the garden.'

'What?' Carrie wheeled round.

'Not there, coming from the wall down by the road from the gate. On that side of the house.' She pointed to the far side of the house, where the bedrooms were.

'Shit, a journalist?'

'I think so.' Jade winced and there was a distinct apology in her puppy-dog posture.

'Did he have a camera?' Carrie rose, indignation burning.

'Not sure,' said Jade.

'Hmm, he wouldn't want to get it wet, now would he?' She paused and then held up her hand. 'Hold up. He wants pictures.' She scanned the kitchen and a slow, vicious smile lit her face.

'Angela, there are some of mine and Jade's T-shirts drying. Can you grab them?'

Without question, Angela sprang into action and returned with two crumpled white T-shirts.

'Put that on,' Carrie tossed it to Jade and grabbed two large dark tea towels. With urgent fingers, she tied one onto Jade's head using one of the fabric bands Angela used to keep her hair out of face and then put the second on her own head. 'Sunglasses.'

Jade frowned, not following. Carrie marched towards the door, beckoning her.

'Come, young Jedi. We have work to do, defending the perimeter. Angela, don't answer the front door.'

'Defending the . . . oh.' Jade's eyes widened in astonished horror. 'We can't . . . can we?'

'You bet we can. Grab The Terminator. We're gonna kick some ass.' She pulled down her sunglasses. 'Shutters down.'

Jade followed suit, grinning from ear to ear. 'You're crazy.'

'I know.' Carrie grinned back.

'Shoot to kill,' said Carrie handing the big purple water gun to Jade. 'If we hide behind the furniture on the end veranda, when he comes around the corner we let him have it with both barrels.'

Jade nodded, hopping up and down on the spot. 'Are you sure we're allowed to do this?'

'Hell no,' drawled Carrie, toting her gun with her best badass gangster swagger. 'I know we can.'

Jade giggled and the two of them, with the stealth of fully untrained ninja warriors, crept towards the veranda, ducking down behind the sofa.

Now they were in position, Carrie's confidence wavered but Jade's hand, tightly clamped in hers, forced her to be bold and fearless. What the hell? How dare this man invade their privacy? She hadn't asked for this.

The seconds ticked by and sweat trickled down between her boobs. At this time of day, the sun shone directly onto this side of the house.

A sudden screech, that furniture-dragging-on-stone sound, alerted them to the intruder's presence.

Carrie jumped up, adrenaline charging through her system, as a tall man in dark sunglasses, dark jeans and a dark shirt came into view. Before she had time to stop and think, Jade had reared up alongside her and, with a gleeful war cry, opened fire, sending a cascade of water all over the intruder. The second Carrie followed suit, it registered, a few seconds too late, that he looked awfully familiar.

By the time her brain caught up, Richard was sodden and Jade's war cry had faded to an embarrassed squawk.

Richard, halted by the sudden torrent of water, stood with menacing stillness, his expression unreadable.

'Oops.' Carrie muttered under her breath, nudging Jade.

'Yikes.'

'He doesn't look too happy,' whispered Carrie, talking out of one side of her mouth.

Jade's lips twitched. 'No, Auntie Carrie, he doesn't. I'm thinking *The Sopranos*.' Her thin shoulders lifted.

'Are you laughing?'

'Trying not to.' Jade's mouth had clamped shut. 'Trying really hard.'

'Me too.' Carrie's breath hissed out as a stifled giggle escaped.

That was all it took to set Jade off and once she'd started, Carrie couldn't stop.

'I should wring your bloody necks,' growled Richard, marching up to them, not that either of them were capable of taking any notice of him, they were still trying to reign in their mirth.

'You got . . . t-to admit . . . it's kind of . . . f-funny.' Carrie held on to her side as she doubled over.

'Not when the world's press is watching.'

Carrie stood bolt upright. 'Are they? Where?'

Richard pushed up his sunglasses. 'I meant the situation.' His eyes, grey-blue today were sombre and shadowed. Carrie sobered.

'Sorry, we thought you were a journalist.'

'There are enough of them camped out there. Phil dropped me off down the road and I climbed over the wall.' He bent and gave his knee a rueful rub. 'They make it look so easy in the films. It would have been a lot bloody easier if you answered your phone.'

'I switched it off. It was in danger of spontaneously combusting at any second.'

Throughout the conversation, Carrie was aware of Jade backing away with exaggerated care, as if not to draw any attention to herself.

'Ah, Richard, you're already here.' Angela skidded to a halt, taking in his sodden clothes. 'Phil's called me to say you were on your way.'

'Yes, I'm here, somewhat waylaid.' He wiped at the front of his wet shirt.

Out of the corner of her eye, Carrie saw Jade bolt into the house.

'Yes,' said Angela, failing to contain her amusement. 'You are. Would you like a towel?' She'd already turned to go back to the house.

'No, I'll dry.' He strode over to Carrie. 'Interesting costume.'

'I like to get into character.'

'*Bugsy Malone. Goodfellas. The Godfather*?'

She giggled. 'I was thinking more *Ninja Turtles*.'

Shaking his head and sweeping back his damp hair, he pulled off the tea towel and brushed the hair from her face. 'Are you okay?'

She nodded, her knees threatening to give way. When he enfolded her in his arms, she melted into the embrace, uncaring of his soggy clothes, overcome by the weight of the stress and strain of today. Tears pricked her eyes. She'd been focused on holding it together, now the prospect of sharing that burden made her weak with relief.

Clinging to him, she buried her head into his neck, inhaling his familiar musky scent.

'I'm sorry about this.'

'It's not your fault. You couldn't have known.' She shuddered. 'I hate the thought that someone spied on us. It creeps me out.'

'Bloody paparazzi. I never saw a thing. Keith's place is pretty private, that's why I took you there. To escape all this. Ironic. The rest of the time we could have been papped at any moment.'

'I guess that wouldn't have been as much of a coup.'

'Sneaky sods.'

'I guess they come with the territory.'

'Yup, although we're not above using them to our advantage when we want to. It's one way to gain acres of publicity when it's wanted, which is why I have a press agent, Caroline, to manage things. She's fuming. Normally we get a heads-up and we could have nipped things in the bud if someone hadn't given them the ammunition to make it such a good story. She's making enquiries at the moment.'

Grim lines fanned across his forehead. A sense of foreboding rattled her.

'It's done now. I need to tell you . . . Alan was here.' She pulled him to sit down on one of the chairs. This shady spot had become her personal Waterloo. The scenic backdrop would forever more be engraved on her memory. This once-in-a-lifetime holiday, where everything changed.

'Fiancé Alan?'

Carrie exhaled heavily. 'Ex-fiancé, Alan. This morning's revelations brought things to a head.'

Richard offered her a rueful smile. 'I can't say I'm sorry to hear that.'

'Thanks,' said Carrie with a touch of tartness.

'You don't love him, do you?'

She swallowed and studied the skyline, imprinting the vivid blue in her head. It would always remind of her Richard's eyes and the first time she'd seen him again – the instant bolt of recognition, sparking a response in every part of her body.

'No,' she said, sadness rippling in waves through her, at the thought of him hurting, compounded by the empathy of knowing you loved someone you couldn't have. 'I thought I did,' she paused, aware of birdsong and the grasshoppers in the garden around them. Why did those sounds, redolent of summer days, make this moment so poignant? 'But not as much as he deserved. I feel bad for him. He was a good man. I'm not the right woman for him.'

'Lucky you found out now.' He took her hand and touched her face, tracing her jawline before bringing his lips down on hers with a kiss of searing gentleness, before lifting his eyes and gazing down at her, serious and steady. '*You* are the right woman for me.'

Her heart almost burst at his quietly spoken words.

'I love you, Mrs Maddox.'

A sob broke through as he pulled her to him, his mouth zeroing in on hers. With heartfelt passion, letting long-banked emotion flood through, she kissed him as if her last breath depended on it. She'd spent too long denying this and even though, it couldn't last, she had now. Time to seize this moment, grab it by the scruff of the neck and wring every last drop of joy out of it, the way she would have done eight years ago.

Winding her arms around his neck, she let her senses take over, revelling in the short spiky hair on his neck, the sensation of hot breath as his lips roved over her face, touching her eyelids, her brows, her cheeks and the sinewy strength of his arms as he pulled her close. 'I love you too, Mr Maddox,' she murmured between gasped kisses as they sank down onto the chair, bodies sliding together in a sinuous fluid movement of limbs, intertwining and flowing in a perfect fit.

Richard's phone burst into life with the sort of insistent ring tone you couldn't ignore. With great reluctance he loosened his hold and dug into his jeans' pocket.

'That's Caroline. I need to answer it.' He dropped a kiss on her forehead. 'You distracted me.'

She nipped at his lip with a sultry purr of satisfaction.

'Maddox,' he said, business-like and alert, all trace of sleepy desire banished from his voice.

With a shiver she wrapped her arms around herself and stood up.

'Tell them we'll issue a statement at,' he flipped his wrist, 'three. No photos . . . no . . . absolutely not. Let me talk to Carrie.'

From the phone came the persuasive, strident tone of a very assertive woman. Richard rubbed a weary hand across his forehead, the corners of his mouth turned down

'I appreciate that but this is a joint decision. I'll get back to you within the hour.' He paced back across the terrace. 'And what about the source?'

With his quiet, grave 'I see', a prickle of foreboding shimmered down Carrie's spine. As if the sun had gone in, goose bumps rose on her skin and she almost shivered at the sight of his sudden granite-hewn profile as he slid his phone into his pocket.

'We need to talk.' Shadows darkened his face, throwing his chiselled lines into sharp relief, transforming him into a rather intimidating figure. 'The whole family.'

'D-does it need to involve anyone else?'

'Yes,' he responded, his tone implacable.

Like a council of war, they convened in the elegant lounge, a rather ragtag band. Angela, clean and neat in a soft print cotton dress, Jade, defiant in a tiny bikini, wearing her outsize sunglasses and a huge floppy sunhat, both of which Carrie suspected were going to be welded on for the duration, and Richard, unusually rumpled and forbidding.

'So, Jade, what have got to say for yourself?' Everyone gasped.

'Richard!' Carrie sprang up and put a hand on his arm. 'Is this necessary?'

'I think so.' He ignored her and turned to Angela. 'Don't you?'

Angela, sitting with her knees together, hands clasped, levelled a quelling look at Carrie, which clearly said, leave this to me, before nodding. 'She's not a child.'

'Er, hello, I am here.'

'Yes,' said Angela, the voice of reason as usual. 'You've been telling me that you're old enough to do adult things. Old enough to drink. Old enough to go to nightclubs. Old enough to almost get yourself into trouble. I'd say you're old enough to speak for yourself and explain what you've done.'

Carrie loved her sister. Despite the heightened emotions in the room, she remained calm and balanced, neither condemning or defending her daughter.

Jade pouted. 'He's not my father or anything. And who says I've done anything?'

'No, darling. Officially he's your uncle but that aside, you know you've done wrong.'

Carrie wondered, if she had a daughter of her own, if she'd manage to soften her voice like that but still manage a slight reprimand. Definitely a mother's skill.

'How do you know it was me?' she burst out, ducking her head and looking everywhere but at the adults in the room.

'The process of elimination wasn't exactly lengthy,' Carrie pointed out, trying to copy her sister's unemotional approach, watching her niece's face go through a series of transparent contortions. To fight or to flee.

'Shall I make it easier?' Richard pulled out his phone,

not about to adopt any of this softly, softly crap. 'My press secretary spoke to the newspaper journalist, who at first, being a journalist, refused to name her source. However, when it was pointed out the possible source was a minor, and the paper could be seen to have been grooming a child for information and offering inappropriate bribes, they handed the name over pretty sharpish.'

Jade shrugged, lifting her chin, and spoke through clenched teeth. 'And? You know it was me.'

'Have you any idea how much trouble you've caused?' His actor's voice carried, resonating anger, irritation and frustration in one neat hit, which made all of them sit up straighter.

Carrie's stomach twisted as Jade's mouth tightened and tears shimmered in her eyes, shrinking back into her chair, her fingers clutching the arms. Despite desperately wanting to be treated like an adult, she was still a child and much as she was a pain a lot of the time, she could also be funny, smart and loyal. Compared to most teenagers, she never got into trouble and went out of her way to conform. She lived in mortal dread of getting things wrong or being given a detention at school.

Carrie frowned. No, this wasn't like her at all.

'Hang on a minute, Richard.' She rose and perched on the arm of Jade's chair, taking her niece's small trembling hand in hers. 'Why don't you give Jade a chance to explain?'

'Explain? I don't need an explanation. I've seen it all before.' For a brief second Carrie saw the flash of hurt there. It had to be hard never knowing if you could trust people. Not being able to let go completely.

Sharp insight brought with it a twist of deep-seated pain. This had been a convenient respite, taking him back to those days when he wasn't famous and when he didn't have those kinds of worries.

'People do it for the money all the time. For what they can get. I'm a commodity. I didn't expect it to happen this close to home.' His business-like description belied any sense of self-pity in what he said, but Carrie couldn't help feeling a little bit sorry for him, even though he appeared so sure of himself on the surface.

Jade muttered something in Carrie's ear, tears spilling down her face as she started to sob.

'Oh, sweetheart.' Carrie's heart missed a beat at her niece's barely coherent confession. Slipping off the arm and into the chair seat, she gathered Jade to her and hugged her tight, bony ribs, reminding Carrie of her fragility and youth.

Angela went over and sat on the other arm and stroked her daughter's hair.

'Do you want to tell Richard why you did it?' she asked, her mild manner conveying implicit trust.

'I'd be fascinated to know. Why you would tell the world and his wife something your aunt and I haven't shared with anyone else, for very good reasons—'

'That's not quite true.' Carrie's quiet voice stopped Richard in his stride. 'The security people knew. You listed me as Carrie Maddox.' She remembered the quiet burn of pride when she realised he'd done that.

'They're security people. Paid to keep secrets and private information – private,' hissed Richard. Although he stood on one spot now, he kept jigging one of his legs up and down.

So much for her secret hope that he'd been making some kind of statement.

'What in the world possessed you?' His sudden yell made Jade jump.

'Don't shout at her. She was trying to help. She was worried about me losing my job.'

'Losing your job! Crap. She's like everyone else, wants a touch of celebrity. Wanted to brag about her celebrity uncle.'

'How dare you?' Carrie spat. 'You pompous . . . pompous.'

'I dare because it's true. I don't suppose you knew there was a tidy reward for anyone with information on the mystery woman.'

'She didn't do it for money.'

'Tell me another.'

'I didn't.' Jade's timid voice cut through the anger in the room as she hunched down into the chair. 'I-I . . . Carrie's done everything for us. We've had such a brilliant time. We never get to do things like this. My friends . . . they always go to exciting places. She came with us so we could come. She drove on the wrong side of the road and everything. She's always doing things for me, for Mum. No one ever does stuff for her. I didn't know she was in *Blood Brothers*. She used to do exciting things. She gave all that up and now she might lose her job. I thought this would help. If her boss knew you were married, I thought it wouldn't look so bad.'

'Seriously?' Richard's scepticism bounced off the walls. 'You thought it wouldn't look so bad. You thought that the papers wouldn't rehash it all again. Or bring it up every time I have new film out? You didn't think at all.'

Carrie bounded to her feet and stood toe to toe with him, which wasn't such a great idea because she had to look up at the arrogant oaf who still had the indecency to be utterly gorgeous.

'Oh get over yourself. She's family.'

She planted her hands on her hips to stop them doing something they shouldn't, either slapping him so hard his teeth would rattle or grabbing him around the neck and kissing the life out of him. 'She did it for good reasons. Alan was worried I'd lose . . . we'd both lose, our jobs, if anyone found out it was me in the picture. She thought if people knew we were married, they wouldn't be quick to judge and that it might save my job. Stop being such a bully . . .'

He frowned in confusion, his blue eyes clouding, and she almost smiled. She bet no one had ever accused him of being a bully or had told him to get over himself.

'. . . and worrying about your precious career. Jade was trying to help.'

He stiffened and then said in voice so quiet that even though she stood almost chest to chest she had to strain to hear it, 'You've always put your family before me, haven't you?'

The simple statement robbed her of her next breath, her cheeks flooding with colour and heat as she met his searing blue-eyed expression of accusation.

'W-what?' It was as if he'd punched her right in the gut.

He turned his back on her and walked towards the French windows. For a second suffocating sadness rolled over her as she took in his dejected stance.

No one said a word. Carrie darted a look at her sister, wanting her to leap in and defend her, but Angela's face had shut down, her expression impassive.

'Where the hell did that come from?' she snapped, anger offering easy refuge.

'Come off it, Carrie.' He whirled around, pushing a hand through his hair, his shoulders hunched. 'You could have come out to the States at any time. You couldn't leave Angela and Jade. Jade was starting school. Angela's condition was bad. Jade this, Angela that. Always a reason. And yet Angela had managed perfectly well when Jade was a baby, a toddler. Suddenly she couldn't do without you.'

'That's not true.' Even as she said it, Carrie knew she wasn't being completely honest.

'I had parts as well.'

'And in between jobs?' She watched his mouth, avoiding looking into his eyes. 'You had six months between *Blood Brothers* and *Hedda Gabbler.* Four months between the Pinter play and another five between seasons at the National.'

God, he'd remembered each play.

'There was always a reason not to come. You were the one that held out on me.'

'So, what? I should have upped and come and hung around your big wonderful career?'

'I could have helped you.'

'I didn't want your help.'

'I know you didn't. You made that quite clear.'

'It would never have worked.' Why couldn't he see and accept that?

'You wouldn't let it. What were you so scared of? That I would be more successful than you?'

Emotion exploded and the temper she'd been hanging onto in case she said the wrong thing suddenly took hold and the words tumbled out. 'I didn't want to hold you back! We were crazy in love. It couldn't last. It was too fast, furious and bloody terrifying. What if I'd come? And it didn't work for you? I couldn't bear it, if I ruined it for you. I had my family. It didn't matter if I didn't make it, but it mattered to you.'

With one hand, he covered his eyes and Carrie regretted all the times she'd accused him of playing a role, she'd rather that now than see him stripped bare, the sadness etched into the lines around his mouth. When he lifted his head, his eyes flashed furious sparks. 'And you made that decision. I loved you. That was what I wanted. Your love. More than my career.'

'No you didn't,' she said, with a touch of desperation, horrified that she'd let too much spill out.

'So you made the decision.'

'There were other reasons,' she said, her voice rising, but she couldn't think of a single one.

'Like what?' His voice gentled as if he wanted, no needed, an answer to the question.

She swallowed and shrugged, unable to give him one.

As the helicopter lifted from the lawn, taking a silent and uncommunicative Richard with it, a dense atmosphere descended on the house. Jade, sobbing incoherently, ran from the room, followed by her mother, leaving Carrie in the lounge with a terrible headache and a horrible emptiness.

When Angela returned, Carrie had taken refuge in the kitchen, brooding into a cold cup of coffee.

'Is she okay?'

'She's asleep.'

'I'm sorry about that.'

'She was in the wrong, even if she thought she was doing it for the right reasons.'

'I meant, I was sorry about Richard shouting at her like that.'

'You can't blame him. He had every right. It's you I'm cross with.'

'Me?' Carrie squeaked. What had she done? 'Why?' She threw her hands up in the air at Angela's accusing glare.

'You used me and Jade as your excuse not to go and join Richard?'

'It wasn't an excuse,' Carrie winced, as her voice pitched into a whine, 'it was hard for you.'

'It's hard for any parent, but I coped. When Jade was a baby, I managed. She's my daughter. She doesn't need another mother. I don't need a mother. We don't need a babysitter.' Angela levelled a stern look at her, reminiscent of the one she'd given Carrie once before when they'd rescued Jade from the nightclub.

Carrie stilled and glared back. 'I . . . I . . .' Like a dam breached, all her defences collapsed as the truth poured in, sweeping away all the misconceptions she'd been hiding behind. With a sob, she sank onto the sofa, tears flowing freely. Angela came over and put her arm around her.

'I'm sorry honey.'

'No, you're right.' She covered her face, wiping in vain at the tear tracks flooding down her cheeks. 'I did use you as an excuse. I lost my bottle. When Richard went, it left such a massive hole. I m-missed him . . . so much.' She sucked in a painful breath. 'I could barely function. Saying goodbye to him at the airport.' She swallowed hard, her stomach cramping. 'I sat on a bench in the departures hall for two hours. When I got home, I couldn't set foot out of the flat for two weeks. The sole reason I managed to get out of bed was for Jade's eighth birthday party. Remember. And only because Richard had bought her a teddy bear from Hamleys. I-I promised I'd deliver it.'

She jabbed at the table with her fingers, tapping out a tattoo to force herself to go on. 'And then . . . when I was at the house with you and Jade, it made it bearable. I could be busy. Not on my own. Except I couldn't admit that, to me or to you. Told myself that you needed me. A big fat lie, but it was the only way to survive. I didn't want Richard to know how much I missed him, how much it was killing me without him.'

'Then I got a part . . . immersed myself in it. I was scared I'd have nothing if I didn't have my work and you guys. It gave me the perfect excuse not to go out and see Richard.'

'And you haven't got that excuse any more,' pointed out Angela, firm but gentle. 'Jade was wrong. Even she knows that. You just defended the indefensible to Richard. You pushed him away. Again.'

Carrie closed her eyes, a band of tension squeezing her chest, so tight and unforgiving it made it hard to suck in her next breath. 'Yes. And it's for the best. When he's finished filming here, he's heading to LA. I remind him of a time before he was famous. It's been a convenient summer fantasy. An escape for both of us. There was never a future.'

CHAPTER THIRTY-FIVE

Swimming, Carrie decided, should be patented as the best therapy in the world. In the final few days of the holiday she must have swum several hundred lengths. Except it hadn't really worked.

Sitting in the head's office now, the rehearsed conversations she'd practised as she pulled herself through the water with her favourite back crawl, came back to her. She crossed her legs and pulled her blazer tighter. After the Riviera, the spartan office felt chilly, even though the temperature outside was up in the sixties. The insipid pale-grey walls contrasted sharply with the vibrant colours her eyes had become used to, the jewel-blue of the sea and the cloudless, endless sky, the warm peach of terracotta and the exotic splash of fuchsia pink Bougainvillea. Her mind's eye conjured up the explosion of brilliant reds, oranges and yellows in the massive bouquet that Richard had sent Jade in a surprise apology. Jade hadn't shared the message and despite almost dying of curiosity, Carrie had refused to ask what it said.

She checked her watch again. Nigel's PA had shown her in five minutes ago. It was plain rude to keep her hanging around. She'd been on time. They didn't need to know it was because she hadn't slept much last night.

The summons, a formal letter full of legalese and HR bullshit, had been waiting on the doormat when they staggered in punch drunk with the type of weariness that comes from endless hanging around in an airport for most of the day. It had given her a few days' grace, of which every minute had been filled with whirlwind activity and detailed planning.

She'd read the Code of Conduct. Skinny-dipping wasn't illegal, she'd been with her husband, she was prepared to fight everything they chose to throw at her and had checked out the situation regarding union representation, which would be her next step.

At last the Head came in, closely followed by the bustling figure of Olive Martin, the Chair of Governors. She had that kind of busy walk that suggested she was always on a mission of utmost importance and carried a capricious handbag as official and important as the PM's red box.

Olive's down-the-nose, double-take gave Carrie a snicker of satisfaction. It had been years since she'd worn these white palazzo pants and the black and white blazer, which she'd dug out from the loft. Today she rocked the Katharine Hepburn look with great pride.

'Miss Hayes. Thank you for coming in,' Nigel smiled, shifting in his chair, with all the ease of a man with a loaded gun pointing his way. Olive straightened and leaned forward.

Carrie didn't fill the obvious silence. She'd read a couple of those books about difficult conversations too.

'I . . . er, invited you in to . . . erm . . . well—'

'Miss Hayes, as you must be aware your behaviour has brought the school into disrepute.'

Carrie met Olive's censorious stare with an unconcerned gaze and waited. Olive glanced at Nigel and inside Carrie smiled, rather enjoying their discomfort.

'We are under pressure to suspend you pending further investigation. Your behaviour has breached the school's Code of Conduct.'

'Has it?' Carrie sat back in her chair and crossed her legs.

'Of course it has,' spluttered Olive, looking at Nigel again. 'The Code of Conduct policy quite explicitly states that members of staff should not bring the school into disrepute, doesn't it Mr Lyndon?'

'I see,' said Carrie. She brought her index fingers together to a point under her chin, considered, calm and in control. Body language made up fifty-five per cent of non-verbal communication and she knew how to use it.

Nigel tugged at his tie. 'The media coverage has been quite extensive, particularly in the local media.'

Carrie raised an eyebrow in silent rebuke. He had been a regular commentator and had rather perfected the art of the sound bite.

'Miss Hayes, you don't appear to be perturbed. You do realise the seriousness of the situation. The governing body wishes to suspend you. This is your opportunity to put your case forward.'

Carrie left a lengthy pause before addressing Nigel rather than Olive. 'Perhaps you could be more specific about what it is I've done that is causing concern.'

His Adam's apple bobbed up and down.

'Well . . . you see . . . impressionable minds. You were in the national press showing yourself in a compromising position. It doesn't reflect well on the school. The parents . . . you know.'

'Have parents complained?' asked Carrie.

'Yes,' snapped Olive.

'Er, no, not really,' mumbled Nigel.

'So, parents haven't complained,' said Carrie, intrigued by the red rash spreading up his neck from the rather tight collar of his shirt.

'Not . . .'

'They're not happy.' Olive rapped her hand on the table. 'It's not what we expect from our teachers.'

'Can you be specific about what it is they are complaining about?' asked Carrie, giving in to an inner imp of mischief.

'That one of the teachers from this school has been pictured naked in the national press,' answered Olive, with a distinct tart touch of spite.

'How many parents are 'not' happy?' Carrie did the little speech mark quotes with her fingers.

'A few,' said Olive, her eyes sliding away.

'A few? Perhaps you can be specific.'

'I'm not at liberty to divulge that information. The fact remains, you have breached our Code of Conduct.'

'How? I was a perfectly innocent holidaymaker on holiday with '*my husband*',' she emphasised the words, 'on a private beach. Those pictures were a complete invasion of privacy and, as such, I deserve your sympathy and empathy, being the victim in all this. Being called in like this has caused me considerable stress and is having a detrimental effect on my wellbeing.' She'd worked long enough in teaching to know that these words were enough to strike terror into the heart of the governing body.

'I appreciate that this unfortunate incident was outside

your control, however you displayed poor judgement in . . . in,' Nigel blushed.

'Exactly,' Olive jumped in, 'so pending further investigation, it has been agreed that you will be suspended on full pay.'

A flood of panic-driven adrenaline coursed through her system and then came to an abrupt halt, like a train running out of track. What was so bad about losing a job? The shame? The loss of security? Not doing something she loved? Insecurity in the theatre had been part and parcel of life, holding no terrors. She'd sailed with the current, taking the troughs and peaks as they came.

What the hell was wrong with her? This wasn't even a job she cared that much about losing. Like the final firework of a display, exploding across the sky in glorious crescendo, enlightenment burst upon her. She didn't want to be here. Not coming into work on Monday wasn't a problem. This wasn't her. Teaching wasn't what she wanted to do. It was time she took control. That pile of manuscripts in her room had been sitting around doing nothing for long enough.

'That won't be necessary.' She rose in one fluid move. 'I resign.'

'Now, now, let's not be hasty.' Nigel's hands telegraphed alarm. 'I'm sure we could conduct an investigation very quickly and you could be reinstated by the beginning of term.'

'No.' Carrie scanned the room, the shelves bowed with the weight of row upon row of lever arch files and one wall was taken up with large noticeboards crammed with timetables and notices, filling every last bit of space. A metaphor for her life, the burden of constant planning, assessment, marking, rules, regulations and the lack of time, never enough spare to explore her own creativity. She didn't want any of it any more.

'You can't leave,' wailed Olive, shooting horrified glances at Nigel.

'You wanted to suspend me a minute ago, surely this makes things easier.'

'But . . .'

'It's by far the easiest solution all around.' She stood up and stepped away from the desk. The subtle shift in power immediately shoring up her conviction.

'Miss Hayes, don't you think you're being a little bit precipitate?' Nigel clicked his pen off and on, the speed increasing. 'Perhaps you should take some time to think about it.'

Carrie smiled. 'No. I don't need to. My mind's made up.' With bone-deep certainty the decision locked into place. Her brain had finally woken up and made her do some straight thinking. For the first time in a very long time, the prospect of losing her job didn't hold any fears. As an actor, every job had been precarious and she'd loved that sense of danger and excitement. The thrill of the chase for a new role, another audition or another break. Life had been full of hope and opportunity. Chances, gambles, risks. She'd relished that. When had that changed? When had she lost her sense of self.

When she came out of Nigel's office, to her surprise, Alan sat waiting for her.

'What are you doing here?'

'I came to try and help. Offer a character reference. Have they suspended you?'

'No.'

'Thank God for that.' Alan beamed and came towards

her, about to give her hug, and then stopped in his tracks, looking awkward. 'That's brilliant news. I'd heard the governors were having a meltdown.'

'I quit.'

'You did what?' The panicked note in his voice hit one of the higher registers. His face reflected his deepest fear, the worst thing that could happen to him — losing his job.

The worst thing that could happen to her already had. With a leaden pang, she clutched her stomach, trying to hold back the horrible black hole of hollowness that threatened to suck her in. Richard had gone with no word bar the briefest kick-in-the-guts text, telling her that if she needed anything, to contact Arla.

'What will you do? Supply teaching?'

She eased the grip around her middle and focused on her breathing. 'I can still act. I can write. I'm too young to settle and give up all those dreams I had.' Complete bullshit. She didn't have a bloody clue, but jumping off the cliff would force her to do something.

With a smile, she realised that the antsy fizz in the bottom of her stomach might be excitement. If not it was sheer terror.

'Don't be silly. Teaching's a good, solid profession. You'd be mad to give it up.'

'I can do supply teaching to make ends meet, but I've been burying my ambition.' She almost giggled. On the outside she sounded grown up and measured, as if she'd given this a lot of considered thought, not jumped out of the plane without checking she'd packed her parachute.

'Is it because of him? You think he can help you?' Alan frowned. 'Of course, that's what this is. He's going to give you your big break.' His voice dropped, almost cracking on a half-breath of a sob. 'Oh Carrie, don't do this. Please don't jack in a perfectly good job on the promise of some film star. You're going to regret it when nothing comes of it. Have you heard from him since came back?'

Carrie shook her head, swallowing back the hideous lump lurking in her throat. She would survive losing Richard again, even though some days it hurt to even breathe.

'No and I'm not expecting to. This isn't about Richard. I'll regret it if I don't. I'm sorry Alan, but you don't know the real me. I've been masquerading as someone else for the last few years.'

'You're being dramatic now. Of course, you're you.'

'No. The real me takes her clothes off on beaches, she takes speed boats out, she kidnaps people, she hops on a scooter and rides off into the sunset, revels in the thrill of a Ferrari tearing up the roads. Acts on the spur of the moment. Doesn't worry about the future. I'd forgotten how to live, or to go after what it is I want.'

'And us? You're sure?' He bit his lip, still hopeful as he pushed his hands into his pockets, standing his ground.

'I'm sure.'

'This blessed cat will not leave me alone.' Her sister picked up Coco, stroking her. 'Honestly, you'd think we'd been away for a year rather than a month.'

'I guess it's a long time in cat years,' said Carrie, setting her bag down on the kitchen table, almost laughing out loud. When she pulled up outside the house, having no recollection of the journey home, her head buzzing with ideas, she wondered what Angela would say.

'So, how did it go?' asked Angela, putting the cat down, her back to Carrie as she put the kettle on. Carrie put an arm around her sister, grateful for her complete lack of drama.

'It went,' she said.

Her sister raised her brows in question, but being Angela didn't ask any more.

'I resigned.'

'I see.' Angela busied herself with mugs, tea, pouring water, before turning and handing Carrie a mug. In tandem they sat down at the kitchen table, the cat immediately leaping onto Angela's lap.

'I'm going to do loads. All the things I should have done. There's a scriptwriting course in London. Two months in the evenings. I'm going to polish up all the scripts I've written over the last couple of years and I'm going to go back to Andrew Fisher and hassle him, push to find a backer. I'm going to make that happen. It's crazy waiting on him.' The words poured out in a confessional deluge.

'Sorry, that's rather stream of consciousness. If I'm honest it's all been there at the back of my head for the last few weeks and then today I realised there's nothing stopping me. Except me.'

Angela nodded and smiled.

'Good for you.'

'You don't think I've gone completely mad?' Carrie bit her lip. She could withstand Alan's concerns.

'Not at all.' There were tears in Angela's eyes.

'Hey, don't cry. I'll be fine. Don't worry.'

Angela laughed. 'I'm not worried. I'm relieved. You've no idea how good it is to see you firing on all fifty-nine cylinders again.'

Carrie stared at her sister. She'd expected her to worry about money and security. 'Seriously?'

Angela rose and came over to her side of the table and looped an arm around her to hug her. 'Yes, you big noodle. It's about time you got off your . . .' As she paused, Carrie loved that she still couldn't quite bring herself to say the word 'arse', 'backside and did something. You haven't been you for a long time.'

Carrie stood up and hugged her sister back, tears seeping out as she held on tight. It felt good to know that someone else understood her. It was time she escaped her own self-imposed bonds.

And what about Richard? Have you heard from him?'

Carrie stilled. 'No. And I don't expect to. Sorry, Ang, that boat has sailed. He's back in the States filming.'

'What about the divorce? You don't need it now, but will you still go ahead?'

'It's about time, although I don't want to stir up the press again.' If Richard wanted a divorce, he could bloody well sort it out. He had people like Arla to do that sort of thing for him.

'Mum, have you been shopping yet? We're out of biscuits again.' Jade wandered in and hoisted herself up onto the kitchen counter. 'What's the goss? Did you get the sack?'

'No, I quit.'

'Good for you. That's cool.'

'Eat some fruit,' said Angela, offering Jade a bowl full of apples and rather wizened satsumas.

Jade pulled a face and selected an apple, checking its skin with forensic intensity before deigning to take a bite. 'So.' She crunched for minute. 'When do you think that Richard will get us tickets for the premiere of *Turn on the Stars*?'

Carrie snorted and spat out her tea. 'You are kidding.'

'He said he would.'

'When?'

'When I asked him.' Jade hopped off the side, matter of fact and nonchalant, and walked out of the room.

While half of Carrie itched to shake the information out of her irritating niece, the other half refused to give her the satisfaction. Instead she sipped at her tea and gave the grain of the wood on the table a very thorough examination.

Angela took pity. 'She sent him a text to say thank you for the flowers. He responded and asked if she'd like to go and take some friends.'

Carrie rolled her eyes, tracing a groove in the wood with one finger. 'That's nice of him,' she said airily, clenching the fist of her other hand under her thigh, out of sight.

'He's a nice man,' said Angela.

'And what about your nice man? Phil. What's happening with him?'

'He's coming over in October for a visit. We'll see each other then. Take it one step at a time.'

For a very brief moment, Carrie envied her sister. Why couldn't she be like that? With Richard it had been all or nothing. Complete and immediate from day one. There'd been no waiting around, taking it slowly or building the relationship. Like lemmings they'd hurled themselves straight off the cliff. And she wouldn't have changed a thing.

CHAPTER THIRTY-SIX

'Hi Andrew, its Carrie Hayes.' She put a big tick next to his name on her list and drew an arrow to the action plan table on the A4 sheet of paper.

'About bloody time too. Where the hell have you been?'

'What?' She stopped doodling around the arrow.

'I called you two effing weeks ago.' That was typical of Andrew. It wouldn't occur to him to call again. 'I was beginning to think you weren't interested.'

'Sorry. With the media frenzy, my phone —'

'What media frenzy? Any hoo, now I've got you. We've got a space. I want to start casting straight away. You never said you knew Miranda. She says you've been collaborating.'

Carrie snorted and threw down her pen. That was kind of Miranda.

'Can you get down here to see some of the auditions? I'd like your input. There'll be tweaks to the script and we'll work on the characters. You need to see who we've cast.'

'Hang on, Andrew.' She jumped up from her desk. 'You mean you've got a backer and a theatre? When did all this happen?' Her heart almost leapfrogged right out of her damn chest. This was all news to her.

'I said, didn't I?'

'No, you didn't.' Sometimes you had to be forceful with Andrew. It had something to do with being a director, too used to everyone doing as they were told. 'Back up and tell me properly.' She walked to the window, pressing her forehead against the cold glass, her fingers clutching the phone so hard they almost squeezed it out of her hand.

'Ooh, I love a feisty woman. You and I are going to work rather well together. There's a space re-opening early after a refurb and another play was due to be put on but the producer's dog got killed or his granny died, can't remember, any hoo, no matter. Ill wind. The space came up and then everything fell into place. I haven't got a backer but it's a matter of time. Now are you coming up for the casting or not?'

If he'd been in the room, he'd now be minus a hand.

When she put the phone down, staring out of the window, unseeing, she let out a huge squeal. Her play. On. In London. In the West End. Miranda Buckley had said nice things about her. This was the start of things.

The casting was, unusually, taking place in the theatre, which she rather liked. It made it more real. Arriving outside, she pinched herself, yep, definitely awake, not dreaming, and with a sigh of happiness, walked through the doors, inhaling the sharp, chemical smell of newness.

She imagined the paint had just about dried on the walls as she picked her way down the corridor down to the auditorium, dodging the obstacle course of ladders, discarded paint tins and downed tools.

It mirrored her life this last week. Dusting off manuscripts from their metaphorical bottom drawers in folders on her laptop, polishing up her words, poring over lists of agents and firing off emails, submitting and researching every last relevant competition or opening. Like the week before opening night, it had been a frantic last-minute kerfuffle to bring everything up to scratch.

'Carrie, darling.' Andrew kissed her on both cheeks, his huge hipster beard rasping across her face. 'Isn't this a fabulous space? God bless Godfrey's granny, or was it his dog? Any hoo. Great isn't? We can use it to our advantage to convey the emptiness of Ella's life.'

She nodded. That sort of thing was his job. She'd given him the story. The words. It would be interesting to see what he did with them. Her skin tingled and her blood raced, a temporary reprieve from the punishing black shadow hanging over every waking moment.

For the next few hours, she could focus on the thrill of being back, working in a theatre again. She'd come home, where she belonged. Choosing a seat in the second row in the half-lit auditorium, she sat down looking up at the lights, the sound box and the stage, forcing herself to enjoy the moment.

'I've asked a couple of actors to read for Ella today, some young hopefuls. I've chosen the final scene, where it's decided whether the shoe fits. I've got four girls coming this afternoon.'

'Okay.' Great. That was a good sign, an omen, he'd picked her favourite scene in the play.

'It's going to be vitally important to get that sense of chemistry between Ella and Mr Charming. I want to fine-tune Mr Charming before we introduce them. Would you mind reading for Ella this morning?'

'No, that would be fine.' She gulped at the unexpected invitation. It had been a while since she'd stepped on a stage. Biting her lip, she hoped that once she got up there, she'd be okay.

'Although I will need a script.' She gave him a light tinkling laugh, hoping it sounded natural. 'I don't know it quite line by line.'

Andrew joined in. 'Wasn't expecting you to, my dear.' He brought his wrist up to his eyes, peering at his watch in a near-sighted squint. 'I'm going to grab a coffee before we get started. Why don't you have a read-through? I'll be back in five. If you can start at the top of Act Three, scene two.'

That sounded like an excellent idea. She waited until Andrew left and then crept up the stairs to the big, white, empty stage. Although she faced row upon row of unoccupied seats, the empty auditorium felt haunted by previous audiences and the actors who'd stood on this stage. The air shivered with an indefinable atmosphere of hope, expectation and mystery that prickled along her skin.

Folding back the pages, she ran her finger down the lines to find her place in the script. It was the part where Ella knew she'd messed up but didn't have the first clue how to make amends, so being Ella she went on the offensive.

Despite the theatre being empty, her first line came out wobbly and high-pitched.

'It's just a shoe.' Her voice shook and tried the line again, taking in a careful breath, focusing on the character she'd created. She knew her inside out.

This time she spoke in a much more strident, more Ella-like, tone, 'Not a happy-ever-after. There is no happy-ever-after, except in fairy tales,' she faltered. The meaning of the words hitting home, hard. She tightened her grip on the script and threw back her head. Ella didn't let herself be derailed by emotion. 'We're running a business here. A successful corporation. We don't do happy-ever-afters.'

'What if we did?'

Carrie dropped her script, whirling around at the deep voice that came from the wings.

Her next words dried in her throat as Richard walked towards her from the shadowed edge of the stage.

Dizziness swept over her and she couldn't, for the life of her, remember the next line, couldn't even remember her own name. The air gushed out of her lungs in one stranded-goldfish gasp.

'What if there was a happy-ever-after for us, Carrie?' The tender caress in his voice sucker-punched straight into her diaphragm.

'That's not the right line,' she whispered, hardly daring to breathe, drinking in the sight of him. Everything switched to red alert, her nerve endings radiating static and tingling electricity running like wildfire over her skin.

To her relief, he kept walking because she couldn't trust herself to move a limb without collapsing in a boneless heap.

'What is the right line?' he asked gently, as he came to stand in front of her, those mesmerising blue eyes focused on her with diamond-bright intensity that made her heart catch in her throat. She sighed, her eyes shimmering with tears and an overwhelming desire to tell him everything in her heart.

'I've never loved anyone the way that I loved you.' She repeated back the words he'd used that night on the boat. Words she'd held fast to, an anchor of hope. Saying them out loud scared the pants off her, making her wince as she remembered how carelessly she'd thrown them back at him that night. She owed him the truth. The whole truth this time.

'When . . .when,' she faltered. He took her hand and squeezed it. 'When you went. When you left me at Heathrow, I . . . it hurt. I'd always sort of thought I was invincible. I wasn't. Suddenly I couldn't function. And I couldn't tell anyone because it sounded rubbish. So, I hid behind my family. Much easier than risking you not loving me any more.' Her voice broke. 'But I can't do it again. With you and me, it has to be all or nothing.' Like an avalanche coming to rest after a downhill torrent, her words faded.

'I'll take all.' He lifted a finger, tracing the tear that tracked down her face, before lowering his head and kissing it away. 'I love you, Carrie Maddox, and there is no way on this earth that I'm giving you that blasted divorce.'

His mouth trailed down before capturing her lips in a passionate home-coming kiss. Her knees sagged as if the rest of her body had finally given permission to stop being strong and brave. She let herself be carried away by the kiss, led by the spiralling sensations of desire, touching and being touched. Nothing quite matched the utter bliss of being so wrapped up and lost in each other that nothing around them registered, until the unwelcome slam of a door in the background brought them swimming back to the surface.

'Ah, Richard. You're here.' Andrew strode down the main aisle, completely unperturbed by their passionate clinch. 'I've brought you coffee too. Didn't know how you take it.'

'Milk, no sugar . . . any more,' muttered Carrie, wishing he'd bugger off.

Richard dropped a kiss on her head. 'How the missus tells me, basically.'

He tugged her with him as he came off the stage to greet Andrew.

'Thanks, mate.'

Carrie screwed up her forehead, shifting her glance between the two men. 'Do you two know each other?' She turned to Richard.

'We do now,' said Andrew. 'Richard is going to be your Mr Charming. I didn't realise, when he first approached me, that . . . he knew you, in the biblical sense or any other sense at all. But I wasn't going to turn him down. Big name like his means we'll have no trouble securing a backer.'

'What? When?' Carrie turned to Richard. 'You said you wouldn't do theatre.'

He shrugged, but something crossed his face. 'I'm still not convinced, but like you said, maybe I need to spread my wings. Try something new. Besides, it gives me an excuse to base myself in London for the foreseeable future.'

'When did you decide to do this?' She didn't know why she needed to know, she just did.

He picked up her hand and with his fingers circled her wedding-ring finger as he laid his cheek next to hers. His lips whispered against her cheek.

'It was the night on the boat when I told you I've never loved anyone the way I loved you.' He paused and kissed the corner of her mouth, before pulling back far enough, that she could see the solemn promise in his eyes. 'I got the line wrong. What I should have said is, "I've never loved anyone the way I love you and,"' he laid a finger on her lips, 'I never will.'

EPILOGUE

'I still think I should have been a bridesmaid.' Jade pouted as she flounced into the bedroom and threw herself down on the double bed.

'But then you wouldn't have got to wear DKNY,' pointed out Carrie, pausing from pinning up her hair in a smart chignon to turn and give her niece a twinkly smile. She could tell the younger girl felt slightly unsettled. 'And your mum wanted you to be with her.'

'I guess.' Jade smoothed down the pencil-straight skirt of the dress. 'Arla has got brilliant taste.' She stuck her feet out like a little girl, to admire her shoes. 'These babies are banging.' She got to her feet and in the mirror's reflection, Carrie could see her pacing. Honestly, it was supposed to be the bride that was nervous.

'And it was fun having my make-up done properly,' Jade peered at Cassie. 'Sally's done a nice job on you too.'

'Why thank you.' Carrie examined her face. She was rather pleased with the results, although always found it ironic that looking this fresh and natural took the application of quite so many lotions and potions. Her face positively glowed, as if she'd been lit from inside or perhaps it was just sheer happiness. This last year had been amazing and today was going to be even more special. She looked at her watch. In another half hour they'd be in the church. Butterflies fizzed in the bottom of her stomach. She didn't want anything to go wrong today, but all the arrangements were in place and super-organised. Angela had done most of the work with her usual quiet, unflustered efficiency, although Cassie worried at her lip, her sister was allowed to be nervous now.

'How's your mum doing?'

'Sally said another five minutes on the make-up.'

Cassie smiled. 'Bang on time.' With make-up done, all that was needed was the finishing touch of the dress. The ivory, heavy silk confection had been hanging up in the spare room for a week, ready to rustle and slither into place. Just thinking about it sent the butterflies rising and swirling in her stomach like a flock of starlings.

'What time is the car coming?' asked Jade, wheeling abruptly to pace across the room once more.

'It'll be here soon. Have you got everything?'

Jade patted the matching clutch that Arla had also supplied. 'Phone, lippy. That's all I need.'

'And is your phone switched off.'

Jade rolled her eyes. 'Not yet.'

'Just make sure it is before you get inside the church.'

'Yes, Auntie Cassie. I'll just go see Mum. See if she's ready yet.'

The three of them descended the stairs in solemn silence, broken only by the swish of the dress as it whispered down each tread. Through the open front door, Cassie could see the chauffeur-driven limousine, with the driver holding open the rear door. A brief smile flitted across her face and she nodded towards the car. 'Just like St Tropez again.'

Angela laughed, the sound bubbling out like effervescent champagne, her face radiant. 'How things have changed since then! Who'd have guessed? We've been blessed.' She paused and gathered Cassie and Jade to her. The three of them stood in a group hug for a minute and Cassie took a deep breath and swallowed hard. She didn't want tears to spoil her or Angela's perfect make-up.

'Here goes,' whispered Angela, giving Cassie and Jade one last squeeze.

The three of them stepped out into perfect wedding weather. The sky had cleared overnight and the sun shone against a brilliant blue backdrop, broken by occasional puffballs of a white clouds.

The journey took a scant five minutes and in no time at all Cassie passed through the church doors. The pews were already full, hats bobbing in anticipation as everyone turned to look at her. She looked down the aisle, feeling a touch self-conscious, but the attention quickly turned back to the film star at the front. With a sigh of relief, she followed the common gaze to find Richard and picked up her pace, her heels clicking on the worn stone slabs. He winked at her as she slipped into the pew next to him and he took her hand, pulling her to him to kiss her on the mouth in front of the whole congregation, as if it had been days rather than an hour since they'd seen each other. Behind them, Cassie heard a collective sigh. As she sank onto the wooden seat, she caught Phil's eye as he peered uneasily over his shoulder from his position in front of the altar. He looked a little pale. His nervous smile lacked the usual wattage she'd become used to seeing since he'd moved in with Angela, as he fiddled with the yellow rose pinned to his morning suit. She gave him a thumbs-up, to let him know everything was fine and that the bride was in position, along with her best girl.

Phil's October visit had ended up lasting through to November before he decamped back to France to collect the remainder of his clothes, dry-dock his boat and shut up his house for the rest of the winter. He'd proposed on Christmas Day and he and Angela planned on living in France and England around Jade's school and, hopefully in the near future, university terms.

The organ's triumphant notes swelled into the air and a frisson ran through the crowd as Angela took her first step into view and they craned their heads to see the dress. It could have been designed for Angela, even though Carrie knew that her practical sister had found it off the peg in a bridal shop on the high street in Tring. Simple and stylish, it suited her perfectly. The full but not too fussy skirt swayed with elegant fluidity as Angela glided down the aisle, her arm tucked through Jade's and her eyes focused on Phil with a serene smile.

Tears welled up in Cassie's eyes and she clung to Richard's hand, her fingers laced through his as she leaned against him, feeling the warmth of his body through the fine wool fabric of his suit. He glanced down at her and those oh-so-blue eyes held hers, his gaze intent with one silent message shimmering between them. They didn't need the words, the concentrated look in his eyes said it all, making her heart swell so hard and fast, it might almost burst with the feeling. She squeezed his hand and edged closer to him, pressing her shoulder up against his arm. His thumb stroked hers, the gentle pressure reassuring, and she knew that his thoughts were in tandem with hers.

The music stopped, the congregation sat down as one and the service started, the vicar's voice ringing out clear and authoritative in the high-raftered church. Angela and Phil's responses were equally confident and strong, as they held each other's gaze with solemn promise.

When they both said 'I do', Richard scooted closer so that they were thigh to thigh, their hands squeezing each other's in silent communication.

'You still sure?' asked Richard, whispering in her ear. She nodded and gave him a beatific, happy smile. They'd discussed this. Whether or not to renew their wedding vows. Richard had been in complete agreement when she decided against it. Their wedding day, all those years ago, held a special place in both their memories and in her mind and heart that vivid emotion of sheer joy and crazy happiness was indelibly burned into place. It could never be eclipsed and neither of them wanted it to be. The informality of that day, the lack of fuss and drama, was a talisman and a juxtaposition to their current lifestyle, where parties, formal gatherings and dressing up played such a huge part and for most of the time held little meaning.

It had been a busy year, premieres, openings and awards events culminating in a never-to-be-forgotten evening at the Royal Opera House, where they both had to look excited and happy for Frank Jeffersen, who pipped Richard to the award for best actor and then, luckily, was able to let rip with genuine cheers of delight for Miranda, who apologised on stage, rather handsomely, for beating Carrie in the best new play category.

The play had been an enormous success, not just thanks

to Richard's name pulling attraction which secured full houses every night but also due to his rather brilliant (and, no, Cassie wasn't the least bit biased, that's what the critics said) performances.

As she and Richard rose when Angela and Phil smiled their way back down the aisle, Cassie's foot nudged something on the floor.

'What's that?' she asked, bending to look down.

'Today's disguise,' said Richard, with a naughty grin, as he scooped up a chauffeur's peaked cap. 'I didn't want to steal the limelight when I arrived.'

Cassie let out a gurgle of laughter. 'Thank God it wasn't the gangsta-rapper look you adopted last time we went shopping.' She cringed remembering the white baggy tracksuit and back-to-front baseball cap complete with gold chain he'd donned for a trip to Harvey Nicks to buy her outfit for today.

'And you think you looked any better in your posh hooker kit?' teased Richard, pinching her bottom, reminding her of the ridiculously skin-tight stretchy skirt she'd worn with gladiator heels and fishnet tights on the same shopping expedition. He gave her a hammy lewd wink, making her burst out laughing.

She nudged him in the ribs, trying to regain her decorum. They were in a church, after all.

'I don't remember you complaining too much when we got home.' They hadn't made the bedroom that afternoon, but that was par for the course.

'I've got no complaints whatsoever. Life couldn't be better.' He gave her a gentle kiss on her cheek and twisted a finger through one of the loose curls around her face. 'It's just perfect,' he paused, and then, with a lightning tug, pulled out the pins securing her sophisticated chignon. 'Apart from that.'

She sighed and smiled up at him, her heart somersaulting at the intent expression on his face as her hair tumbled down. 'I wondered how long it would last.'

'It was a deliberate challenge and you know it.' He tweaked the curl again.

They giggled together as they followed the rest of the congregation out of the church to the top of the steps. A light breeze lifted her hair, blowing across her face.

'But it gives me an excuse to do this.' With tender hands he brushed the dancing curls aside, his thumbs stroking her cheekbones as he lowered his head to kiss her. He'd done it a hundred times in the last year and it never failed to make her insides curl up in heated delight and he knew it. Some things between them had never changed and with a contented sigh, she sank into the kiss, knowing they never would.

ACKNOWLEDGEMENTS

My biggest thank you goes to the ever-sunny Charlotte Ledger for championing this book from day one and for her never-ending supply of enthusiasm and encouragement (truly awesome.)

Nearly as big thanks go to the fabulous Donna Ashcroft, Prosecco partner extraordinaire, who when the going gets tough, kicks my arse and pours me another glass. I'm also indebted to lovely Louise Wilding, my go-to Riviera expert, for local knowledge and tips on the locations of Ramatuelle, Gassin and St Tropez and Nicky Duffle, additional Riviera consultant, for the helicopter idea.

A big shout out to the real Phil Hillair-Brady for allowing me to use his name, which was his prize in a raffle held for the Alzheimers Society organised by fab friends Shane and Jenny O'Neil. Hugs and more thanks to my family Nick, Ellie, Matt, and dear friends Justine, Alison and Candy, for their endless support. They put up with erratic housekeeping and dodgy diary keeping when I'm writing . . . and never complain (or look bored when I tell them about the latest plot).

Special thanks to my dad and beloved step-mum, Tricia. You may well have been coerced into buying this by her in a bookshop somewhere (proud doesn't begin to describe it). They share the delusion that I'm somehow brilliant. Long may it last.

A massive shout-out to the amazing, supportive organisation that is the Romantic Novelists' Association, and all the wonderful friends I've made among its members.

Thank you to you for investing your hard-earned pennies in buying this book. I hope you enjoy it. I'm always thrilled and grateful when anyone takes the trouble to get in touch or leave a review. I promise you, it's always appreciated.

And last, but not least, grateful thanks to the fantastic team at Avon, who've done so much work behind the scenes.

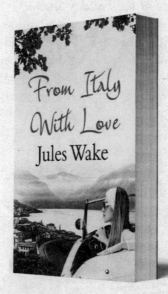

Jet off to Paris with Siena and Jason and experience the magic of the holiday season!

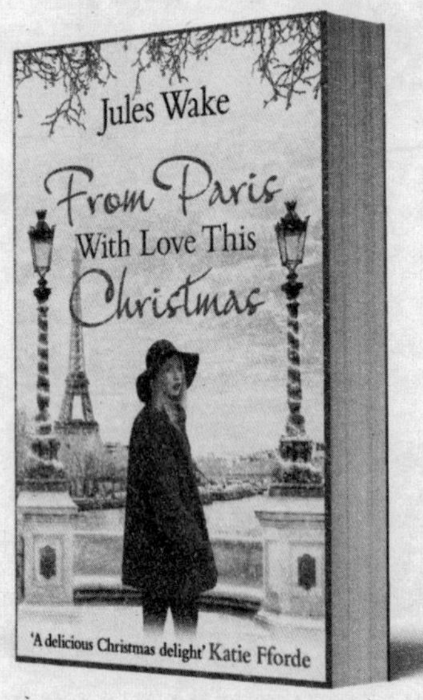

The gorgeous, Christmassy feel-good follow up to the Summer best-seller *From Italy With Love.*